SHADOW AND DARKNESS

AMANDA CASHURE

Book Design by – Inked Imagination then updated by The WordSeed Guild
Line Edits by – Michelle Motyczka
Bibling by – Adriel Wiggins
Continuity Edits by – Cate Ryan
Cover Designer – Laercio Messias
Cover Image Copyright 2020

*To Jaymin for being a listening ear when your work inspired me. Thank you for
the direction and guidance you offered. I'm grateful to you for a ton of things
over the years, supporting my wild imagination is just one of them – and I hope
you know it. And Jane, if you ever read this, your Curse of the Gods changed my
life.*

And with special thanks to all the alpha and beta readers who saw this book
in its 'bad' and 'ugly' stages.

To Michelle who has been with me from the beginning, Adriel and Cate for all your hard work, plus the arc readers who hunted through for slip ups and typos.

Never last and never least
To Jaz, I'm so grateful to have you in my life.

CONTENTS

TRIGGER WARNING

2 OUT OF 5

The stories of the *ShadowVerse* contain violence, typical
warriors and battle type stuff, as well as typical servant-
treated-as-a-slave stuff.

There is no dubcon or noncon in this book.

This is the one and only trigger warning in book one.

Other books in the ShadowVerse may contain triggers,
where possible the darkest of which have been flagged.

HIRANA

BLACK CASTLE

DRAYGON

WHITE CASTLE

MANOR

EFOS

RENGURRA

CAVE

LACKSHIR

DESAYER

REALM

JAI FOREST

INSO FOREST

TANAKAN PRISON

AQUA RIVER

CRIMSON CASTLE

THE KINGDOM

OF SILVA

SHADE TWO

a Shadow Verse novel

DAY ONE

3RD

DAY OF

SNOW MOON

PROLOGUE
IN THE DAYLIGHT
SOMEWHERE WITHIN THE RENGURRA FOREST

S hade is with them. With Killian and Seth and Roarke. She's *supposed* to be safe.

I'm supposed to keep my distance, leashing myself. If that were even possible. It could be, if she could stay out of trouble and not get attacked by lizards. *Not* need to be rescued.

We need to talk – I tell my demon.

Currently – he says, words muffled by layers and layers of pain and distrust – **killing things.**

He finishes the man, ending his life. What's *ours* can't be harmed. Can't even be touched.

And then? – I demand, the man's blood between our teeth.

Then we talk –

I sit back, unable to offer more than my opinion unless I want to get into a very heated argument. And at this point, I agree with every move he is making.

Until he turns toward Shade.

Beautiful – I think, unintentionally sharing the word with the beast.

She has a name? – he asks, because of course he hasn't bothered to pay attention.

Shade – I say.

Beautiful – he agrees.

In a sharp rush of power, we turn from beast to man, and I move toward the one thing we both want more than air or life or peace inside our own minds. The one thing burning through our joined souls with irreversible need.

She falls into my arms, the crimson-gold threads entangling, fusing, becoming whole. I can't see them like Killian, but I feel them.

Mine – we agree.

She must be. There is no other option.

SHADOW

I 'm on a short gray mare, and yes – she has reins. Those reins are being controlled by Roarke. The long-haired guy on the chestnut gelding to the side of me.

Majestic Silva trees have surrounded us all night. They were shadows and darkness as we raced from probable death and certain pain until the early morning light began to creep between the reaching branches. With a gentle shawl of mist lifting from the leaf litter, the day promises more peaceful things.

Promises it, but I know better than to believe it.

My four companions have slowed, their horses easing into a relaxed amble. We're no longer moving at the speed of running-for-our-lives, and I'm no longer in danger of being thrown from my horse.

I don't ride, never have. It's one of those things that most servants, especially a servant from the soot side of the border, just don't do. When the order came in from a mysterious Sealer who turned up in the middle of the night, telling us to get our asses out of the White Castle and as far away from the wrath of Silva's crazy DeathSeed ruler as possible, riding lessons were a luxury I didn't have time for.

Killian is riding the big black thing behind us. Pax, on a dapple-gray, and Seth, on a bay gelding, are riding ahead. All the horses are as different as their riders, but everyone is in their usual order.

One – Pax. AlphaSeed, badass, and commander.

Two – Seth. ChaosSeed and the biggest pain in my ass.

Three – Roarke. AllureSeed. The guy who knows everything, which is helped by the fact that he can draw information out of your mind at any time. As well as make you take your clothes off without saying a word. It has taken me a long time to trust this guy.

And Four – Killian. DarknessSeed and the worst combination of sweet and deadly I've ever had the pleasure of knowing.

I've known sweet before. Jake, an indentured servant like me on Lord Martin's estate, was sweet. That was back when Silva was nonexistent, and the Enchanted Forest was just a scary forest off in the distance. I had no idea a whole realm was hidden in here, cloaked by magic and somehow much bigger on the inside than you'd think possible.

Martin – the Manor Lord – on the other hand, was the kind of darkness that still twists my insides into knots. Knots of fear which curl through my limbs and take hold of my mind.

"Don't," Killian orders.

I jump a little in the saddle. Then wince, because saddle plus legs plus riding like crazy through the night equals pain.

When did he even get there?

Killian grunts, but I can't tell if it's a pleased or displeased sound.

Roarke twists and runs his gaze over me, a concerned little crease in his brow. I just want to make it to the end of this ride, to our destination, and eat, then sleep, then eat again.

"Don't," I grumble at Roarke. Why not? It works for Killian.

Roarke's gaze doesn't shift. "Shade needs to stop."

Apparently, it doesn't work for me.

I know what I look like; I don't need to see it reflected in his eyes. I was asleep when the assignment arrived. Comfortable and warm.

Then my life went from bed to horse. My blonde hair is pulled back in a ponytail, but after riding all night, strands have broken free and dangle in front of my eyes. I huff at one in frustration.

On a lucky note, I had fallen asleep fully dressed, in a shirt and pants made of soft Silvari cotton, and I did manage to get my boots on my feet. Under the long sleeves, my left arm sports a thin blue length of cloth, tied around the old scars left by Lord Martin's chains, and my right arm is bandaged securely around the wound I received from an attack orchestrated by Logan, nephew to the Crown of chuckin' Death.

Orchestrated by Logan, but carried out by Asanta – Seth's stalker and the woman who wants me dead on a personal level – and her brother, Thom.

Yep – life's been peachy.

We pick our way through the trees. Then, without discussion, Pax stops, swings down, and starts fishing in his saddlebags. No one else is surprised. We're on a rough track, the kind made by animals, not horses and carts. That wouldn't stop a cart getting through here though, if one wanted to. The grass is flat, the trees well-spaced, and the low brush is scattered away from the track.

Seth turns his horse in a circle, seeming to consider where he wants to get off, before stopping next to a tree and tossing the horse's reins over a branch. The guy pops up onto his feet, standing in the saddle, and leaps straight up into the branches.

"I'm getting a better look," he says, then he's gone.

The Elorsin brothers have both the super-fast and super-strong thing down pat. They also have deadly fighting skills, and their own individual arsenal of abilities – Seeds of power that they were born with.

I'm too busy watching Seth climb from limb to limb to realize that Roarke's dismounted and tied my horse's reins around the nearest tree. "Get down, stretch your legs."

"Can't," I respond under my breath, still trying to spot Seth in the canopy.

Killian makes a chuffing noise as he rides up beside me. That's his this-is-going-to-be-funny sound. I turn to glare at him – and at the same time, he scoops down, grabs my foot, and tips me off the horse.

I flail, then hit the ground flat on my back, gasping for air through the ache that vibrates down my whole body.

Killian rises up in the stirrups and glares at me over the back of my horse. "No time for this." Then he's walking off.

It takes me a few more gasps before the air actually reaches my lungs. Roarke's long hair falls forward to frame his face as he holds a hand out to me.

I accept with my good arm, and he pulls me to my feet. He doesn't let go of me, though, clasping my fingers just enough to make me look up into his eyes.

"Kitten, you know I can take it away?" His voice drifts between us, soft and tempting – but lacking the intensity of his Allure magic.

By 'it,' he means my pain. The numb ache that has now settled in my broken arm, the throbbing in my head from hitting the ground, and the burning down my legs. Saddle versus skin apparently leaves the skin worse off.

But I shake my head, slipping my hand free from his. It will all pass. Minor inconveniences, and not the end of the world.

"No, thank you, but please fix him up." I wave toward where Killian is grabbing a piece of bread from Pax.

He's taken off his cloak, and I can see his left shoulder has begun to weep. Sections of his black linen shirt have stuck to his skin. I've had a burn before, but not one that covered my whole shoulder and was caused by barging into a magically warded door to try and save some girl who can't even defend herself – me. Regardless, I still know that leaving a weeping wound to dry means peeling skin off later.

Roarke nods and moves off to collect supplies from Killian's saddlebags. Killian, the man who likes to hurt things, is also the man who can feel when you're hurting. That makes him our resident healer-of-sorts. The guy is really bad at looking after himself, though – maybe he likes being in pain. I don't know. I've never asked him.

"Here," Pax says, closing the distance between us and offering me a roll. "You should eat something."

I sigh with pleasure, wrapping my fingers around it and taking my time with the first delicious bite.

His sleeve falls back, drawing my eye to the seal on the palm of his hand. It looks like an angry black stick-figure frog, the style of drawing I might have done in the dirt with the kids from the Manor. Though, those were never burned into anyone's flesh by a SealSeed. It has a head pointed like an arrow. Arms and legs that curve and swirl. No body, though. Just lines. And over that, in red, are more curves and swirls, finished with three dots on either side.

"Where are we?" I ask while chewing.

"About an hour from Rengurra," Pax explains, putting the last piece of his own roll into his mouth.

"Which is where, exactly?"

"About a day's ride from Potion Master Eydis'."

It's pretty much just him and me, and my new horse, in

this conversation. Seth is still up a tree, and Roarke's a short distance away, about to argue with Killian.

Through the night and half a day to get here, another day to get to the border. When they snatched me from Martin's estate – long story – I was knocked unconscious in the morning and woke in the White Castle two nights later. Thirty-something hours unconscious on Pax's horse – I put a taco in his boot for that pleasure.

"Why, when you guys can run faster than the wind, do we have to ride horses?"

He runs his hand along the sweaty side of my mount. "That only lasts for short distances. Horses last for long distances. We'll have to get you something with more stamina in Rengurra. This little pony isn't built for this kind of travel."

Killian finally gives in to Roarke and tugs his shirt up over his head. My mind switches gears. The guy is tall, built for battle, toned, and tanned. Two scars mark his body, one that cuts clean across his face and another across his chest. Scars he earned defending his mother until her last breath.

"What else don't you get?" Pax asks, partially dragging my mind away from the definition of Killian's abdomen, where it vees and dips into the front of his pants.

"Sex." The word escapes – because apparently my mind wasn't dragged far enough away from Killian's complete hotness.

Crap!

My eyes widen, and I turn sharply to walk away.

Pax practically chokes on his laughter, coughing to try to cover it up, but he catches my wrist before I can get too far. Stopping me, then stepping in close. Heat radiates off him, sinking into my skin at the points where he's almost, but not quite, touching me. He dips his face down next to my ear, his breath skimming along my collarbone.

"That's going to be complicated from now on," he says softly. "You can't lay with a Saber. Our magic would devour your soul. Your own kind would be safest, and you could possibly satisfy yourself with a Silvari, but my AlphaSeed isn't going to let that happen. It's complicated."

I'm on the verge of explaining that I have no desire to climb into bed with *some random Silvari*, because everyone in this realm, every Silvari I have met, has been an asshole. Almost everyone. Clara was nice, but she's the one exception, and I'm not climbing into bed with her either.

But before I can get any of that out, he's dropped a new rule into my life.

No sex.

And instead of saying something sane and rational, I turn on him, yanking my arm free from his grip, and proceed to poke him in the chest.

Which always pisses him off.

"You don't get to tell me who I can and can't sleep with," I growl.

"I'm only telling you because it's a fact." He sounds almost casual, but the slight glow in his golden eyes warns me that calm Pax is very close to becoming bossy-as-bralls Pax. My head tries to tell my mouth to shut up – but my mouth never listens.

"You don't get to shape the facts. I can sleep with whoever I want," I shout.

And the instant I hear my own voice, I regret it.

Seth drops down out of his tree. "I don't know how this started, but that's the wrong thing to say to our Alpha."

"I don't care." I try to keep my voice even, but all I manage to do is muffle my words until they come out like a growl. "I'm not your toy," I snap, waving a hand toward Seth but keeping my gaze on Pax. "Or your shadow." I point at Killian. "Or anyone's pet." I point at Roarke. "And I'm damned sure not your property." I point at Pax, poke him, actually.

He wraps my hand in his and holds it in place. Tight enough to hurt. As he steps forward, I step back until he's walked me into a tree and pinned me against it. He's taller than I am, and he maintains his full height, looking down with his eyes glowing.

I can't move, with the tree behind me, Pax in front of me, and my hand being bruised in his grip. As if I'm not already blocked in, he presses his other hand against the tree, next to my head.

The bones in my hand begin to creak, and I let out a hiss. I've seen this guy crush metal in his palm, and a bolt of fear shoots through me at the prospect.

"Pax," Killian calls loudly, but no one moves.

Pax opens his mouth to speak, and I watch as his canines slowly extend into the kind of thing found in a wolf's jaws. A really big wolf.

That's new.

"We're not discussing this again." His words are accompanied by a low growl that rolls up from deep in his chest.

He doesn't move, though, just stares at me like he's waiting for an answer.

I close my eyes against the pain and just try to breathe. Finding words when someone has you pinned and hurting is hard. Everything in me is thinking, *Just wait until it's over*.

Pax growls, loud and sharp and forcefully. The tree shudders, and a wood-splintering crunch fills my ears. Then he's gone. The heat from his presence sucks even the warmth from my own body away, leaving me with a cold chill.

At first, I don't move.

Then slowly I open my eyes and uncurl my fingers before taking a shaky step away from the tree. There's a chunk missing from the thing. Pax literally ripped it out with his bare hand.

My hand, however, feels numb, and I wriggle my fingers to try and get the blood flowing again.

Pax is nowhere to be seen. Roarke shoves the last of the medical supplies back into a bag, and Killian pulls his shirt down into place. Seth approaches me, leading my horse over.

"Where'd he go?" I ask, a little afraid that Pax is going to reappear at any moment.

"To blow off some steam. Did he hurt you?" Seth gazes down at my hand, and I wriggle my fingers again to assure him they're all intact. "Don't tempt the guy. MateBonds aren't supposed to work like this –"

I cut him off right there. "Mate? He's not a Brahman bull, and I'm not a cow."

The guy doesn't even crack a smile – which is the complete opposite reaction to what Seth should have. So I suck in a shaky breath and search for something better to say.

"We weren't talking about mating. We were talking about sex, and he was telling me I never get to have any, which is not how I plan to live my life."

He cocks an eyebrow at me.

"What?" I demand.

Roarke strides over to stand next to his brother. "Let me explain this to you. AlphaSeeds were the original Silvari rulers. All Seed bloodlines are kept pure because only two parents of the same Seed can pass on the gift. Alphas only mate with Alphas. They have almost no say over who their mates will be. Not like instant love, but an unbreakable bond. It worked fine when there were a hundred or so different families. Over time they joined the long list of extinct Seeds. Our mother found two, hidden in different parts of the –" he hesitates, before deciding on, "– world, their powers

13

suppressed for generations. Pax as a young man, and years later, Jessamy."

"What happened to her?"

"She died of a broken heart," Seth says softly. "Before Mother died and Lithael usurped the throne. Before assassins started removing council members, and the grimm were pulled through the Veil to lock down the Black Castle. Before we were sealed into the White Castle and kept caged."

"Before all of that, Pax married her," Roarke cuts to the point. "Jessamy was with child, and someone paid a CataclysmSeed to make all of that go away. CataclysmSeeds were rare, but those that were still alive had become weapons for hire. They've the power to make anything they touch dissolve. With one touch, the baby was... well, dissolved... a few weeks before she was due to be born."

I choke, a cold, hard fist squeezing at my heart.

Roarke continues, "Pax hunted them down. Killed all of them he could get to. I was there that day, on the other side of the market. I saw the woman who brushed her hand over Jessamy's stomach and ended everything. I traced her to the Hyll family line, but Pax had already been there, and the bodies that were left behind... nothing could be made of their faces. He'd always been a bastard to live with. His power has an innate need to classify people as either *his* or *other*. If you're his, then he needs to protect you."

"Becoming a part of his pack took me two decades and drove Mother mad," Seth adds. "I slept in a glorified cellar for twenty years because the bastard couldn't stand the smell of me in the house. I did take a lot of pleasure in finding particularly rotten things to line my clothes with, though. Probably didn't help."

"What happened next? After he lost Jessamy?" I ask. This guy can get seriously off track.

Seth shrugs. "He went back into the Saber ranks, and we all went back in with him."

The information tumbles through my scattered mind. I focus on parts of Roarke and Seth's revelations, and the sparse details that I'd gathered before today, to distract me from feeling pain and sympathy. Not because I don't care – but because Pax just walled me in, ripped the tree apart, and threatened me with lifelong virginity.

"You've said before that he shares his bed with plenty of women. If he gets to have sex, then so do I," I grumble, heat flashing in my cheeks as my words sink in. So I blurt some more stuff out to try to fix it. "I don't even want to have sex, but I don't want to be told by him that I can't."

Seth's smiling like I'm his toy again.

"He's slept with plenty of women, you're right. Sabers – Silvari wouldn't survive – but to him they were all *other*," Roarke insists.

"You two get to have sex, right?" I demand.

"You want to have sex with us?" Seth asks, his eyes so alight with amusement that I have to warn myself that slapping him is only going to hurt me, not him.

"No, shut up. No, I mean if you guys being with other people doesn't worry him, then he can just get over the idea of me being with someone else."

This is ridiculous. I don't even have a 'someone' that I want to get into bed with!

"I don't pretend to know what's going through his mind," Roarke says. "He didn't take as long to accept me as Seth. I was seven, and I spent three years sleeping in a cot on Mother and Father's floor, but it took you minutes."

"What do you mean it took me minutes? I'm not actively trying to sleep with the man. That wasn't even the point of our conversation."

"It took minutes for him to break you free from Martin's chain."

"That was his fault," I insist, pointing at Seth, because it was Seth who originally stepped in and saved me from the death grip that Lord Martin had on my throat.

"I saw you as a shiny new toy – Pax was right about that. And if I'd chosen anyone else, he would have let me play my games."

I scowl at the man, hating that his lopsided smile is dimpling, just one of his cheeks, and taking away some of my reaction, because playing with people should not be okay. But against my own judgment, I let that slide. What he's talking about is practical jokes, a dash of humiliation, and the end result of being me in the stocks. We've already been there.

"How does this have anything to do with –" The right words elude me so I resort to waving my arm around and growling incoherently.

"Silvari," Killian grunts, and we all turn to listen, "grow up with their families. They go into service for fifty years, then return home. They marry, have kids, go to universities, and bicker over the best professions and the best meaningless jobs. Their lives are hollow. Sabers grow up with their families, then get called to the White Castle to train and eventually fight and protect the realm."

He stops talking, but I keep my gaze on him, waiting for the important part. The guy never says anything unless it's important.

"If someone dies, the triune is broken and the surviving members become inactive. Sometimes they fight their way into posts as guards, or eventually get offered positions as Master Apprentices – maybe one day becoming Masters. The only other thing that allows a Saber to leave their duties is love."

"Love? Or this forced mate thing?"

Roarke shakes his head. "Only Alphas have MateBonds. A few other Seeds develop their own kinds of bond connections. The uncontrollable, instinctive, deeper than magic kind. A mate is the one other person who will stop our souls from searching."

"The rest of them just fall in love and get married and try to make it work," Seth adds.

"Seeds who form bonds can only do so with a perfect match of their own kind. When there's no more of your kind, you can still hope for love and marriage."

"Which is harder for the Seductions," Seth says, pulling a face at his brother.

"Chaos and Trickeries make a mess of things just as much as we do."

I set my glare on Seth first, making sure his vibrant blue Chaos eyes meet mine before I ask, "You've been married?"

"Not married, but in love – sure. I've left six times, but they weren't true bonds."

"That's impossible for you, Seth," Killian adds, a smirk on the corner of his lips.

"What happened?"

I've yet to find a 'one time' love – and yet at the same time, I'm falling for four of them at once. Four guys with three hundred years of experience. They have pasts. They've had lovers, even wives. *Of course!*

And of course they're not going to like me in return because magic has a loophole to keep them locked down to their own kind.

"Didn't work out." Seth interrupts the Seed of Dumbass growing in my chest.

While Roarke runs his thumb over his short beard looking thoughtful. "Well, you did steal that horse from the Royal Races on your first official date with Illwyn and left her to take the blame. Was that in the middle of you two being intim–"

Seth cuts in, "Roarke has had ten partners and three wives."

I gasp, and have to press my lips together to stop my jaw from dropping. "What happened? Were they all, ah, bonds?"

"No, nothing that special. They just didn't work out," Roarke echoes, timidly running his hand through his hair and avoiding eye contact.

"Doesn't help that you had some of those partners *while* having some of those wives. Plus almost draining the life –" Roarke sets his gaze on his brother, and Seth shuts up mid-word.

I turn to Killian.

He doesn't even answer me, just grunts and walks away.

So I turn back to the other two. "And Pax?"

"Once," Seth says. "More than two hundred years ago."

I grit my teeth. Now is not the time to feel sorry for Pax, and I'm not going to let this go. These guys might live for a thousand years – I will not. I'm going to get a normal human's fifty or so years and then be too old and broken to care much about love.

"He can still get over it," I snap. "He's made it pretty damned clear that intimacy stops at making sure my clothes smell like pack, and that's it. What I do with my body is my decision."

Seth looks at me with a hint of sympathy, then he grabs a stick and draws a line in the dirt. A line with a dot either side of it.

"This is Pax, this is you, and this line is his stubborn Alpha impulses. You need to stay as far away from that line as you can."

I groan, because I've done some really stupid crap over

the past week, including dropping my towel in front of them all.

Stuff that crosses lines.

And at the same time, longing unfurls itself inside me because being near Pax feels good. The idea of belonging to him makes my core melt.

In the background, Killian rinses his mouth out with water, then climbs into his saddle. With a gentle clicking noise, the horse kicks into a canter, and they're soon out of sight. Roarke and Seth start to move toward their own mounts, and I get the picture.

"Does this mean you rescind your previous ultimatum?"

We did have a deal, what feels like a long time ago now, when I got stupidly jealous of their gorgeous female servants and demanded they request guys instead. Around the same time, I learned that Elite Saber and mortal interactions always ended in mortal deaths. That fact isn't new to me. I did order them not to have any guy/girl interactions at all – unless they were in mortal danger and the interaction ended in death.

That whole deal wasn't supposed to develop into my permanent virginity.

"Sure," I say, not wanting to be the one laying out rules for them the same way Pax is laying them out for me. "After me. New deal, no one gets any sex until I do."

As soon as I've said it, I regret it. Deep, devastating regret. Partly because discussing my sex life was at the bottom of my to-do list today, but mostly because the idea of any one of these guys being in the presence of any other woman makes it hard for me to breathe.

It's followed sharply by the realization that I can't compete. Like Pax said, I might be able to share a bed with a regular Silvari – might. Sabers are out of the question. Elite

Sabers like these guys are so far out of my league I might as well be considering learning to chuckin' fly.

Seth steps up behind me. "Need help?"

I glare at the stirrup, the saddle, and the short horse that were acquired for me seconds before we raced from the castle. Running my fingers over the bandage on my broken arm, I curse two things – that I suck at anything other than washing dishes, and that I break so easily.

Because if I were to be honest, I don't just want to be close to Pax. I want all four of them.

And that's about as crazy an idea as a soot-servant girl can have.

They're stuck with me, a potion gone wrong, and some cryptic message left by their mother that has put me into their lives. Stuck. And maybe they need me. Maybe they're good people, and they treat me better than I ever have been – bruises and all. But ultimately, they're right – I'm not the kind of person who's going to live for very long in this realm.

Surviving should be my number one priority. Not sex, and not pushing Pax over the edge.

Darkness

My world is Darkness. I live with it. I'm good with that – I'm good at it.

Choosing the light in the dark takes strength.

Choosing to stay in the dark breeds evil and ash and death. Killing or wishing to be killed. Suffering and the infliction of it.

Pax is by the stream, prowling in his wolf form. The wolf hasn't walked for so long, I'd almost forgotten the way the molten metal shines underneath his coat like his skin is metal, and it's mixing and melting before my eyes. Being revealed in glimpses under his coffee and ash fur.

He swivels sharply, snapping and making my horse skip backward. I dismount, tie the horse's reins hastily to a tree, and approach him on foot.

He goes back to pacing, turning to look at me every five or ten steps, growling and showing canines. All teeth and all bite.

I let out a sound in comradery, sensing that every snap of his jaws is actually him angry at himself. Angry at the voice of the wolf coming alive inside him.

Arms crossed over my chest, I stare past him at the tree line on the other side of the stream. Something dark settles itself uneasily into the pit of my stomach. Something we're riding toward – and that *wants* us to ride toward it.

A flash of light engulfs the wolf, and Pax is left in its place. I grab a set of clothes from my bag and toss them at him.

They're big, but he needs to be clothed if the boys catch up – if the girl catches up.

"Hm?" I ask.

"Leave it," Pax grumbles. I glare at him, giving him a second to add, "It can't happen."

"Already is," I grunt.

He leaps at me, trying to stand over me, with his fist clenching the collar of my shirt, and his eyes glowing with furious magic.

"What do you know?" he demands.

Knowing isn't really something I do. I do *feeling*. I feel their needs, feel their pain, feel their wants. I feel his ache. The way any distance between him and the girl is beginning to gnaw at him. Not just him – Roarke and Seth are the same.

The girl has no idea. She still swings between feeling safe and afraid.

Afraid is good. She needs to be afraid.

"We have to get rid of her."

He slams his fist into my stomach, sending me flying back into a tree. I grunt on impact, slipping to the ground before beginning to pull myself to my feet. He doesn't advance on me, returning to pacing and looking like he's on the verge of going wolf again.

"We need to reverse this potion and put her somewhere safe," I try again, stalking toward him. This time, I'm ready to be attacked. "You can't let these bonds seal. If your power claims her as a mate, she will not survive long."

"I know that." Frustration leaks into his voice, and a touch of pain laces through the threads that reveal his heart, but all body language screams of rage. "I'm not going to touch her."

"You don't have to touch her to get attached."

"I'm already attached," he says, growling at himself.

"Push her away, before it's too late. Scare her back. Order her back. Whatever it takes."

"I tried," he cries, launching himself at me.

Twisting, I throw him to the ground and pin him down. In a burst of light, he's all wolf and has my arm in his jaws. I grunt in pain, both from the bite and the pull of my burnt shoulder. Same arm. Followed by the taste of my own blood as it fills Pax's senses. His anger ebbs, and he releases me.

My ability to exist in the dark places lets me sense through him – feel and taste too. So I know what his motives are. Deep down, in the place where only brothers understand each other. But the clothes are a different story. They're in shreds on the ground, ruined, and I doubt he has any regrets about it.

His wolf angles himself, ready to attack again at the slightest provocation. I'm not here to poke the beast. I'm here to make him think.

"Not talking to you," I tell the oversized beast, ignoring my pain – ignoring my arm altogether as I focus on the unpredictable animal.

Nothing.

"You won't reason. Put Pax back in his skin."

The wolf growls, light flashes, and Pax is back. Crouched on the grass, fully naked again – and this time I'm not giving him any more of my clothes.

"She's not safe with us."

The glow in his eyes dims slightly. "We're the strongest Sabers in existe –"

I cut him off. "And we have a realm to save. She will die if we take her into that battle."

The glow extinguishes, leaving his normal golden eyes and a hint of sadness behind. Sadness has a scent, almost a taste. It's like dew is to grass in the early morning.

"I need her to be safe," he insists.

"If these bonds seal, will you be able to walk away?"

"It's complicated," he growls.

"Uncomplicate it. Give her the order to stay back."

"I've tried. I can't." He pops to his feet, waiting for me to climb to mine. "You keep her safe. I will keep my distance."

"Can you do that?" I ask doubtfully.

I can already feel the way his soul has recoiled at the notion and his wolf is rebelling against it.

"I have to," he says through gritted teeth. "We have to."

Then he's fur again, sprinting from the bank straight into the water and across to the other side.

He doesn't understand.

Fate wants her to die – one way or the other. And not that half-dead shit Roarke did to her. I've known since then, that moment when she remembered her birth.

Ash and pain.

But the prophecy is pretty damned clear – if I don't let her die, our Realm will burn.

Maybe this mating is the thing that ultimately ends her life. Or maybe leaving us will make her too vulnerable. Pax is right, we are the strongest Sabers.

Maybe I don't know which is more important anymore.

Her – or the rest of the Kingdom.

SHADOW

N obody talks.

At first, it's because Killian returns from wherever the bralls he went with some kind of fruit that makes my tongue go tingly, but is too damned sweet and juicy to stop eating. I don't even bother asking what they are – past double-checking that he's not trying to kill me.

Three of the large oblong things later, and still no one is talking.

Roarke raised an eyebrow when we found Killian riding slowly along the narrow path we're classifying as a road, but when Killian just kept riding, the whole conversation was dropped.

With Pax nowhere to be seen, Killian takes the lead. Seth maintains second position and Roarke moves into last. If you don't count me behind him, still being towed along on my little gray pony, or Pax's mount, which is tied to the back of my saddle and ambling along at the back of our line.

"Seriously, guys, where is he?" I ask, for the third time. I twist in my saddle to scan around us – even *up* the trees. "As far as I'm aware, vanishing is not part of an AlphaSeed's repertoire."

"How do you know?" Roarke asks.

"Because he would have used that ability already.

Someone needs to tell me or I'm getting off this horse and not moving until…" I trail off.

It's obvious my threat isn't bad enough for them. None of them have even turned to look at me. Roarke gathers his hair up into a tie, knotting it on top of his head, then adjusts the various buckles down the front of the leather vest he's wearing.

Seth begins to whistle the kind of tune that reminds me of a lullaby, just not a lullaby I've heard before. He's leaning back in his saddle, hands clasped behind his head, and his gaze stretched up toward the treetops and the blue sky beyond.

Killian reaches back and flicks his hood up over his head, drawing my attention to the smear of blood across the back of his hand.

Okay, time to make my threat bad enough for them.

I've always had a knack for going up – something I mastered when tethered to Martin's torture post, and various other times I had to scale out of windows and across the manor's roof. Not the same as a tree, but since I'm not very good at much else, up will have to do.

Mimicking Seth's using-a-horse-like-a-ladder trick, I pop to my feet, almost fall flat on my face, and just barely manage to grip an overhanging branch before anyone notices what I'm trying to do. Roarke keeps moving, my horse keeps moving, and within a heartbeat, I'm dangling from a branch with air beneath my feet and the ground way down below that.

Pain thrums through my broken bone, and I struggle to swing my legs, gain momentum, and hopefully throw myself up on top of the branch, with only one arm.

Struggle. Hurt. But succeed.

Go me!

"What is she doing?" Killian growls, just as I manage to straddle the branch and sit upright.

They spin their horses around sharply. Killian glares. The threat emanating from his presence balances with the shock on Roarke's face and the joy on Seth's.

While Killian might be inclined to keep walking and let the magical-potion-gone-wrong bubble that I'm trapped in knock me to the ground because that's how magical walls work, I'm just hoping Seth and Roarke stay where they are.

My bubble is of no consequence to them. They are completely unaffected – actually, that's not true. It is having some minor effect on their magic – which is more to my disadvantage than theirs. But for the most part, they can do whatever they want. For me, the bubble is real.

The bubble is *very* real.

When they get too far away, it presses against me like a physical barrier. If I get caught between the wall and some other solid object, then I get squished – that's all there is to it.

Right now – Killian would squish me. He has before.

I'm just lucky that if Seth and Roarke stay here, it doesn't matter what Killian does. I'm tethered to whichever Elorsin brother is closest.

"Pax," I declare, swallowing hard because my climb has left me puffing. "I need to know where he is."

And there it is. The honest truth. We can't keep riding endlessly away from the last place I saw Pax, because in my mind that means we're actually physically riding away from *him*. Which I know we're not. Not really. Or probably not.

I'm losing my mind, but that doesn't change my need.

"I *need* to know where he is," I repeat, because none of them have said anything.

Roarke glances at Killian, then scratches the back of his head, muttering, "Awkward," under his breath.

Killian rides toward me, nudging his big black horse between the others. My legs are dangling on either side of the branch, and I can see that, with his large horse and larger frame, I'm in trouble. Before he can reach me, and probably grab my leg to pull me down off this branch, I shimmy closer to the trunk. Standing, using it as balance, I stretch to the next branch and struggle up just high enough to be too high for Killian.

About a story and a half up – the height of the window out of Lord Martin's chambers.

Killian growls, turning to Seth. "Get her down."

"Just tell her where Pax is," Roarke suggests.

"Yes, tell me."

"Tell us all," Seth adds, but he's already standing on the back of his horse. He balances for a second, then in two strides – not even proper leaps, just big steps with a little spring to them – he's standing on the branch that I have struggled to get to.

I press my back into the trunk and wrap my legs around the limb to keep balanced. My gaze stays locked on the blue in Seth's eyes. For one of the bigger brothers, the guy is practically unaffected by gravity.

He squats down, balancing on the balls of his feet with his hands clasped in front of him.

"Don't throw me out of the tree," I almost plead.

Actually, not almost – I'm definitely pleading.

"I won't," he says, the corner of his mouth tweaking into a smile. "I mean, he would, but I won't."

He gestures down to Killian, then we all turn to lock our eyes on the one brother who might have my answer.

"Talk," I order. Being out of his reach has given me some weird boost of confidence.

"Not here," Killian grunts.

"Why not here? We're not at the White Castle anymore.

There's nothing but trees. If you can't tell me here, then where can you tell me?"

"We're not stopping here," Killian says, slowly.

Right, he didn't mean we weren't talking here; he meant we weren't stopping here. We're *never* talking. Ever.

And I'm not ready to go anywhere without talking.

"Answers. Now. Where is Pax?" I try speaking slower, mimicking Killian's tactic, which gets a soft chuckle from Seth. I turn my full attention onto the youngest brother. "Tell me."

"I don't know, but he's a big boy. He doesn't need a mother."

I shove him in the chest, hard. He wavers for a second, then lands on his ass on the branch. Still chuckling, and not falling to his death.

"Right, is this forest safe?"

I'd rather not admit that I'm acting like a child who's lost her dolly. Or maybe a stalker. A really bad stalker who's chosen to have a tantrum because her stalkee has vanished.

"Safe enough," Seth says with a shrug.

"We're a fair way off the main roads in the Rengurra forest. There is a spring here, so sometimes nasty things get lured this way," Roarke adds.

"So you're saying he *could* be in danger?"

"Seth, get her down," Roarke calls up. "We can talk and ride."

"Just tell me where he is, Killian. And why is your arm covered in blood?" Neither Seth nor Roarke turn their attention to their brother – which means that this isn't new information to them. "Tell me what's going on!"

The emerald-green sheen to Killian's dark eyes fades, leaving only pits of black, and his lips twist into a smile, part manic and part pleased.

"Shit." Seth spits the word out.

"Stay up there," Killian orders, pointing at me.

The horses whinny and pull on the various reins that are tied between them as Killian spins his mount in a hectic circle. The big black animal's eyes widen in the kind of anticipation that experience has taught him.

Roarke dismounts, throwing his horse's reins loosely over a branch next to Seth's abandoned bay gelding. At the same time, he pulls a bow from behind Seth's saddle. The weapon and a quiver of arrows sail silently up into Seth's hands.

Before I've even managed to breathe, never mind take stock of the action, Seth has an arrow loaded, and Roarke has not one, but two short swords drawn and ready.

Something red flashes between the trees. Not like a shirt or cloak, but skin. Something with red skin.

I spot more on our left, then our right.

Seth curses again, turning carefully on our branch and scanning in sweeping motions over the forest behind us.

He shoots an arrow and the creature lets out a wounded hiss in the trees. Quickly, Seth fires three more arrows. Whatever the thing is, and it's sure not human, it takes more than one arrow to slow it down.

Killian growls, going into battle mode, and draws his sword at the last second. The deadly curved blade rips through one of the things as soon as it darts into the open.

The red skin over its face is so tight that its features are flattened – but even so, it looks incredibly human. Eyes like mine, cheekbones and a nose like a man, and a solid jawline. At first, its massive ears look like bat wings, but as it turns to try and fight Killian, I get a glimpse of something more like gills on the side of its head. Arms and chest like a man, with rudimentary leather armor on. But it has a tail. No legs. No pants. Its bottom half is like a giant chuckin' snake.

"No matter what happens, stay up here. They can't climb,"

Seth says, loosing arrows with the kind of speed that makes it hard to track his movements.

The horses dance around in fear, their eyes wide and their nostrils flaring. Pulling at their reins, until finally one of the ropes gives and half the animals break free. They bolt down the track, only to stop suddenly before they're out of view.

While the action below me, with half a dozen red-snake-things fighting my guys, is crazy scary, the fact that the horses have stopped draws my attention.

A man steps out of the forest to take Roarke's horse's reins. A normal guy, with normal skin and normal legs. He ignores everything else, patting the horse on the shoulder and running his gaze over the saddle and various bags and packs attached to the animal with a satisfied – or maybe excited – smile on his face.

This isn't just an attack. This is a robbery.

Seth shoots his last arrow, then literally steps off the branch. He lands with a thud that's almost lost among all the other noises: swords and screams and a few angry words that aren't even in the common tongue. He dashes for his horse, whose reins are so tightly hooked around a tree branch that the animal can hardly move, and pulls a spear from under the saddlebags.

The horses are important, but my guys are all in the middle of keeping their heads attached to their necks. I like their heads on their necks.

Helplessly, I watch as the three horses are led out of sight.

The battle is moving further and further away. Every enemy the guys cut down, every scream of pain followed by loss of limb or life, drives the creatures away in an intricate dance. One of the creatures shoulder-barges into Roarke – tossing him back against a tree. Seth puts his spear through the thing's chest. Then the two of them turn and step toward

31

the next wave of ugly-red things. More of them coming out of the forest.

And I'm pretty sure that puts both of them outside my range. All I have left is Killian – and he's surrounded. Five of the things keeping him busy. Pax would be handy right now.

Where the chuck is he?

I've got two options: wait for a wall to knock me to the ground – which given the super-speed and crazy jumping distance of these guys, could knock me clean across the forest and into unconsciousness – or climb down and creep closer.

Leaving my tree is a horrible idea, but being knocked out is worse.

The ground is a long way down. I hadn't factored that in when I got up here, and there are no good holds or branches between me and the bottom. I hug my branch before dangling my legs, inhale deeply, then let go – landing in a crumpled ball of pain. Not something's-broken pain, but man-that-was-a-bad-idea pain.

Someone grabs my ponytail and yanks me to my feet. The guy has long blond hair that's matted into permanent chunks, a smile that's missing three teeth, and brown eyes that pierce into me. He's not a red-snake-thing, but he's not much better. He steps in close, forcing my head back. Then leans against the tree, my hair still in his fist.

"Shade," Killian growls, his voice slicing through the battle noise, but not affecting this guy at all.

I hear him, and somewhere in the back of my mind I register that Killian's yelling at me, but he doesn't have me pinned against a tree right now, so anything he's shouting sits low on my priorities.

My captor licks his lips. "So you're the slave they're talking about," he drawls, his breath rancid against my nose, brushing my lips, and burning my throat.

His fingers trail along my collarbone before snapping up to grip my throat. My heart's racing so hard that I might pass out just from the blood rushing through my head. I try to speak, but can't. Try to swallow, but can't. Try to inhale, but can't.

"They never mentioned you were pretty. The one who broke the Saber laws. The woman in a team of men. A pentad, no less."

He leans down, and the last thing I'm expecting is for him to run his tongue up the side of my face – from my jaw to my hairline – slowly.

I glimpse the pleasure in his eyes as he pulls back, then a giant wolf leaps from the forest and slams into the guy so hard that I'm sent flying from the force.

The leaf litter crunches underneath me as I land and roll. Not caring that I need to move or even breathe, I rub at my face, scrubbing the moisture away and then scrubbing some more to try and remove the sensation.

Then I inhale.

The wolf has its teeth bared and the man pinned. The guy's screaming – screeching – then the wolf's jaw snaps around the man's neck, and his body goes limp. The only movement I make is the continued scrubbing at my cheek with the sleeve of my shirt. Even though my gaze is locked on the wolf-thing – too big to be a wolf, maybe a wolf-bear-thing – out of the corner of my eye, I see the last of our attackers being skewered and falling to the ground.

I struggle to my feet, hugging myself and realizing that my heart is still pounding so hard that I can feel it against my arms.

The wolf turns, its golden eyes boring into me. He looks familiar.

Then Killian steps between me and it, taking my full attention. A blade so covered in blood that red droplets fall from the steel still in his white-knuckled-fist. He lifts his other hand and points at me. The scar that cuts across his face is practically glowing with his anger. Roarke and Seth move in, but none of them try to stop their brother. I hope that means I'm not about to die – therefore they don't need to step in. Or it could mean that my death is inevitable and stepping in is futile.

None of them pay any attention to the wolf-bear-thing as it prowls forward, if I don't count Seth bouncing on the balls of his feet and shooting the animal brimming smiles between frowning at me.

"You didn't fight," Killian growls. "You have to fight."

"No." The word escapes my lips, hoarse and struggling. "I have to survive. That's all. Just survive."

I have a mouth that lets out stupid shit, but a body that understands the need for self-preservation. Growing up as Lord Martin's servant has taught me that if I can't run, submit – and it's always worked.

A snap of light makes me slam my eyes shut and shy away, but I force my eyes open as soon as I can. Seth actually claps, just once, then pumps a fist in the air. His smile is so big that his face can hardly contain it.

Roarke sighs, relieved, then walks off toward the two remaining horses.

Killian doesn't move, still pointing at me, his fist open and his fingers tense like he wants to grab my shirt and shake me. Pax, with his eyes still glowing and absolutely no clothes on, steps up beside him and gently rests his hand on his brother's arm. Killian responds, lowering his arm before stepping back and storming away.

Pax.

The tension inside me melts so suddenly that my knees go weak. I throw myself at him, wrapping my arms around his neck and burying my head in his chest.

"Don't ever disappear on me again," I whisper.

"Too late now," Killian grunts, followed by the sound of horse's hooves tearing down the road.

Slowly, Pax's arms wrap around me. His fingers slip through my hair and press me closer to him.

Darkness

S eth's unruly bay gelding thunders behind me. Dashing in and out of the trees, detouring to jump over a fallen branch, snorting and pulling at its reins. Seth's gaze is focused, but the fool's smiling. Happy. No clue to the danger our brother is putting that girl in.

"Shut up, Seth," I growl.

My black gelding rushes to eat the distance between us and the thieves.

"Didn't say anything, brother."

"You don't need to say it," I grumble.

Seth lets out a whoop, spurring his horse faster for a few beats. They zig across the path ahead of me, then slow to almost match my pace.

"But he's back," the fool says.

I overtake him, and he zags back across the path behind me.

"Not a good thing," I mutter.

"Don't tell me you haven't missed that beast!"

"It's the wrong reason."

"She's a pretty good reason. This shouldn't even be possible – which means it's amazing."

I pull up sharply, but Seth keeps racing past me. It takes a moment to swing his mount around and backtrack to stop right next to me. If we've done our thinking right, we should be ahead of the thieves. Now we wait for them to cross our path.

"You like her?" I question Seth.

I feel his pulse of excitement. The air carries the slightest hint of lilies – possibly lust – as the man turns the question over in his mind.

"She's. Mortal." I push the logic onto him.

"I. Know."

"Mortals. Die."

Conflict grips at him. There's a bitter edge to indecision, and I don't like it.

"Thieves almost had her – highway bandits. The least of our enemies. They almost ended her without a fight," I say.

"She's stuck with us," Seth insists, as if that should be the end of it.

"She's not stuck with *all* of us. Who do you think will stay behind with her, while the rest of us ride against Lithael?" His face hardens, some of his smile shifting into a combination of fear and misery, I go on. "We end Litheal. End this battle his father started. Lucif wanted death – and it will be his son who dies. Either our Shadow rides into that battle – or we ride into it without Pax."

Silence. Maybe now the guy gets it.

The echo of a heartbeat reverberates through time, giving me the slightest glimpse of the man riding toward us. Or men, rather. Three of them. Good.

I dismount and place myself squarely in the way, a fallen tree to one side and a clump of brambles on the other. Seth vanishes to a vantage point that will end up being behind them. After a few breaths, the thieves, one on each of our horses, ride into view. That sight – those scum on my brothers' horses – twists me up inside. With a wicked smile I suck the feelings in, inhaling them, fanning the fire. Pulling my magic into seeing the world through the lens of Darkness.

The men thunder to a stop in front of me, and Seth slips

in behind them. He stays on his horse, the crazy thing miraculously moving silently through the brush, blocking their exit without them even knowing.

A short man with calluses on his left hand and hamstrings coiled tightly, and his friend who has a slightly larger right bicep and a subtle limp, slip down from their saddles. They hand the reins off to their third companion, who considers turning and leaving but spots Seth and cringes.

My targets draw their weapons, stepping to my left and right. They think it's possible to surround me. My fists curl as I sort through their Darkness. Their desires. Their pain.

I pick my first target and leak the Shadows into the other – forming crippling nightmares in his mind to keep him occupied while I end his comrade. The air cools to mist on both their breaths.

I turn to my left-handed attacker as he fakes a right swing, but at the last minute switches his weapon. I'm already there, already so close to him that his swing is useless, knocking his sword from his hand.

"Silvari scum," I hiss, my fist clenching around his wrist.

The bones crush.

The threads that form his mortality glow, spiraling around each other. Only four. Four threads to this man's life. Vulnerability dimmed the first. Pain dims the second. I slam my fist into his jaw and watch him fall, smiling down at him. Ego dims the third.

Before he can recover, I push tendrils of Darkness into his mind. Creating a pool that will drag him to a slow moment when his desires turn toward his own death. That the end would be a mercy. That his life is in my hands, all manner of Darkness clawing up inside him.

I leave him and turn to face the other guy. He breaks free of my Shadows to swing an axe at my head, which explains the larger right bicep. Doesn't explain the limp, though. I block, then stomp down on the toe of his boot and feel no resistance. The guy's missing half his foot.

And still, he rides with thieves. I tilt my head a little to the side – analyzing what this man is made of. Determination.

Lots of determination.

Inhaling slowly, I suck every last bit of that strength straight from him. His eyes go wide, his arms limp. The axe in his hands falls to the ground, then the man drops to his knees – crying.

Seth has left the third man unconscious. I can still see his threads, swirling and spiraling. Fear. Lust. Hate. He has them all, but not a single whiff of the cinnamon scent of regret.

"Wait, I need to ask him a question," Seth pants, covering the distance to the crying man at my feet.

"Why didn't you ask him?" I growl, waving a hand toward the guy my brother has knocked out.

"I did, but he ran out of information."

"Information?" *What could common thieves possibly know that would benefit us?*

"What were you trying to steal?" Seth asks, grabbing the man by the hair and hauling him to his feet.

"Everything. We got the spoils, and Xylon got the status. Legends. Infamous. The ones who took down the Elorsins."

"So you knew who we were?" I ask.

"Twenty-two lizards should have been enough," the man gasps.

"Xylon is your boss?" I demand.

The guys nods, tears still streaming down his face. "Xylon paid us for the manpower. This is the first time we've worked together."

"Paid you in what?" Seth asks.

He waves toward where the horses have begun to pull tufts of grass and chew loudly.

"In your secrets."

"Lithael," I growl.

But the guy shakes his head, hard. "I don't know who sent Xylon."

"Who else could it be? There's really only two types of people in this world. Those who love us, and those who love Lithael."

I really want to slap him up the back of the head, and the way this guy's eyes go wide confirms my opinion. The world is far more complicated than that.

"I don't support Crown Lithael. I support myself. The money would have been worth it."

"Those bags are filled with our clothes. What things of value do you honestly think we would be traveling with?" Seth asks.

"The reason you turned a soot slave into a Saber," the man says.

"Oohh," Seth exaggerates the sound. "Yeah, I can see how that would get your interest. So Lithael sent this Xylon to kill us, but Xylon needed more men. You had the men, and were willing to risk your lives in return for the slim chance we'd be traveling with some kind of secret in our bags?"

"I don't believe him either," I drawl, lifting my blade a little to get the man's attention. "I could start cutting things off until he tells the truth."

"No, no, no," he stammers. "We didn't really have a choice. Xylon's a BeastSeed. The lizards were susceptible to his powers."

"Fuck." The word slips between my teeth.

"Pax." Seth catches the same thread of thought.

He hauls the guy toward the horses and practically throws him on before we're riding hard back toward the others.

Back toward Roarke, Shade, Pax, and his wolf.

But this isn't the Darkness I sensed earlier, that gnawing feeling in the pit of my stomach. It didn't quite *taste* the same.

No, there's something worse waiting for us.

"What were those things?" I demand.

"They were lizards," Roarke says.

"No, they weren't. I've seen lizards. They're small and cute and don't carry weapons."

Roarke leans down, grips one of the thing's oversized gills-that-might-be-ears, and pulls its head back.

"Also a lizard," he says, before running the edge of his blade across its neck.

The wound spills out blood, as well as an assortment of gunky things – what looks like a half-eaten fish and seaweed. Gagging, turning sharply to look for an escape, I eyeball the track out of here that Seth and Killian tore down minutes ago. Nearby, Pax paces, back in his wolf form. I try not to stare, mostly because all I can picture is the guy naked, and all I can think about is being close to him while he's naked – again. When his arms were around me, it was like the world seemed to stop – the only moment where things felt right since we left the White Castle.

Roarke wipes his blade clean in a clump of grass before slipping it into the sheath at his side.

Pax trots up behind me, his breathing heavy. His coat is that shade of coffee and ash that his hair goes when he gets angry. Now I know why.

He takes a few long strides, sniffs at my back, then backs off until there's distance between us again.

It's unnerving and weirdly comforting.

And having both of those emotions inside me at the same time feels like insanity. I haven't had much to do with wolves, but I imagine they're like large dogs. He's bigger. When Pax stretches forward to sniff at me, his nose almost touches the middle of my back. His legs are almost as long as mine. The thick, brownish-like-coffee and dusty-gray-black fur moves like silk. I clench my fists to remind myself that I can't touch it. Can't pat him – that would be rude, wouldn't it?

I mean, I wouldn't scratch the man behind the ear normally, so I probably shouldn't go scratching him behind the ear while he has sharp teeth. But the swirls of molten gold that dance underneath his coat are too beautiful not to want to touch.

Pax turns sharply, eyeballing the road in the direction that Seth and Killian had vanished. A few breaths later, the horses thunder into sight, both of them riding into our midst.

"Human, now," Killian growls.

Pax doesn't obey – snapping and snarling in defiance as if Killian isn't his long trusted brother.

"BeastSeed," Seth says, pushing a man from the front of his saddle.

Not just any man. A thief with thick black hair, eyebrows that stretch across to form one long line of hair, and tears streaming down his face.

"What did you do to him?" I gasp.

And get ignored by all of them.

In a flash, Pax is human again, human and wrapping an arm around me to pull me back tight into his chest... Nope, wait. I barely brush his chest before being shoved behind him and into Roarke's arms.

43

Roarke, however, does pull me into his chest and continue to hold me close, while Seth reaches down and pulls his hostage to his feet.

"Which one?" Pax growls.

"What's a BeastSeed?" I whisper, tilting my head back a little.

"Their power is like Allure, but to animals."

"Eww." I cringe at the idea.

"What? No. Not like *that*. They can make any animal do anything they want."

"There," the hostage is saying, waving to the torn-up body on the other side of our bloody battlefield. "That's Xylon."

"Well, he's clearly not a problem anymore." Seth lets the hostage fall back to the ground, rolling his shoulders and looking like there was some genuine tension there.

Killian reaches across and presses his palm to the hostage's forehead, knocking the guy backward in a fit of tears.

"What's he doing?" I whisper, obviously too loudly, because Killian meets my gaze.

"Getting answers."

"By making the guy cry?"

"By playing with his Darkness," Roarke explains.

Pax, still naked, crouches before the man and asks, "Who sent you?"

"Xylon," the man sobs, waving a hand toward the torn body of the man who tried to lick my face, and who Pax tore to pieces as a freaking ginormous wolf.

"Who sent him?"

"The Crown, I guess. All I know is that he wanted to get to you first. There are others."

Roarke covers my ears before saying, "***Tell us every detail, free your soul from the burden***." Then adding, just for good measure, "***Not you, Shade***."

"That is everything I know," the thief wails.

My guys look from one to the other, like they're silently agreeing on something, before Killian reaches across and smacks the guy over the head hard enough to knock him out.

"I can't make out his features anymore," Pax grumbles, inspecting the body of the man now known as Xylon, but previously known as the face-licker.

I avoid looking. The lizard things are gross, but in a surreal kind of way. That other thing… It's human – or at least it *was*.

"When's the last time you saw a BeastSeed?" Pax asks, coming back to stand with us.

"Never," Roarke answers.

"That time when you were fifty-six and –" Seth begins, but Roarke cuts in.

"Oh yeah, there was that one."

"Two," Killian grunts.

"You mean there's another one of him out there?" I ask.

"Brothers, from my memory. But the men we knew weren't the attack-you-in-the-forest type," Seth says.

"In all fairness, we didn't actually *know* them. They weren't residents of the White Castle, and I can't even remember their names. If this is one of those brothers, I can't imagine they'd keep a grudge over losing a few tournaments for more than two hundred years. But the other is most certainly going to be pissed off now."

"They're attacking us for revenge?"

"Lithael," Killian grunts.

"Oh, yeah. Everything happens because of Lithael," I mutter. "Lithael and revenge."

"Roarke's right – this isn't revenge. Sabers lose in tournament all the time. Every time, actually. There can only be one winner on the sand, so there is always a loser," Seth explains.

"So this is purely because of Lithael?" I ask.

"No doubt," Pax growls. "But where did Lithael find this BeastSeed hiding, and where's his brother?"

Because, like Roarke said, if this wasn't already personal, it is now.

"You," Killian snaps, pointing sharply at Pax, "better get that wolf up out of his primitive darkness before we find out."

In a flash of light Pax is a wolf again, turning to glare at me like maybe he feels all of this is my fault.

Great.

"Why?" I ask, but the word is choked, and only the nearest Elorsin, Roarke, seems to hear me.

"BeastSeeds control primitive creatures. Pax, at full strength, shouldn't be susceptible." He nudges me toward the horses, and I take the hint.

I'm the reason he's not at full strength.

Killian walks up to Pax's horse, pulls out some clothes, and pretty much throws them at the wolf. I'm expecting some more growling, but the wolf picks up the clothes in his jaw, then disappears into the trees.

I watch the empty forest for several long minutes before turning back to the horses – which are nowhere near as interesting as where Pax has gone.

By the time I've played with my horse's reins and gotten to the point where I think I actually might be able to do this, Pax walks back out to join us – dressed and *human* Pax. With his golden eyes troubled, and looking anywhere but at me, he mounts up, then kicks his horse into a gallop and tears off down the track. I feel like the wind's been knocked out of me.

Sucking in a sharp gasp, I walk straight into Roarke. Because he, of course, was standing still, but I was trying to walk forward while looking backward.

He steadies me, not looking down, his attention still on

the remaining two of his brothers. "What are we going to do?"

"Maybe warn me before you suddenly stop next time," I mutter, but he was clearly talking to Killian and not me.

The big guy doesn't respond though, mounting up and riding way back down the track. Way back. Almost out of sight back. Like he doesn't want to be here, but he doesn't want to go too far away either.

"Reach the inn before dark. I need a drink," Seth suggests.

"Not about that," Roarke says, but there's a smile on his face – he wants a drink too. "And not about the BeastSeed either. About her."

Me?

That's why Pax rode off. That's why Killian is way down the track.

Me.

Roarke grips my waist and hoists me up. I go from being on the ground to being in the saddle before I can object. Moving toward his own horse, he begins to tie us together.

"Nope, give me the reins. I'm sick of being led around," I grumble.

Because if Killian and Pax can't stand to be near me right now, then it's more than okay for me to also demand some space.

What little of it that my bubble will allow, anyway. If bubbles had feelings, I'd be letting this one know exactly how much it sucks.

Roarke eyeballs me, hesitating.

"She's got to learn." Seth makes a clicking noise and urges his own mount forward.

"Pull back to stop, little nudges with your feet to go," Roarke says, looping the reins over the horse's neck and offering them to me. "Pull back to stop, little nudges to go."

"I get it. Pull back to stop, little nudges to go," I repeat, which seems to make him happy.

He mounts up and starts moving. Just walking. And without any instruction, my mare moves too.

My mare. Probably should think of something better to call her than 'my mare.'

And I try, but my mind keeps swinging from Pax to the dead guy with his throat ripped out, to said dead guy running his tongue along my face and back again.

Shivers rake over me, and I pull my thoughts to a small gray bird that lands on a nearby tree. A tree just like the one I was pinned to.

Killian sidles up next to me, and I jump because I hadn't even heard him coming.

He grunts.

"Don't," I mutter, because that's his usual command. "I know."

"You should have fought," he says softly.

I fix my gaze on him, trying to judge whether he's rubbing my nose in it or chastising me. "Fighting makes things worse."

"Fighting never makes things worse."

"That's because you *can* fight! You don't even need to fight! You have Saber strength and Elite speed and chuckin' magical powers. I have nothing. Submission is my only defense."

"Submission is defeat."

"Not if it keeps me alive." Even as I say it, doubts creep over me. Alive, but broken.

Damaged, like the marks left on me by Lord Martin. Beaten again and again. Scars around my wrist so bad that Pax can't even stand to look at them. Ridges and depressions in my back from lashings over lashings until my flesh was torn apart. I've learned to live with that. But the lord never went any further.

He wanted to, and I evaded him. At first, he wanted me to kneel and enjoy it – and he didn't chase me when I ran. That was when his wife was still alive. In the two years since the woman died, the willing part of Martin's desires had morphed into demand, and I had become better at hiding in the shadows.

This other guy, the one strewn dead across the forest floor... I refuse to weigh up the price of survival-through-submission if Pax hadn't intervened. Refuse to weigh it up – because I know that no matter what the cost, my actions still would have been submit, submit, submit.

Killian grunts again.

Grunting. The guy survives on grunting and four word sentences. *Is that what it takes to battle the Darkness, grunts?*

I try it out. A soft noise rolls over my vocal cords.

He looks sharply at me, one eyebrow cocked. Then grunts.

The sound is forced up from his chest like he's pushing the air out. Mine sounds a little like I'm saying a raspy, "Herm."

I try again, with a bit more volume, and he echoes my noise. He still sounds better than me, more determined. His grunts always say something – express something. What is my grunt trying to say?

I'm confused, and it sucks.

Everyone seems mad at me, and it really sucks.

I'm vulnerable and that's messing with their lives, and I hate it, and that sucks too.

It all boils down to 'it sucks.'

I grunt again and get a full face, eye to eye, clearly happy about something smile from Killian.

"I like you," he says, and I grunt a thank you. At least I hope it interprets as 'thank you' and not 'chuck you.'

He laughs, a heavy comforting sound that seeps into my soul and settles the nerves rattling around inside me. Settles everything. I breathe a sigh of relief, even though I'm not sure why.

He fishes through his saddlebag with one hand, producing two long strips of dried meat and holding them out to me. There's a chance that one is meant for me and one for him, but I snatch them both up anyway.

"You should rest. I can tie you to your horse."

I look down at the mare in horror but have to swallow my mouthful before I can say anything. "That sounds like torture – not rest. Besides, I thought you'd be the last person to offer rest."

"I want to see you push yourself. Struggle and thrive. No one can do the impossible. You've had two hours of sleep in two days."

"Thank you for noticing – but no, I'd rather stay awake for another week than get tied to anything."

He grunts, nods, then slows down to ride at the back of the line once more, too far away for proper conversation.

I'm not tired. Not tired, I tell myself as I chew through the rest of my meat.

Seth is at the front of our line, then Roarke, me, then Killian. The youngest brother leans back in the saddle, almost laying flat, and looks at me upside down.

"You know, I should call you Splat."

I look at him blankly.

"Because the way you fell out of that tree was like you went 'splat' – or maybe 'rock.' You did drop like a rock."

"You do that, and I'll start calling you Asshole," I say.

"You can do better than that." He lets out a chuffing noise, sitting up and nudging his horse to the side of the track, so he can snap a twig from a spindly little plant.

He twists, throwing it, and even though I know it's coming and try to block it, it still smacks me in the forehead.

I moan, rubbing my face with one hand and stretching out to break my own stick free. A bigger one than his, which I'm rather proud of. I toss it at the guy, he's only a horse length in front of me... and I watch helplessly as it sails off course and hits Roarke in the back.

"Sorry," I burst out, but the words are lost under my laughter.

"What are you hitting me for?" Roarke demands, rubbing his lower back.

"It was his fault," I say, pointing at Seth. "It's always his fault."

"Not this time, Splat. You only have your own crappy aim and weak mortal arms to blame for that."

"I'm not Splat. Roarke, tell him to stop calling me Splat."

"I could call you Shit-shot."

"Shit-shot is pretty accurate," Roarke agrees, still rubbing his back.

"What's wrong with Puppet?" I ask. I don't add that I rather like Roarke calling me Kitten, but have no fondness for being called Puppet. But if my options are Puppet and Shit-shot, then it's a no-brainer.

"Nah, Puppet doesn't suit you anymore. Pretty sure puppets do what they're told."

"Shade. My name is Shade."

"Yes, but technically that's a pet name too. One your cook gave you," Roarke corrects.

"Cook, her name was Cook – she wasn't *my* cook."

I don't have the energy for this. They're not making any sense. I let my eyelids droop shut for just a second. A long blink.

Okay, so sleep would be good right now.

"That can't have been her real name," Seth says.

I open my eyes, checking first that Seth doesn't have a new stick aimed at my head. He's right. Fifteen years living with her and I have no idea what her real name was. Which makes me feel crappy.

"We met the woman – Cook was a fitting name for her, plus she was also your cook," Roarke says.

"Right. That's the rule then. You can't call me something unless I am that thing."

Seth chuckles.

"Useless."

"Pain-in-the-ass."

"Trouble."

Killian, then Roarke, then Seth.

I don't reply, because I'm too busy yawning. Yawning is more important than dealing with these three.

"I like Trouble," Seth decides, that wicked grin on his face. "What's another word for trouble?" he asks Roarke.

"Disturbance."

"Don't you dare," I growl.

"Annoyance."

"Asshole," I counter.

"Bother."

"Fool," I say.

"Are you naming yourself?" Seth asks. "Because they're pretty shit names."

"No! I was naming you," I shout, but then I have to smother another yawn.

"Unpleasant. Vexation. Worry," Roarke continues.

"Wait, vexation," Seth declares. "Vexy. I like it."

I glare at Roarke's back. "What does vexation mean?"

"Something that worries, annoys, irritates, makes you angry, that kind of thing," he says.

"Is that what you think of me?" I demand, specifically of Seth.

"Yes," all three guys answer.

I start ticking through my options. Things to call them. Annoying things.

Or at least I try to, as my eyes droop shut and my legs relax.

"Whoa," Roarke suddenly says, his horse knocking into mine and jolting my eyes open.

I'm leaning on him. If he wasn't right here, I would have hit the ground. And he wasn't right here a moment ago – he was a little ahead of me. Technically I should have fallen into his horse's ass.

I blink up at him, asking, "Not that I'm complaining, but where did you come from?"

"Just luck," he murmurs softly.

He puts one arm around my back, and the next thing I know I'm in his lap, my little pony's reins dropped and forgotten about.

I lean into his chest and admit Killian was right. I need sleep. But this is so much better than being tied to a horse. This is soft and secure, with a gentle rocking motion as his horse continues to walk.

"Roarke?" Seth asks, and through one partially opened eyelid, I see him ride back to retrieve the pony.

"I can hold her," Roarke says, tucking my head into the space underneath his chin. "We're only walking, the horse will be fine. We don't need sleep for days, I'm focused – I can control it, and she's in pain."

I stick my hand in the air like that will help get their attention. "I'm not in pain – just tired."

Roarke grabs my hand and guides it down into my lap. I'm not sure how he's holding the reins, or if his horse is well enough behaved to keep walking – no reins needed right now. But he has one arm wrapped around my back, hand resting on my stomach, and the other comes up to brush the hair from my face. The main reason I'm not completely sure what's going on is because my eyes are closed, and I'm leaving them closed.

Roarke puts his palm on my forehead, and my world turns to white spots and weird sparkles. The tension in my chest, the ache in my arm, the raw burn of my legs – all gone.

"Okay, I was in pain," I mumble…

Darkness

The land feels wrong.
 Tormented.
Drained.
Suffering.

Still looks the same. Same kind of green paints the leaves. The blue in the sky is unchanged. Azure and cobalt.

But there's suffering in the bones of this realm.

I flick my attention back to the girl. To her sleeping features and Roarke holding her like a treasured pet. He meets my eyes, his expression pressed thin.

He fears himself. That no matter what distance he keeps, or how tightly he has his magic locked down – only letting out a few lines of Allure, or a few minutes removing the pain – that he will hurt her.

He can fall in love. I cannot, but maybe if I could, I would understand his fear.

The Darkness seeks a mate – the magic intervening and forging a soul-bond. When a person can taste the fear in others, and you can see the way they see you, it's hard to be near them for long periods of time. And I can't expect anyone to be near me. But bonds between two Darkness souls make us see each other differently. It once made love possible.

Once. Not anymore. A soul-bond requires two Darkness-Seeds, and there is only one left.

Me.

Not saying that the BloodSeed, or Elite SeductionSeed

with a death wish, or that one time with the BlaiseSeed that set me on fire, weren't good. That I can't enjoy another's company in short doses with no long-term expectations.

And maybe the only reason I'm even thinking about all of this is because I'm jealous.

Of Roarke. Of his feelings.

Of them all.

Of *my* Shadow.

SHADOW

I 'm not sure how long I've slept. Only that Killian's in my view and something feels off about him.

"Why's he in a bad mood?" I ask, my voice soft from sleep.

"I thought I felt you stirring," Roarke says, before his gaze moves from me to his brother. "What makes you think he's in a bad mood?"

"His horse is kind of stomping," I explain.

Roarke lifts the reins and guides his horse toward my pony; the guy looks like he's half-considering Killian as we move.

"Awake, Vexy?" Seth asks, his voice so gentle I have to look twice to work out if he's teasing me or not. And I'm still not sure.

I push myself free from Roarke, slip out of his arms, and land on my feet. With help – but I'm going to ignore the fact that he bent to the side to guide me down. "Yes, Sethy, I'm awake."

"Oh, Sethy. I like it," Roarke chimes in.

Roarke's on his horse behind me, and Seth, holding my pony's reins, is mounted in front of me. Both are glaring at each other, a look of challenge in Seth's gaze. I opt for the only exit, which involves practically chasing after Killian, as the two guys start trying to kick each other off their horses.

Killian stops and turns to watch, his brow drawing down with annoyance.

I twist a little as I run, trying to glimpse the action. What Killian finds annoying, I generally find funny.

That is exactly the moment I smack into my invisible wall, bounce off it and land in the dirt.

I groan.

Killian laughs – followed by Seth and Roarke laughing even louder.

Pulling myself to my feet involves a lot of dusting dirt, leaves, and twigs off my clothes. By the time I'm standing, Roarke has ridden past me, and Seth has stopped in front of me.

He dismounts, still laughing, then grips my waist and hoists me onto the mare.

"You can call me anything you like," he says softly, guiding my foot into the stirrup. "But he can't."

He pats my thigh before leaving my side and throwing himself onto his horse, clicking to get us both moving.

Our little track grows wider and begins to smell heavily of a campfire. That might just save us from the two younger brothers still spontaneously trying to tip each other out of their saddles. Killian rumbles, and suddenly I have Chaos riding close on my left and Allure on my right.

"What is it?" Seth asks, after moving into bodyguard position. Note to self, that specific rumble from Killian translates to 'something's wrong.'

My pony is dwarfed between their two full-sized horses, and I have to crane my neck to scan the forest around us. But there's nothing. Just trees, trees, and more trees.

And a smoldering pile of…

"What's that?" I ask, covering my mouth and nose with my sleeve.

It's not wood, and it was never intended as a campfire.

Whatever it is, it's lying clean across the track, and it was once some kind of living, breathing creature.

"A wolf," Killian grunts, steering his horse around it without a second glance.

"A what!" I gasp.

Roarke's hand comes down heavy on my shoulder before I can... I don't know, dismount and inspect the creature. Does it have coffee and ash fur? Golden eyes? It doesn't look nearly big enough, but...

"It's a timber wolf. Native to these woods," Roarke explains.

I inhale. Just a regular wolf.

We can't all go around the tortured creature – it's right in the middle of the track – but Roarke moves forward, grabs my pony's reins near her cheek, and guides us quickly to the edge of the path, while Seth stays back.

"Why is there a barbecued wolf in our path? Can Beast-Seeds set things on fire?"

"No, but they can make a creature stand still while they burn to death," Roarke answers.

My stomach flips low, bile rising in my throat.

"Where's Pax?"

"Rengurra," Killian calls back, his horse trying to move into a trot or canter, but Killian holds him back. Which makes the thing throw its head around in defiance.

"How do you know?" I demand.

"Because he already pissed on the carcass," Killian says.

Oh. Well, okay then.

Killian gives his mount his head, and we all surge forward with a fresh urgency to make it to our destination sooner rather than later.

We emerge from the forest onto a road at a canter, and the first sign of Rengurra appears through the trees soon after. The town is somewhere beyond the tall wall, made from planks of wood fitted with spiky-studs bigger than my head. Clearly they want to keep the forest creatures out.

The boys slow to a walk and ride calmly ahead. I try to mimic their composure. Massive gates sit open, hugely tall but only wide enough for two horses at a time. Killian drops back to ride behind me, Seth in front of me, and Roarke at the lead. Their new order is unsettling.

It shouldn't be; they can line up in any order they want. Just because when I first met them, they were in a line that went Pax, Seth, Roarke, then Killian doesn't mean they have to stay that way.

But they do stay that way, most of the time. Right now they're not, and Pax isn't here at all, and this place is huge and full of people. It feels wrong. Nerves bounce around inside me, making me long to hear Killian laugh again.

Swallowing them down, I focus on the details. The peeling black paint on the wall. Short tufts of grass growing between the base of it and a very well-trodden track alongside it.

A guy in leather armor steps out of a small shelter next to the gate. "Halt. All visitors from the forest must declare themselves," he announces.

"Why?" Killian grunts, stopping right beside me.

But Roarke and Seth swing down off their horses and hold their arms out to display their weapons. They turn in a circle then hold out their hands to clearly show the Seals burned into their flesh.

"Why did you travel through the forest and not around on the main roads?" the guard asks.

"We had word that lizards were causing problems and wanted to see if we could deal with them on our way through," Roarke explains. He doesn't hesitate at all, and the half-lie sounds genuine.

"They don't know who you are?" I whisper-ask Killian.

"Why would they?" he grumbles back, too low for the nearby guard to hear while Roarke is continuing to explain that they did, indeed, deal with some lizards on the way through.

"Our faces aren't painted on walls. Do you think we ride around with announcements on our asses?"

"There's plenty of problems in those woods," the guard mutters, turning to Killian and adding, "Well, you too."

Killian snaps his sleeve back and thrusts his hand out for inspection.

"Any new problems on the road ahead?" Roarke asks.

"Nothing new here, but plenty of stories further along the trade routes."

"There's always trouble on the trade routes," Seth says, climbing back onto his horse. "That's what enforcement is for."

"And her, what's her story? She aint' no Saber."

"Neither are you," Roarke declares, mounting up. "*But your memory can be patchy, can't it, old man? How about you forget about her?*"

The man's eyes glaze over, his face going slack, and he lifts an arm as though half-asleep to wave us through the gates.

The street is churned up, but not currently muddy. It makes me think that when it does rain, it rains hard, and the ground stays wet for a long time. All of the buildings are made from timber with wide verandas and bridges from one to the next. They sit on short stumps to keep them just above the ground. The scattering of people moving about on the bridges and walkways in the late afternoon sun barely look up or notice us. All of the people are on the walkways. What is on the road *is* so much weirder than people.

Centaurs, that's what Cook's stories used to call a being with the top half human and the bottom half horse. When I was a kid, I pictured a big plough-horse and a hairy old man. I never pictured silky fur, perfectly toned abs, and hair like it belongs on a goddess. There's six of them on the street, all women, and too far away for me to properly admire, but we walk straight past two wearing loose satin shirts in bright blues and pinks, which barely reach to their belly buttons. Their horse lower-bodies are both white, one with braids through the tail and the other with sections painted in red.

I admit, I'm staring.

And right on cue, they look over at me. Their attention is quickly pulled past me and onto Roarke, like he's a magnet, and they're drawn to him. He doesn't seem to notice, though.

After they cover their mouths, whispering and batting their long lashes, their gazes move back to me. Their smiles pull tight in disgust.

I lift my hand, in a way blocking my view, but pretending to tuck a stray strand of hair behind my ear and doing everything but whistling to act like I don't care what they think.

Seth does start to whistle, sidling his horse next to mine. "Ignore them," he says softly, then shrugs. "Or watch."

I catch a glimpse of the twinkle in his eye and glance over my shoulder, expecting to see one, or both, of the centaurs slip over. I guess they can't technically fall on their asses, but any falling would be good.

Nothing happens.

I twist back to look at Seth.

He winks. "I don't normally get specific about my Chaos, but this feels like a slow revenge moment. Watch."

I obey, twisting further in the saddle as we move down the road at a normal walk and they continue to amble along like they're too pretty to move any quicker.

Their tails are already swishing, as horses' tails do, so it takes me a minute to spot the strands stretching from one to the other. Reaching, entwining, and knotting. Within seconds, the two are so thoroughly threaded together that they're going to need scissors to fix it.

I look back at Seth to see the guy's beaming.

We keep walking and soon turn a corner. A high-pitched scream erupts from the street behind us.

I don't even bother containing my laugh.

"That's what I was waiting for," Seth says, clicking loudly so his horse skips ahead.

We ride through the rest of town, past the buildings built too close together, until the town begins to sprawl. Goat and pig pens fill the space between homes. A few more centaurs walk past – all women. They're pretty gorgeous, and a part of me is keen to see if the male versions are muscular or hairy. I still expect them to be hairy, but that's a pretty big gap in equality. If the women are divine and the men are not, I really pity the women.

The road snakes around, a forest on our left and the last building on our right.

A shepherd's crook slung on a crooked angle hangs from the roof. No two guesses needed on the name of the place. 'The Crooked Crook.'

The forest has been cleared, lush grass growing in its place, with the squat two-story building in the middle. Outbuildings hug its walls and speckle the yard behind – a woodshed, cellar, outhouse, bathrooms. The guys ride straight for a timber-fenced yard where Pax's dapple gray stallion is grazing lazily alongside a black gelding. No, not quite black. Just very, very brown. His mane and tail are a golden-yellow. Not the glowing metal type like in Seth's hair or Pax's eyes, but a gentle sandy color. I could stare at him all day. He's unlike anything I've ever seen.

Pax, his bags, and his saddle are nowhere to be seen.

Roarke hops down and opens the gate, then pushes it shut behind us. I slip awkwardly to the ground, running my hand over the pony's soft neck. My legs ache, my bum aches, and my arm aches. Man, does my arm ache. I hadn't noticed the pain slowly seeping in, being strained by the cool evening air and general use, but it has. Hugging my arm close, I rest my forehead against the saddle, just grateful to have made a destination. Not our final destination, but a safe stopping point, anyway.

After a breath, I collect myself and begin a one-handed struggle with the buckles on the saddle, using the guys around me as a model. Nearby, Seth lifts the side of the leather, reaches under, and in one smooth motion has the stomach-strap-thing undone.

I try to do the same, wriggling and wrestling and making no progress.

Roarke settles his saddle over the railing, hooking his horse's reins over the post, and moves in my direction.

"Here, let me," he offers, but my hand's already in the air – held out to stop him.

"Nope, I can do it."

"Or I can do it," Seth says.

"No, leave me to it. I'm not useless," I tell them, then before Killian can grunt I add, "Not a word, Killian. I am *not* useless."

Killian lets himself out through the gate. He has saddle-bags over one shoulder, cloak in one hand, saddle over his arm, two swords attached at his belt, bridle hanging from his neck and a bow and his arrows resting against his back. My jaw almost drops – the guy makes it look easy, ambling up and into the inn.

Meanwhile, I manage to get my own saddle free and struggle to slip my left arm underneath it, hoist it from the horse's back, and set it down on the fence.

I'm pretty proud of that effort, smiling and all.

"Good job," Seth says, clapping.

Okay, sure, a five-year-old could probably get a saddle off – but I have all of twenty-four hours experience. Let's not talk about the one arm thing.

Seth springs from the ground up onto the fence railing and proceeds to balance along it until he's next to me, then he sits with his legs dangling and his dazzling blue eyes watching my every move.

"Bridle now," he announces, waving at the horse's head.

I roll my eyes at him, setting about undoing the buckle under the horse's chin. The animal moves away as soon as she's free, tearing up chunks of grass and chewing them slowly. Roarke's already left with all of his gear, and Seth's stuff is sitting nearby. He pops to his feet, perches on the railing for a bare second, then springs into a backflip and lands lightly on the grass beside his bags.

"Show-off," I drone.

"Want me to teach you?" He's smiling so big that both his cheeks dimple.

How can I say no to that?

I slip through the fence, over one railing, and under the other. "Is it going to hurt?" I ask, lifting my broken, bandaged, and splinted arm to highlight my concerns.

"Nah," he says, offering me a relaxed shrug.

"I don't believe you."

"You never believe me."

"Not true. I usually believe you, and that's what gets me into so much trouble."

He steps up close, which makes me lean back a little to keep eye contact. Roarke has silver strands among his dark hair. Seth has gold so vibrant that I'm willing to bet it's actual metal. It always catches my eye, but this time I reach up and pluck one from his head. I roll it between my fingers. It's thicker than a normal strand, smooth as silk, and so bright it shines in the dwindling copper sunset.

The guy smiles down at me, a lopsided smile full of curiosity.

"What?" he asks.

"Could have sworn it was real gold. Why is it that no other Silvari I've seen have shiny hair like you and Roarke?"

"Last of our kind."

He says it so dismissively that it takes me a beat to register the weight of his words and a second after that for the shock to settle into my features. Pax is the last AlphaSeed, Killian is the last DarknessSeed – I already knew that – but Seth is the last ChaosSeed, and Roarke is also the last AllureSeed.

"What happened? Did your parents decide to have an exotic collection of kids?"

He shrugs, dismissively. "I never asked."

Of course he didn't. The carefree streak in his nature is much larger and more in control than the slim vein of common sense and the even slimmer trace of logic.

"Our pentad is made up of four almost extinct Seeds and a mortal. Our mother sent us to find you for a reason. The same as she found the rest of us."

"Don't say that." I swallow down the lump in my throat. A lump of longing-to-belong-but-knowing-I-don't.

"What? That our mother sent us to find you?"

"No, that you four risked your lives in a stupid tournament to have the powers-that-be remove my status as a soot-servant from the Desayer realm and consider me an Elite Saber and part of your team. I'm not part of your team, Seth." A stab of pain hits me as each word forms and escapes my lips. "On the inside, I'm still a soot-servant."

The smile slips from his lips, and he caresses the backs of his fingers over my cheek as if wiping away tears that aren't there.

"No, you're not. Part of you is Silvari. Part of you belongs here, and all of you belongs to us, Vexy."

"Not your toy," I rebuke.

"You like being my toy."

Before my mouth can spit out something stupid – like the fact that he's right – I grab at a whole new conversation. "Teach me to flip."

I hold my broken arm in the air – hoping my gesture conveys the threat that if he hurts me, I will be hurting him back. Not physically, because that's not even possible, but I'll find something nasty to put in his boots or down his pants or in the hood of his cloak.

"Can you jump?" he asks.

"Of course I can jump!"

"Show me."

I roll my eyes and jump.

"Higher."

I try again, I need to get higher, but I still want to land gently.

"Like this," he says, and I swear he looks exactly the same as I do. "Arms must go up."

Throwing my arms around is a new concept. So is jumping up and down in public on the grass beside an inn, but I do it anyway.

"You're not going to make it around like that. You'll land on your head. You have to jump like the landing isn't going to hurt."

"That makes so much sense." My voice drips with sarcasm.

It makes him chuckle. "If you jump like it's going to hurt, then you'll make it hurt. Focus, tell your body exactly what to do, and then wait and see. Doing things any other way is like willing them to go wrong."

That sounded smart – but I'm not about to tell him that.

Instead, I listen. Pushing the awkward feeling out of my mind as I jump up and down, again and again, and swing my arms to reach for the sky over and over. An ache slips through my damaged bone, but I'm too busy thinking about the fact that every minute of this could just be Seth playing a joke on me.

"Okay, stop," he says, stepping in behind me and resting his hands on my hips. "I'm going to stand here, and you're just going to jump up and look at the sky – then go back down again."

"Really?"

"Really." He nods, smiling stupidly big.

He is definitely jesting with me. All right. I wonder how long he can keep this up if I just play along? At what point is he going to get bored and suddenly start laughing?

Does playing into his joke when I know it's a joke actually make me the one pulling the prank?

I jump, lean my head back and glimpse the darkening sky, then he takes my weight and lowers me back to the ground.

"When you come up this time, I want you to lift your knees to your chest – but don't try to roll backward. Just jump, pull your hands up to your face, look at the sky, and lift your knees. Then I'll lower you back to the ground."

As instructed I jump, look up, lift my knees, then find myself lowered back to the ground.

He spins me around to face him so quickly that I almost fall over. His hands on my hips are the only thing that keeps me steady. I'm just waiting for the punchline.

"No matter what, you have to follow through. If you bail out halfway, jerk, hesitate, or second guess yourself for just a moment, you're probably going to break your neck."

"Yep, all right, in that case, let's go get dinner," I say, pulling away and taking a fake let's-give-up-now step backward toward the inn.

He tilts his head a little to the side, his blue eyes searching mine. Then he just nods, stepping as if agreeing with me. Agreeing that I'm incapable of doing this, too weak or stupid to learn to do a backflip.

"Fine," I declare, pushing firmly on his chest. He stops in his tracks. "What's the next step?" *Your stupid prank better get to the point soon, or I really am out of here.*

He spins me around before I can change my mind. His hands remain on my waist as he positions himself a little behind me and a little to the side.

"This time, commit. Follow through. All the way around. Don't stop until you've landed on your feet or your ass. Probably your ass. I always landed on my ass. Ready?"

What person learns to backflip by jumping and looking at the sky? Or jumping and leaning back against someone else?

"Seth, if you hurt me –" I begin.

"You'll put a taco in my boot?"

"No, I'll get Killian to kick your ass."

He chuckles. "Pretty sure I can outrun him."

"Pretty sure you can't run forever."

"How sure? I've got a good thousand years in me yet, Vexy."

"Fine." I growl.

"Then jump."

I jump. Look up at the sky and lift my legs – fully committing and at the same time completely disbelieving of everything he's said. My body follows through, rolling back over his shoulder. I feel a push against my hips, then he steps forward – I continue backward and for a blissful split second I'm mid-air and spinning. The world rushing by.

Then the ground rushes up, and I land smack on my ass. The pain should affect me, but it doesn't – because I just did it. I flipped.

Not too weak. Not too stupid.

I pop to my feet and let out a cheer. Jumping around like an idiot.

"Again?" he asks, arms out ready.

"Yes!"

Again, and again, and again. Until it's too dark to see the ground and people begin to wander out from the town to the inn. Probably something to do with the delicious smells wafting out of the place.

Darkness

"Hardly a palace," Roarke mutters, running a finger along the dusty mantle.

"That's because it's not a palace – it's an inn," Pax snaps.

Roarke drops his bag in the corner and lays his sword on the dust. The room is simple. Big bed. Big window. Big hearth and a small fire. There are tattered canvas curtains over the window. I don't even need to pull them aside to watch the two out in the yard. Seth, smiling like a kid with a toy, and Shade jumping around like a toy with a kid.

Happy.

Which contrasts Pax's anguish. The guy doesn't say anything. He's not even doing anything, specifically. But he's hurting.

"Good horse." I nod toward the silver dapple Silvari gelding in the yard. It doesn't take a genius to work out that's why Pax rode ahead. That's the excuse he gave himself.

Pax glances at the window, pulls his gaze away, and then tosses his own bag across the room to crash into the wall beside the bed.

"I'm out," Roarke announces, slipping from the room and closing the door behind himself.

My attention stays on the two in the yard. On their laughter. I can feel it even from here. Not normally some-thing I can do – but this bubble is messing with all of our magic.

"How's your arm?" Pax asks, sitting heavily on the bed somewhere behind me.

"Healing," I say. I don't even move to show him.

"Was unintentional."

"I know."

His thoughts turn dark, or something in them does. I can't read his mind, but I can feel the way his emotions change. Something happening inside his head has gripped at his heart, tainting the air with the smell of a lingering memory. Of fear.

"Don't," I grunt.

"But I should have left her there. Every single thing we need to do to save this kingdom will come crashing down around us because of me."

"Hm," I mutter. "Done now."

I turn away from the window. The guy is on the edge of the bed, his head in his hands, massaging his brow, frowning at the ground. A knowing frown.

"You already knew," I press.

"Not really, not when I first saw her. I knew she was worth saving – but there are lots of people worth saving, and we don't have time to go around rescuing people individually."

"But you did. You rescued her."

"Yes, I did."

"And you'd do it again." I feel his wolf bristle to life deep within his soul.

"Of course, I would," he snaps – no wolf in his voice, though.

Interesting. The two have already found some balance. Neither one is playing master to the other. Which means they both agree – they have both bonded with her, and the damned girl doesn't even have a clue what this means.

Pax lets out a long sigh and joins me beside the window, in time to watch the girl flip right over Seth's shoulder and land on her ass. She's on her feet quicker than I thought the mortal could move, not a tinge of fear or the flicker of apprehension in sight.

Happy.

She moves in close to Seth, his hands gripping low on her hips. Her back to him, so she probably can't see the way he's looking at her. The quick glances that slide low over her chest, the lopsided way he's grinning. I'm not willing to bet on it, though, because women tend to know all sorts of things that I'd think impossible.

She jumps, he rolls her back over his shoulder, and this time she lands on her feet. He can't get his hands back on her hips quickly enough. There's a tension in the kid that I've never seen before. Roarke gets nervous. He has the kind of power that hides it, and he has a gift for getting what he wants, so he never has to face uncertainty. But with Shade, Roarke is always edgy. Seth doesn't tend to get worried about anything – but he is right now. Worry that smells like desire and hope mixed together.

"What about him?"

Long seconds stretch out before he answers, "Not a problem."

"What do you mean *not a problem*?"

"I don't know," he says. "It just isn't. Which one of us she spends time with isn't going to be an issue."

I don't believe him. Squaring off with my full attention on Pax, who's almost a head shorter than I am – but then so is almost everyone – I focus all of my power on him. On his threads and the way his darkness moves, shifts, ebbs, and flows around the other things that make him tick.

"Look at them," I order, pointing out the window. "What if he kissed her right now? Grabbed her tight, pulled her in, and passionately kissed the fuck out of her?"

"Doesn't," he says slowly, "bother me."

His emotions mirror his words.

Two Silvari guys walk quietly up the road, glancing curiously at Shade and Seth and their antics.

"What if they kissed her?" I ask, pointing at the Silvari.

Pax's lips curl and fangs drop. Threads of protection unfurl – ready to attack.

"No," he growls, the word barely discernible amongst the raw aggression.

"Back here," I order, pointing at Seth and Shade again. Not sure if I'm talking to Pax or his wolf – or both. "Seth and Shade," I repeat, trying to focus them. His canines retreat, his threads settling like his protection isn't needed because Seth is there to do the job. Almost. There's a hint of Alpha still in the air. An amber smell that is lingering.

Then I decide to press him a little further.

"My Shadow," I begin.

Nothing. No reaction.

"Imagine she's immortal. Imagine she could handle being with one of us," I continue.

Pax settles a wide-eyed look on me, a small muscle on his jaw ticking with the threat of harm to come.

"No."

"Imagine." I raise my voice – we need to finish this conversation. "If she could survive. What would you do to Seth?"

Because for any other guy, any other girl, sharing would be out of the question. I've known Pax a long time, and he does not play well with others. None of us do. But for an Alpha to see his mate with another man, it would only end in death – no matter how close the men were. The MateBond is stronger than family.

I need to know how long we can all stand to be near each other before Pax becomes too dangerous.

I need to know who he's going to try to kill first.

His wolf retreats. His threads settle. The tension ebbs away.

"Nothing," he says, and he means it. "Assuming she were a true Saber, and immortal, and she wanted to be with any of us, I would do nothing. We aren't in competition."

"Huh," I muse.

I leave the guy with his window and his swirling emotions. Going out the door, down the stairs, and straight to the bar.

He didn't just say 'Seth.' He said *any* of us. And that idea is its own kind of dangerous.

S eth leads the way up the stairs onto a narrow veranda and through a double set of doors. Past a growing crowd inside a common eating and drinking hall, then up another set of stairs. When we reach the top, Killian steps out of the third room down the corridor.

He grunts on his way past, but keeps moving. Seth ignores him, opens the door his brother just came out of, then motions for me to enter first.

The bed's huge – all Silvari beds seem to be big – with four pillows across the top and a thick, patterned blanket all puffed up and looking like heaven. A gentle hiss and crackle fills the room from the fireplace opposite the bed. There's a painting of a chicken on the wall – which is just odd – and a small rectangular rug woven in grays and blacks on the floor.

Pax is on the other side of the room, inspecting the contents of his saddlebag.

The door clicks shut behind us. The one bed thing doesn't worry me – these guys sleep about once every moon cycle, and I'm betting we're only staying here for the night, which means I'm the only one who will need the bed. Because I'm the only mortal in the room, and mortals have needs.

According to Pax, intimacy just isn't one of them.

"Where are your clothes?" Seth asks.

"In your bag," I say, pointing to the bag he's just put down.

He raises an eyebrow. "In my bag?"

"You would have known if you weren't off making a mess of the bottler's office," Pax points out.

"You're welcome," Seth says.

Both Pax and I groan.

Yes, the prank Seth pulled on the bottler did inadvertently provide us with the distraction we needed to escape, but no – no one wants to hear him gloat about it.

Seth runs his gaze over his brother, then – for some reason I fail to understand – he retreats.

"I'll send up a servant and some water," he says, then he's gone and the door's shut and I'm alone with Pax.

I turn sharply and bend down to Seth's bag, setting about gripping the fabric in my teeth and trying to unzip the thing with one hand. Gripping and pulling with my right is out of the question. I'm just about to get my foot in on the action when Pax crouches next to me.

Even though I knew he was in the room, I still jump. Not scared, not like waking up with Lord Martin leaning over me, but still kind of scared, like looking up and seeing a spider right next to the toilet.

I, however, am "not on the toilet."

And I just said that out loud!

Crap, crap, crap.

Of course I'd say something like that out loud – because that's the relationship my brain and mouth have. I groan, burying my face in my hand.

Food, my problem is food. These guys seem to be constantly eating. Only sometimes it's three course meals at lunch and other times it's a single piece of fruit. My brain needs more energy to keep control of my mouth.

At least, I wish it were that easy.

Pax just smiles, unzipping the bag with ease while saying, "There's one downstairs."

"You didn't tell me you could turn into a wolf," I blurt out the first thing that pops into my mind, hoping it's better than the *last* thing I let escape.

"I can't."

"I saw you do it."

"We kind of co-exist."

The Alphas only mating with Alphas thing suddenly makes sense – if their wolves are separate beings, then they would have to fall in love with each other too. How I fit into this equation, however, is still a mystery. The kind of mystery that makes me very nervous.

"Am I in trouble?" I ask, referring to the going-to-get-myself-killed kind. "I mean, if your wolf decides he likes me, that sounds –"

Pax takes my good hand and pulls me up with him as he stands. Time seems to slow, and I feel every subtle movement… Him letting go of my hand finger by finger, pulling himself to his full height, which draws him that bit further away from me, his hand falling back to his side – putting more distance between us.

Back the bralls up, I tell myself. *I do not need his touch.* Needing a guy is not the kind of thing I do. Enjoying the company of these guys – yes. Not managing to exist without them because of a bubble, that I can handle.

Wanting to tackle this guy, pin him down, and rip his clothes off? That is a whole new emotion.

I just answered my own question – we are in some serious trouble.

I take a step back, but there was only one step between me and the wall, so I take three steps to the side and end up in the corner between the bed and the far wall. This isn't a very big room, but somehow this distance feels wrong. It's made worse by the small crease of disappointment that runs across his expression.

"I'm sorry about the hugging you thing," I blurt out. "I didn't mean to make things harder for you... or your wolf."

He scratches the back of his head, hesitating on whatever words he wants to get out.

"I'll keep my distance from now on. I'll stay over here, you stay over there." I swallow hard on the lump in my throat and force air down past the pain in my chest – because no part of me wants to hurt him, or see him hurting, but I don't think I would survive the affections of a wolf.

"Too late," he says.

Killian said that in the forest too. Right when I hugged just-saved-my-life-but-still-naked Pax.

"I'm sorry," I whisper, because this is all my fault. I deflate onto the bed before asking, "Can we reverse it? Is there a potion or a seal or something to fix my mistake?"

The door opens, no knocking, and four servants walk in. Three girls and a guy, all wearing leather aprons and looking nervous. The first two are carrying a round wooden wash tub. They look up, spot Pax, then turn completely white.

"Wait, put it by the fire," Pax orders, waving them in before they can run back out the door.

They obey. The young man looks like he might be about to vomit. He, and the last girl, are carrying an oversized bucket of water in each hand. They avoid looking up as they place everything in front of the fire.

Roarke saunters into the room, also without knocking. The guy's wearing a black towel, his dirty clothes clutched in one hand. Gorgeous face, slim shoulders with the defined muscles of someone who can move, fight, and run, and a scattering of hair across his chest.

Roarke offers Pax a look that I don't even have a name for. A tilt of the head, a crease over one eyebrow. Maybe a 'What do you want me to do?'

Pax looks at me, looks at his brother, then nods. He grabs

some clothes from his bag before leaving the room. I dash after him without thinking, only to have Roarke hold his arm out and catch me on the way past.

"Let him go," he says softly.

When I struggle and manage to block the servants' only exit, Roarke lifts me up and physically holds me back. He sets me on my feet again when the Silvari servants have left the room, but doesn't remove his arm. So I'm still attached to him as he moves to the door and flicks the lock over to seal us in.

Then he lets me go, placing himself in the doorway as a further barrier from me escaping. Not that the magical bubble wouldn't do a good job of that anyway – but maybe he's worried about me making a scene.

"What?!" I demand, because he's acting like I'm about to murder someone.

"Give him his space."

"He's had plenty of space. The guy's been running off from me all day. I need answers." It occurs to me that Roarke is the answers guy, and I fix him in my gaze. "*You* can answer me. How do we undo this mating thing?"

I poke him in the chest, hoping that the action emphasizes my point.

He doesn't look impressed by the idea, but I stand my ground while he runs his thumb and forefinger over his manicured mustache-beard combo.

"You asked him that?"

"Of course. We need to fix this. Is there a potion – or a seal? I'm good with a seal if it'll fix this."

"That had to sting," he mutters, not referring to my suggestion of a seal. Yes – sigils and seals hurt, but for Pax I'd do it.

I'd do anything for any one of them.

"Being trapped with me is hurting him. You've seen him,

he's all over the place, angry and avoiding you all. That's because of me. We have to fix this."

Roarke shakes his head in sweeping motions that makes his long hair, mostly tied in a band at the base of his neck, sway.

"There is no *fixing* it."

"Then how can I make things right?!"

"You can stop hurting the guy's feelings, to begin with."

I drop my hand and stop poking him.

"You walked all the way through the inn wearing that?" I demand.

Roarke's practically naked body is a very good distraction from this whole conversation.

"Of course I did. I like the attention," he says, then he makes a spinning motion with his hand, and I do as I'm asked, turning to face the wall and give him some privacy. The sound of a zipper opening fills the room, followed by the obvious shuffling and rustling noises. I tune them out, wallowing in the mess of feelings inside me instead. I can't work out if I don't want this mating for the right or wrong reasons. Is it because I'm scared for him – or for me? "He has rules," Roarke continues, making me jump.

I hadn't even heard him approach. The guy's right behind me, leaning in so he can talk softly in my ear.

"I know he has rules," I mutter.

"He won't hurt you," he adds. "And he will keep you safe."

I spin sharply, feeling like he's only giving me half the truth, but also like he's only understanding half the problem. "*I'm* hurting him. I'm making his life worse."

"That's not how he sees it. It makes things more complicated, and we don't really understand what's happening, but we can work that out."

"Tell me how he sees it?" I ask, only just managing to muster a whisper.

"You should probably ask him that."

He searches my expression for a moment, but I'm not sure what I look like. "When he lost his child, then his love, his wolf receded out of reach. I can't pretend to know what that feels like, but I imagine it's close to losing a limb and a brother at the same time." He stops abruptly, before adding, "Your bath's getting cold. I'll wait outside the door."

He's out the door, and the door is shut again, before I can even open my mouth. Not that my mouth has much to say. My mouth is stunned silent. It's my heart that's screaming at me.

I steel myself enough to approach the door and tap on it lightly with one fingernail.

"I'm still here," Roarke says from the other side.

If it were Seth, I'd be worried that he'd wait until I'm naked and walk off – making my invisible wall force me out of the room while stripped bare. Which he would think is hilarious.

But Roarke is not like Seth.

The bath is big enough to sit in, hot enough to relax in, and smells sweet, like they've poured soap directly into the water. I scrub gently over my bruised ribs and raw legs – minor injuries that sting like bralls. At some stage, I'll need help to re-wrap the bandage on my arm. Holding it stiffly in place keeps the pain at bay, but the fabric and thin metal splints have loosened over time, leaving room for movement. A job for later, when I've stopped driving my guys away from me and won't feel guilty asking one of them for help.

The fire crackles in front of me, small logs glowing and occasionally shooting sparks up the chimney. The room is littered with bags, saddles, and weapons, but rather than feeling small and cramped, it feels comforting, almost familiar. Despite the fact that we're in a new place, facing a new challenge.

These guys' lives must have been so boring before they met me.

I don't linger in the water. Food awaits, and even though the guys packed various rolls, pastries, fruits, and meats for the trip, more eating never hurt anyone.

I dry with the towel that Roarke discarded, the inn's towel. Black is a really odd color, though. Before fetching fresh clothes, I fold my old ones – and something crunches within the fabric.

I pull it out. *It* is the paper Jada had slipped into my hand while the boys grabbed their gear and prepared to run into the night. The Sealer seemed like the guys' friend, even referred to their mother endearingly. But there was no time to ask someone to read the note, or even risk pulling it out before we left the White Castle. Or during our rushed midnight ride. Then Pax stole all my thoughts away.

Even if I could read Common, this thing would still be lost on me. It's in Silvari scribble. I fold the thing back up, or rather, half-roll, half-fold, and stash it in the small pocket on the front of my pants. That's one of the ways to tell if a garment is made for servants or masters. Servants' pockets are big enough for rags and cleaning supplies, everyone else has these tiny little things – what does a normal person even put in there? A shopping list? Emergency monthlies cloth – because when that goes wrong it's a genuine emergency?

Getting dressed and undressed one-armed is a little more time-consuming than I'd like – but not impossible. Putting my hair up into a presentable band, however, is impossible. I open the door, then jump out of the way as Roarke stumbles backward. He flails for a second before regaining his balance.

"Were you leaning on the door?" I ask.

"Yeah."

"That's a stupid thing to do."

"Apparently." He looks me up and down, then settles his gaze on my hair.

"Help?" I ask, holding the thick piece of elastic out for him.

His cheeks dimple. "My pleasure."

Then he snatches a brush up out of his bag and expertly pulls the knots from my just longer than shoulder length blonde locks.

"Can I cut it?"

"What?"

"When's the last time you took care of your hair?"

I run my fingers through it, trying to process what he's talking about. "A few weeks ago, actually."

"No, I'm not talking about the last time you hacked it off."

I shrug. It's not something that's ever worried me.

"Cook's method of hair cutting was to gather it all up in one hand and use a knife to saw through it," I explain.

"Why? Didn't the woman own scissors?"

"Anything to look less appealing in Martin's eyes."

Anything.

"I see," Roarke says, slowly, like other, more important thoughts are rushing through his mind. "I'm cutting it."

He steers me toward the fire, then fetches scissors from Killian's saddlebag – not sure why Killian packed them – and gets to work. As the hair comes away in his fingers, he tosses it into the fire.

"Stay still," he orders.

"I am. You really don't have to do this. It's fine."

"Yep, I do – it's not fine."

I leave him to it, listening to the rhythmic snip-snipping noise and scrunching my nose up at the faint smell of burnt hair. I give the almost-healed line on my arm a scratch, the one left by a knife when my bubble and I first met.

"Done," he eventually declares.

I run my fingers through the light locks. There's something almost giddy inside me at the feel of it. I can't even see it – but it feels *so* good. It's shorter, just above my shoulders, silky through my fingers, and a little wavy.

"What's it look like?" I eventually manage to ask, still shaking and combing my fingers down the strands.

"Like hair," he replies, smiling with delight. "Real hair, not a rat's nest in a band."

I'd mention that I've woken up with rats in my hair, and that's a million times worse than you'd think. I'd also hit him, but I still need him.

I hold my splinted arm up, again asking, "Help?"

"Here, rest it on a pillow."

He grabs one of the pillows and lays it on the edge of the bed. Kneeling, I do as instructed, and he kneels opposite to me, gently unraveling the bandage.

"If it hurts, tell me," he says.

"I will," I agree, but I'm going to try not to. Not because his offer isn't welcome – but because I'm more than confused about what I want from these guys.

He twists my arm, making me grind my teeth against the stabbing reminder that I can't fight, can't even bloody fall, without hurting myself. Then it's gone, so subtly drawn away that white specks barely touch my vision. My jaw relaxes.

"I was fine," I mutter.

"I shouldn't be using my power on you." It actually sounds like he's arguing with himself.

"Then why did you?"

He refuses to look up from his hands as they gently brush along the length of cloth, unraveling it.

"If you'd stop getting hurt, I could stop intervening with your pain."

"Have you ever considered that I hurt myself at timed

85

intervals in our relationship just so you have to let your guard down around me?" I blurt out.

He freezes, his gaze snapping sharply to meet mine.

I stare back into his beautiful dark eyes and wait for him to realize that I'm not serious. How could he even entertain that someone might do that?

Unless that *someone* was Killian.

His lips press together, trying to smother a smile.

"You and Seth were cut from the same cloth," he says, turning his attention back to the bandage.

It feels like a compliment, though I'm not sure if it was intended to be.

"Thank you."

"For comparing you to Seth?"

I snort a little. "No, for the hair and the arm."

"I was going to thank you, actually. None of the others let me near their hair."

I open my mouth to ask about the note – after all, words and knowing stuff is Roarke's thing – but then there's a tap on the door. After the briefest pause, Pax and Killian wander in. They're clean-shaven and wearing towels, with wet hair and the day's dirty clothes in one hand. Pax runs his gaze over me, stepping close to examine my bare arm. It's bruised down the middle, but the swelling's gone, and really, it doesn't look broken at all.

Roarke grabs the hair-cutting, and possibly other-stuff-cutting, scissors off the bed and tosses them toward Killian. A normally deadly action, but Killian snatches them out of the air like it's nothing.

Which Roarke must have expected, because he wasn't even looking.

Pax and Killian stow their things away in their bags. Everything neat. Everything ready to grab at a moment's notice. There's even a clean escape straight out our window to the horses – I just hope they don't expect me to make a two-story jump in the middle of the night.

Roarke straightens the splints on either side of my arm and rolls the bandage to firm everything into place.

"Done," he says, getting up and offering me a hand.

I'd accept, but I'm already halfway up.

He heads for the exit, and I hurry to follow him out into the hall where Seth is waiting.

The youngest brother gives me a lopsided smile, the kind that says he's up to something. I have just enough time to take a step back, but not enough time to run. He reaches out, grabs my shirt at my middle, and the next thing I know I'm pinned to the nearest wall. He's still smiling, his grip on my shirt instantly releasing.

Chills run down my spine. Good chills.

Maybe that's exactly the reason I don't run – that, and the second of hesitation in his eyes.

"Sorry, not sorry," he says, his voice a silky whisper.

His lips are on mine, his body pressing into me.

Chuck, my head shouts, but my body presses into his, raising up on tiptoes. My fingers thread through the waist of his shirt. Searching for skin. Finding it and brushing along his side – up his back.

He pauses, letting out a shuddering breath that whispers across my lips. One hand in my hair, the other gripping my hip tightly.

"What the chuck…" I gasp. The words should be full of shock, and I should be pushing him away, but I've only enough energy to gasp.

"Can you just go with it?" he whispers.

"Go where?" I ask.

His seductive smile is so full of emotions that it lights up his blue eyes. Midday sky-blue. Gorgeous.

"Wherever you want to go," he says, pulling his hand

through my hair, then trailing it down my neck, down my spine. Pressing the palm of his hand against the small of my back. "And can I come too?"

My hips are pressed to his and my *everything* responding to his curves – one curve actually. The curve in the front of his pants.

Subtle but warm power floods through me. Alive. His power makes me feel alive.

I open my mouth – then there's a flicker of movement. Someone walks out of the room, and Seth presses his lips into mine again. I let him, soaking in every second of him. Every touch and sensation. My body melting in his hands. His power washing over my skin.

My stomach does a backflip – this can't actually be happening!

"You hurt her, Seth, and I will kill you," Pax deadpans, walking past.

Seth pulls away, turning to his brother like I'm not even here anymore. Without him to keep me balanced, I stagger, my knees weaker than I'd realized.

"What? That's all you've got?" Seth demands, chasing after his brother. Pax says nothing. "No bite? No blood?" Seth adds, completely abandoning me.

I stand dumbfounded, watching all of them disappear down the narrow stairs and toward the dining room below until an invisible wall slips in behind me and starts pushing me in their direction.

What the chuck?!

Darkness

Five heart threads.

Not possible. And in a few hundred years, I've seen bloody everything. But not this.

Not her.

Pax has two – but Pax has a wolf. That's something else entirely.

Seth pulls back, leaving her with wide eyes and short, desperate breaths.

I almost feel sorry for her. Crimson, nearly gold threads recoil from her every fiber to settle back deep within her chest. Actually, I think I *do* feel sorry for her.

What an interesting emotion.

Those threads will never connect. Never reach from her being into Seth, into Pax, into whoever else they are meant for and entwine with the heart threads meant for her.

How does the mortal world have the word love when their bonds are so devoid of power?

In the dining hall, Pax chooses a table closest to the stairs. Twenty-seven Silvari are seated around us. Seven of them scrutinize me and Seth. They don't know who we are. Why would they? Without royal colors on – not an option anymore – we're just Sabers passing through.

Eight women flutter their eyes at Roarke, sending the heavy scent of lilies and roses across the room. Lust.

Normal.

Roarke smiles at the nearest lady, a youthful beauty wearing a shift that sits low across her cleavage. He even blows her a kiss before sliding into the seat opposite Pax. I inhale twice to check – and confirm.

No burnt rose scent – the tell-tale sign one of them will be in his arms tonight. A sign that his power has latched on and it will be a fight to keep the girl alive.

Pax's gaze flickers to meet mine, and I shake my head slightly.

No, he's not interested in any of them.

They're all merely Silvari, so we'd have to stand in his way. He'd try to fight us. He always has. If his lust latches onto someone, the results are often deadly. He tries to control it, and we all try to stop the worst. Mostly. We can't keep him entirely from his desires. He can't keep his damned self completely or permanently from his power any more than I can lock away my connection to the Darkness or Seth can stop acting like an idiot.

Which means he *should* at least be interested in the big-busted woman – but he's not.

Because of Shade.

"You're responding to her, too," I say as I cross my arms over my chest and try not to look aggressive. Roarke shuts down when I get aggressive.

He swallows hard, looking to Pax for his opinion. Pax remains neutral.

"I can keep my distance," Roarke insists – but he's not denying my accusation. He could try. I was expecting him to. But he's not denying that he has feelings for her, and he's not fighting us about it either.

Pax steeples his fingers and presses them to his forehead. "I trust you."

"Maybe you shouldn't. Maybe she's only letting me near her because I've used my power to take away her pain too many times."

"Or maybe she actually likes you," Pax shoots back, not looking up from between his fingers.

And he's got the self-control of a throwing knife in mid-air.

My opinion comes out as a low growl.

Roarke runs his hands over his face.

"New rule," he says. "I'm not to be left alone with her."

Pax finally looks at him. "I trust you."

"Please don't," Roarke replies.

The conversation hangs like that, and I have no clue what to do. Pax needs to control this. He's the Alpha, so he makes the rules. If he says it's a rule, we obey, unconditionally, uncontrollably.

"Why don't we let her decide?" Seth asks.

"No," we all agree.

Silence.

This conversation is going to be left open.

Seth turns toward the stairs.

"She's fine," I grunt. The girl's sitting just out of view – it's not like she can go far, and we can all sense her there.

Seth turns back and sits down on the bench next to Roarke.

With one last glance at the room I note seven swords, twelve concealed knives, three bows on the bow rack by the door, and one man fidgeting with a long dagger that he has resting on his table.

People are usually wary of Pax. He tries to rein it in while in public, but the heavy feeling of something deadly sharing a room with you is hard to completely remove. Having been in his wolf form today, it's probably even harder for him to suppress the sting it would have on these common folk.

But I'm not sure if that's the only reason for the heavy firepower among the locals. They have walls between them and the dangerous side of the forest. Why do they need to be armed just to walk from their homes to the inn?

"Are you sure he's mated with her?" Seth asks, looking to me for the answer. "I kissed her and didn't even see teeth, and he's practically giving Roarke permission…" He trails off, clearing his throat instead of finishing his sentence.

I let out an 'of course, I'm sure,' noise, then slide onto the seat next to Pax and pull back the sleeve of my shirt.

The Release Seal is still fresh and bright on the palm of my hand – but more important than that are the four puncture wounds that are still visible on my forearm.

Pax reaches up and lowers my arm to the table, not looking at the marks that sit pink against my skin. He lets out a long sigh, tinged with a hint of morning dew – sorrow.

I grunt at him, because I just as much put my arm in the wolf's mouth as he had control over the thing in that moment.

"Why'd he do that?" Seth asks, and seeing no response in me, he turns to Pax. "Why'd you bite him?"

"Killian suggested her removal from our company," Pax says, swallowing the beginnings of a growl. "Which isn't happening. She doesn't go anywhere without one of us."

"And you trust *us* with her?" Roarke asks, each word soft and slow.

It's not like Pax's protective wolf never allowed us near his last mate. I held her hand to walk her daily through the market when she was heavy with child, supporting her weight when she grew tired. Their babe was an unknown exercise – the toll it took on a full Saber Alpha female was extreme. She labored to walk, sometimes to breathe, because the babe was so strong.

But the way Pax lost them both, I had fully expected he would be inseparable from his next love – even though that love was unlikely to be a true mate. I expected that he would remove himself, even from us. Unable to trust this world at all.

And over the next eight hundred years, finding another love was inevitable. Surely some of the other Seeds would be strong enough. An OverrideSeed or even a HealingSeed – both of them have powers that can accommodate those around them. It was bound to happen, love. Not a mating. But love. When it did, we would let him leave us.

But not now, not with so much at stake. Not a true mating and *not* a fucking mortal.

Pax nods once. "Because she needs all of us to protect her."

"You've got a problem, though," Roarke begins. I flash him a warning glare – which he ignores. "You and your wolf are barely going to be able to kiss her. This guy might be able to." He slaps Seth on the shoulder. "The luxury of having a power that seeks to affect *things* – not people. But a kiss is about all he's going to be able to steal, and you or I... I don't even know what would happen to her. I wasn't expecting her to survive when you took her into the bedroom that day. I felt your release of power."

"I was trying to warn her away."

"You were barely restrained," Roarke points out. "I've seen the way she looks at you. She wants you."

She wants you too, dumbass.

"I was very restrained. We need to remember the consequences," Pax says in a low growl. "All of us."

"Well," Roarke begins, scratching the back of his head. The cinnamon scent of regret laces the air. "If you pick a strong one, full of determined lust – which she isn't – they can usually hold out until you're fulfilled –" He stops, faltering as Pax begins to growl.

Conversation cuts off at the tables around us. The fear grows thick. They can leave if they want, I don't care.

I hold my hand up, getting both Pax and Roarke's attention. "You need to hear this. Pretend it's some mortal named Ellerian."

"Ellerian isn't a mortal's name," Seth says. "Try Anna."

"How would you know?" I ask.

"He brought back an Anna once." Seth waves a hand at Roarke.

"I did?"

Seth just nods.

"Okay, Anna," Roarke begins slowly, getting a nod of approval from Seth and no growl from Pax. "Sabers absorb each other's powers in equal share, which is much more satisfying. Anna's heart would probably have kept beating until the morning, but most of her soul would be gone. I would absorb it all – and even though my power would be trying to give back, she would be unable to absorb any of it. Not properly. It would just burn through her body. I mean, if she died, she'd die happy."

Seth nods. "She died. They all died."

"Remind me why we let you do this again?" Pax asks.

Roarke shrugs, his attention turning toward the bar and trying to summon a server.

"We were all grieving," Seth says.

No one responds.

We know the theory. We've watched it happen. But Pax needs to hear the details, the things only Roarke can elaborate on. Pax needs it fresh in his mind – and so does Roarke.

Roarke waves his hand in the air and holds up five fingers. A few seconds later, two servants approach our table.

We need to talk about the lizards in the forest, and the BeastSeed, but not here. Not when our combined knowledge is made up mostly of speculation and shards of memories. We need answers, but they're not going to come from any of us. Not unless one of us is keeping something secret.

SHADOW

My wall ceases pushing me about halfway down the stairs. Which is exactly where I stop, lean back against the invisible force, and take a few deep breaths. The boys must have stopped somewhere down in the dining room, out of sight.

It's not that I'm not starving. The sweet smells of pumpkin soup, roast meats, and spiced bread that fill every inch of this place are more than a little appealing. But I can hardly walk down there and take a seat at my own table – away from the guys – and eat in peace.

Can I?

A pang of something sharp, something annoyingly painful, vibrates through my chest. Like my soul is warning me not to entertain the idea.

But my soul is only a small part of the equation; my head gets a say too. And so does my heart and my body – though both of those are going to agree with my soul right now.

Walking out into the dining room, I search table after table of Silvari, all dressed in fine cotton, linen, and silk. Some of the ladies are in beautiful dresses that flow over their unnaturally tall and slim figures, highlighting every perfect curve. The men are all similar, tall and lean, so my four guys stand out. Although Roarke is the leanest of the group, he still has more muscle than the average Silvari.

The walls of this place are oddly lined with stained glass windows. Not actual windows, but rather the panes of glass are being used like pictures against the timber paneling. I have no idea why they wouldn't just have regular windows that people can see out of – but there are none in here. The images in the stained glass are of trees – no surprise there – but each one features a different kind of tree. Different colors and different types of leaves.

To the left is a bar, several patrons sitting along its length with drinks in their hands. Next to that is a serving window with chefs working away in the kitchen beyond and four pretty women delivering the plates around the room. To the right is a double set of doors propped open to let the cool night air in.

Would it be rude if I walked over there and shut them?

It's too cold for cool night air, I think, my skull humming like I just stood up too quickly or something.

The guy closest to the doors gets up, kicks the small stops out of the way, and pulls the doors closed. I almost say 'thank you' out loud – but this dull ache in my temples makes me squeeze my eyes shut and take a deep breath.

When I open my eyes again, I'm back to my original series of thoughts. *Where to sit?*

Sighing heavily, I realize that there are no empty tables. Not even an empty seat with the guys. The four of them are taking up all the room on the two benches.

I'm no stranger to stealing food from a kitchen after they've closed, and I'm pretty sure Seth will find it fun and join me later – so I turn to leave. Waiting quietly on the steps, just out of sight, feels very appealing right now.

"Sit," Pax says, part order. There's definitely some Alpha in that tone. Or maybe it just sounds that way because he's being demanding.

All of the nearby tables go quiet.

"Please," Roarke adds.

Seth stands, and before I have a chance to decide exactly how I'm going to respond, he grips my shoulders from behind and begins to steer me toward the table. It's only Seth, and I relax in his grip – letting him slide me onto the bench seat between him and Roarke.

The seat's not very long, and I'm shoulder to shoulder with both of them. I've been squished between two of my guys before, Seth and Killian actually. They pinned me into place with an arm over my lap and one behind my back during Sigil class. But these two, now, are almost wary. Like they're trying to negotiate a line that none of us can see.

Two servants cross the room, a plate in each hand. The shorter girl giggles, setting her first plate in front of Roarke and the second in front of Killian. Killian, she completely ignores, but she can't take her hazel eyes off of Roarke. The guy smiles back up at her, and just when I begin to think I might slap him, he flutters his eyelashes.

What the chuck?

So I do slap him, hard and right on the thigh.

He jumps in his seat, turning his dark gaze to meet mine. His hair's tied back, with just one lock hanging free in front of his face.

"Careful," he says to me, but his gaze darts momentarily to Pax – who's ignoring us and taking a plate from the other young woman.

"Leave the poor defenseless girl alone," I order.

He curls his fingers around my knee then very deliberately shoves me closer to Seth. But his hand stays there, on my knee, holding me tight, and I wonder for a split second if he might change his mind and pull me back closer to him.

The girl lowering a plate in front of Pax is lingering, her

hand gently on his arm. Her gaze is still on the bowl of pumpkin soup, fear in her fake smile, but her intention is clear. She's trying to flirt with him.

My blood boils.

I stretch my leg underneath the table and kick the guy.

His golden eyes meet mine, a smile dimpling one cheek. But he doesn't take the pretty blonde's hand off his arm.

He looks up at her. "Thank you. There was one more."

I hadn't even realized they didn't bring food for me.

Minor detail. I don't even care.

What I do care about is getting this girl to move her ass on. There's plenty of other Silvari to serve in this place.

She turns her gaze in my direction, but very deliberately looks over my head, then turns back toward the bar.

"Oh, your servant wants to eat too?" she asks, her voice fluttering as much as her eyes. She tilts her head a little, acting coy, then walks off. "I'll be right back."

The servant on the other side of the table does the same. Roarke's hand leaves my knee, so he can eat. My jaw aches, and I realize I'm grinding my teeth.

"You're not entertaining that, are you?" I demand, my jaw barely relaxing enough for the words to get out.

"Why not?" Pax counters, watching her walk away for a moment. "It's amusing." He pulls his gaze back to me.

Which makes my insides absolutely melt.

And that infuriates me more. Is that what she's feeling right now? After Pax held her gaze and fed her lust? And I don't even care if that's not his power – he's male and hot-as-melted-chocolate and giving her all the wrong signals.

I'm going to rip her hair out.

Killian grunt-chuckles, then clears his throat and offers up a real chuckle.

The amusing part in all of this is going straight over my

head – just like her gaze. She reaches the serving counter, collects three plates, and crosses to the other side of the room.

"The risks Silvari will take to try and marry someone in power," Seth mutters.

"Silvari crave power," Killian adds.

"I thought you said the Elite Saber and Silvari relationship dynamic was impossible," I say, still watching her.

"Some Silvari think the issue lies in winning us over, and not a matter of magic. The younger Sabers, those that haven't been called to the castle yet, their power is timid enough that there are no problems. And the Sabers called to the castle hardly stay in the villages long enough to inform the locals of the risks. Enforcement are all in steady relationships before being released from duties at the castles. Silvari deaths are definitely illegal, and –" Roarke shoves his spoon in his mouth like the next words he was going to say needed to be physically stopped from coming out.

Seth tilts his head to the side, catching my attention. Like me, he's watching the servers and probably noticing that none of the girls have any desire to deliver me a bowl of food.

"I'll take care of this," the guy says, sliding his bowl in front of me. "You eat."

He leans in, kissing my temple. The spoon's in my mouth before he's pulled away, and it takes me a second to register that he kissed me at all. Servants don't turn down food, and after eighteen years as a servant, that lesson is ingrained in my muscles. No thought required.

Which is good, because every fiber of awareness in me has zeroed in on the tingling sensation left by his lips. I hope I'm not grinning like a stupid love-struck Silvari – because then I'd really be pissed at myself.

Seth gets up and ambles through the room. No one notices, no one turns to look at him or even pauses in their conversation. It's like the guy has all but vanished. He approaches the pretty blonde at the serving window, but before he can get to her, she turns and walks purposefully toward a far table with three plates in her hands. Three plates, but the table only has two people at it.

Two men, both with brown hair and plain faces. One's got a few freckles across his nose, the other a short beard. They're both smiling, talking animatedly, as the bowls are placed before them and the girl walks off. Seth slides into the currently empty third seat, picking up the spoon and taking a mouthful. He's nodding and smiling excitedly, jumping right in on their conversation as if he belongs there.

The two guys' eyes go wide and their gazes dart around the room, trying to decide where Seth belongs. Seth keeps talking, laughs like he's said something funny, then takes another mouthful.

My eyes bulge.

"What is he doing?" I whisper.

"Being Seth." Roarke shrugs, still eating, not even looking.

"Does he know those people?"

"Nope," Pax says, and I realize that he's not looking at Seth either, he's looking at me.

I turn to face him. "Should I go sit over there too?"

He frowns a little.

"I mean, if you all are going to go flirting with every Silvari that approaches you, I feel like I'd be better off over there." I point my thumb toward where Seth is still eating and still telling jokes – not that I can actually hear what he's saying.

The room fills with his laughter, and I take that opportunity to pull my gaze from Pax's.

"New rule. No flirting," I declare.

"I thought the rule was 'no touching anyone unless we plan on killing them?'" Killian asks.

"That *was* the rule," I agree. And that rule worked fine when we were trapped in the White Castle. "This rule is on top of that rule. Rule number one – no flirting. Rule number two – no touching. Got it?"

There's also rule number three, *no sex*. But now's not the time for bringing that one up.

Killian straightens, putting his spoon down. Across the room Seth takes notice, standing.

I keep eating. I'm not as fast as they are, but I'm pretty sure I'm just as hungry.

"Great talking to you," Seth says loudly. "We should do this more often."

A guy approaches the table as Seth walks away – their third dinner companion. All three of them watch Seth's back as he crosses the room, brows creased in confusion. Just blank confusion, not frustration or anger or even spite.

"What is it?" Pax asks, his voice angled toward Killian.

The servants approach, placing plates of roast meat, potatoes, and green vegetables on the table. The pretty blonde steps close to Roarke, leaning in as if to whisper something into his ear. Killian grabs her by the arm, and she freezes, blanching.

Has she stopped breathing?

"Back to work," Killian growls.

She runs off into the kitchen, shaking and sobbing. Killian's looking deadly, and I almost feel like a horrible person. But I'm pretty sure that had nothing to do with me. The other serving girl falters for a second but stays. Leaning over, she puts a plate in front of Pax in a way that angles a peek down her low-cut top.

Pax locks his gaze on mine, not taking notice of what she's offering. He smiles like whatever he's seeing in my expression pleases him. The air bristles. It takes me a second to realize that there is something physical going on, and it's not just my own personal reaction to his gaze. Power spikes over me, and my body grabs at it – like warm skin relishes a cold breeze.

The servant, however, squeaks and runs.

With her out of the way I should relax, should be able to pull my gaze away, but I can't.

"What is it?" Pax asks.

I struggle with an answer, then Killian begins to speak, and I realize the question wasn't even for me.

"Tonight," he says, standing, that glazed black look still in his eyes.

Roarke stands too, and without any further explanation, the two of them head for the stairs with Seth close behind.

I reach across the table and snatch Pax's plate from him, which finally breaks the grip he has on my gaze. Forgetting about cutlery until a piece of meat is in my hand – and I figure it's too late now – I start eating.

"What was that about?" I ask, pointing toward the stairs.

"Something dangerous is going to happen tonight. Killian usually senses these things. They're going to saddle the horses."

As he speaks, the guys reappear. Seth and Killian are carrying a saddle over each arm. Roarke's in the lead with the last saddle, shoulder-barging the doors open. People turn to look, and a plate crashes to the floor, smashing. The serving girl who was flirting with Pax scurries to clean it and offers apologies to the nearest tables.

"And what did you do to her?"

"I can make people feel fear – it's one way to ensure my authority isn't questioned. Not something I do often."

"That didn't feel like fear to me," I mutter around my mouthful.

He drags one of the plates across, picks up his knife and fork, and starts cutting his meat like a normal person.

"I noticed."

Darkness

The world is heavy with nightfall. Roarke is in the lead, already unlatching the gate for us, followed by Seth. Then me.

Three Silvari, armed with cut-and-thrust swords, are slowly walking a small dog back into town, and two other patrons saunter across from the wash-house into the back door of the inn.

People of no consequence.

Shade and Pax are inside the inn. They stayed there when the tang of Darkness swirled and licked across the floor. Seth and Roarke came with me to prepare the horses for a non-specific danger. A *something* that is coming.

I'm never wrong.

I sling my saddles over the railing and turn to watch the point where the road out of town molds into the trees. Seth does the same, perching on the top railing, eyes intense, posture deceptively relaxed. Roarke leans against the fence from inside the yard, looking between me and the trees.

Whoever it is smells of death and Saber power – but not Darkness.

I look at Roarke, then nod toward the trees. He can deal with it.

He lets himself through the gate, then leans back against the post and oozes calm, his stance and posture inviting. All that power he's been locking down is let free to stretch its cramped limbs. I ignore him, and them, as best I can, moving to the far side of the yard and tossing Shade's saddle onto the new gelding. Fixing everything in place before moving onto my own mount.

The Sabers spot us quickly. Three lithe females on black geldings. Their hair, the women's and the horses, is braided tight, and there's no blood in sight. They're wearing chest guards made of black leather, a short sword at each of their sides, and all of them have a bow slung across their backs. No arrows are left in their quivers, though.

Roarke has drawn them over, probably without having to do anything. The two that dismount do so with a pompous huff. Their chins tilt up, their lips in thin lines.

Roarke gets them talking, but I'm too far away to hear the specifics. So I approach, which makes the women still and Roarke work harder.

"I told you – our orders are to report first and not share gossip on the way," one of them repeats.

"I know," Roarke says, the smell of jasmine painting the air. "*I know. But what I say is far more important than any of Lithael's rules.*" I scrunch my nose at the sweet scent of Allure – but the girls almost swoon when their lungs fill with it. "*And you desire to tell us what your assignment was.*"

The woman on the left runs her hand down the length of her braid, pulling the tail of it around onto her shoulder. There are needle-pins in the weave – an effective weapon, if she had any control over her mind right now. I know she doesn't because I can see the threads of lust reaching for her fingertips, begging to close the distance and press them against Roarke's skin. Like an instant addiction. A need.

"Robberies in the Red Canyons," she says, her fingers shaking against her hair. "Important shipments going missing."

Roarke shifts, smiling at her and sending her heart into a flutter. A flutter! *What kind of Sabers are these women?*

"They sent a Saber triune from the White Castle to deal with a bandit? Sounds like overkill," Seth mutters.

"It was reported to be five rogue Sabers, and reported that they were well-armed and brutal. Not the one man that we found," the still-mounted woman snaps out. No Allure needed to get her blood boiling. She's so easily made herself into a liability for the team. "Back on your horses," she growls. "We're leaving."

"Who gave the assignment? Who signed it? Who are you trying to impress?" Roarke asks, the words ordering her to stop, to stay, to drop her guard and lose her focus.

"Arland, Zanda, and Lithael."

Lithael. I almost smother my growl. Almost – but not quite. Which sends fear trickling through the women.

"Here," Roarke says, lifting his hand and snapping his fingers to grab their attention. *"Lithael was worried about a handful of Sabers and some missing trade – and he didn't think the local enforcement could handle it?"*

"It was *five* Sabers. The Black Castle has been whispering. Calling them the Black Pentad – the mirror of the White Pentad."

That makes even Seth straighten and focus.

"We're the White Pentad?" he asks.

Breaking Roarke's spell. The three women look between us like they're only just realizing who they're talking to.

"Who knows, Seth? Servants gossip. Damn, the whole kingdom likes to gossip. There can't be any other pentads, though – all Sabers are called to the White Castle. No teams are formed at the Black Castle," Roarke says, as he runs his hand up the muscles on the back of his neck.

"But? I'm sensing a *but*," Seth pushes.

"But, I guess technically they could be formed outside the castle walls if they managed to avoid the patrols and be at exactly the same spot, at the same time, but for some reason not at the front gates where the magic calls to them. And they'd have to form their bonds without the Castle's magic as a kind of lynchpin, and then for some crazy reason run away from the castle. Weirder things have happened – there's those four guys a few months back who got the calling, but never met the remaining two to form their triunes. They were even tested as a tetrad, but the castle rejected them. Pretty sure they're still drinking at the local pub, waiting for the magic to release them."

"Roarke," I grunt.

"Right, sorry. *You don't need to remember that. You don't even want to. Forget you know who we are, and instead tell us what you found when you adventured to this single bandit's location. The bandit who was rumored to be five Sabers.*"

"A single ShatterSeed," one woman says. The rest just nod.

Silence sits between us – which these Sabers don't even notice. They don't realize the weight of that declaration. They're young, barely released for assignments. Wouldn't surprise me if they passed their third trial last week.

"ShatterSeeds are extinct." Roarke frowns. Adding, with compulsion in his voice, "*This story is getting more and more interesting. Why did Lithael send you on this assignment? There's no chance it was to stop the robberies. He's not the caring-for-his-people's-wellbeing type. Come on, help me understand.*"

I smile a little as the girl in the middle fights to decide what she wants to say and what she doesn't. Roarke's power crushes that indecision, and she succumbs almost instantly, her lip quivering as she speaks.

"We're all TrackerSeeds – if we want to find someone, we can. We were sent after missing shipments on the trade route. Important weapons destined for the White Castle – we found a ShatterSeed."

"Our order was to eliminate – hunt and eliminate," one of

them says. "The traitors and Kyra are on the top of our Crown's priorities."

"Kyra – Lithael's niece? She's supposed to be under lock and key at the Black Castle."

The girl shrugs.

"*I'm sure what you know about Kyra is very interesting. Do share?*" Roarke asks.

"We were not the only Sabers summoned and given orders," the woman still on her horse explains. Her tone is almost completely void of emotion. "We heard the others. We shouldn't have, but did. Sabers without triunes. Sabers not from the White Castle or the Black Castle. And Logan sent to hunt her. But to us, the Crown simply said that Kyra has been ordered to stay at the Black Castle until she gets the call, and he simply wants assurance that she isn't taking liberties."

"Sounds more like she *should* be at the Black Castle, but isn't, and Lithael wants her found without anyone knowing that his own niece isn't obeying his orders. She should have had the call by now – but hasn't. I already like her," Seth says, before switching gears to ask, "Who were these other Sabers?"

All three women back up, glancing toward the road.

"*I've never seen prettier eyes*," Roarke coos. "*And I know you have an answer for my brother.*"

Despite looking the most ferocious, with her jaw tensed and her teeth grinding, it's the one still on her horse that is giving up most of the answers.

"We only heard the end of their conversation. That Logan was hunting Kyra, and these others are to hunt the traitors."

"*What others?*"

"It was a list that began with the threat of evil, then mentioned Daryan, Gartil, Sromma, and Xylon."

"That's only four Sabers, and Xylon we've already met," Roarke muses.

The woman shrugs. "That's what we heard. We couldn't see anything."

"No two guesses who the traitors are," Seth mutters.

"We didn't hear specifics on that either," the woman says.

So there are three more on our tail. Xylon was hardly an obstacle, but the BeastSeed was chosen for a reason.

"Where's the ShatterSeed's body?" Seth asks.

"*Yes, do share the location*," Roarke coos.

"The afternoon worth of riding back that way, unless you go straight through the forest," she says, pointing straight into the trees behind her. "But we burned it. He was using a cave in the ochre to hide out in.".

She's not looking at me – most people don't – but I level my gaze on her and breathe in the scents she's swathed in. Death, uncertainty, exhaustion, and truth.

"Who else knows of this cave?" My voice cuts through the Allure that Roarke has woven, making them flinch and almost cower.

"Robberies have been happening all along the western trade route. We tracked him from Lackshir markets to his cave, but still couldn't recover the weapons. You are the first we've seen. No one else will know of this until we reach the castle and put in our report."

"And we'll be the last," I grunt, turning to finish prepping the horses.

"*You remember*," Roarke says, Allure pooling so thickly around him and the women that even Seth shuffles further along the railing and out of the magic's heavy touch, "*Hunting the ShatterSeed east of Lackshir. You found and killed him on the Arch-Straight Cliffs on the northern coast. You are riding directly back to the White Castle from the cliffs – which actually means you're traveling in the wrong direction. I suppose you had better be on your way."*

They swallow, moving their tongues as if all moisture has been sucked from their mouths. I remember that feeling from when we were all much younger and Roarke's power had some effect on me.

Triunes are bound together when they are called to the castle. Usually they're strangers up to that moment in time. The magic hits them. Ties their threads. Anchors them to the castle and reels them in like fish on a line. Those threads tangle together when all three Sabers stand in a circle on soil laced with the castle's magic. Releasing the team from the anchor to the castle and instead anchoring them to each other. Except now Lithael adds a seal to their flesh as quickly as he can to hammer them in place. There isn't a Saber team alive who's strong enough to stand against him and *not be* tethered to the damn White Castle. There are triunes, mostly those who are broken, who work as enforcement in villages, but they still wear castle seals, and release seals to counter the magic and tether them to their posts.

All those Sabers that arrive as strangers have to rush to form brotherhoods just to survive the trials. Lithael makes each team choose a commander, but that was just to piss Pax off. Even in a team of three, there are still rules to be made and weaknesses to be exploited. All the things that push and pull at relationship bonds. There was always a leader, but there used to be only one commander.

We were different. When we were called, we'd already worked out our differences. The trials force new Sabers to tap into each other's magic to survive, but to do it well takes practice. Centuries of it. Something my brothers and I have – and one female mortal has managed to shatter.

I clench and unclench my fist in frustration. My Shadow

is on the castle's documents as a member of this team. As a defining point in Saber history.

She has changed the landscape for Sabers – but she can't take the trials. Can't learn to tap into our powers the way we can with each other. Roarke's Allure will always poison her. My Darkness will always eat at her soul.

Pax can't change that. He can't make her into something she's not. Getting Shade to hit something in self-defense, other than Roarke's balls, even feels out of our reach.

"*And what is Lithael planning to do with Kyra once she is returned to the castle?*" Roarke asks as the women mount up.

"I heard him yelling to Logan. Call or no call – pretty sure she's going into the Saber trials by the next full moon," someone replies. I'm not sure which woman, because I'm not looking and don't particularly care.

Roarke waves at the women as they ride off back the way they came.

"Does that count as flirting?" he asks Seth, throwing me a glance like maybe he's asking me too.

I grunt, then swat at the cool trickle sensation running over my shoulder. Damn Shadow.

Ignore it, I order myself.

"Does it count if it was a side-effect of getting information?" This time Seth doesn't bother to check my reaction.

"Caves."

"Caves?" they both echo me.

Pulling the last buckles on Pax's big gray stallion into place, I nod.

"Right, caves," Seth says. "And extinct Seeds. The Beast-Seed was a worry, a ShatterSeed even more so."

"Not extinct. There was one," I correct him. "We put him in Tanakan Prison."

Roarke sucks in a sharp breath, a sure sign he's just pulled something into place in that racing brain of his.

"Our first summer. I remember. But if one Seed got out of Tanakan, then there could be more," he says.

"Or he was *let* out," Seth offers, finally slipping from the railing and picking up his saddle. Only to stop when he realizes that both Roarke and I are staring at him. "What? I'd do it if I were Lithael. It's the perfect army. All those Seeds desperate for freedom, willing to do anything, already evil. It's not a big stretch of the imagination."

He's right.

Too right.

Roarke runs a rough hand through his hair as he speaks. "And if four Sabers were sent after us, there's a chance all four were freed from Tanakan. All Seeds that were put away for being evil to begin with over hundreds of years. We don't even know for sure what's in there. We have no idea what they can do, or what they're willing to do."

Fuck.

Daryan, Gartil, Sromma, and Xylon. Three of them are still living. I repeat their names, committing them to memory.

Which one is going to attack us tonight?

M y appetite melts away, and I put the last piece of meat down. Picking up my fork gives my hands something to do, pushing the food around the plate, but that doesn't occupy my mind or my mouth.

"I'm going to suck at this," I say, not looking up.

"At... what?" Pax asks, very slowly, hesitation filling the gap between his words.

"At the whole mate thing. I know it was kind of out of your control. I'm sorry if I did anything –"

"You didn't."

He reaches across the table and stills my hand, taking my fork from my fingers and laying it onto the plate with a gentle clang. Then he draws one finger along the skin under my chin, encouraging me to look up – to look at him.

"Your brother keeps messing with me. All of your brothers do. They keep flirting and stuff."

I leave out the part where I *enjoy* them messing with me. Want them to. Which makes me the worst almost-mate in the kingdom.

He offers me a lopsided smile. This clearly isn't worrying him the way it's worrying me.

"Seth did that to test me."

"So he didn't want to kiss me?" I blurt out.

Crap. I hope I didn't just sound as hurt as I feel.

"I'm sure he did."

He did?

Not exactly the response I was prepared for, and I rush to alter the course of our conversation – otherwise, the next thing I say might include *'can he do it again?'*

"But that's not why he did it?" I ask.

Pax shakes his head, slowly chewing through a forkful of beans before answering. "It was far more likely that he'd lose a limb than be able to kiss you as I walked past."

My eyes go wide. "You'd attack your own brother?"

"Not me. My wolf."

"That's still you."

"Not exactly. The wolf lacks the same kind of logic and reasoning that I have. He's… lacking."

I swallow hard. "So that's what you meant when you said I'm not allowed any kind of relationship with anyone else." I leave out the important part – sex.

He nods, and I groan. Because at some stage in my life, I want a husband, kids, to grow old with someone.

"Roarke told me to ask you how you feel about all of this."

He lifts an eyebrow, a hint of surprise in the expression. "Roarke told you?"

"Well, I tried to ask him first, and he told me to ask you. So, how do you feel about this?"

"Like I'm putting you in danger."

"Scared?" I press.

He nods, then adds. "I would be scared no matter who you were. Silvari, Saber, even Elite Saber."

I sit on that knowledge. Pretty sure I'm scared too – him feeling the same only makes it worse.

He pushes the dishes aside to grab my hands and hold them in his, evoking death stares from the servants hovering nearby. For a moment I itch to pull away, then something shifts, and his power seeps into me like thin tendrils of lightning sliding through my veins. I'm not even sure he knows he's doing it.

"It would help if you weren't so damn desirable. If you looked and acted like one of them, this wouldn't be a problem." He nods toward a servant before continuing. "We're going to remove this barrier and work out how to keep you safe."

Which brings me full circle to the main problem in my life. Problem number one – the bubble.

Break this bubble, and everything changes.

Problem two – why the bralls did their mother send them to find me?

Three – what's in that letter?

Four – what's in Pax's big bad past that makes the sight of my captive scars such an issue?

"I need some answers," I begin, hijacking the conversation. "I need to know why I'm here."

Pax shakes his head, not even a full shake, more like snapping his chin to one side while fixing me with the full intensity of his gaze. Meaning – 'no'. His hands stiffen over mine, and I gently pull them away before his grip makes escape impossible.

"We need to talk about this," I push.

"Not here. The closer we get to the border, the safer we'll be."

"I thought the border was more dangerous?"

"The enemy of my enemy type thing. Not many Sabers linger close to the border, and there'll be no Silvari there."

Before I can respond, his gaze lifts and fixes on something behind me. The second they step inside my bubble I can feel them. Confidence, wisdom, and safety. I can't explain it. It's not a sound, not exactly an emotion, more like something I *sense* – the same as that rare moment when a person can feel rain coming. It fills your body in a way that can't exactly be described.

Killian meets Pax's gaze, but all he does is grunt and walk past our table.

Pax jumps to his feet and follows his brother up the stairs – so that grunt must translate to 'follow me.'

Which leaves me gawking after them in pure confusion.

"What's that about?" I whisper, leaning into Roarke as he sits next to me and pulls one of the plates toward himself, the white ceramic scraping across the timber.

"Killian has bad news," he says, filling his mouth with potato before I can press him for more information.

So I lean in the other direction, toward where Seth is sitting down in the spot Pax just left. Reaching out, I grab the last plate before Seth can get it.

"Spill. Now."

Seth smiles at me, that twinkle in his ice blue eyes and a dimple on one cheek. Great, I think I just challenged the guy.

No going back now.

"You need to watch your figure anyway, princess," I say, pushing the plate completely out of his reach.

His other cheek dimples.

"Whoever gets the plate first wins," he declares, pouncing across the table.

I dive after him, grabbing a handful of something mushy on my way over the table. Potato, by the feel of it. Which I instantly regret, not because of the potato but because I use my right arm to propel myself off the table and have to swallow down a grunt of pain.

I *am* putting food in his hair, no matter how much my arm is throbbing right now.

The table of Silvari behind us stand and scuttle out of our way, looking at me in particular like I'm a wild animal. I ignore them, jumping at Seth and wrapping my legs around his waist – then massaging the potato all the way through his hair and down to his scalp.

"Ew, Vexy, come on," Seth groans.

But he's the idiot with one arm wrapped around me, holding me in place.

His other arm darts out, and I twist just in time to see him grab a small jug of gravy.

"Seth – no. Don't you dare."

He pinches his bottom lip in his teeth to try and subdue that damn gorgeous smile.

And those damn gorgeous lips. My gaze hovers on them, my own lips tingling at the memory of our kiss. That was my first real kiss – ever – and I want more.

Just not right now, because right now he has me trapped against him, and he's armed with gravy.

"Sethy, you wouldn't," I say with real pleading in my voice.

He raises the gravy slowly, hovering it in the air above my head. For a moment I squirm, trying to wriggle free, with absolutely no effect.

Then the gooey liquid tickles down my back. I would squeal, but I'm too busy hugging closer to Seth in a useless attempt to get away. I reach up his back and grab a handful of hair – clenching and pulling.

"Aw, ow! That hurts," he cries.

We topple backward, saved from falling to the floor by Roarke.

"Come on, you two, you're scaring the locals," he says softly.

I can't see the locals over Seth's shoulder. All I can see is Roarke's partially amused face and the side wall of the dining hall, but Seth must agree because he turns and carries me toward the back door. As we move, I slip the first thing I can grab off the nearest table – a small bottle of red Silvari wine.

Just in case I need it.

Seth puts me down in the hallway, and I follow him outside, the wine half in my hand and half up my sleeve. My other hand is busy over my shoulder, trying to hold my shirt away from my back. Which makes me twitch and squirm just from the gooey feel of the gravy.

Roarke is relatively clean, just a bit of splashed gravy on his sleeve. Seth isn't even that bad – just potato in his hair.

But I'm covered in gravy, and it's a nasty, nasty feeling.

The small patch of grass outside the back door of the inn gives me just enough time to weigh my choices. Wine over Seth or wine over Roarke.

I slow, letting Roarke overtake me slightly. His luscious hair is loose, a slight breeze blowing a few strands across his cheek.

That settles it.

I lunge for him, and Seth turns at the same time, pulling roast meat smeared with gravy from somewhere. We surround Roarke before the guy can react. Seth smears the food all over his head – and through his hair – and I pour the wine over the top.

Roarke screams. Trying to shield his head and run at the same time, he sprints across the yard, ignoring the stepping stones.

"That's childish!" he shouts, ripping his shirt over his head and vanishing into the wash-house – not quite quick enough for me not to get lost in the sudden desire to follow him and watch him take the rest of his clothes off.

Um, no. I order my body. *No jumping on Roarke. Not now. Not ever. No.*

But I can look, can't I?

A door on the inside slams shut, and the sound of running water drowns out most of his growls.

"What made you do that? You've hurt his feelings." Seth looks at me with a stern expression and a raised eyebrow.

"Me? You attacked him too," I argue, following Seth to the wash-house door.

He takes two steps in, then two steps backward. "Are you coming? You can't go to bed like that."

He waves a hand to indicate all of me.

I run my hands over my hair, shoulders, and arms. They feel fine. My back, however, is not.

"But I can't go in there," I argue.

Because Roarke is in there and he's naked – logic says that's how a person would usually shower.

"Wait." Seth vanishes inside before returning. "There's no one else in here – and the showers have doors."

I relent because being covered in gravy is not fun.

The building is pretty basic, timber floorboards, stone walls, four shower stalls, a shelf of clean towels high up on the wall, and two sinks. There's a lantern in the middle of the room, but as the night darkens, the lamp is creating just as many shadows as it is light.

I reach for a metal bucket under one of the sinks.

"Just throw water down my back," I say, handing it to Seth.

"With pleasure."

"*Warm* water," I warn.

But I haven't even got the full sentence out before cold water is dumped on my head.

"Seth!" I genuinely scream this time.

He laughs.

"Not funny!"

"Very funny," he corrects, rubbing his hand up and down over the back of my tunic. "It's not going to wash out though. Take it off."

"What?"

119

"Don't turn around. Just pull your shirt over your head, and I'll scrub it in the sink. Here, let me lock the door."

"No," I say, but he's already turning the lock.

"Why not? That innkeeper would love the opportunity to kick you out, and his daughters are pretty keen on securing themselves a Saber and skipping right past their bonded serving years into the fantasy of prestige and power. If you walk inside wearing that, I'm pretty sure he's going to tell you to sleep with the horses."

I growl, grip the hem of my tunic, and pull it up over my head in one sharp movement. He slips the soggy garment from my fingers but doesn't say anything. Just moves away and flicks the taps on. I hug my arms across my chest – partly to keep warm and partly to save some modesty. I had no idea how revealing being topless is – even from the back.

"Hurry up, I'm freezing thanks to you."

And being cold and shivering makes a broken bone cranky and achy.

A warm cloth presses to my back, and I both jump in surprise and relax into the pleasant sensation at the same time.

He runs it down my spine, then lifts my hair and trails the warmth along my neck. Shivers rake through my body, and I rub my hands over my arms to wipe them away – to no effect. With his hand in my hair and his body heat so close that it's caressing along my side, I don't care that I'm half-naked anymore.

The cloth melts away the cold on my skin, in my muscles, and moves deeper into that knot of fear that has always existed inside me. Daring me to relax.

Because his touch is gentle. His breathing is smooth in the room where the only other sound is the patter of water in Roarke's shower. For this moment, I know we're safe, just him and me, and that there's no reason to hold on to the barriers between us.

Except there is, I remind myself. *He's a Saber and I am not.*

Besides, he's wiping gravy off my back.

Hardly sexual, I try to tell myself.

But I don't believe it. If it were, my breath wouldn't be getting caught up in my throat and my eyes wouldn't have drifted shut.

Just admit it, Shade, you like this. You like Seth... a lot.

I have to bite my lip to stop myself from letting out any sounds that might completely give away the desire unfurling inside me.

"Don't let Pax see these," he murmurs, his voice low as he runs the cloth down my spine again, all the way to the waist of my pants.

His words cut through my inner bliss. "These?" I press.

With one finger he traces a ridge just under my shoulder blade. Whip scars. A side effect of having Lord Martin as a master for a very long time.

"I don't know how he didn't see them when you dropped your towel," Seth says.

"How do you know he didn't?"

"Because I didn't see them – and he would have left holes in the walls, and people too."

"I guess I pulled his shirt on quickly."

"You moved pretty slowly, actually."

My cheeks flush red, hot, and shamed. Because only I could try to regain some of my dignity by dropping my towel in front of them all. I mean, it was an act of defiance – because they were ordering me to get changed in one of the bedrooms, and I was sick of being ordered around.

"How much of everything else did you see?"

"Only everything. But I closed my eyes, mostly. Honest."

His words are normal Seth, humor poorly hidden in his tone.

But the raspy way he's struggling to speak, the hesitation between sentences – that's not normal Seth.

Goosebumps run down my arms again, and I hug myself tighter.

"Seth, tell me why Pax would lose his shit over these?" I ask, holding my left hand with its bracelet of blue cloth that covers even more scars.

"His need to protect the small number of people that are his pack extends into retribution," he says.

"Come on, give me more than that. Is it like an allergic reaction?"

He chuckles. "No, Sabers don't get allergies."

Jokes aside, I try for serious reasoning. "He was a slave, wasn't he?"

"His reaction has to do with his AlphaSeed," he replies, avoiding my damn question. "It's as hard for him to control as it is for Roarke to stop being a dick."

"I heard that," Roarke calls.

His shower flicks off, and without so much as a breath of hesitation, he flings the door open. It smacks against the wall.

"That could be a problem. When Seth said Pax shouldn't see you naked, I hadn't realized they were that bad," Roarke says, his voice is gentle, but it still makes me cringe. "Even I want to murder the f –"

"Seth," Pax calls from outside.

I twist my head in time to catch Roarke's worried gaze – not looking at my eyes or my face or my arms folded over my chest, but my back.

"Quick, get her in the shower," Seth declares.

He heads for the door, and Roarke, wearing nothing but a towel, storms over to me. Using his body to shield any view Pax might have if he gets past Seth. With a stern wave of his hand, he orders me into the nearest shower cubicle. I move.

"Just stay in there," Roarke says softly, his hand against the small of my back as he nudges me inside.

I turn the lock before relaxing my arms. Clenching and unclenching my right fist – the broken bone currently not throbbing in pain.

Huh? Odd... I file that away for later, pretty sure it has something to do with Roarke and that there's a boundary here he's crossing – but now's not the time.

Twisting, I try to get a view of my own back. I know it's scarred – about a million whippings does that to a person. I can feel where the skin was torn and Cook fixed thin pieces of cloth in place with honey. The times Martin brought down the whip again and again until it started to flay the skin from my back. But I have no idea what they were seeing – not exactly. I only know what it feels like.

"She tripped over the table," Seth begins to say, his voice floating in through the vents near the roof.

"I heard her scream, and I heard your name," Pax counters.

"Oh, that. I kind of helped the gravy pot to follow her."

"Gravy?"

"Yep, a gravy bath actually. I'm going to grab her some fresh clothes."

Silence.

"She's having a shower," Roarke explains from inside the doorway, making me think Pax has entered the room.

"I organized a bath, so we wouldn't be playing these games," Pax groans.

I move away from the door and flick the hot tap on as far as I can bear it. I slip my mostly-clean pants off, hanging them on the hook, then step into the water – my bandaged arm held out and above my head to try and keep it dry.

I can't hear the guys anymore, but several times I glimpse Pax's boots under the door. As soon as a fresh tunic is hung over the top of the frame, I turn the water off – then catch a towel with my face.

"Thanks, Seth," I mutter.

"How'd you know it was me?"

"You're the only person who throws stuff at me."

"Huh, hadn't realized," he says.

Dry, and with pants and a fresh tunic on, I step out of the cubicle.

My hair hangs wet around my face, the water almost pulling its rough waves straight – but not quite. Exhaustion tugs at my limbs. Sabers might not sleep more than once a week, but I much prefer sleeping every night. More than once a day would also be nice.

Seth and Killian are standing near the door. Killian's balancing the tip of a short blade on his hand, ignoring the trickle of blood dripping from his palm as he spins it like a child would a ball.

Seth smiles at me, waiting until I'm right in front of him before whispering, "Are you okay?"

My brow furrows.

"Why wouldn't I be?" I whisper back.

"Yes, Seth. Why wouldn't she be?" Killian stops spinning his blade and shoves it into the secret sheath on the inside of his belt. He grabs his brother's elbow before the guy even looks like moving.

I try to walk around them, but one of Seth's arms snakes around my waist and I find myself pulled into the struggle. He draws me in until I'm pretty much standing between them – very closely between them.

"Explain," Killian demands, his gaze now on me.

"No," I declare, pulling far enough back to free myself from Seth. "*My* past is *mine*. You guys don't get to join in."

My embarrassment ebbs, and what's left is fear. I'd like to say fury, I'd like to say fire, but it's not that

124

strong. I'm not that strong, and I don't need them seeing that.

"Let me past," I growl, pointing a finger at the two of them. "I will never, ever take my shirt off in front of Pax. Ever. And we'll never speak of this again. Got it?"

Seth runs a hand through his wet hair – when he got a chance to wash it, I don't know – then he turns and leaves without a word.

Immediately, I feel horrible, but I bury that under my gnawing fear. I'm stuck with these guys; I can't change that and I can't fix it – but what I can do is try not to make it worse. Or any more complicated than it already is.

Which includes not falling in love with Seth, and not triggering Pax into a rage.

Killian stares at me for a few long moments, then turns and walks off like I don't even exist. I chase him out the door, hoping he's heading for the bedroom, because I just picked the crankiest brother to get myself stuck with. If he's going for a jog in the woods, I'm screwed.

It's completely dark, but there are lanterns everywhere. Across the back of the building, alight in every window, around the small fenced paddock or horse yard, in long strings between the inn and the nearby town. Four young Silvari are sitting on the grass, talking, one of them lying back and pointing up at something in the sky. Two girls who were patiently waiting for the showers shuffle inside, one of them whispering and the other giggling.

The clang of steel against steel echoes from the space behind the horse yards. Just grass, lit by a single lantern and punctuated with the silhouettes of three guys trying to kill each other. My three guys.

They move in a complicated pattern, fast even when they are at normal speed and impossible to track when they throw bursts of their own kind of super-speed into the mix.

Pax is in the middle, blocking strikes from both Seth and Roarke. The two younger brothers are working together against the eldest. There's no clear winners or losers; each man seems to be expecting their sword to be blocked, then they step into the next move.

"Why are they fighting?" I ask.

Killian stops and follows my gaze.

"Training. You tell me. Why do Roarke and Seth think Pax needs to let off steam before he goes near you?"

I grit my teeth so hard my jaw hurts, turn, and march toward the inn. The back door is narrow compared to the front, with a single stone step up and a heavy red door that is hanging open. It's right when I notice all of this that I bump into an invisible wall.

My bubble.

I slip backward with the force, landing partly on my ass, but mostly on my back.

Groaning is the first reaction I have. Getting up could be my second, but Killian is already standing over me, and the guy is chuckin' smiling.

"What?" I demand, but the word is more like an accented groan.

"Bubble," the man laughs, stepping over me and into the building.

Leaving me to struggle to my feet on my own.

"You *would* find that funny." I half stagger down the hall, rubbing my forehead and my ass. "I just want to go to sleep."

"Mm," he says, which might mean 'I know'. "I'll stay with you."

He leads the way through the dining hall, which is still packed with patrons and the same girls madly trying to serve them all. Then up the stairs, down the hall, and into our little room.

I haven't even shut the door behind me before he's

pushed the window open as wide as it will go, stuck his head out, and sniffed the air.

"What do you smell?"

"Something dark. Tonight."

"Then why don't we just leave?" I ask, snatching my boots up from where I left them when I had a bath.

"No point running from Darkness, Shade. Wherever you think you're going – it's already there."

I drop my boots again, stepping out of the way as the man systematically collects the bags and lines them along the wall closest to the window.

"Can I sleep, then?" I ask.

"Boots on."

"Sleep with my boots on?"

He nods, and I obey, slipping into the boots before staggering the few steps to the bed.

The bed has four pillows – four. When a person only has one head, four pillows is a little beyond luxury. I flick back the covers and begin tugging down the top sheet.

Killian pulls his shirt off, fishing through his bag for one with more leather down the chest. I'm powerless – stuck. Watching his muscled biceps with the tingling urge to wrap my hands around them.

Do these guys not understand how that affects me?

They're all about rules and boundaries and me being untouchable, and yet they go just pulling their clothes off without warning, whenever they bloody please.

Killian's head snaps up. The emerald sheen to his black gaze reflects some of the fire's gentle light, and a smile spreads across his lips. The scar on his face alters most of his expressions – frowning makes him look angry, sighing makes him look angry, yawning makes him look angry, even his blank expression is fifty percent angry. But the scar from one brow, over his nose, and down to his cheek, doesn't alter his smile.

Not to me.

"What?" I demand.

He gathers his shirt up, slipping his arms into the sleeves before pausing.

"You should get some sleep," he says, turning as he pulls the shirt up over his head.

I get the barest glimpse of his healed shoulder before the shirt's in place.

"Your burn's gone?"

He rubs the spot as he answers, "We heal quickly. Sleep."

My body obeys, dragging me into the bed and under the covers. I'm pretty sure I'm asleep within one beat.

And awake in the next.

Awake, and screaming as a deafening boom makes the whole building shake.

I spring to my feet, rushing toward where Killian is tossing the bags out the window. Four bags, then four sets of saddlebags. The floor tilts back. Stone and timber creaks, cracks, and splinters around us. Killian grips my arm, pulls me into his chest, then rolls backward out the damn window. I'd scream again if I weren't so scared. Flames explode through the window behind us, shattering the glass and sending it into the air. The pieces reflect the flames like sparks of orange and red in the night.

We roll to the edge of the veranda roof, then straight off the thing.

To my death. The world is ending, and I'm going to be crushed by Killian.

He scoops me up in his arms in mid-air. Then the guy lands on his feet. Easy.

Why didn't I think of that?

Probably because right now breathing is a priority and I'm failing to get it right.

I'm set on my own feet, and in the same motion he grabs at the bags. Two saddlebags over one arm, and two duffels in each hand.

The moan of the building is drowned out by screams and mayhem, then crashes as it begins to fall apart. I grab the last two saddlebags and run, not even stopping when I hit the gate. I yank it open for Killian, then quickly shut it behind him. My little gray pony is dancing around with fear in her eyes at the far end of the yard – but she doesn't have a saddle on. Five other horses do, and I recognize the boys' mounts straight away. The new horse is either mine, or I'm stealing it.

Killian launches into his super-speed to tie the bags and packs into place on the respective mounts, and while he's wasting time doing that, I scramble up onto the new horse's back, biting back the ache in my arm – because that ache has nothing on a building being blown to pieces by gods know what.

There are plenty of people running, lots of screaming, a fair few signs of blood and injury, but nothing that looks like the cause of it all.

"What's going on?" I shout again.

Killian doesn't respond as he throws his leg over the saddle. All of the animals are unsettled, but his gelding stands still. Solid, unfazed. The damn thing seems calmer with all of this than he is when there's nothing going on.

The building shudders. The stones from the chimney begin to topple in all directions. It was one of two things keeping the place from falling flat. The chimney on the back, and the support posts on the front veranda.

I follow Killian's line of sight and find Pax standing between the back of the inn and the wash-house. He waves a sharp arm at us, shouting something that's lost in the roaring flames and crumbling timber and stones. He's still wearing what I saw him in last, still holding the weapon he was using. There is a very real chance that I just slept for all of five minutes.

Killian leans over and snatches the reins from my hands. My horse jumps about a bit – which in turn makes his horse want to bite or kick mine. Possibly both.

An arrow bolts right past my face, and I dive for cover – straight off the horse. Hitting the ground, I struggle to get myself out from under the stomping and kicking horses.

"Get on the horse!" Killian growls.

"People are shooting at us," I shout back.

My horse breaks free from Killian's grip, and I rush to capture the frightened animal. When I turn, reins in hand and desperate to lay eyes on the person firing arrows at my head, Killian has his sword drawn and an opponent on either side of him. He makes it look easy, battling with two armed men. I mean, the Darkness guy is smiling as he draws blood. But my heart's doing nothing but hammering in my chest.

The building groans again and people still running from the front door are suddenly cut off by falling timbers. Seth bounds onto the veranda and blows a freaking kiss at the flames. They twist, rise, and burst into a cascade of chuckin' flowers.

The rest of the building is still on fire, but the people inside now have an exit.

Pax runs down the slope, vaulting over the fence and cutting down one of Killian's attackers. But he's not alone – behind him, two more guys are in close pursuit.

That makes three armed men against my two. I'm scared, but still quite like our odds. That is, if I don't look up the hill at the mess, destruction, and more Sabers with powers and swords.

"Elorsins," shouts one of Pax's attackers.

He's the same height as my guys, but his skin is pale – like it has lacked sun exposure for a few hundred years. His smile is more like a scowl, but deep joy and pure malice fills every crease on the guy's face. He rolls his shoulders in his crimson shirt and stretches his neck.

"Sromma," Pax announces, pointing at the guy in the red shirt. "Daryan, and Gartil," he adds, pointing at the other two.

One with a heavy beard, and his teeth sharpened to points. Next to him, the guy with short blonde hair and a ring through his lip looks almost plain.

The two men point at each other.

"Daryan," the bearded guy says.

"Gartil," lip ring guy adds.

"It's nice to put faces to Lithael's scum. Which one of you wants to hear how we tore your brother to pieces?" Pax asks. Daryan lifts his lip in a snarl and Pax turns toward him, swinging his sword in a wide arc past his shoulder. "And I **enjoyed** it," he snarls, with a whole lot of wolf in his voice.

Goosebumps have covered my arms, and the combined fear and adrenaline are making it really hard to get my ass back in the saddle. I'm not even sure I want to be in the saddle – there's still an archer out there somewhere.

"Sit," Daryan growls, and Pax freaking does. "Horse – still," he adds, and Killian's horse pretty much freezes.

I don't know what to deal with. Or what I *can* deal with. Killian's horse chuckin' pretending to be a statue and making it very hard for Killian to defend himself? Or Pax dropping to one knee with his sword uselessly stabbed into the ground at his side?

Killian's silhouette is growing darker and darker – the night playing tricks on my eyes as shadows rise and fall along his shoulders and biceps. Every time his sword crashes against one of the attackers, the earth under us booms and vibrates – threatening to knock me over.

Fur visibly shimmers over Pax's skin, an internal struggle lacing through his physical form. I probably should be running, or at least preparing to run – away. Away is the safe direction.

"Stay," Daryan orders Pax.

Nope, not me.

I run straight at them. Gartil swings his sword toward Killian, making Killian block or lose his leg, while Daryan is lowering his blade on a direct course with Pax's neck.

And Pax is not moving. Not blocking. Not fighting.

So I tackle Pax – hard.

It knocks us both to the side and we roll out of the way of Daryan's immediate swing. All the way to the edge of the yards. We stop with me on Pax's chest and my back to the action, the glow strong in his eyes.

"Control," Pax growls, but he's not talking to me. "Or she dies."

He pinches his eyes shut, then opens them again with no sign at all of the glow.

"Or you chuckin' die," I gasp.

The ground shakes underneath us, like the earth itself is angry.

Suddenly, Pax grabs the chunk of wood beside us and lifts it like a shield, behind my back. Immediately, it's smacked into with a metal against wood thud.

"Run," Pax gasps, rolling me to the side in time to block another attack from Daryan. "Get her out of here," he shouts, his voice completely human.

Killian thunders toward me, still on his damn horse – apparently Daryan's instructions last mere minutes. His sword drips with blood, and Gartil's body is in a heap on the ground. The other guy, the one in the crimson shirt, is nowhere to be seen. And for a few long breaths, Daryan staggers back and looks around in disbelief – then anger.

It's enough time for Pax to get to his feet and me to get to mine.

"Where's the other guy?" I demand as Killian tosses his sword to Pax.

"He's about to blow this place to pieces," Killian growls. "Get on the horse!"

"I have this under control," Pax shouts, still human.

He needs to stay human.

I do as I'm told, fear and danger driving my clumsy mount up. With one last look toward where Pax is fighting, Killian kicks his horse forward, and I'm forced to follow.

"Buck," Daryan shouts and my horse's ass-end kicks into the air.

Pax rushes Daryan, thrusting and swinging and forcing the man to focus completely on Pax or die.

"Hold on," Killian orders.

I grab two handfuls of mane and pull my whole body as low down on the animal as I can.

Then we're tearing toward the fence, sailing over it, and straight into the forest.

Not down the road, not into the safety of the town, not back there to help the others. No – we vanish into the trees.

Darkness

F ight.
  Run.
Fight.
Run.

The impulse to fight rips through me. Battling against the logic – run. Get Shade out of here.

This isn't like last night, when we ran because Lithael was riding toward us. Lithael, we can't fight. Not yet. Whoever this is, we can. And we can destroy them.

But I force my gelding to jump the fence. Force Shade's gelding to follow me over it. And force us both into the forest. Into the night.

The canyon and the caves are a few hours away. I know the canyon well, and I've heard of a cave system up in the cliffs, but I've never gone looking for it.

When the deep red and golden ochre cliffs come into view, I allow us to slow. The horses don't object.

Even in the dark, this place is impossible to miss – any moonlight practically makes it glow. I follow the scent of burned body, an acrid sensation in the back of my throat. We move further away from the road we've been shadowing, around behind the first cliff reaching up to form the canyon walls, and up a gentle slope. Half an hour later, we arrive at a grassy patch between two stories of cliff at the back of the canyon.

Except for the small horse yard, made from felled and lashed branches, I'd say it's nearly perfect. But if the choice is between being completely invisible and having a horse nearby, I'd keep the horse. We stop, and I twist in my saddle, taking in every shadow on the cliff, every angle of the trees, every scent of the night – of nocturnal animals and things slowly growing. But no danger.

The charred remains are just inside the horse yard – meaning the girls probably killed him as he tried to flee. I ignore it as I dismount and stretch out my limbs. They burned the body to the point of being nothing more than ash. Likely Shade will think it's an old campfire. It's also likely the Sabers who killed him carried firedust, and they didn't want evidence of a body – otherwise, at least a portion of the skull or femur would be left among the charcoal.

"What the bralls was that?!" Shade whisper-screams.

"Lithael," I growl. The man pulling the strings.

"No, they were Sabers."

"Sent by Lithael. I smelled blood."

"I saw blood. Lots of blood. Whose blood did you smell?" She gives up on the whisper part and just full screams.

I set my gaze on her, trying to still her, waiting for the shaking in her torso to settle – but it doesn't.

"A BloodSeed."

"What does a BloodSeed do?"

"Manipulate blood."

She lets out a loud, torn growl. "Whose blood?!"

"Not ours."

She lies flat on her stomach, swings her leg over the saddle, then slips to the ground with all the grace of being half-dead.

Her legs are shaking too. *How much can a mortal shake before they fall apart?*

I lead her horse and mine into the yard, unclipping my bag and packs as she continues to talk.

"Seth's? Roarke's? Pax's?" Her voice hitches.

"Not their blood," I assure her – I'd know the minute one of them was close to death.

Know it. Fear it. Can't dwell on it.

She sighs, "Good," as she wraps her arms around herself, cradling the broken one with the strong one.

A broken right arm is a disadvantage – but not much when neither hand can wield a sword. Has she ever held one? Or a knife? Or any kind of weapon other than her mouth? She's good at cowering, good at running, good at hiding in the shadows, marginally good at climbing trees, but useless at any of the important skills.

Here we are, clearly being targeted, and all it would take is another lizard attack…

And I might not be able to keep her safe.

If I can't keep her safe, and she can't keep herself safe, then all we have is fate. Even Mother couldn't alter fate, and she saw everything before it happened. She saw thousands of years unfold in minutes. She ordered me to run – but I stayed, and I still could not save her.

If we get rid of this bubble, Shade will have free will again – she'll be able to make stupid decisions.

"He told Pax to kneel, and Pax did it," she says.

"BeastSeed."

"I worked that bit out. His teeth were pointy."

"Filed down," I explain. Popular in Tanakan.

"How much danger is Pax in?"

"Pax is in control," I point out.

She had to have seen that, Pax taking back control of himself.

"For how long?"

I don't answer. I don't have one.

"Which one of them was making the earth shake?"

"The dead one."

"What can the other guy do? The one in the red shirt?"

"Sromma can take your power and mimic it. Use it against you."

"So he could turn into a wolf?"

"No, but he could use our blasts, if and when he sees us use them. Or our speed. That kind of thing."

She glances back the way we came, and even though her whole body is rejecting being upright, I can see she wants to go back.

"They will find us," I tell her, referring to my brothers.

I walk past her, toward the cliff. I can't see the entrance of the cave yet, but I can smell a secret. Smell is the wrong word – sense is, too. Track might be a better description. My gut feeling directs me to a small path that leads up. A few rough steps zig-zag back and forth, to a lip almost at the top of the eroded rock formation. From below it looked like a seam, a spot where wind and rain had worn a track in the soft stone. But it's an opening, and I step inside without fear.

Darkness is my thing, after all.

Shade, however, lingers outside.

I drop my bags, feel around for a lantern, and click the flint at its base.

As soon as there's light, she staggers in, scans the room once, spots a small pile of blankets that was possibly passing as the dead guy's bed, curls up on top of them, and falls asleep. That shouldn't bug me – I'm not Pax – but it does. Fishing around in my bag, I pull my cloak out and drape it over her.

Only mildly better.

Clean inn sheets are one thing. They're nothing more than the scent of soap and servants in a temporary capacity. The smell of a thief and a murderer – entirely different. It's like having an itch I can't scratch.

I fetch my short recurve from my bag, pull the string tight, and collect my full quiver of arrows. Roarke and Seth have wicked skills with their bows, but from this vantage point and with the night hiding no secrets from me, no one is going to survive approaching us.

Someone approaching us is only half my worry – the danger still lingering in our future is my other half. I still can't put my finger on it, but something worse than the attack tonight is devouring our exits. Corralling us.

Waiting to pounce.

If Pax or Roarke don't accidentally kill the girl first.

DAY TWO

4TH

DAY OF

SNOW MOON

CHAPTER EIGHT

SNOWMOON · 1 · 2 · 3 · 4 · 5 · 6 · 7 · 8 · 9 · 10 · 11 · 12 · 13 · 14 · 15 · 16 · 17 · 18 · 19 · 20 · 21 · 22 · 23 · 24 · 25 · 26 · 27 · 28 · 29

ROUGHLY 52.5 MILES FROM POTION MASTER EYDIS

Morning comes and goes. I know because the light is streaming directly in through the cave door, piercing through the gloom and into the corner where I'm trying to sleep. I pull the cloak up over my face – Killian's, I'm guessing, because it wasn't there when I curled up.

I sleep until my bones stop aching and my eyes can open without the world being blurry. It's my growling stomach that finally makes me get up. I take Killian's cloak with me, fastening the top few buttons and pulling the heavy black fabric around me to hold the cave's innate low temperature at bay.

"Where are we, exactly?" I ask, my voice a little hoarse.

Killian is sitting at the mouth of the cave, his back pressed against one wall and his feet against the other.

"In a –"

"Cave, I know. But whose cave?"

I sweep my arm around the room, indicating the huge collection of boxes, crates, bags, canvases, and even framed artwork around the room. Then I regret moving my arm at all. It's been broken for three days – or maybe four, my mind's a bit too sleepy for doing math – but it's still instinct to use my right arm for things like pointing. And it takes me a little by surprise when I awaken the ache.

"Either this is a pirate's hideout, or you four have been living a double life," I say. My mind is on my arm, but my mouth can usually run the show on its own.

He grunt-laughs, climbing to his feet but leaving the bow he was cradling by the doorway.

"Sabers recently removed a ShatterSeed from here," he explains.

"Removed – as in killed?" He nods so I move on to ask a new question, "What exactly can a ShatterSeed do?"

"Shatter things. Anything he touched. The wheels on a cart, the side of a cliff, a person."

"Right, so the guy sets the perfect traps."

I climb to my feet and move around the room, looking for a box that might contain food and stopping sharply when a picture of a small brown bean on the side of a long, shallow crate catches my attention. I unclip the edges, the metal fastenings making a groaning sound as they give way. Inside is a thick layer of shredded brown paper and a thin layer of wrapped bars about the size of my hand.

"Chocolate." I drool. Leaning forward, I inhale the smell before mumbling to myself, "I was thinking about chocolate when we passed through the border."

"You were unconscious," Killian says, startling me.

I'd forgotten he was even here – everything lost in the idea of chocolate.

"Not fully. I could hear you all talking," I mumble, pulling one of the bars free.

"You heard me tell Allure that you're not a pet?"

I nod. We had half-established that much... a long time ago. Well, not technically that long ago. As I unwrap the brown paper, it fills the cave with the most delectable shredding sound. I break a piece off with a loud, crisp pop. The sound feels like it's echoing through my tastebuds.

Killian steps in close to me, the kind of close that's new for us. The pull of his brow and tilt of his chin hints at curiosity – but the kind of curiosity I'd normally reserve for watching a confused chicken run up and down the fence line until it finally found the gate and ran inside the pen.

"Want some?" I ask, holding the first row out to him.

He takes it, then turns away and practically nibbles at it as he explores the rest of the boxes. Nibbles. Never thought such a big guy would be capable of nibbling. I take a large bite, rolling the piece around my mouth as its creamy bitterness starts to dissolve, and the dark cocoa becomes sweet and juicy.

I don't continue talking until every bit of flavor has flowed down my throat.

"I was awake enough to hear you all talking, and to feel the pain of being bounced around on a horse –" Which seems trivial now, given the steadily-growing-more-extreme pain I've been in since then, "– then something knocked me out properly. Felt like it smashed into me, whatever it was."

Killian hauls back an oiled canvas to reveal more crates. "The border does that to most. That's how it keeps mortal things out and immortal things in."

I push aside the mess I made with the shredded packing paper and jump-shuffle backward until I'm sitting on the crate next to the chocolate. The note in my pocket bends and digs into my leg.

"Killian."

He grunts but doesn't turn from popping lids off boxes. I can't see what's in most of them, but whatever it is doesn't interest the big guy. My fist closes around the now empty chocolate wrapper, crunching it into a ball, and I throw it at his head as hard as I can with my left hand. It bounces off his temple, and his gaze moves to lock onto mine. He doesn't turn his head or his body, just glares at me from the corner of his eye.

"I have something to show you," I go on. He huffs, like he doesn't particularly care, so I try harder. "You," I order, pointing for emphasis. "Here. Now."

He ambles over, one corner of his lips tweaked just enough to show amusement. I pull the note from my pocket.

"You have to read it to me. Read it out loud." He grunts, so I hold it out of reach. "You have to say each word as you look at them. Don't read it in your head first. Promise me."

He grunts again.

"Promise me in words!"

"Promise," he snaps.

I look at him critically.

"What does a promise mean to you?" I ask, checking that our definitions of a promise are the same.

"Everything."

I wait.

"If I promise something, then I will do it."

"What if you think that things will turn out better if you don't?"

"That's my decision."

"Then how can I trust that you'll read this out loud?"

He crosses his arms over his chest, which at first looks like he's penning up anger – but after a breath I realize it's genuine contemplation.

"You want me to follow your instructions without question?"

I nod.

"You sound like Pax," he grumbles. "Is that what a promise is to you?"

"I wouldn't have put it that way, but you've got the right idea. What *exactly* does a promise mean to you, then?"

143

"That I've considered your request," he says.

"But not that you agree to it?"

"I don't have to agree. I just have to uphold it – like a bargain."

"But you don't have a problem with breaking it?"

"I don't have a problem with making good decisions," he counters.

I pull the paper well out of his reach, just in case he tries to grab it. Pushing it deep into my palm with my thumb and wrapping my fingers around it.

"Would you follow a promise if it turned out to get you, or someone you loved, killed?" he asks, a gravelly softness to his voice.

I chew on my lip, sensing pain underneath his words.

"Killian," I start talking even before I'm sure what I think. "My life is pretty simple. Soot-servant." As I talk, I point at myself. "Make promise – keep promise."

He smiles, teeth, cheeks, and all. My soul practically dissolves at the sight.

"Killian promise Shade – Killian keep promise," he says, tapping his chest over his heart.

His words seep under my skin like a power or an energy – even though I'm pretty sure it's not magical. Just emotional – an emotion that I don't have a word for.

"Promise you'll read it out loud, each word, immediately," I manage.

"Promise," he says.

I unfurl my fingers, holding my palm out and offering him the paper.

He eyes the thing, hesitating before accepting it.

"Jada gave it to me."

He unfolds and unrolls it. I haven't exactly kept it in good condition.

As soon as the paper is opened, his brows draw together, and his jaw sets so hard that the muscle tics.

I'm not sure what I was expecting – perhaps confusion, not sharp anger.

"You promised," I say softly, because Killian is within fist-throwing range.

Not that I think he'd deliberately hurt me, but that maybe he'd forget that I break easily.

He growls as he speaks.

"The one thing to fight a grimm is something that's finally dead.

Wait until your grief has passed, then – Seek the remnant beyond the border.

Speak to a man named Martin but believe the word of a bird.

Let your reflection go hazy in clear waters and see instead through a gray lens.

In Silvari glass is a blade that can pass, a soul that can kneel, and a world that can heal.

This is not a battle that can be won. Before this time can pass, the mortal soul from its beginnings cannot last. There is no way a soul can rule and live.

Because I heard what the Origin Spring said to the tallest forest tree – the key will be in the last of me."

Before he's even finished reciting it, he sets the note on the crate beside me, palm over the majority of it and one line overhanging. Then he rips that line off.

I gasp, about to open my mouth, when he closes his fist

around the torn piece of paper, and the thing turns to black smoke. Poof. Gone.

Along with the warmth. The air's like ice.

"Never speak of this," he growls – crazy scary, and so intense that I recoil to the point of falling backward off the crate. "Never."

Then he turns and leaves. Storms from the cave, letting out a deadly growl that echoes through the space.

I gasp, able to breathe again – and I wasn't even aware that I'd stopped. The man can make things go poof!

Like smoke.

Gone.

Can he do that to people?

I clamber to my feet and pick up what's left of the note, hyper-aware of the fact that my bubble will be closing in on me any moment now. Twenty-two paces, that's all I get. Well, twenty-two small paces. Maybe my stride is getting longer?

Not now, not my problem right now.

The one thing to fight a grimm is something that's finally dead – I'm guessing that's the line that's missing. Just the top bit.

The rest is still here, I think.

Wait until your grief has passed, then – seek the remnant beyond the border. Speak to a man named Martin but believe the word of a bird.

Let your reflection go hazy in clear waters and see instead through a gray lens.

In Silvari glass is a blade that can pass, a soul that can kneel and a world that can heal.

This is not a battle that can be won. Before this time can pass, the mortal soul from its beginnings cannot last. There is no way a soul can rule and live.

Because I heard what the Origin Spring said to the tallest forest tree – the key will be in the last of me.

I run the words through my mind, again and again, to commit them to memory.

I frown at the rough edge left behind, then give in to my anger. Scrunching the note and shoving it back into my pocket, I storm out after Killian.

"What was that about?" I shout before I've even stepped out into the daylight.

I blink back the brightness and almost trip down the natural steps, but I don't slow. Killian is standing on the overhang, like he'd just barely managed to stop himself from going any further, but as soon as I'm outside, he bounds down the slope in three leaps and lands on the grass below. He pulls his sword from its sheath and swings it in arcs over his head, by his side, even behind his back.

Now would be a good time to walk away, I realize. I promise to regret this later – but right now I need answers. I'm sick of this.

'Wait until it's safe,' they keep saying. 'We'll tell you everything.' Brahman-bullshit.

I want answers *now*.

"You're inept," Killian growls at me.

"I am not inept – I'm human," I shout back. "I make an awesome human, and you'd make a terrible one. People don't go ripping up other people's property."

I jump down the last few feet of path and land on the soft grass. My boots are still on – because I didn't have the energy to strip them off last night – and my steps are a soft whisper through the grass.

"That was not yours to read," he says, stepping toward me.

Just two steps, with his sword lowered and the tip scraping a path into the dirt.

"Of course it was mine. Jada gave it to me."

"My mother gave those words to *me* seventy-eight years ago." He stabs his sword into the ground, burying it up to the middle of the blade.

"Then she gave them to *me*," I growl back.

He steps into me, but I hold my ground.

"You aren't worthy of those words," he snarls.

So I slap him.

His face doesn't flinch, but in one sharp movement, he has a short blade drawn and pressed flat against my chest. The kind of flat I would have expected closer to my neck.

I refuse to step back. Refuse to pull my gaze from the dark depths and emerald sheen of his eyes. So long as the emerald is in there, I know he's not in full deadly killer mode.

I hope.

"If you can't run, you must fight."

He shoves me backward, and I'm no match for his strength. It takes me a few steps to recover my balance. The blade's fallen, embedding its point in the grass with the hilt sticking straight up in the air. Relief floods me – not being stabbed is a good thing.

Killian walks away, pulling the shirt, with its armor-like leather sections, from his back and dropping it to the ground, before he turns and stalks back to me.

"Pick it up," he orders.

I was doing okay at not freaking out – until now.

He rolls his shoulders, and the muscles across his chest

flex and tense. No matter how long it's been, the scars on his body still look raw and fresh. Reminding me that everything this man does, everything he says, he's serious about.

I lunge for the blade and have it in my hand, my left hand, my weak hand, at the same time as my mouth begins spitting out rushed and desperate sentences.

"I'm not fighting you, Killian. I can't. You'll crush me." *He's a Seed of Darkness. The Seed of Darkness. When he's through with me, I won't even be recognizable.*

He draws a blade from his boot, running it back and forth between his fingers like it's a magician's coin. There's a twist in the corner of his mouth like he's proud of this idea. His chin's lowered, making his gaze heavier, more intense. And the way he walks is like he's ready for me to attack.

Me, attack him?

I should turn and run, but a rush of nerve-tingling excitement pulses through me.

Chuckin' excitement.

Go away, I tell the feeling. *You're going to get me killed.*

He lunges, and I step back too slowly. Automatically, my left arm lifts in defense of my face – forgetting all about the weapon I'm holding. My skin stings, the rush of pain giving me enough speed to get some distance between us. I look at my arm in shock. Blood is visible through the cut in my shirt.

"Too slow," he declares.

Of course Killian wouldn't pretend. He wouldn't miss me and chide me about how I *could* have gotten hurt. No, I'm going to *know* when I've messed up because I'm going to feel the pain.

"I don't like this," I say, circling to the left and ordering myself to block with my right arm next time – maybe the bandage will protect my skin.

I try to keep back, but I'm running out of space.

"I know."

"*I* don't like being hurt," I clarify.

He lunges forward, and since trying to move backward didn't work for me last time, I try sideways instead. Sideways, in, closer, thrusting my knife toward his arm – let's see how he likes it – and get myself shoved backward. I hit the ground, and the wind is knocked from my lungs.

"*I* don't like feeling your pain," he retaliates.

He walks up to me calmly, while I lay on my back gasping for air, trying to get my lungs to work again. The blade I was holding is... who knows where, and the sunlight above is stinging my eyes – so his sudden flash of motion takes me completely by surprise. I might not have much practice with a blade, but I've had a bit of practice trying to avoid being grabbed.

Killian is not trying to grab me, he's trying to thrust a knife into my chest, but the avoiding part still works the same.

A sharp sting sears down my shoulder. Same arm. Should make bandaging it easier.

Yay, I've always loved bandage fashion, I cheer inwardly.

Killian laughs, not moving. He points his blade at me like a person would normally point their finger.

"I like you," he says.

I skip back, ready to dodge again.

"No, you don't!"

"Yes. I do." He points his blade down, and I follow his line of sight to find my blade nestled in the grass.

"People who like each other do not draw blood." But as I speak, I dive for the knife, wrapping my fingers around the hilt, and as soon as I've got it, I raise it in defense.

He flips his blade, so he's holding it by the sharp end, and in the same split of a second he throws it at me. I don't even have time to dodge it before the hilt smacks into my forehead.

I crumple to my hands and knees. Pain thrums through my skull, and a ringing sound is vibrating in my ears. My blade's in one hand. His is not far from my other.

He walks up, and I make no effort to move. I'm pretty sure if I tried to stand, I'd just fall over again. The whole world is spinning. All I can see is his boots and the bottom part of his legs.

He's not coming to help me up, I tell myself.

Forcing my arms and legs to move, I grab his knife, and drive it toward the toe of his boot.

He moves his foot, and the knife buries itself in the ground. Squatting down next to me, then bending over further, he tries to look me in the eyes.

"Pain can be comforting," he says.

"That's a stupid thing to say." My voice is somewhere between a gasp and a groan.

"It can be fuel. If my opponent is in pain, then I am doing a good job."

"Congratulations."

"But I like the feeling of determination better." He grips his blade in a slow, deliberate movement, and pulls the thing from the ground. "I like the thing that grows out of the Darkness toward the light."

He stands up, rests his boot on my shoulder, and kicks me over. Those boots are the kind with multiple buckles down the side, and before this journey is over, I'm going to find something particularly nasty to put into them. Or just cut the buckles and watch how fast he moves when his boots start falling off.

"I like you," he says again, right before lifting his boot and trying to crush my skull.

I roll.

"I like my head," I growl, scrambling to get to my feet, to find balance, to think through the pain. "And I swear if you don't rethink this twisted version of a teaching moment, I'm going to run myself into the bubble so hard it knocks me out."

He stills, his head tilted to the side like he hadn't considered that as one of my options.

"You," I say, waving my blade around like some magic wand. "You need to show me how to hold this thing first."

He looks at my grip, then nods. "You're holding it fine."

Then he lunges at me again. This time, he swings his shorter weapon and clips mine right out of my hand. Gone. Flying through the air and smacking to the ground way over by the trees.

I run for it, picking it up and turning to face him in time to get the thing stripped from me again. I try to block his attack with my own weapon but get cut for my efforts.

I'm panting, gasping, hurting, chasing my blade and trying each time to hold it better, to move faster, as he effortlessly relieves me of the thing again and again. Leaving small nicks on my fingers and palm.

He kicks me behind the knee, and I fall backward, smacking to the ground. My hand slaps down on a stick. I grab it and smack the thing into his legs as hard as I possibly can. It breaks. Killian doesn't even wince – he just moves. I don't see where his blade is heading until after I've felt the pain and a long slither of blood runs down my arm to mix with the trickles from all the other cuts.

But I roll – because hurting isn't nearly as bad as dying – and throw myself to my feet. Then stagger to get my balance before hearing the sound of a knife through fabric and feeling the sting of steel across my shoulder, overlapping the cut that was already there.

They're not deep cuts. Probably not even worth calling them a cut at all. More like the kind of mark left by a piece of glass.

Every time Killian moves, he has complete control. No matter what I do, he's there, and the tip of his weapon moves through my skin as easily as it would slice through water.

I've been hurting since this dance begun. Sweating and gasping for breath since he tossed me on the ground the first time.

But when did everything go fuzzy?

"Killian," Pax booms.

The word echoes off the cliffs, making everything stop. Even breathing.

Even Killian. In the same second, I sink to my knees. My whole body is shaking with the effort to not fall flat on my face even as black spots invade my vision.

"She's not okay," Killian realizes, letting out a string of curses under his breath. His shadow looms into me, and I lift my blade toward it. It's not even a solid shadow, fluid on the edges, scary fluid. Like his outline is alive. "Easy, lass," Killian says, his voice different. Softer.

Cold fingers wrap around mine, trying to ease the weapon from my grip. I hold it tighter.

"Let go of the blade, Shadow," he whispers.

"Mine," I declare – try to declare, kind of just groan.

I feel pressure on the end of the blade, and hear the sound of a sheath sliding over it.

"Yours," Killian agrees before I'm scooped up.

My eyes have given up working. I think they gave up long ago. But I can feel that I'm in Killian's arms – because I feel safe.

"Why didn't you stop?" Pax demands.

"Because she kept getting back up."

Darkness

W e leave the other two to settle the horses. I can smell blood on Seth and Roarke. On Pax too, but it's not his own.

He bounds up the side of the cliff, sniffs, then tracks our scent directly into the cave. Followed by the pounding sound of his fist hitting a wall.

Three times.

One of his knuckles cracks – the pain sears through him as if it is searing through me too.

I settle Shadow on the bed while Pax kicks my saddlebags across the floor. I'm fully prepared for him to pounce and rip chunks out of me. Teeth and muscles tearing and pain.

He needs to.

But after I've fixed Shade.

Her sleeves are shredded. Her left, from shoulder to fingertips, and her right would be the same if not for the bandage in the middle. I grip her sleeves one at a time and give them a sharp tug – tearing the stitching at the shoulder and tossing the fabric out of the way. The bandage on her arm is barely holding together. Three cuts have made light work of it. They're the type of cuts that tape will fix. Shallow. Drawing a little blood but doing no real damage. No damage – if there were just one or two. Healed within hours if she were a Saber.

There's seventeen. Not counting the little ones that dot her fingers.

I pull the destroyed bandage from her wrist, using it as a

swab. Drenching it in alcohol and wiping every inch of her arms clean.

She flinches – but doesn't wake.

I dry her arms, then fix the adhesive cloth tape from my kit over the wounds.

My own cloak smacks into my back, and I pull it around to cover the girl, before standing slowly and turning to face the guy behind me.

His eyes are vibrant, the kind of glowing gold that means his magic is bursting at the seams.

I step away from Shade, putting some empty space behind me, and wait for him to attack.

"What. Did. You. Do?" he demands. Growls. Canines extending.

I draw in a slow breath. Then another.

But he doesn't strike.

"Check her pocket," I say. "Check."

He moves to her, his hands trembling as he pulls back the cloak and feels through her pockets. She sighs, her body relaxing, and rolls to snuggle into the cloak.

Pax brushes a loose hair from her cheek, the glow of his eyes calming a little. He pulls her tunic into place – his hand hesitating over the blankets that stink of murderer. But there are more pressing things devouring our energy than the lingering smell under Shadow's damaged body.

He returns to me, the paper in his hands.

"You should reprimand me," I tell him.

"I know."

"Do it."

He grits his teeth, his jaw muscle ticking with the effort required not to crack his own teeth.

"I trust you," he finally says, though I can tell he's having trouble getting the words out. "Doesn't mean I agree with you."

He unfolds the paper and scans over the delicate black ink. I've only seen Pax blanch twice before. When we lost Mother. When he lost his child.

Not when he lost his wife. That news reached him while he was a wolf, and a wolf's reaction to death is… different.

"This is in Mother's hand," he realizes. "How did *our* Shade get this?"

"Jada."

"You read this and decided she needs some fighting skills."

I grunt, stepping out of the way as Seth and Roarke drag themselves and their bags into the cave.

"You're right," Pax agrees, holding the paper out for Roarke. "But she needs to survive the training. We've got bigger problems."

"Like who attacked us?" Seth asks.

"We didn't get them all," Roarke adds.

Seth shakes his head. "I didn't see anything but flames."

"I smelled a BloodSeed," I say.

"Well, I killed him," Roarke replies.

Pax nods. "Seth ran the rescue, though I don't think we got everyone out, and Sromma and Daryan got away."

I roll the knuckles of my left hand against the palm of my right.

They're all looking at me, and all I have to do is nod. *Yes*, there is still a Darkness lying in wait for us. But I don't think it's any one of the men that we have so far met.

It's something, or someone else.

SHADOW

"Will everyone stop knocking me out?!" I scream, sitting up way too fast and using the smooth cave wall beside me for balance. "The next person to leave me unconscious will be getting castrated."

I stop long enough to draw in a breath and hunt the four of them down. Killian is by the door, and he looks back over his shoulder just long enough to frown at me. The other three have pulled most of the crates apart, thoroughly searched through them, and left a big mess. Seth's perched on top of the biggest crate. Roarke is sitting on the floor using Seth's crate as a backrest, and Pax is sitting on a metal box beside them – looking at me with his chin lowered and his gaze darkened.

Pax.

He's alive.

They're all a-freaking-live.

My heart does two things simultaneously – suddenly feels whole again, then becomes seriously pissed off.

I don't care what they were just talking about – they need to believe I'm serious.

"I mean it! I've castrated the Brahmans before, and I don't imagine you guys are all that different anatomically. "

Seth laughs, cutting through the tension in the room.

I lift one hand to point at them and catch sight of the

layers of tape over my fingers. Seth leaps down from his crate, and shaking his head like everything I just said was a great big joke, he heads for the door.

Killian swats at his shoulder like there's a great big bug underneath his shirt, then leaves with Seth. Disappearing from the cool dim of the cave, into the evening light. I can tell by the change in angle and the gentler glow, so I might have been out cold for an hour. What I can't tell is where they're going or why.

The other two haven't moved, so I turn back to them.

Pax leans forward, resting his elbows on his knees, no longer looking at me. His sleeves are speckled with blood. The top three buttons of his shirt have been ripped open, and bruises dot both his knuckles.

He picks something up from beside him and holds it out between two fingers.

"When were you going to share this with us?" he asks, and he actually sounds hurt.

Inside I feel bad, guilty maybe, but my verbal self-defense system kicks right in. I pull myself out from underneath Killian's cloak, and three others – why did they all layer me in their cloaks? It wasn't that cold.

I ignore that, getting to my feet as the words start tumbling out.

"I already did. I showed Killian, and he clearly showed you, which means I shared it, and that was such a pleasant experience."

"You've had this for two days."

Roarke clears his throat, standing slowly and heading toward the exit with a limp.

I hold my hand out to Pax. Out and up like I can freeze him in time for just a moment while I ask Roarke, "Are you okay?"

"It's nothing," Roarke says, without turning around as he waves vaguely in Pax's direction. "Fix him."

Then he's gone, hobbling out the door.

Fix him? I turn back to Pax, who has stood up and who looks like I've managed to make him even angrier. Note to self – Pax doesn't respond well to hand gestures that translate to 'shut up.'

My heart skips a beat, telling me that running might be a good idea right now, as my mouth opens and my hands settle on my hips. The two notions – run or stand my ground – are battling inside me.

"When were you going to tell *me*? Clearly something in that –" I wave a hand toward the note that has slipped from his fingers and fallen to the floor. "Affects me, and I deserved to know."

"It. Wasn't. Safe," he growls, his deep tone sending chills down my spine.

Damn this mate thing – I can't even decide if they're good chills or chuckin'-scary-save-yourself chills.

I step backward, just a little movement toward the exit. He steps forward, and I find myself taking a bigger step in response. The floor of the cave is sandy and loose under my boots, making a little crunching noise with each motion.

"Then," I begin, my brain happy that my mouth is supplying a distraction. "It wasn't safe to share that note either. This works both ways, Pax. You don't get to lay down all the rules and not follow them."

His shoulder muscles tense, a sure sign that fists will be following. Throwing a punch is more something I'd expect Killian to do, but Pax is really pissed off, and the last time I saw him like this, he ripped a chunk out of a tree. I spring into a run, angling myself for the exit while trying to keep one eye on him. All I see is a blur, then he's in front of me, and I rush to alter my course and keep a safe little pocket of space between us.

He closes that distance, getting his hands around my waist and pinning me against the wall. The one furthest from the exit, shrouded in shadow because the lantern light hardly reaches around the boxes and crates.

"You can't keep secrets." His words are low and heavy. Each one of them is laced with the threat of a wolf entering this conversation.

I can keep secrets, and I did. I'm not about to apologize for that – but now would be a really bad time to open my mouth and say anything but an apology. My gaze darts toward the exit. He puts his hand on the wall beside my face, blocking my view. Power spikes against my skin, filling the room. His golden eyes are alight with a glowing ring around the iris.

This keeping secrets thing is a really big issue for him.

I bite my lip to keep anything stupid from coming out while I try to think of something not-stupid to say.

But there's a lot going on right now. My heart's beating so fast that it's interrupting my ability to breathe. He's clearly not in control of his power, that thing that can kill me if this goes too far, and despite all of this, he's looking at me like I mean something to him. Like I'm important.

The idea sends a rush through me that is almost too much to bear.

He growls, his fingers clenching against the wall and crumbling away chunks of ochre.

Before I can gasp, he's leaning in, pressing his lips to mine and snatching the air from my lungs, the thoughts from my head, the beats from my heart. He doesn't hesitate, doesn't start soft and build to passion – every movement is firm and determined and claiming.

His fingers leave the wall and trace along the back of my neck, soft with crushed ochre powder. Finding the spot where his hand fits perfectly just beneath my hair. Tilting my head back, pushing in closer.

I rise up on my tip-toes, even though some part of me knows that this is probably not a good idea.

But not a bad idea, I tell myself.

The power in the room settles over my skin, warm and inviting. Joining and twisting with the need that is coursing up from deep inside me. The zap of it runs over my skin – like it's waiting for an invitation.

He tugs me off the wall and pulls me in close to him as his tongue brushes across my teeth and his fingers run through my hair, tilting my head back a little further. I consider that maybe I need to stop, that maybe breathing is important, but my fingers curl through his shirt and I press myself against him instead.

His hand leaves my hair and returns to my hip – lifting me off the ground and pressing me back against the wall so I'm exactly the same height as he is. His body is against mine, holding me in place as his kiss moves from my lips to my neck.

Down my neck and onto my shoulder.

I moan and am delighted in the sound leaving my own lips. A sound that says *'yes'* and *'more.'*

The sound is still rolling over my throat when pain sears through my shoulder – pain that fills me with heat and makes my muscles quiver. Pain from his teeth, or rather his wolf's teeth, buried into my flesh.

He withdraws, a low growl vibrating through his chest and into mine. If I could respond, I would. I want to.

I swallow hard to stop the impulse. Me growling in return would just be weird.

He tugs at the front of my shirt – either ripping or popping open my buttons until my chest is bare. I don't bother looking to see if the shirt is ruined.

Don't care.

The cool air of the cave whispers over my flesh and dampens some of the heat from his magic. Delicious, intense, passionate heat. I want that heat – want more of it, want more of him.

My right arm keeps ahold of his shirt, using it as support to keep the damaged limb out of the way. My left hand slips under it, along the curves of his muscles, exploring the way he feels and wishing I had the strength to just rip his shirt off too. Instead, I push it up, and he grips my wrist in response. Pulling it from under his shirt and pinning it against the wall. Between the pressure of his body against mine and the hold he has on my hip, he manages to lift me up a little higher. Putting me where he wants me.

His teeth scrape over my shoulder with just enough intensity to leave a trailing sensation. Then they push through my skin again, biting harder.

I gasp and grit my teeth and enjoy it all at the same time.

He presses into the bite, all canines, exploring the moan that escapes me, the way my back arches and my breath quickens for a long moment before releasing me. Leaving me with four punctures and a thin trickle of blood – and wanting more.

His tongue trails over the blood, over the second bite and up to the first. I realize I should be caring about the heavy effect of his magic, about the way it's making my hand twitch as his power sinks into my body. But everything in me just wants more.

Him. More. Him. More.

"Pax," I gasp. "Don't stop. But if you leave me. Unconscious. I will cut. Off your balls, and put them. In your boots." I practically have to stop and gasp in a breath between every second or third word.

A chuckle rumbles through him, then he leans in and draws up a long breath.

"You smell like desire."

"Yes, desire."

His fingers uncurl from my wrist, from the spot where he was pinning me in place and stopping me from pulling his shirt off.

"You smell like hesitation," I tell him, using his phrasing even though I can't smell anything – just him, which is a combination of saddle, horse, and hard work.

His gaze meets mine for the first time since he pinned me here, eyes still aglow.

"Control," he corrects.

"You don't need to control me."

Which in my head goes something like, *you are not allowed to control me.* And to prove it, I push off the wall just enough to lift my legs and wrap them around his hips. Pressing myself hard against his loose cotton pants and everything underneath and almost regretting it when my body responds with desperate zaps like lightning. I thread both my hands through his hair and link them behind his head so he can't pull them apart. My fingers tremble a little, a side effect of his power. Small consequence for his lust.

He grips my arm just above my elbow as if he's going to try and pull them off him, a contrast to the low groan that's escaping him. I seal my lips against his, controlling the kiss for all of half a second before he gives up on my arms and grips my hair instead.

Tugging my head back to break the kiss, he asks, "Do I smell like danger?"

"No."

"You were trying to run."

"You were angry," I counter.

"I still am."

A smile creeps across my lips as I realize what this means. "I like this kind of angry," I admit.

He lets go of my hair and leans forward to rest his forehead against mine, his hands moving under my ass to support me. The two of us are rising and falling with each heavy breath he takes.

His eyes close as he speaks. "I bit you."

"I think I want you to do it again," I counter, letting my eyelids close too.

Falling into my other senses, like the feel of his breath whispering over my skin and the power still prickling inside me.

"You can't keep secrets," he says softly.

"It wasn't intentional."

"You can't let me do this."

There's a touch of pain to his voice, which sparks a vein of fury inside me. I snap my eyes open, grasping desperately at all those lovely things I was experiencing just a moment ago, but still feeling them slip away. Anger fills the space.

And maybe disappointment.

I let go of his hair and try to push myself away from him – being this mad is most effective when stomping and finger-pointing. But he holds me tighter, carries me to the nearest crate, sits me down on it, and then turns to walk away.

Bralls no. He's not having the last word on this. He's not chuckin' leaving without me getting to say all the shit I want to say!

I spring to my feet and throw myself at his back. It takes him by surprise enough to make him stagger. Somehow, between floundering in mid-air and hitting the soft ochre floor, he manages to twist and get on top of me. Straddling me with his full weight on my hips and his hands pinning down both my arms.

Both of them.

I groan through the pain, trying to ignore it, trying to keep my eyes on his because this argument is bigger than a broken arm which, if I could stop agitating it, should be healed in weeks. This argument could change the course of my mortal life. A short life compared to Pax's, so I don't have a whole lot of time to prance around things.

As soon as the sound leaves my lips, he takes the pressure off my break, gently bringing my arm up to rest across my chest. Half my torn shirt has settled into some kind of modesty, but the other half is wide open and his gaze is momentarily lost on my bare breast.

Power still crackles around him. Not that I can see it, but I can definitely feel it. When I inhale, I swear I can breathe it in, mixed with the cave's cool air.

"I want you," he says. "But if I go too far, you –"

I cut him off. "Will die. You've said that a million times. Maybe I won't – have you considered that? My mother was a mortal, and she survived loving a Silvari."

"We don't know that for sure."

True, the Allure-induced memory of my birth was vague and short on details, but I'm getting really good at using vague to my advantage.

"I've seen what my power does to you. If there is any Saber in you, it's buried way down under the mortal part."

He lifts his weight off my other arm and trails a finger down the smooth underside of my wrist. For all the taped-up cuts Killian has left me with, there are none on the underside of my arm and his finger moves slowly, unobstructed.

My fingers jerk involuntarily – a lingering effect of his power. He has almost knocked me out with that power before, left me with whole limbs shaking so badly I couldn't get my own clothes on, so a few finger movements doesn't even worry me.

165

"Roarke was right. You don't absorb my power. It's like a poison to you."

"I'm going to kill Roarke." My fist clenches at the idea.

Pax smiles at me, gentle and amused. He leans in and presses his lips to mine for the barest hint of a kiss.

"I am going to wait outside, and you are going to get dressed – because I really want to bite you again right now."

He's up and off me before I can try to convince him that biting me again is a really good idea.

A really, really, good idea.

The exasperated groan that escapes me as I roll onto my stomach and stare after Pax is unavoidable.

Yes – his power has left me feeling weak and my muscles spasming, yet I'm failing to see why that's a problem. Nope – that doesn't make any sense.

I pull myself up, dusting ochre off my breasts and taking stock of my torn tunic. The buttons are a lost cause, and the sleeves are gone, the latter being Killian's doing, I'm sure.

"I don't have any more clothes," I groan.

I had three sets. The one I wore as we fled the castle, the one Seth poured gravy down, and this one.

"Wear some of mine," he calls, not turning back.

And we're back to this again.

Darkness

Roarke stumbles out of the cave, struggling on his right leg. *Blocking a sword with your leg is a shit strategy. I stitched it. It will heal.*

He limps down the side of the cliff, and both Seth and I watch him intently. Him, then the cave entrance, then him.

No one else comes out.

Pax was mad as bralls. A fear has awakened inside him – dark and gnawing.

Prisoners from Tanakan released and hunting us. Which means they're hunting Shade. Two still out there. Sromma and Daryan. Daryan is Xylon's brother and Sromma will inform him of his brother's death. When things get personal, they always get messy.

There used to be three layers to the law. Try to bend it, and the local enforcement – Sabers stationed permanently in each major town – would apply a punishment they saw fit. Crack it, and you spent time in Tanakan. Break it, and someone would hunt you down and make sure you never did it again. We spent more time dealing with magic and monsters than Silvari – and the younger triunes would cut their teeth on chasing bandits after their trials.

But Tanakan was locked down a hundred years ago. What used to be clear and structured is now a maze of reports to a dwindling council, Lithael's whims, and the power of the local enforcement.

The only thing left in Tanakan was the worst of the worst

and the 'last-ofs'. When you're the last Seed of your kind, no orders can be officially made for your death.

Lithael can push us, try to make us vulnerable in tournament, send us on ridiculous assignments, strip us of our ranks as punishment – but he cannot have a hand at killing us.

How many of those Seeds are out? Destroying our realm. Harming our people.

Seeking my Shadow.

And that fear inside Pax is like a knife to the thin threads of control that he's managed to string together since Jessamy.

"What's going on in there?" Seth demands before Roarke has made it across the open grass to the shade of the trees.

Roarke turns, watching the cliff for a moment. "Give them a minute."

He rests back against a tree, taking his weight on his good leg and sighing in relief. "If I sit down, I think I'm going to need help getting up."

"Then don't sit," I tell him.

"I'll help you," Seth offers, and Roarke lowers himself to the ground.

Two minutes pass.

"They've been in there too long," Seth says, popping to his feet.

Power ebbs through the air, brushing against me a moment before the other two realize it's there. Seth offers Roarke a hand and has the guy on his feet with one tug.

"Leave them," I order, standing much slower. "Maybe it will put fear where fear needs to be."

"Or maybe he kills her," Seth counters.

Both of them settle their gazes on me.

"You can sense it better than we can. Get over there and tell us what's happening," Roarke orders and points.

"No," I grunt, because I have no intention of playing this

game, and I have even less desire to feel what's going on in that cave.

"Yes," Seth demands, drawing his sword.

I look at it and smile, wanting the challenge.

"Because," he starts, pointing the tip of his blade toward the cliff. "If he kills her, none of us are going to be able to control our reactions."

The truth ripples through me. One of us ending Shade's life will kill us all.

For a stupid guy, he's said the one thing that makes me move. Because he's right.

My own fear is pushed aside as I move closer, their emotions ebbing over mine. I stop at the base of the cliff.

"And?" Seth asks.

I turn to face them. They've stayed over there, under the shade.

Cowards.

"What's going on?" Seth pushes.

The things I feel don't always have names. Life isn't as simple as happy or sad. I take a second to sift through the information.

"They're kissing," I say, careful to keep my volume down.

They're not far enough away to make me shout, and Pax doesn't need to overhear.

"And?" Seth pushes. That guy is really pissing me off.

"More kissing!" I growl back.

They look worried, sizing me up. Seth still has his sword drawn. Pax might be trusting us, but I'm not sure all of us are trusting him.

I growl, giving in to the feelings and forcing the descriptions. "He's in control, and she's enjoying it."

"I know that much – and that's part of the problem," Roarke mutters.

"They've stopped."

The guys sigh.

"They're arguing again."

The guys bristle.

This is fun.

"She's pinned him down – and he likes it."

Anger flashes in their eyes.

"He's letting her have control."

Seth tilts his head like he's trying to picture how exactly that would unfold.

"He's trying to escape, and she's trying to stop him."

Their brows raise, and a small wave of confusion pulses from them. I have to concentrate to keep the smile from my face and my attention on the emotions coming from behind me, not the ones I'm orchestrating in front of me.

"He's trapped her again," I say.

Seth steps forward, fury and desire warring inside him. He's struggling.

So I continue, "He's tearing off her clothes."

Roarke draws his sword.

"She has his pants off."

Seth lets out a growl, fist clenching on his hilt as he moves closer.

"They're fully naked and all over each other."

My attention is so thoroughly on Roarke and Seth, and the slip of a cold Shadow down my spine and away across the grass, that I miss the first signs that Pax is finished playing with Shade. I only sense that he's approaching a split second before he emerges.

I run my fingers through my hair, mustering an 'act casual' walk, and starting to whistle.

Seth's eyes go wide and flash past me to the mouth of the cave. In a rush, he turns to Roarke, raises his weapon, and spins it in an arc past his shoulder a few times. Roarke mirrors the action.

"You shouldn't be sparring," Pax declares, standing sentry outside the cave entrance. "You're still injured."

"We were just stretching out," Roarke protests.

He's a really bad liar. He thinks his Allure covers for good execution, but his powers don't work on us.

CHAPTER TEN

I kick Pax's bag a few times before bending down and struggling to pull a shirt out of it. The first one I grab is black with buttons down the front and leather from wrist to elbow. I pause before putting it on, tracing over the tender skin where Pax's teeth had pierced right through my flesh – it had felt so good.

The feel of them makes me shiver with a kind of excitement, even though they hurt.

I'm losing my mind, I decide.

Which is a problem – I've only got one.

I slip into the shirt, adjusting the four silver buckles on the leather sections until they fit comfortably. My pants are okay, just a few drops of blood below the knees. I can't quite imagine how blood got there. Possibly flung from my arm or fingers as I tried to run, dive, and fight.

Tried, and failed.

The knife, in an unassuming brown sheath, is lying on the edge of the rough bed. I pick it up, pull it from the sheath, and imprint its details into my memory. Killian is right. Not being able to fight has already gotten me into all kinds of trouble – and pain. I'm pretty sure being able to fight will be an advantage.

And I'm pretty sure gaining any skills in anything with Killian involved is going to chuckin' hurt.

Why do I like these people?

Pax thinks I'm a chew toy.

Killian thinks I'm useless.

Seth considers me entertainment.

And Roarke… He just wants to be himself, even though he can't because I'm here.

And then there's the matter of the note. I snatch it up, shaking the red dirt off before putting it into my pocket.

I'm not wearing a belt, but I am wearing high ankle boots, and I slip the knife into them, pulling my pants leg into place around it, before storming out into the daylight. Or what's left of the light. Pinks and oranges are painted across the horizon, reflecting off the ochre cliffs and making their peach and red hues even brighter.

Martin's estate was surrounded by dead land, with barely enough struggling weeds to feed the cattle. The prettiest things there were his rose garden and the wild green of the kitchen garden.

But this. This is beautiful.

I suck in a deep breath and muster some attitude before turning toward the boys. I almost trip over Seth.

Of course one of the guys was standing in the doorway. Someone had to be.

"Easy," he says, grabbing the back of my shirt and saving me from going over the narrow ledge.

The other three are over by the horses. Pax is running a brush over the horse I may or may not have stolen to get here. Roarke is sitting on the ground using a tree as a back rest, and Killian is on the other side of the yard, leaning against a railing and using a knife to take chunks out of the piece of wood in his hands. They're all out of my bubble's range.

"After you," Seth says, motioning down the cliff.

It's not a huge drop. After all, the guy who was living here was able to haul boxes and crates up into the cave. I probably would have survived the fall, and the roll over the rougher parts of the cliff, but I'm grateful not to have to find out.

"They've been talking about you," he murmurs, following me as I negotiate down the natural steps.

"Why?" I snap.

"Might have something to do with that piece of paper you were harboring."

I grit my teeth. "Good. If they're so keen to talk about it, they can answer all my questions."

I step onto the grass and march toward the others, my fist clenching and my jaw hurting. I need answers. I need to know what is going on, and, bralls, I've needed to know since day one.

A small shadow darts under my foot, gone before I get a proper look at it. Then my forehead hits something solid. The impact vibrates through my whole body and knocks me to the ground.

Chuckin' bubble, I think, as I groan and rub my stinging head. Tears fill my eyes, and Seth's laughter fills my ears.

"Slow down," he says, catching up to me. He crouches down beside me, waiting patiently as I wipe the tears away.

"Why?" This time the question is a groan.

"Why were you keeping secrets?" he asks, ignoring my question. He's smiling, but there's a forced edge to the corner of his lips.

"We were busy," I grumble, sitting up in the soft grass. "You know, running from people, and things, and stuff blowing up." He doesn't look convinced, so I go on. "Don't forget, I can't read. I had no idea what this thing said."

I wave it in the air, watching as his gaze follows the paper, then moves back to me. To my legs curled under me.

Then my hips.

Then my shoulders – okay, maybe my chest too – then

along the line of my neck, past my lips, and finally settling on my eyes.

He's given me goosebumps, and he hasn't even touched me.

"I can read," he says softly.

But before I can reply, he stands and offers me a hand up.

"Why'd you make me walk into the wall?" I grumble, which is my best attempt at changing the subject.

And I'm very aware that it sucks.

"I hadn't seen you walk into the thing for a while. Thought I'd check if it was still there."

All impressions of Seth leave me pretty certain that the only thing going on inside his head is reruns of past pranks and the planning of new ones. And he just broke that mold.

Seth has feelings.

And I hurt them.

"Because you wanted to get back at me?" I ask, brushing my shirt and pants – even though there's not much dirt on them.

"Like, revenge? Harsh, Vexy. You should know, when I get my revenge, there are more fireworks than thuds."

I hesitate on the verge of hugging the guy, but movement by the horses catches my eye. Pax, clearly avoiding looking at me, gets my blood back to boiling point.

"After you." I motion.

He starts walking, and I fall into place behind him. When we reach the others, I position myself so I can see them all.

Roarke has begun pulling up single blades of grass and slowly tearing them to pieces.

Killian hasn't stopped scraping and chopping at his piece of wood. Pax moves to the other side of the horse he's brushing, and nudges her so he can keep grooming – but with his back to me. Seth hops up on the railing – a tree branch, really, which bows under his weight.

"Hope that breaks," I tell him.

"Ouch," he says, taking a block of chocolate from his pocket.

I lunge, reach out, and wrap my fingers around the chocolate. He tries to pull it free, leans back, loses his balance, and falls in a mess of flailing arms. He hits the ground with an oomph that sends the nearest horse skittering away. But he loses all grip on the chocolate.

As tempting as it is to eat, this is my weapon, and I hurl it as hard as I can at Pax's back. Hitting him between the shoulder blades.

He turns sharply, anger flashing across his face.

"Wasn't me," Seth declares, slowly picking himself up off the ground.

We both ignore him.

"We're safe now," I say, annoyed at the quiver of desperation in my tone, but hoping to see understanding in Pax's gaze. He remains still so I press on, "I deserve answers,"

Yes – I'm desperate. No – I don't want them to know that.

"Liars don't get answers," Pax growls.

I'm halfway through the railings when Killian says, "Stop her."

Seth wraps an arm around my waist and lifts my feet off the ground. I push forward, trying to get to Pax, but he puts one hand on the top of the fence, then jumps over the thing! One movement, taking me with him.

I scream.

"Easy, Vexy," he says, putting my feet on the ground.

"Tell her," Killian says – suggests, really – then he walks away, taking his weapon and his wood with him.

Off into the trees, like going for a stroll was always on his agenda for this evening.

Pax slams the brush down on the fence post and hops

over the thing. Just like that. One jump, with his hand on the railing, no run-up needed. *How do they do that?*

I swallow and try not to show my shock. These guys are so gentle, so restrained around me, and I'm just no match for the things they can do. Without effort. Without practice.

The churning sensation in my chest has a few possible labels. Jealousy is definitely one of them. Envy. Inadequacy. Longing. Disappointment.

"We'll tell you what we know," Pax says. "But you can't go running off with this information and some half-cocked plans of your own."

"Since when have I ever done that?"

Seth raises an eyebrow at me, relaxing his grip for a second – then, seeing I'm not about to try and attack his brother, he lets go of me.

"When?" I demand.

"You traded shirts with a servant and thought it would be a fantastic idea to kneel before Lithael," Seth explains.

Moments before Lithael sucked the life out of the other two servants in the room.

I swallow hard.

"Right, I promise not to do that again."

It wasn't exactly intentional the first time.

Seth shakes his head, like he doesn't believe me, then moves to collect his chocolate bar from the dirt. He dusts it off on his pants before slipping back through the fence.

I wave the note in the air.

"I won't use this information to do anything – except stay alive."

Roarke waits for Pax's nod before holding his hand out to me. I give him the paper.

"Wait," I say, just before letting it go. "You're not going to rip it up, are you?"

His brow creases. "Why would I?"

Right, this is Roarke. The guy who squealed like a child when I tried to tear a picture of the Origin Spring from his book.

"No reason," I say, letting him take the note.

He reaches up, grabs my wrist, and yanks me down to the ground.

Okay, I'm sitting.

Then he unfolds the paper and points to the writing about halfway down the page.

"*Let your reflection go hazy in clear waters, and see instead through a gray lens,*" he reads. "Mother wrote that on a slip of paper and stowed it in my bag the day we were branded with the Return Seal and ordered to the White Castle."

He passes the note over to Seth.

"*Wait until your grief has passed then – Seek the remnant beyond the border. Speak to a man named Martin, but believe the word of a bird.* She sent a courier to deliver this message to me. He was ordered to ride the long way around. It took the message three weeks to arrive – two weeks and six days after she died."

He passes the note across to Pax. For a moment, I'm not sure the guy is going to accept it. His expression is pinched with uncertainty, his jaw held tight like he's trying to fight back what he really wants to voice.

"Whether you like it or not, we have to do this," Roarke says softly.

Pax doesn't bother to take the piece of paper. "*In Silvari glass is a blade that can pass, a soul that can kneel, and a world that can heal. This is not a battle that can be won. Before this time can pass, the mortal soul from its beginnings cannot last. There is no way a soul can rule and live.*" Pax's tone is soft, gentle, and reverent of the words.

Of the person who first spoke them to him.

"We," Roarke begins. He clears his throat and tries again.

"We thought that maybe the thing we were collecting from Martin was a weapon or a tool. Something that could safely release the souls in the glass vials around Lithael's neck. The minute we attack, he'll release souls. Silvari – even those without Seeds – don't whisper quietly, becoming ghosts if they get lost on the way to the Aeons. We become balls of energy, volatile and angry. If he breaks even one jar… we are as good as killing half this realm. We can't make our move against him until we have a way of forcing those souls through the Veil."

"But what you found at Martin's was just a statue of a knightsing. Are knightsings weapons?"

"And you," Pax says softly.

"No, knightsings are not weapons, Kitten. The birds are extinct, and the statue was just a poorly-crafted wooden impression."

"What were they like? Maybe it's a clue?"

"They were," Roarke hesitates, rubbing his mustache-beard combo as he thinks. "Like the phoenixes from your stories, but their wings were made from glass, and they could manipulate their size. From something as small as a bee to something as large as a dragon."

I smile at the idea, though I'm not sure why. I've never been much for stories and fantasies, but the image that paints its way through my mind leaves a warm feeling in my chest.

"Why the riddles? Why didn't your mother just give you a checklist? Lists are so much easier to follow."

"She was a ProphecySeed. They see a thousand different possible outcomes in uncontrollable flashes. The words they choose to describe them have to accommodate variables and allow for multiple futures to unfold," Roarke explains.

"We don't know if we were supposed to find you or not. We don't know if there was another option. If we'd arrived

179

ten years earlier, you would have been a child and not sitting on top of a post," Seth points out.

"I still would have been up there," I mumble, not expecting Pax to tense in response.

"Or," Seth says loudly. "If our grief had dragged on for another fifty years, you probably wouldn't have been alive."

Which does nothing to calm Pax. He crosses to me, crouching down and balancing on the balls of his feet to look me in the eye. My world narrows. Just me, a handspan of air, and then him. His chin is a little stubbly, his hair a little mussed, and his full attention is on me.

"You might not be the key to all of this. Mother left Jada a note to deliver to whoever was in our presence at the time. In an alternate future, that could have been a servant or one of Roarke's lovers. Your existence could still just be a mistake created by Chaos," he suggests, stabbing his thumb toward Seth.

"Ouch," the guy gasps, patting his chest to emphasize his emotional pain. "Not for me, for her. Way to make a girl feel like shit, brother."

I swallow hard. "What he said."

Pax shakes his head, looking down at the grass between us.

"I don't want you to be here."

Seth snorts. "That was actually worse."

Pax turns sharply to face the guy, a wolf-ish growl escaping. Seth throws his hands up in submission, and after a beat Pax turns back to me, canines lowered and a slight glow to his eyes.

"*Before this time can pass, the mortal soul from its beginnings cannot last,*" he says slowly, the words partly a growl as his lips try to move around teeth made for a much bigger jaw.

I swallow, finally understanding the root of his fear, and

scramble for the next thing to say before I do something stupid – like pat Pax's face.

Why is that even an option right now?

"What about Killian?" I ask. "What did your mother leave him?"

Pax shakes his head. He doesn't know. But I do – *The one thing to fight a grimm is something that's finally dead.*

Putting all of these clues together as many ways as my soot-servant brain can muster still brings me to one conclusion. Lithael is a bastard that needs to die – and making that happen means I will die.

"Maybe that mortality part means Lithael will die?" I offer.

"He's immortal. If that were the case, then it would say, *'Before this time can pass, the immortal soul from its beginnings cannot last'*," Roarke explains.

"So, your mother left out two letters."

"Two very important letters, Kitten."

"But Lithael *can* die?"

They all nod. "We can recover from a lot, but we're not completely out of death's reach. Both Lithael's father, Lucif, and Lithael's son, Kuornos, are dead."

"How did they die, then?"

"Lithael ran his son through," Roarke says, "Killian saw him do it. And Lucif died somewhere in the battle. So many bodies were burned, the whole wing of the castle turned to ash, and we can't exactly have a sit-down with Lithael and get the facts."

"But if souls go through the Veil, and Lithael can already do that, doesn't that mean DeathSeeds don't truly die?"

Roarke actually laughs at me, and I feel like an idiot.

"On this side of the Veil, he would be nothing but a silver ball of energy. Hence the name Silvari."

My mouth opens wide in a big 'o' as the answer to a question I didn't even know I had clicks into place.

"On the other side, he would have a corporeal form," Roarke begins, looking at Pax and not me. The AlphaSeed gives him a sharp nod before Roarke continues. "People on the other side of the Veil look like people, but spirits look like the shadows of their former forms. Not many people can exist over there and not turn into decaying corpses themselves."

"Only those that belong," Pax growls.

"Well, a DeathSeed sounds like he belongs."

Pax shakes his head sharply, his skin a little blanched – or the light was just playing tricks on my mind. "Those like the Queen. Those destined to rule," he growls.

"But a ruler needs to be living, which Lucif is not anymore," Roarke argues. "So even if his soul is still beyond the Veil, it would be corporeal and tortured, and likely unable to recognize his own name."

"It's been seventy-seven years, so he isn't even corporeal anymore. They would have sucked the energy from his soul by now," Pax counters.

"So your mother's messages have nothing to do with him?"

"We didn't know that all of these individual messages were supposed to form the one prophecy," Roarke says, but neither Pax nor I avert our gazes from each other. "We were hoping that Seth's and Pax's would complement each other and provide us with a weapon. Not only are we still missing a weapon, but we have gained more riddles."

"*Because I heard what the Origin Spring said to the tallest forest tree – the key will be in the last of me.*" I pull the words from my memory. "I'm not the last soot-servant, but you four are all the last of your lineages."

"And the attacks happening have all involved Seeds which should have been extinct, or very close to."

Roarke keeps talking, but I still can't pull my gaze from Pax. His canines retreat, and the intense glow in his eyes slowly dims. I swear if he doesn't give me some space, I'm going to tackle him to the ground and kiss the bralls out of him.

"This bandit was the last ShatterSeed that we know of, and he was supposed to be locked away in Tanakan Prison. Gartil was a TremorSeed – also a last of. They would have been in the glass wing."

I gulp, repressing my desires long enough to twist my head and look at Roarke. "How?"

"The prison guards let them out. Gave them one order, and then said they were free after that. Orders which could only have originated with the Crown."

"How do you know?" I ask.

"The same way Allure knows anything," Pax offers, getting up and walking away.

"Explains why our chocolate bandit was hunted down. Clearly he didn't fulfill his end of the bargain," Seth says.

"Chocolate bandit?" I ask, but my attention is mostly on Pax.

Pacing.

Making me nervous again.

Seth points down at the wrapper in his hands. Okay, makes sense.

Dream job, chocolate bandit. Just minus the Crown having you on his hit list. Which we seem to have anyway – but at least this bandit had something good to eat.

"Is that how you were wounded Roarke? Asking all these questions?"

"Trying to question them as the inn burned to the ground – yes. The ShimmerSeed took me by surprise," he explains.

Then, seeing my look of confusion he adds, "They move through shimmers of light and can remain invisible to the naked eye for long periods of time. I had two Blaise sisters under control, but the Shimmer came out of nowhere."

"Are Shimmers extinct?" I ask.

"No. But he's dead now. And so are those two BlaiseSeeds."

"How many Sabers were there?" I ask.

But no one can answer me. There was too much going on. No one can say for sure who was there. But we know who got away – Daryan and Sromma.

Daryan, whose teeth were sharpened and who brought Pax to his knees with one word. And Sromma, whose skin was pale white and whose shirt was bright crimson.

"How did he control you?" I ask. Which is a bit off-topic, and gets stunned silence from them all.

I meet Pax's gaze – he knows what I'm talking about – but "It's complicated," is all he says.

"Can he do it again?" I demand.

"I'm working on it."

Dread fills me, right down to my core.

"How many bad guys were in Tanakan?"

"A lot," Pax snaps, not stopping in his pacing.

"How many like Daryan?"

"None. He'll be the last one. But there are other things," Roarke says.

Pax growls, punching the fence post next to him and breaking the damn railing. The two broken halves fall loose, making the horses dance into the far corner.

Yep – scary shit resides in Tanakan.

I don't even want to paint that picture.

The one thing to fight a grimm is something that's finally dead. I think through the words that Killian has forbidden me to say before opening my mouth to recite the rest.

"Wait until your grief has passed then – Seek the remnant beyond the border. Speak to a man named Martin but believe the word of a bird.

Let your reflection go hazy in clear waters and see instead through a gray lens.

In Silvari glass is a blade that can pass, a soul that can kneel, and a world that can heal. This is not a battle that can be won.

Before this time can pass, the mortal soul from its beginnings cannot last. There is no way a soul can rule and live.

Because I heard what the Origin Spring said to the tallest forest tree – the key will be in the last of me."

"I thought you couldn't read?" Roarke asks.

"I can't. Killian read it for me."

"Then what was the point of Mother giving you the message if you couldn't read it?" Seth muses.

I ignore him. How was his mother supposed to know I wouldn't be taught to read? "Did anyone know the last few lines, before today? *Because I heard what the Origin Spring said to the tallest forest tree – the key will be in the last of me."*

They all shake their heads.

"So, that was the point of the note. To turn your fractured messages into something whole, and give you the final lines. Maybe my being here was just a timing thing. Like the last cog turning into place in a clock, allowing the hour chimes to ring out. If I wasn't at the castle, you would never have gone into that tournament. That got Lithael super mad, and was the trigger for Jada turning up and the assignment that got us all out of there. Maybe my role in all of this is already done?"

None of them look convinced, but I refuse to entertain the idea that their dead mother has locked in my funeral date. Trying to survive is a daily activity, but a determination hums through me as her words echo in my mind. I'm not going to die.

None of them say anything.

"What about Logan? Is he, or Thom, or Asanta, after us too?"

"I doubt they've left the White Castle. Kyra, however, is a mystery. She's up to something, and I'm not even sure it has anything to do with Sabers, or Logan, or even the castles," Seth says.

"She's probably run away, like a spoiled rich kid with daddy issues," Roarke offers.

Which Seth snorts at. "Says the spoiled rich kid."

I roll my eyes at them, moving the conversation right along. "Fine, what's next on our plan? Find the Potion Master and get rid of this bubble?"

Pax shakes his head. "We need to get to the bottom of the Tanakan escapes. We can't risk assassins following us to the Potion Master, and we can't bury ourselves in research and experiments when people are dying."

Of course we can't.

"We could split up," Roarke begins. "Shade and I ride for the Potion Master's, and..." he trails off, taking Pax's long, slow, head shakes as a 'no'. "I wasn't too fond of the idea either."

"We'll ride into Lackshir. It's a few hours' detour, but the merchant markets will be an easy place to gather information. For now, we stay together."

"Are we leaving now?" I ask.

"No, we'll eat. Killian will be back with meat soon. You

can sleep here tonight, then we'll ride out in the morning. Roarke's leg needs more time to heal," Pax says, motioning for me to follow him back toward the cave.

Sleep is an ongoing issue; they need so little of it, and I keep getting these interrupted naps followed by unconscious slumbers at really odd times of the day. What I wouldn't give for just one night where I fall asleep at sunset and wake up, uninterrupted, at sunrise. No injuries, no Saber magic involved, and no alcoholic tranquilization.

So I don't argue about the plan and follow them like a good little shadow.

As I walk, I do a reshuffle of my list of questions. Finding out why white-haired Silvari Masters drowned me as a baby and why the Elorsins' mother sent her boys to Lord Martin's estate are still at the top of the list. Working out why Killian ripped the top line off the prophecy is reaching for a top spot, though, followed by discovering Pax's dark past. The most important one should be discovering an exit out of these boys' lives before I get myself killed – or get them killed… but it's not.

I might have entertained for an instant that I *might* be someone important, that I *might* be able to make a difference and help bring down Lithael, but I fear Pax is right. If I have any part in the future of this realm, it will be to die.

And sitting right up on the top of my list is stopping a BeastSeed before he gets close to any of my men ever again.

No freaking idea how a soot-servant is supposed to be any help with that.

Darkness

We cook small game, a rabbit and three bush chickens, in the low coals of a fire, then move into the cave with its superior defensive advantage.

Shadow curls up on the old blankets and rags in the corner, not taking notice of the state of them. She pulls our cloaks over her shoulders – the things are long enough to be full length blankets on her. They're thick Silvari wool. Cool in summer, warm in winter, waterproof.

The girl needs her own cloak.

And her own bed.

I scrunch my nose at the scent of a killer, not even realizing I've stopped midstride.

A bed is a bed.

Pax lets out a small snarl, pacing two steps forward then turning to walk one step back. There's no pressing business to do with me knocking her out or a note from our dead mother. Nothing to pull his attention.

And it's clear in the way his jaw is clenched, his lips pressed thin, his hand bouncing as if trying to tap out a tune on his leg – as if itching to move closer, pick her up, and carry her away with him. That scent is really screwing with him.

Roarke and Seth glance between the girl and me – the two of them fanning out in the room, collecting various foods and a few weapons, before moving toward the cave's entrance. A few more glances back. A twitch of Roarke's nose.

The scent is digging at all of our nerves.

It bugged me when we first got here. Seth even stopped breathing through his nose while she slept off the nicks from my blade. But we all had other things on our minds: Roarke was bleeding, Seth was bruised, and Pax still wanted to hit me.

Things that have passed.

Pax sets his gaze on me, and I nod.

It'll actually be amusing to watch her wake up with his wolf in close proximity. I picture screaming.

He strips off his gear, folding it into his bag before his wolf takes over. The beast pads over and makes himself comfortable at Shade's back. His head nudges into her hair, huffing deeply.

She sighs, her body responding to his presence.

I wait a moment longer to see if she'll stir. But she doesn't.

As the scent of evil is overridden, and the imminent dangers are all behind us, we all take a deep breath of relief.

"Triple in a row, my roll," Seth says, pulling three dice from his pocket and letting them drop one at a time onto the red dirt of the cave floor.

I grunt, sitting to form the last corner of their triangle. Kicking his ass at dice sounds rather relaxing.

DAY THREE

5TH

DAY OF

SNOW MOON

Roughly 52.5 miles from Potion Master Eydis

SHADOW

I sleep like a rock. Like a warm, cozy, safe rock.

And I have no idea if that's how rocks normally feel, but my sleep-lulled brain likes to think I'm right.

Always right.

I'm so good at chuckin' sleeping I can do it with my eyes closed.

I yawn. Stretch. Roll slowly onto my back, then yawn again.

The sun's up, a funnel of light falling blindingly onto my face, but there's still a pink hue to it – so I'm going to guess it's early. Five-thirty or six kind of early. Jake's milking the cows. Cook's pulling out the early rolls for the servant's breakfast. Someone let me sleep in, so it's probably my birthday.

Must be spring then. Nineteen. Crap, that came quick. I'll be twenty soon. I was born at a young age, and so far this is the oldest I've been.

And I need to get my ass moving, or it's going to be the last birthday I see. I've a list of chores a mile long, and the first on the list is crawling into Lord Martin's bedchamber to stoke the small fire in the corner. Crawling. The man likes to sleep in – but he's also particular that only the female servants are allowed to attend him.

And I'm particular that if the choice is between me and fifteen-year-old Beth or sixteen-year-old Lucy – then it will be me.

Because if Martin wakes early, he's on you like a snake on a mouse. He's never managed to pin me, or lock me in, which has little to do with my own skill and a lot to do with his old age and complete lack of fitness.

Okay, maybe a little to do with my ability to climb out a window and up onto the roof.

But I'm so damned comfortable.

I stretch again, reaching to flick the blanket off of me.

My fingers brush dirt, and my mind tumbles over the new information.

The apple cellar is stone.

Where the fuck am I?

A silhouette moves through the sunlight, and I throw myself to my feet, my heart racing as I stagger, trip, land on my ass, then try to shuffle backward until I realize I'm pressed against a wall.

In a cave.

Looking at Roarke.

Now that I'm not directly in the sunlight, I can see his long hair is out, he's wearing a fresh black cotton shirt, and he's frowning.

I take a deep breath, my eyes drifting shut as the fear ebbs away. Leaving me shaking instead.

Footsteps approach.

Just Roarke, I tell myself.

I'm in a stupid cave, somewhere inside the stupid Enchanted Forest, and I'm feeling really chuckin' stupid. Just took all my darts and threw the lot at the board and watched them all miss – that's how stupid I feel.

Roarke stops, and I open my eyes to see him crouched down just out of arm's reach. His brow furrowed, his lips pressed thin.

"I have my power clamped down," he says slowly, his gaze scanning over my face as if looking for even the slightest reaction.

"Why?" I ask. Actually, I gasp.

My heart is still struggling back into a normal rhythm, and I have no idea what the guy's talking about.

"I shouldn't have scared you like that."

"Why would having your power locked down affect what I'm afraid of?"

"Because you're scared of me. Of what I can do. And you should be."

I shake my head very slowly, closing my eyes again as I will myself to calm the bralls down. *Why are my fingers still trembling?*

"I'm not scared of you," I whisper, not even bothering to open my eyes. "I thought you were someone else."

He moves, his knee whispering against the dirt, his fingers coming to brush against my cheek.

"Who?" he asks softly.

I shake my head. "Not you."

When I open my eyes, my gaze is immediately drawn into his. Into a depth of sadness that I wasn't expecting to see.

"Not you," I repeat.

He drops his hand from my cheek.

"Do you know what I am, Kitten?" he asks, his tone low and even – but somehow still hinting at pain and fear.

"An asshole," I mutter, almost mumble, my throat left dry as the fear settles. "But you're my –" I swallow the last word down.

Yep, that was going to come out wrong.

The corner of his mouth pulls into a smile, just a little.

"Mortals have stories about sirens, beings who crave lust and desire to survive. I don't get a choice in what I crave. There's no line between what I am doing and what my power is doing – they innately work as one unless I have the presence of mind to lock it down. It's a short-lived solution."

He stops, leaving something unsaid.

I take a guess at it. "Because you need your power to survive."

He runs his finger through the sand, drawing a spiral, stalling.

I don't mind. Swallowing a few times to wet my throat and hoping he'll start talking again before my nightmare jumps to the next visual. Because I hadn't stopped before to wonder which of the other girls would be stoking Lord Martin's fire in the mornings now that I'm not there. And whether they can run and hide as well as I could.

Or how his hands on their flesh would feel.

"I don't want you to look at me like that," he says, grabbing my focus just in time. "I don't want that fear you had just now to be because of me." He grips my elbow and pulls me to my feet before I can object. "Pax is coming," he adds, but I'm stuck on the thing he said before that.

"You know when you found me under your bed and thought I'd be fun to play with?" I ask.

He nods.

"Why didn't it bother you then?"

He runs a hand through his long hair, pushing it back from his face before letting it settle into a mess around his shoulders. "Because I didn't care about you then."

It sounds like he's going to leave it there, so I raise an eyebrow and press him, "And?"

"I was probably going to humiliate you – I admit, that was a dick of an idea. It would have pissed Pax off if you'd walked out of my room naked – but he deserved it because he brought you back in the first place, and we had more important shit to be doing than drawing that kind of attention among the dignitaries at the White Castle. But making you walk naked out of our suite was all that was going to happen."

"All?" I blurt out. "Then what? Was I going to walk naked through the whole damned castle until I found some more clothes?"

He gives me a sheepish look. "Hadn't thought about that."

"I might have been afraid of you then, but I'm not now," I say, almost expecting him to see it as a challenge.

But he's not Seth.

He turns slightly, looking toward the cave's entrance, as Pax walks in.

Pax, also dressed in fresh clothes and with the look of someone who's just had a shower, steps inside, then stops.

"What?" he asks Roarke.

It's like I'm not even here.

"Something scared her," Roarke explains.

"And it's none of your business," I growl, pushing past Roarke and storming toward the crate of chocolate bars.

Because chocolate for breakfast just screams of the perfect solution to this nonsense.

"Roarke?" Pax presses, still not talking to me.

"Not Roarke," I grumble, pushing the lid off the crate.

"Apparently," Roarke says.

I don't bother to turn around, but by the gentle footsteps retreating, I'm guessing he's left. I grab a chocolate bar in my left hand, not wanting to find out how easily my right is going to start throbbing today, and turn sharply.

Yes – Roarke is gone.

And yep – I feel like crap.

"Tell him I'm not afraid of him," I insist. There's a worried little crease in Pax's brow. When he doesn't say anything, just walks closer. I add, "He didn't do anything. I just had a bad dream."

"He's affecting your dreams?" Pax demands.

"No," I cry, pointing at him with my block of chocolate. "No. The dream had nothing to do with him. I did have a life before you threw me over the back of your horse and dragged me into this mess."

He grabs the chocolate bar, stopping me from pointing with it. Apparently pointing with chocolate also pisses him off.

I don't let go, though. This sugary goodness is mine.

Okay, so there is a whole box of bars behind me, but that doesn't mean Pax can just take this one off me.

"I trust him. If you say his power isn't affecting you, then I believe you," he explains, his soft voice contrasting the death grip he has on my chocolate. "What was in your dream?"

"Who," I correct, giving the bar a yank but failing to get it free.

"Who was in your dream?"

"It wasn't really a dream. More like a split second where I forgot that I was no longer in an apple cellar."

Pax scans over me. His gaze is so intense that I freeze, and goosebumps rush over my skin. Finally, his eyes settle on my left wrist. On the thin piece of blue cloth tied over an old scar.

I let go of the chocolate bar and try to retreat, but he has my arm in his grip before I have even begun to move. The bar falls to the ground with a soft thud, but that's still louder than I dare to breathe.

"Killian says no," I mutter.

He nods, like he's listening, but still tugs me closer. Twists me, then slams my back hard against his chest. With one arm wrapped around my waist, he has me pinned. I want to fight, even squirm a little, but within a beat my body has stilled and submitted.

I have no chuckin' idea what's made him snap or what's going to happen next.

"Pax," I begin, tentatively. "Remember what I said about castration. I will use a chocolate bar as a blunt instrument if I have to."

He huffs into my hair, and his fingers splayed across my stomach relax just a little.

"Show me," he says.

"Tell me why you're holding me like this first."

"Show me," he presses, the words pulling at my mind, daring me to argue so his power can rip into me and snap my thoughts into submission.

I close my eyes against the pressure – but my mouth is functioning fine.

"Answer me," I growl back at him. "Why does the mark of someone held captive make you turn into a wild animal?"

Slowly, like he's fighting against himself, he extends his arm underneath mine. His hand lets go of my wrist, inches from the blue cloth. My arm rests on his, my elbow in the crook of his, my hand open and his unfurling.

I've spent a lot of time looking at this guy. At his eyes, his expressions, his ass.

But not his hands – or his wrists. They all wear a lot of long-sleeved shirts, except when they're wandering back from the showers, which is also one of the times where my attention is on other body parts.

His fingers are calloused, the nails chipped short from hard training, but his hands are freshly washed, and every scar is clearly visible. Small, like they've had a few hundred years to heal, but white against the natural light tan of his skin. Slivered lines in distinct patterns.

Chains. Cuffs. Manacles. Canes and lashings.

I want to turn my hand, wrap my fingers around his wrist, and smooth away the pain that still seeps from him. But I can't move.

"You have a past too," I say softly.

He nods, and I can feel the movement against my hair.

"Do you have bad dreams? Moments when you wake and think you're somewhere else?" I ask.

"Not anymore." He moves his arm so he can cup my wrist, his thumb hooking underneath the blue cloth.

"Is this going to make things worse?"

He nods. "What's mine needs protecting."

"You can't protect me from memories."

"That doesn't make sense. Of course I can."

"If seeing these little scars is going to trigger you into a rage, then my wrist is staying covered," I declare, but the minute the words have left my mouth, claws extend from his fingers, and with the brush of his thumb, he cuts through the cloth.

I groan, and wait for him to get over his 'me Alpha, you obey' shit. His hand turns human again – human is good. Human is safe from a rogue BeastSeed.

"These," he says, brushing the cloth aside to join the chocolate on the floor, "are not little scars."

He takes long, measured breaths. The kind that sound like he's controlling something, but I feel like he's losing that battle. He's right – against the thin lines that mark his skin, my rough, jagged reminder of days left in chains are not little.

But compared to the mess the Manor Lord has made of my back, my wrist looks almost pleasant.

"I told you the wolf has much simpler logic," he says. His muscles begin to shift, subtly moving against my back. Sometimes man, sometimes trying to be wolf.

I nod, but he's already started talking again. "The wolf doesn't know forgiveness. He remembers."

Pax's fingers on my stomach flex again, the tips of claws pressing against my skin with the barest sting of something that could cut – but doesn't. Not yet.

He leans lower, his lips brushing against the exposed skin along my neck and down toward my shoulder.

"He wants to know if you're all right." As he speaks, the sharp tips of his teeth nick at my flesh.

I nod furiously, my body so full of a rush of fire and flames that my words have been burnt to ash. The air escaping my lungs is rough, pulsing, struggling. I suck in a fresh breath and run my tongue over my lips before trying to speak.

"I feel like maybe we shouldn't be this close right now," I manage.

And find myself pulled in so tight that the air's pushed from my lungs.

He moves, and suddenly I'm between his weight and the nearest wall, my hips and chest glad that the ochre isn't rough and sharp. He lifts my hand, pressing it to the smooth stone and forcing my fingers apart. Then slowly he draws his own hand away – leaving just mine and my scar on display.

We had a Brahman once who nearly died from a snake bite. Since then, anything moving in the grass made him run. Sometimes it was just a breeze, but he ran like death was on his heels.

Sometimes things happen, and our reactions get branded into us for later use.

And breaking that, healing from it, might mean facing it to regain control. Or it might mean hiding from it to safe-guard our souls.

I have no idea what Pax needs right now.

And all of the logic in the world doesn't stop Pax's power

from seeping into me. Or the way my legs are beginning to go weak, and my pinkie finger is twitching from the excess energy.

"Cut it off then," I say, and am immediately horrified by my own suggestion. Because that just sounded like I'm giving him permission to remove a limb.

Crap. Not what I meant.

Before I can blurt out anymore stupid shit, Pax lowers his teeth into my flesh. Driving deep at the point where neck becomes shoulder. Making my knees give way, and my inside pool into molten heat.

I fall, and he follows me. Pulling me in tighter to him, cradling me, keeping me from escaping.

I gasp. Then groan, pain giving way to the buzz of his power. Falling, giving way to the feeling of being his.

Purely.

His.

His teeth retreat, taking some of the pain with them, and his tongue runs over the wound.

"I need to taste that you're still mine," he says, his voice rough, partly wolf.

Not sure what happens next, except that at some point everything goes dark, and in the next beat I'm tossed to the floor in one direction, and Killian is throwing Pax in the other.

Pax, the man, flies through the air, but after a snap of light, it's the wolf who lands on his feet.

I roll in the dirt, my mind fuzzy and the world barely making sense.

Killian draws his blade, his feet settling shoulder width apart. Every inch of him is between me and Pax and poised in a mix of ready-to-fight and trying-not-to-antagonize-a-beast. He points the tip of the sword into the ochre floor and waits.

I scramble to my feet, rubbing my neck and running my fingers toward my shoulder until they brush against tender flesh and sore muscles. Barely a trickle of blood – not even enough to coat my fingertips.

Pax snaps his jaws at the air – then dashes for the exit, knocking Roarke over just inside the door and, by the sounds of things, knocking Seth over just outside of it.

"You," Killian orders, pointing his sword toward Roarke. "Should know better. And you –" He turns sharply to me. "We told you to keep that covered."

I wave my trembling hand toward the sliver of blue against the red floor.

"I didn't cut it off," I try to yell, but my voice is shaking.

Killian grunts, his sword slipping into its sheath with a smooth metal against leather scrape. Then he walks off.

I run after him, slipping past Roarke as he climbs to his feet and into the daylight.

"We can't keep doing this," I yell at Killian's back. "I can't keep hiding, and I can't keep hurting him like this."

I leave out the part about there being worse damage to discover on my skin, because making Pax run back here is on the bottom of my to-do list right now.

At the top of my to-do list is not crying.

Suck it up, I tell myself, giving the corner of my lip a bite just to get my point across.

I'm barely two steps out the door, and just noticing that Seth was literally knocked halfway down the cliff – lucky the guy's got great reflexes – when Killian turns.

"He's had that trigger for nearly three hundred years. He's always going to have it, and you're not going to be around long enough to fix it," Killian growls, and for a beat he just stares at me.

Then he turns again and storms down the slope like I've somehow offended him. But I'm not sure how. By bearing the flesh that sets off Pax's trigger or by not arguing with Killian over my short life expectancy? Did he expect me to argue over whether or not I can, in some way, fix Pax?

"I'm going after him," he growls. "Before something else does."

I stagger a few steps backward – he's right.

All of it.

Killian's right.

It's only thanks to Roarke being right behind me that I don't end up slipping straight over the edge.

Seth looks up at me. The narrow ledge he's on has left him with two choices, scale up or jump down. That's an easy prospect for him – he could bloody just step out and then land on his feet. If I got knocked down there, I'd go splat.

My cheeks crinkle as I try to smother the smile that wants to break free. Seth would love another reason to call me splat.

The guy glances at the down option, then turns and launches himself high up on the wall. He plants one foot then propels himself up again, grabbing quick holds and not waiting to catch his breath or check that the soft rock is going to hold him up.

In a few short seconds, he's bounded over the edge and landed lightly on his feet in front of me.

Roarke runs his fingers down my neck, pulling my shirt aside to view the bite marks and making me shiver at the unexpected touch.

"You're still shaking," Seth realizes, taking my good hand and pressing it firmly between his.

"He's bit you before," Roarke says, tapping on yesterday's bite, making it sting just a little.

Is it bad that I like that sting?

I try to step sideways, to get away from their attention – but of course I'm on a narrow track on the side of a cliff.

"Lots of touching going on here, guys," I say, still trying to bend myself out from underneath Roarke's fingers and trying to pull my hand free from Seth.

Seth looks up from inspecting my wrist, his gaze meeting mine sharply with a little tilt to his head like I just surprised him. Then he smiles, yanks me forward into his chest, and wraps his arms around me like a snare.

"Yes, Roarke, one at a time," he agrees.

I groan, pressing my hand to his chest. He relaxes his grip and lets me push free from him.

"Not what I meant."

"And not the time," Roarke says, grabbing my shoulders and twisting me around to face him.

I spin so fast that I almost lose my balance and the drop over the edge suddenly feels too close to my feet. Neither of them seem to notice.

"You can't let him do that. He's trying really hard to keep his distance from you, just like the rest of us –"

"Not me," Seth chimes in.

"But," Roarke raises his voice over Seth's. "You have to do the same. We're trying to keep you alive."

"Make up your mind – first you tell me I can't undo this mate thing, and that I shouldn't hurt his feelings, now you're telling me that I should try to hurt his feelings." I grit my teeth and almost fail to form coherent words.

"Respect. His. Space," Roarke says slowly.

"Screw. That," I counter, pushing past him on the wall side of the path – not the cliff side, of course.

I march into the cave, snatch up a fresh chocolate bar, and before anyone can dump it in the dirt, I tear it open and take a bite.

A very big bite.

That turns out to be rather difficult to chew.

After a moment, Seth follows me inside. I'm still working

on my first bite and pacing across the floor. My pinkie is twitching every now and then.

"Why is my finger doing this?" I demand, holding my hand up and watching as the little finger jerks violently.

He gives it a curious look.

"Pax's raw energy is like being inside a lightning bolt. When lightning hits something, it fries it. It sets trees on fire and leaves charred marks on the ground. It..." He stops to search for a word. "Zings."

I nod – *zings* works. He could also have gone with drives-me-crazy, makes-me-want-more, and could-possibly-be addictive.

"The effect it has on you is not the same effect it would have on anyone else. Might be the mate thing," he adds. He must be reading my expression because he can't read minds.

"Wait, can you read minds?" I check.

He chuckles, shaking his head.

"No, but when we were younger, Pax could drop me to the ground and leave me writhing and shaking for hours. You probably should consider yourself lucky that he's losing control, and you only have a twitchy pinkie."

I don't *only* have a pinkie problem. I definitely have the smoldering feeling of being pissed off. Sure, he's Commander Pax, scary-ass AlphaSeed, and I'm just a sootling. But sootlings have rights.

Including the right to do stupid shit.

I scan the room, spotting Pax's boots lined neatly beside his bag, before frantically looking from box to box.

"The boot thing's getting old," Seth says, popping up to sit on the crate beside me.

"If bossing me around isn't getting old, then putting crap into people's boots isn't getting old either," I counter, still looking for inspiration.

A crate of blank paper, another of folded fabric ready to

be sewn, another of feathers dyed in multiple colors and cut, ready to be turned into decoration…

"Did this guy go around stealing the most unusual crap he could find?" I wonder.

Seth shrugs. "It's all worth money."

I cross the room to the feathers, running them through my fingers. Smooth as silk, their tips carved into fine points.

Seth follows me. "I didn't pick you for the prissy and pretty type."

"That's because you know nothing about me," I say, my fingers running over the sharp tips of a short, vibrant blue feather.

"You're right. What's your favorite color?"

"Blue," I reply, holding the feather up. I leave out the part where it's the same color as his eyes and that just might be the reason my favorite color changed from far-off-Enchanted-Forest green the first day I met him.

"What's yours?"

"Gray," he says, slowly.

I scrunch my nose. "Gray's a horrible color."

"I don't agree. Before we stole you, what did you like doing in your spare time?"

"Sleeping."

"No, be honest."

I chew the corner of my lip for a second. "I liked lots of stuff."

"Well, pick one."

"The kids. I liked playing with the kids. What about you?"

He hesitates, a curious look on his face before he steels himself to answer. "Gambling. Dice, cards, anything really."

"Of course you do," I say, threading the tip of my feather into the fabric of his shirt.

It slides in easily. Straight through the weave.

He looks at it and smiles, but doesn't alter our conversation.

"Favorite food?" he asks.

"Anything I can get my hands on… and chocolate."

"Mine's bacon – but it's so damned hard to get ahold of pork on this side of the border."

"Are you telling me you ride into Drayden to buy bacon?"

He nods. "What do you dream about when you're not asleep?"

I sag a little under the weight of that one. "Wow, Sethy. That's deep."

"I'm not one-dimensional, Vexy." As he talks, he plucks a feather from the crate and pushes it into my hair.

"I didn't say you were. I just expected you to ask me about the first mud-in-boots incident, or my breastband size, not this."

Crap, now I've given him ideas.

He chuckles. "That's next."

"No, it's not."

Which makes him laugh harder. His dazzling blue eyes don't break their connection with mine.

"Tell me?"

Running my fingers through my hair, I pull the feather free, then pluck the one from his shirt.

"I don't have time to dream, Seth. When I think about things, it's either planning survival or… you know, things from the past."

"And revenge?"

I shake my head and smooth feathers into a stack in my hand, one neatly on top of the other. "No, I don't really think about that – I just do it."

"What about you?"

"I don't think about revenge. I'm more of a cause and

effect kind of person, and I usually do the thinking part days – or years – later. Or centuries."

"Well, I *am* thinking about revenge right now – you want to help me?" I say, holding my handful of feathers up.

"Anytime, Vexy. Anytime. What's the plan?"

Darkness

My Shadow rubs at her shoulder every few minutes. Sometimes like it's hurting her, sometimes like she's making it hurt. Poking at the bites Pax has left there.

Wolves like to fight for dominance.

Pax likes it too.

She is the picture of submission, bowing to his command. But Pax can't have her, and his power, his wolf, will think that's her fault. That someone else has claimed her. And that she might submit if he just presses a little harder against her.

Just shows her a little more that he's strong enough for her.

That he can protect her if she'll let him.

Stupid wolf doesn't even see that she's mortal.

That this kind of power will kill her.

"Rein. It. In," I order, through gritted teeth.

Pax looks over his horse at me, the saddle almost in place and the buckles in his hands. He drops them and runs a hand down his face.

"She pushes too many buttons – all at once."

"Can you control it?"

"I'm trying," he practically growls.

"There's too much at stake."

The last time, Daryan told Pax to sit, to stay. Next time, he might tell Pax to turn his weapon toward one of us – or Shade. To seize her and run his blade across her throat. To use his power and blow her mortal soul to whatever wasteland their dead are sent.

"There's a Sigils Master in Lackshir."

His eyes glow involuntarily. His wolf objects.

"That animal doesn't understand," I tell him, pulling the girth tight and then double-checking it.

My gaze is lowered – because looking at him now would be a challenge to his wolf – but my full attention is on his every breath. The first hint that he's coming after me, and I'll be ready.

"I don't understand why," he says through gritted teeth, "I can't keep control. Every time I have it, it slips again."

"A sigil would work."

He growls, his fist clenched but resting on the top of his saddle.

"What are we riding into?" he asks.

"Darkness."

"And what's been chasing us?"

"Only a hint of what's to come."

His chest heaves in measured breaths. He needs to understand that what waits ahead of us is so much worse than what we've been running from. I just can't put my finger on what it is.

It tastes like venom.

Secrets and deception. Pain and death.

"Protecting her can't happen while the wolf's impulses rule your decisions. He's right, but he's doing it wrong. Find your balance – by any means necessary."

Silence.

Pax finally nods. "The wolf agrees."

I press my foot into the stirrup and hoist myself up into the saddle. I'm so close to making it before Killian pushes my ass on his way past and almost tips me over the other damn side.

"I can do it myself," I growl.

He lets out a disbelieving grunt, not even turning to look at me.

Pax is right up front. Killian behind him, then me, then Seth and Roarke side by side behind me. Everyone settles themselves into their saddles and adjusts their reins, offering their mounts a pat or stroke. Especially Killian. He loves his big black gelding, despite how it fusses and complains like a noblewoman.

I run my fingers through my gelding's mane. The coarse hair is a creamy color, while his coat is a dark almost-black. He shakes his head, snorts, and then twists a little to look me in the eye. I like him, even if there is a chance that he's stolen.

I click my tongue and nudge him forward until I'm next to Killian.

"I'm never going to learn if you're always pushing me in the wrong direction," I tell him.

Pax's dapple gray starts moving without any obvious instruction, and the rest of us follow his lead. Moving away from the horse yard and ochre bandit cave and toward the road.

"I like pushing you."

"He thinks it's funny," Seth says behind me.

I twist a little and just manage to spot my partner in crime threading a feather into the back of Roarke's shirt. Chaos winks at me.

"I don't," I mutter, not breaking in my conversation with Killian.

He grunts.

I growl.

Then he smiles.

"Yes, you do," he counters.

With a lift of his reins, his horse pushes into a trot, pulling away from me to ride up beside Pax. When we step out onto the road, Pax sniffs the air, searching for who knows what. But he doesn't say anything. Roarke and Seth make clicking sounds, and as soon as their horses move, so does mine. All of us catch up to each other, then fan into one line on the wide road through the canyon. It's a road designed for large carts, surrounded by cliffs with the kinds of vantage points that would make a single file line an exercise in waiting to see which one of us gets shot first.

I frown at the guys to either side of me. Two to my left and two to my right, with me wedged in the middle.

Not that I would rather be on the outside – but I would have liked to be a part of the decision. If I ever manage to get my hands on a weapon or a skill that I can actually use, preferably both, I'm going to make it very clear to these guys that I'm to be consulted on… everything.

It's only fair.

My new normal involves practically begging one of them to escort me on toilet breaks – how would they feel if they had to get my permission to pee?

I should just be able to say, 'toilet break,' and have everyone stop and let me pee. It should be that simple.

"Toilet break," I declare – just to press Killian's buttons, because there's no way we're stopping in the middle of a canyon.

And apparently my mouth thinks pushing Killian's buttons is a great idea at this time of morning.

"Hold it," the guy grunts.

"I'll pee my pants," I threaton, channeling full Seth – calm in the face of impending stupid-shit-coming-out-of-my-mouth.

"Hold it." Killian's grunt has grown more like a growl. His gaze flicks around the canyon, like us talking is making him nervous, before settling on me.

"Should I pee *your* pants instead?" I ask.

I've never seen his brow draw together or his mouth slacken so quickly.

Did I go too far?

Seth's cracking up, and the sound bounces off the canyon's walls, making the vast space feel hollow. Pax growls, and all the noise makes Killian's horse skip forward before the guy gets him under control and back into the line.

I chew my bottom lip, trying to control my mouth as I wait for everyone to fall into place, and the threat of me getting someone shot has passed, before I slip a feather from my pocket and flick it at the back of Killian's shirt. It helps that my horse has slowed, and we're a few inches behind him, but the shot still requires a moment to aim and a flick of my fingers.

I'd forgotten how good it feels to throw a dart – even if these feathers don't have the same weight or flight precision.

Killian reaches across and grabs my horse's reins, pulling her a few steps forward until I'm shoulder to shoulder with him again. No reaction.

He didn't notice.

I smother my smile. Wait a few minutes. Then slow down again.

I probably should be watching the vibrant red and orange cliffs for danger the same way Killian and Pax are. But if there's something up there, I'm going to be the last one to spot it.

Once we leave the cliffs, the road winds through oaks that stretch to impossible heights. Purple flowers unfurl along vibrant green vines, and the odd scuttle in the leaves hints at small wildlife.

But for the most part, that's all just background noise as I flick feather after feather into Killian's, and even Pax's clothes. Seth tries to flick a few, but after the third one completely misses its mark, he resorts to sleight-of-hand.

I run out of feathers at about the same time as the road vanishes into open space, the ground dusted with a scattering of leaves through which tracks have been made. The trees are spaced much further apart, and it's clear that the area gets a lot of traffic, but there are no defined roads. Just tracks in the leaves between several stables, and way off in the distance what looks like market stalls, with colorful buntings blowing in the breeze, and a few stone walls that could be buildings, but I can't really tell from back here.

The guys stop, and my horse halts with them, but my attention is on three women who walk across our path toward the base of the nearest tree. Two of them are wearing vibrant hats with a mixture of feathers and flowers cascading down into their flowing auburn hair.

I bite my lip to smother any sound that might escape me – like laughter. Bralls, they look funny. But these guys beside me look worse.

The women step onto a wooden platform, and the thing starts moving – up.

I watch, my head tilting back and my jaw dropping. Up past the lower branches and into a tangle of timber bridges, decks, even houses.

Roarke crooks his finger under my jaw and closes my mouth.

"I'm guessing she's never seen a sky-village before," he says.

"Not likely. The border's mist would have kept all of this hidden. I'll get us a room," Pax explains.

He dismounts, unbuckling one of the short swords from beside his saddle and adjusting it to hang around his waist.

This is it – the moment they realize I've decorated their backs in feathers.

Pax tosses his reins at me, and at the same time Killian's mount lunges forward into a canter.

I have to pull my horse back sharply to stop him from following him before I can look around in surprise at Seth and Roarke. Pax has vanished between the trees, and Killian's gone. There wasn't even time to admire my handiwork on either of their backs.

"What could be that important?" I demand.

Seth shrugs.

Roarke isn't even watching. He's twisted to fetch coin from his saddlebag.

"Probably something Pax has asked him to do," Roarke mutters. "I'll hire some stalls. Follow me."

Seth rides up and takes Pax's horse's reins from me. Good – I don't have the skill to be steering two animals at once.

Now that I know to look, I can see that the ropes and ladders and platforms that lift into the trees are crawling with activity. Suddenly, lights flicker on in a rush of glowing lanterns. Up the trunks. Along the bridges and walkways. In the windows of homes way above my head.

None on the ground around us, though, except for the various stables – like the ground isn't even a part of this city.

Each tree trunk has Silvari writing carved and then painted into it. Which means I'm going to get very lost in this place.

Roarke rides straight into a small stable, one normal-looking for something in Silva. Which means it's on the ground, not suspended in the air. He dismounts, awkwardly with his injured leg, in the middle of the corridor and looks around at the stalls on offer. I dismount and very slowly flex and curl the fingers of my right hand in a bid to push some of the ache away. Roarke reaches back, his arm going around my shoulders as he pulls me forward to stand next to him. A sensation that gives me little goosebumps and makes me forget all about the ache in my arm.

The building is made of the same branches-twisted-together style as the White Castle stables, but they're in desperate need of a polish. I should know, I'm good at polishing stable branches.

The ground is compacted dirt – but it's raked clean. The lighting is poor, but we are inside a building and underneath a dense canopy, so that's to be expected at night.

A girl saunters out of one of the stalls, a rake in her hands. Black hair is pulled into a tight braid and her no-nonsense-got-work-to-do clothes are smudged in dirt and speckled in straw. But they're made from fine Silvari cotton, so she's not a slave or a servant. Just a girl doing a job.

She looks like she's about to casually greet us but freezes instead. The rake drops from her grip and crashes to the floor.

"Saber," she gasps.

Next to me, Roarke levels his dazzling gaze on her. His chin lowers a little so his hair frames his face, and a seductive smile hangs in the corner of his lips. The scent of roses fills my nose. Which is odd, because I haven't seen a rose bush since I left the manor – maybe she has rose soap.

I elbow the guy hard enough to make him grunt and break his gaze with her.

"We need five stalls for the night," I say – but her gaze barely flicks to me before it's back on Roarke.

"What she said." He waves one hand at me while the other hugs his ribs.

Good.

He turns away, gripping his horse's reins and limping to claim the nearest stall. The girl chases him.

I consider sticking my foot out and tripping her over, but as she nears, I feel the telling pressure of magic and consider that tripping an unknown SaberSeed is probably a bad idea.

"You don't understand," she says, leaning against the divider between the stalls and trying to catch his eye over the back of his horse.

And she is definitely bathing in roses. A whole chuckin' garden of them.

"Understand what?" Roarke asks, but his focus stays on unclipping buckles and sliding his saddle free.

Seth scoops my reins up from where I dropped them and sticks them in my hand. A quick nod indicates that I should take the stall next to Roarke's. So I do.

"You know horses can run off if you just let them go?" Seth asks.

"Yep," I reply, too focused on the girl and Roarke.

She looks just a tiny bit younger than me – which possibly means she's forty Silvari years old. Who knows with these people.

"I've never met another Seduction before," she coos, her voice lilting with awe.

She rests her arms along the railing, then her chin on her

arms, smiling at him like he's the sun and she's a delicate flower.

Roarke glances quickly at me, maybe checking I'm not close enough to hit him, but his attention is drawn across to her pretty face and breathtaking smile.

"You're waiting to be called to the castle," he guesses. "SeductionSeed."

She nods profusely and Seth lets out a slightly disgusted huffing sound, muttering "Bloody Seductions," under his breath.

"I'd like some time to talk to you. Alone, preferably," she swoons. Bloody swoons!

"You think you can handle me?" Roarke asks, his tone sizzling with want.

A rush of heat surges in my chest, and I forget all about unsaddling my horse. Sure, jumping this fence is going to hurt, and tackling Roarke isn't something I've done before, but I start moving anyway.

I just narrowly avoid an object as it sails past my face and whacks into the side of Roarke's head.

"Bottle it," Seth orders. "I don't care how much it hurts."

Roarke rubs the side of his head, settling his gaze on me.

Me, with my one leg over the railing.

"Not a good idea," he suggests, wrapping an arm around my waist and guiding me back to the ground on my side of the low stall wall. "I'm not a SeductionSeed, and your pretty little power wouldn't survive five minutes," he says to the girl, then lowers his voice to add to himself, "Besides, it isn't you I'd lose my control with."

He grabs the brush off the ground. I try to force myself to unsaddle my horse while my brain demands I stop acting like a jealous idiot. What the bralls was that anyway – was I going to launch myself at Roarke?

Or at her?

Definitely her, followed by eye gouging, I try to tell myself.

But more likely Roarke, followed by kissing.

I groan inwardly, grab the saddle, and struggle to move it from my horse's back to the railing.

"That's disappointing," she says, then immediately launches into a new series of thoughts. "What does the call feel like?"

She keeps her face at a delicate angle against her arm, her eyelashes fluttering every so often.

"Impulsion," Seth declares loudly. "You'll just start moving. You won't even think about it."

"And what about meeting the rest of your triune? What's that like?"

"Like meeting family," Seth answers again.

She scowls in his direction, but the ChaosSeed has his line of sight on Roarke.

I'm... not jealous... But I'm definitely pissed. I've got great reasons to be – Roarke's mine.

Okay, that much is clear, but I can't pin down why Seth would be pissed.

"We have two more companions to arrive," he adds.

Roarke unlatches the gate to let himself out of his stall, but stops short at the look of surprise in her wide eyes.

"You're an Allure. *The* Allure," she gasps, followed by a swift bow.

Neither of them react.

"We'd blend in better if we picked up one more companion," Seth says to no one in particular. "We'd look like two triunes."

"Not her," I growl, tossing the bridle over the railing and hastily letting myself out of the stall.

"He wasn't being serious," Roarke assures me. "But maybe the Seduction has some potential. If she can sense the difference between Seduction and Allure, she could become Elite."

Seth moves to join us, a horse brush still in his hand.

"She didn't, though. You told her you weren't Seduction, and she did the math on the rest."

"I'm right here," she says, but her voice is still too awed for either guy to take her seriously.

Then, as if a little ashamed, she bows again.

Doesn't make me like her, though. "What does it matter if she worked it out? She still has an agenda. The Silvari servants at the inn wanted to marry you because you were Sabers."

"Sabers, yes. They didn't have the brains or the presence of mind to wonder which Sabers we were," Roarke explains.

"And that was before the place was blown to pieces by people trying to kill us," Seth adds.

There's a moment of silent communication between the two. The girl is starting to look pissed that she's being talked about but not included in the conversation. She plants her hands on her hips and opens her mouth – but Roarke cuts in.

"Kitten, cover your ears."

I don't hesitate, sticking my fingers in as far as they will go. Seth steps behind me and presses his hands over the top. Roarke's words are muffled, but the feeling of magic in the air still washes over me. The roses in the room dissipate, replaced by the scent of jasmine.

My head is released from Seth's grip, and a little gingerly, I pull my fingers out.

The girl nods, and I turn sharply to face Roarke.

His brow is drawn down and worry, maybe stress, paints his expression.

"What did you say?" I ask.

"What did you hear?" he counters.

"Nothing."

"Good," he smiles. "I just redirected her suspicions.

Removed the knowledge that we're Sabers. Convinced her we're just travelers. Nothing special."

"Wait, I don't understand why you were entertaining her in the first place?" I demand.

Seth leans in next to my ear to answer as Roarke collects his bags, plus Pax's saddlebag.

"Not him, just his power," he says.

Something twists in my chest, my jealousy mixing with a kind of disappointment. What gets the final say on who Roarke takes an interest in? Him, or his power?

Seth has already grabbed his own plus Pax's duffle – and I don't own anything, so I have nothing to grab. The girl is just shaking off her dazed look when Roarke leads the way toward the door.

"What's with the feath –" she begins, pointing at Roarke's back.

I grab her arm and push it down.

"Nothing," I say. *Shhh... You can't see any feathers.*

Her eyes glaze over again, and I rush to get away from the tingling scent of jasmine. Too much jasmine, it gives me an instant chuckin' headache.

Roarke has walked off – but Seth's waiting for me at the door, half a smile on his lips and half a question in his gaze.

"What's with all the flowers?" I grumble, trying to explain why I'm practically running from the stables.

"Flowers?"

"Yeah, she stinks of roses one minute and jasmine the next."

Seth cocks his head to the side. "Hadn't noticed."

"How could you miss that?"

He doesn't get a chance to answer as we step out the back door of the stables and directly onto a platform. Roarke drops his bags down, tugs a rope attached to a bell, and the platform immediately starts moving. It jerks upwards, and my stomach does a flip.

I squeak, grabbing onto the nearest thing I can for balance.

That nearest thing is Seth.

He chuckles.

"Anytime, Vexy," he says, putting one bag down so he can wrap an arm around me.

"There are no railings," I gasp.

"You're not supposed to fall off."

"Falling down is exactly what happens when people go up. Maybe not every time, or every day, but it would have to happen."

"Practice," Roarke murmurs. "And a dose of immortality."

"I'm not immortal!" I object. "You're not even immortal. You guys can die – that makes you mortal."

"Our souls live on in a physical existence," Roarke says.

"Not helping," I growl back.

Branches envelope us, and the platform stops sharply, level with a timber deck. Roarke steps off. Seth goes to collect his bag, but he can't really move because my grip is like a vise – I'm even hurting myself.

"Here," Roarke says.

He must have already dropped his bags because he grabs me around the waist and pulls me free from Seth.

"Drop me, Roarke, and I'm going to cut your hair off."

"Ghosts can't use scissors."

"This ghost will find a way!"

He sets me on my feet on the deck, and I take three quick steps to the point where the timber meets the tree. Also known as the furthest point from the edge.

The deck's round, hugging the tree in a big circle. Three rope bridges stretch out from here, and there's a guy on the pulley system watching me like I've lost my mind.

AMANDA CASHURE

He's got short black hair, brown eyes, and two previous breaks making bumps in the line of his nose.

"How do you die, then? If the fall won't kill you?" I demand of the random guy at the crank.

His eyes go wide.

"She doesn't mean it," Seth chuckles.

Both his hands are full of bags. Same with Roarke. Which means I have to walk on my own two feet. Or my hands and knees. Crawling is an option.

"Yes, I do. I mean it."

"Come on, before the guy calls enforcement and has you arrested for conspiring to commit murder," Roarke says, moving toward the nearest bridge.

The bridge is made from a net of ropes on either side and planks fitted so closely together that there's barely a gap between them. It's actually pretty safe-looking.

Safe, I try to tell myself.

I don't believe me.

Roarke is already halfway across, the whole thing bouncing a little with his every step.

We're almost twice the height of the manor roof. Which is freaking high.

But it's beautiful up here. I suck in long breaths – scanning out over the people and across a sea of ropes and bridges and buildings dotted with the golden glow of lanterns. And the real world so far below.

This doesn't feel real – houses in trees is not part of my world.

Or wasn't.

Is now.

I try to slow my breathing, and the way my mind is jumping around.

One breath.

Two, I inhale.

222

Three, exhale.

Four.

I relax enough to realize I actually like it up here.

It's just a pity that there are all these other people up here – destroying my 'up is safe' mentality. Making things swing and sway and bounce.

I wait until Roarke's off the bridge, grip the ropes on either side, and start moving.

"I really do want to know how you people die," I declare, because my mouth loves giving my brain distractions.

"Mortal wounds," Roarke offers.

"Like a sword through the heart, or deep enough that it can't heal before your organs fail," Seth adds, stepping onto the bridge behind me.

The thing shudders, and I let out a squeak.

"How else?"

"If someone fell from the top, it would kill them. Or fell badly from this height. A broken leg isn't much consequence. Even Silvari heal faster than mortals," Roarke says.

I make it to the other side, and I have to force my fingers to unfurl from the rope because I'm sure Seth is deliberately making the bridge bounce around.

"Are you okay?" Roarke asks.

I nod.

We're on a much wider deck. The thing spans between two trees, and at the far end, a set of stairs leads up to double doors and a building almost as big as the inn we were in last night. Hoists, ladders, more bridges, they all crisscross through the trees. Stacking higher, to more buildings that stretch up in narrow stories either between the trees or with a tree growing up the middle of them.

"Are you scared of heights?" Seth asks, a little teasing in his tone.

"No, not normal heights. One or two or even three stories

223

up. This is not a normal height. And I'm not scared – I'm cautious. How is that even staying up here?" I demand, waving at the building before us.

Seth shrugs, but Roarke offers, "Ingenuity and a few millennia to perfect it. Come on, Pax will be waiting."

A tall, and way too bouncy Silvari passes us. He taps Roarke on the shoulder, saying, "I love your fashion." Then keeps walking straight into the inn.

Roarke straightens his shoulders, reveling in the compliment. I swear the guy even holds his head higher.

I start to giggle.

Seth puts his bag down and slips his hand over my mouth, whispering, "Shhh," in my ear.

Shhh is harder than it sounds, but I swallow the noise down and nod my head. Then I slide my hand under his and pull it down from my face. Pretty sure it doesn't need to be there anymore. He's smiling at me, a dimple on one cheek, barely containing his own laughter, as he threads his fingers through mine then gives my hand a little squeeze.

Inside, the inn is very similar to any other. Thin stools instead of seats. Narrow tables that will barely be able to fit Killian and Seth's legs underneath them, and no walls between us and the kitchen. Light, that's what the design is – as little weight as possible.

Pax is near a narrow spiral staircase, looking back in our direction.

"No sir, we don't have the kind of laundry service that could care for your unique garments," says a male servant with broad shoulders and less than lean muscles, giving him a disproportionate look.

"Fine. If you can't have our clothes washed, we will take one room, one bed, and one bath."

The guy nods as we approach – then we all turn to hear Killian thunder into the room.

"Why did a stranger just ask who my tailor is?" he demands – his gaze boring into Seth.

Seth throws his hands up, a complete surrender.

I scuttle a few steps to the side, getting out of the way.

"Honestly, I have no idea," Seth says, his smile too big for honesty.

Pax turns to the frightened-as-bralls servant.

"Why did you say my clothes were unique?" Pax demands, while Roarke runs his hands down the front of his shirt – looking for anything out of place.

Then finally looks over his shoulder and tries to glimpse his back.

He stretches one hand around and plucks a brilliant purple feather from the fabric.

"How many of these are on my back?" he asks, flicking the thing at Seth.

"Maybe thirty," Seth suggests. That bright sparkle in his blue eyes momentarily steals my attention – before Killian growls and pulls his shirt over his head. Abs... damn... fine...

I swallow hard.

With his chest bare, and his second big scar on full display, the servant blanches and practically runs from the room – from the whole damn building.

Pax acts like he's too mature to look at his own back, like all of this is below him, but by the twitching of his fingers I'm pretty sure he wants to.

Killian scrunches the shirt up and pegs it at Seth's head.

"I didn't decorate you two," Seth insists, catching Killian's shirt then throwing it at me.

"Don't try to blame her," Pax growls.

"This has your Chaos written all over it," Roarke says.

I start plucking the feathers from Killian's shirt. Every muscle in my face is too busy being amused to say anything.

"You expect me to believe she threaded feathers into my shirt without me noticing?" Killian growls.

"And why not?" I demand, dropping his shirt, but keep ahold of the feathers I've pulled out.

"Because you have the speed of a mortal, the stealth of a mortal-child, and the dexterity of a mortal-infant," Killian accuses, crossing his arms over his chest and never once looking from Seth to me.

"Oh, wrong thing to say to a woman, brother," Seth chuckles, feigning fear as he dives for cover.

Killian turns slowly, and I wait until I have a clean target before throwing one of several feathers in my hand at his forehead.

He doesn't even bother trying to catch it – and I'm pretty sure he could. The pointy end hits between his eyes and for a moment, it sticks. The guy goes cross-eyed as he looks up at the red feather.

I smile, and toss my words at Seth, "Pick a spot, and I'll hit it."

"Left wrist, left shoulder, right ear, right nipple," he says.

I start throwing as soon as he starts giving directions. Left wrist, done. Killian remains frozen. Left shoulder, perfect hit. Right ear, the thing bounces off his earlobe and flutters to the floor. Right nipple…

"What? No," I declare, stalling.

"Too small a target?" Seth teases.

So I throw the feather at him instead, wedging it into his hair. He laughs, not bothering to pull it out, and Roarke is smiling. But the other two are not.

"You can throw?" Pax asks, his brows drawn in a curious mix of why-didn't-I-know-this and I'm-impressed.

"Everyone can throw," I tell him, tossing a feather toward his top button.

He catches it mid-air, uncurling his fingers to inspect the thing. "It's just a feather," he says. "No shaft, no weight."

Killian glances at it, then back at me, deadpanning, "You. Can. Throw."

I roll my eyes. "What? Did you guys think my whole life was dishes and bubbles?"

"Yes," Pax and Killian say in unison.

Then Pax quickly adds, "No." Running his hand down his face. "Let's find that servant and get our room."

I almost growl at him. Only Pax could take something I'm good at and make me want to… slap him.

Darkness

Wylym is a Sigils Apprentice with his two front teeth missing and an empty scabbard on his belt. His past smells of betrayal, and his hands begin to shake at the sight of Pax and me.

We *did* let ourselves into his house – standing around outside people's doors is not something I do.

So the guy did look up from his dinner to an AlphaSeed and a DarknessSeed. Spoon dropped. Stew splashed.

Which burned him and led to some amusing cursing.

Pax and I seated ourselves at his dining table and waited until he could control himself once more.

No family. No love. Just this empty hollow of a Saber.

"We need a sigil. A very specific sigil," Pax begins, struggling. "I need to null a MateBond."

"That's not possible," Wylym stutters.

"Then make it possible," I say firmly.

The runt of a man swallows hard before straightening, with an air of stupidity masquerading as ego.

"I am the only Sigils Master in Lackshir, and I'm telling you this can't be done," he repeats.

"Apprentice," I correct.

"Apprentice is all these people need. They're simple Silvari. They need a Fertility Sigil, or a Stop Fertility Sigil, or something to help a baby sleep. What you're asking me to do *is* impossible."

"Why are you only an apprentice?" Pax asks.

The guy runs a hand over his almost bald head before

deciding which words to speak.

"We struggled as a triune for three hundred years – then an assignment went wrong, and I was the only survivor. That was four hundred years ago. I spent another two hundred years training with Sigils Master Arrentas, until he vanished."

"And you decided not to complete your training?" Pax queries.

"I decided the gods put the wrong blood in my veins. I wanted to be a rope maker – I never wanted this power or the call or to fight, so when the exit door opened, I walked through it."

Truth.

Even if it is laced with self-centered fear.

"What *can* you do?" I demand.

This is already taking too long. We're on the other side of Lackshir and it's a twenty minute dash back to the inn even with Roarke's speed. She's eating dinner with Roarke and Seth, and you'd think that would be a safe activity for her – at least Roarke has some sense about him. But those other two, Seth and Shade, they're just trouble.

And Roarke, his power smelled off before. The lingering scent of lilies and roses when I entered the inn – which could surely only have come from him.

And that makes me nervous. I curl my toes in my boots, tapping out a rushed tune on the table before realizing I'm doing it and stopping myself.

The guy shrugs.

"I made a Stop-and-Think Sigil for local enforcement a few years back. It's designed to guide youth with too much energy and not enough sense into making better choices. That was before the Crown sent new Sabers and mercenaries to run the enforcement here. They have a new way of doing things now."

"When?" Pax asks.

"Two phases back. They arrived on a Wednesday morning, and it was made clear that my assistance was no longer needed by that afternoon."

I watch the threads of truth and the lick of morning dew that he barely manages to keep from filling my nose.

"There was a young woman, Teryl. She was barely eighteen when she moved here with her aunt, and within a week she discovered she enjoyed being chased, then scaring the crap out of people as she defied gravity. Jumping from rope to rope, level to level. She was a fledgling EddySeed, but her use of air currents was becoming destructive. To start the chase, she'd usually steal something. A hat off a lady's head, the coin purse from a man – she always gave it back."

"Your Stop-and-Think Sigil worked?" Pax asks.

"It has a lifespan of a phase – if a person doesn't burn through it quicker – and gives the wearer a ten minute pause in which time they can't do anything that might harm themselves or another."

"That would leave the wearer vulnerable," Pax points out.

"Needing to use the bathroom all of a sudden or sneeze, that's not a problem. But anything linked to a surge in adrenaline or endorphins will trigger the sigil. The effect takes a second, so the wearer gets enough time to jump out of the way of a runaway horse, for example. In terms of your Mate-Bond, in theory it should put a ten minute gap between your desires and your actions."

"Will I be able to defend her?"

Wylym's lips pull into a thin line. "If you know something is coming, I suggest you plan ahead, so your actions are no longer impulses – in which case, you can probably just plan…" The guy stops to awkwardly clear his throat. "Um, whatever it is you desire romantically, ahead of time too. Making the sigil useless."

"Not the issue. If I am wearing this, and someone attacks

her, I will have to watch for ten minutes before I can help her?"

Wylym moves his head in a deliberately slow nod. "If that is your fear, then perhaps she should stay in his company," he says, pointing at me.

Then, seeming to realize he's pointing, he quickly pulls his hand away – as if I might bite it off.

"I can give you the seal, and any Saber can activate it – I designed it that way so enforcement didn't need to knock on my door late at night." He stands and shuffles out of the room as he talks, returning a moment later with a small metal token painted with the fine gold symbols for instinct, control, and time – among others. Deciphering this thing would be easy for Roarke, but on my cursory glance, all I know for sure is that it stinks of power and yet, still feels like the lesser of two evils.

Pax folds the disc into his left hand and pays the man with his right.

"Tell me more about this new enforcement."

"I've avoided them. They made it very clear that they are the law, and that pure obedience is required. The trial sands have never seen so much blood."

"Why?" I demand, the muscles down my back growing tense.

"No crime by a Silvari, no matter how petty, is left unpunished. The Sabers of enforcement, however... I will warn you to circumvent them at all cost."

Which is about all the useful information this man possesses. I grunt, Pax says something more polite, and we leave.

Once we're on the dual-plank link between the third tier sleeping district and the more heavily trafficked trade district, I make a sound to emphasize the question on my mind, '*Can you do it?*'

The planks move slightly underfoot, but they're double the width of my boot – plenty of room. And there are two other tiers below me – plenty of things to slow my fall.

"The problem is that this beast battles for my skin with nothing but impulse. I can handle watching you defend her. I can't handle the notion that you have to defend her from me."

We hop from the dual-plank onto a slow-lower and grip the single strand of rope as it moves in a continual loop between all six tiers. A straight lower. The idea is, as the rope moves past on its way down, you pick a knot to grip your hand above and step off the platform. I find a knot near my feet to grip between my boots as well – the rope is doing all the work. Taking us down what would have been tedious in stairs and ladders.

The Silvari men going up have to use two hands and considerable strength to keep themselves from falling. Probably not to their deaths, but certainly to considerable pain and a healer.

Inwardly, I laugh at them – but I'm not enough of an ass to actually let the sound out.

The next guy to pass me on the upward rope has a small bag of carrots pinned between his teeth, his gaze lowered in concentration. He should have taken the lift, but he probably didn't want to walk that far. There are plenty of slow-lowers, but only a few lifts here and there. The lift wouldn't have made him sweat with effort and smell of ash-scented fear.

I poke the guy on the forehead. He startles so badly that he lets go of his bag of carrots, and it falls to the ground as he clambers to keep his grip on the rope.

I let out a laugh – maybe I am that much of an ass.

He keeps going up with the perpetual motion of the ropes.

"Stop playing with the locals," Pax says.

I step to the side on the second tier and make room for Pax to step off behind me. The rope goes to the bottom and bridges down there branch off in all directions, through the food districts and the taverns, but the zip-line from here will take us all the way to the inns. The last time I was in Lackshir was somewhere in the vicinity of a hundred and eighty-seven years ago. The place hasn't really changed since.

I grab the handle of the zip-line, push off, and race toward the inn. The niggling sensation of danger in the pit of my stomach begins to settle its gnashing jaws the closer I get to the girl.

If whatever it is doesn't hurry up and attack us, I'm going to go hunting for it.

A BeastSeed on our tail should be my only focus, but I know there's something darker out there.

If we use that sigil, Pax not being able to fight will be a new disadvantage.

Pax losing any more of his grip on himself and ripping the life from her because of his power is worse.

If I were Seth, and willing to put my money down somewhere, I'd bet that no matter how she dies, my brother is going to destroy this realm in his pain.

Maybe that's what fate wants – what Mother wanted.

Maybe that's what I'm trying to stand between – winning this with our souls intact, or losing everything because this kingdom needs Lithael dead, at any cost.

I envy Roarke, his world is clear. A line on the same curve will always find itself again. He just has to follow those lines of logic.

All I get is a scent, a color, a sensation, one thread amongst many – there are too many variations. Too many options.

Too much at stake.

SHADOW

Before Pax and Killian return, I've climbed toward what counts as a bed when one is in the trees.

The stretch of material is somehow firm and yet still flexible, fixed between four posts in the inn's room. The room itself is about the same size as the last one. The fireplace has been made from steel, not stone, with a glass door to keep any loose embers contained. The flames reflect around the room and eliminate the need for any kind of lighting even though the night outside is black and heavy.

The lack of a bed frame or mattress are also clear measures to keep everything up here as light as possible. The thing flexes a little as I climb onto it, bowing underneath me like a cocoon. I don't even bother trying to get under the blanket, just grip one corner and pull it over me – adding to the cocooning.

My sigh is loud enough to make both Seth and Roarke turn from their tasks – Roarke rolling his pants leg up and beginning to unravel the bandage around his thigh, and Seth throwing a small rubber ball at the wall in an annoying little rhythm.

"Comfortable?" Seth asks.

I make an 'mmm' sound, my eyes about to drift shut when the guy bounds across the room and launches himself through the air. I squeal, curling up in the hope of protecting myself from being squished.

The bed flexes like the thing is freaking going to break.

The poles creak, ropes pulling tight, then it springs back up into place. But it takes my thumping heart a little longer to realize I'm not about to fall to my death. The thing's stronger than it looks.

One muscle at a time I relax, slowly straightening from my ball.

"Seth!" I finally manage to yell.

"Want me to do it again?" he asks.

"No!"

He shimmies in close, pulling me – blanket and all – toward him and fitting his body around mine. One arm over my waist and curled up to rest over my fingers, which finally relax and let go of the blanket I was using for cover.

"Good, because you're right. This is comfortable."

I make another 'mmm' sound and relax into his arms. If I keep him close, I've got a better chance at not getting jumped on again.

Roarke is shaking his head at us, then his gaze shoots to the door. Without a knock, or even the hint of boots on timber, the thing opens and Pax stomps in, followed closely by Killian.

Killian doesn't even look at me, his attention on Roarke and the pink line of stitched-together and half-healed tissue on his leg.

"Leave them in," he mutters, fetching a bottle of burns-like-bralls from his saddlebag and passing it to his brother.

Roarke nods and begins to clean the wound. All of that happening in the background as Pax closes the door and settles his attention on me.

"Sleeping," I tell him, pointing with the arm not currently being held in place by Seth.

Killian's gaze moves to the arm, my broken arm, and he grunts.

"Not now," I moan.

"It's not hurting?" he asks.

I shake my head. "Just a little ache."

Both guys look across at Roarke.

"Why does she need to be in pain?" Roarke asks, tying off the end of the bandage. Before anyone can respond, the guy sighs and gets to his feet. "This is harder than it sounds, guys," he says, leaving the room.

"Yes, why do I need to be in pain?" I ask, watching the door as I talk.

What did I miss? Because if there's a new rule that involves me and pain, and I wasn't involved in that decision, I am going to be really pissed.

"Allure needs to keep his distance," Seth explains, his breath fluttering my hair.

"We all do," Killian grumbles, moving toward me.

"Not me," Seth says, his tone about as slow as his breathing is.

"Are you falling asleep?" I ask him.

He mumbles something, which is nothing like any words I know.

"Just because you're not in pain doesn't mean you're healing right," Killian says, pulling a stool close.

"Gentle," I plead, because I can't escape.

Seth has me pinned, his weight the perfect mix of comforting and… just more comforting.

Killian grabs my elbow and jerks my arm clear of the blanket.

"I could have moved it if you'd asked," I hiss.

He grips my index finger and gives it a firm pull.

I gasp in pain, making Seth sit up and glare at the both of us.

"Did that hurt?" Killian asks.

"What's going on?" Seth demands, but I growl over him.

"Yeah, it hurt."

"Good," Killian grunts, pressing his palm to Seth's fore-head and pushing the guy backward. "Go back to sleep."

"You have three minutes," Seth says, wrapping his arms back around me, his cheek resting against mine.

"Can I just go to sleep?" I ask, because assuming Killian's not about to elicit more pain, I'd really just like to sleep.

"In two and a half minutes, Vexy," Seth says.

He's watching Killian like a hawk watches its dinner. Killian unravels the bandage and lines the splints back up. Behind him Pax is leaning on the mantle, his shoulder pressed into the timber frame around the metal, turning a small gold coin through his fingers, over and over.

"One and a half minutes," Seth says.

Killian just grunts at him, not hurrying to fasten the bandage in place.

"Half a minute," Seth sing-songs.

"You can't count," Killian grunts.

I feel Seth shrug behind me. "I don't mind if my clock ticks faster than yours."

Killian tucks the edge of the bandage in neatly, and as soon as he's let go of me, Seth's grip tightens, and he rolls me clean over the top of him and onto the other side of the bed. A squeak escapes me, then I realize that nothing else has changed. He's not about to push me onto the floor or start jumping on the bed. We've just rolled over.

"Go to sleep, Vexy."

The blanket is still around me with Seth behind me. The only way to get under this blanket is in front of me.

All I can see now is a wall. The painting of consecutive images of the moon, from waxing through to full and then back around to waxing, has been done directly onto the wall and covers half the space. Shuffling noises tell me Killian has moved away. Followed by the sound of zippers, weapons being collected, and things being laid down on the timber floor.

Then polishing. I'm sure that sound is polishing.

A new rhythm settles through me. Breathing and polishing. Everything in me relaxes.

Seth moves, his hand digging underneath the blanket until it's resting against the skin on my chest. I stop breathing, waiting for it to move, to hunt lower.

The gentle rhythm of cloth on leather stops, and the room feels like it's holding its breath with me. If I weren't hyper focused on the sensation of Seth's skin against mine, taking me completely by surprise, I might realize that the reason the polishing has stopped is because Killian has sensed something. He probably knows what I'm feeling right now better than I do.

Seth lets out a little snore.

The guy's asleep.

Genuinely asleep.

He's not discreetly trying to feel for my boobs – and I let out a groan for having thought that he was. And having freaked out trying to work out how to react. *Why did I do that?*

He jolts, moving his arm to rub his head. Which is exactly the moment I realize I liked his hand there.

"Who's throwing shit?" he grumbles.

"Shade?" Killian growls.

I've a feeling that the unspoken part of that sentence goes something like, 'do you want me to kill him?'

"Am I crushing you? Do you want me to move?" Seth asks before I can answer Killian, his voice deep and sleepy.

He starts to sit up, taking some of the weight off me. Before his hand is out of reach, I grab the thing and tug it in close to my chest. There's him, a blanket wrapped around me, and then me still fully dressed.

But his body wrapped around mine, even through all of that, still feels incredibly close.

Intimate.

Perfect.

"Nope," I say, gripping his fingers and pushing them to my chest, exactly where he had them a moment ago.

He chuckles, then relaxes and nuzzles his head back down behind mine.

"See, Darkness. There are benefits to being on the bottom of the power-food-chain," Seth mumbles.

Three breaths later and he's snoring again.

Damn, do all these guys snore? Killian mentioned that his room is magically warded for sound, maybe it's because he chuckin' snores too.

These thoughts, and a whole lot of others that are equally useless, dance through my mind between bouts of sleep. Every time Seth or I move, the whole bed sways, and I half wake up before I realize where I am and what's going on.

At some point, Seth sits up and perches on the edge of the bed, making me roll toward the middle. Roarke returns, his soft voice joining the others.

The smell of freshly baked cakes fills the room, and I moan, cracking one eyelid and holding my hand out. Not to anyone or anything in particular – just out.

Lates, the last meal in their way-too-long Silvari day. It must be about midnight.

Seth laughs at me, nestling a cupcake in my palm. I pull it inside my blanket, because I'm too tired to eat it – but if I don't claim food off these guys, I'm left to starve.

"Is she sleeping with that cake?" Roarke asks.

Seth chuckles. "I think so."

"It's for later," I mumble. "Later lates."

"There'll be more food later," Pax says, his voice coming from the other side of the room.

I hadn't really opened my eyes long enough to work out where everyone was.

"Maybe," I mutter.

"Unquestionably. We always feed you," Killian grumbles.

"Sometimes."

"Mortals need food, sleep, water, medical attention. We give you those things. You're fine."

"I know you try," I say, or try to say. I might only be whispering at this point.

Killian grunts. "What's she talking about?"

"Clearly we don't feed her enough," Roarke decides.

THE NEXT THING I hear is some kid squealing in delight as they run down the hallway – right past our door.

I open my eyes and push myself away from the sticky thing pressing against my neck. The blanket is still kind of wrapped around me, tangling me, and it takes a minute to get free enough to see the remains of a jam-filled cupcake pressed into the blanket and smudged all over me.

"Ew," I groan. "Why didn't someone tell me it was full of jam?"

There are only two people in the room. Seth, who's still sitting on the edge of the bed, and Killian, who's literally sitting on the windowsill.

Killian doesn't react, but by the relaxed angles of his shoulders I'd say he's amused.

Seth, however, won't chuckin' stop laughing.

I dig my fingers into the remains of jam and cake on what was once a big, fluffy white blanket. Then without even looking at the guy I dive, my fingers threading through his hair.

"Vexy!" he cries, jumping as far from me as he can.

I topple forward, grabbing the blanket to try and stop my fall, but the damn thing comes with me. With my chin tucked to my chest, I roll from the bed onto my back on the floor, and the blanket falls on top of me. I just did a front flip out of bed... Okay, I shouldn't give myself that much credit – it was more of a front crash.

I'm laughing too hard to move until the sound of the door opening cuts through the room. I push the blanket off my face and find myself looking directly up at Pax.

The guy crouches down next to my head and brushes the wild locks off my face.

"Hi," I say.

Giving him a little wave, or more like a wiggle of my jammy fingers.

"I'm going to have another shower," Seth complains somewhere in the background.

"Morning," Pax says, ignoring Seth. He runs his finger through the jam on my neck, sending a rush of tingles down my spine, then sticks it in his mouth. "Interesting way to eat," he comments, a teasing little smile in the corner of his mouth.

Pax.

Eat.

Me.

Bite.

Yum.

My brain completely malfunctions.

He laughs at me, standing up and heading back toward the door. "I'll send the servants up with a shower. Shower, dress, then we leave for the markets."

Then he's gone, and it's just me and Killian, who's still

smelling the air outside the window like each breath contains new information.

I stay where I am, until the servants arrive and a hose is hung over a drain that I didn't even see in the far corner. They plug the hose into the wall, then leave. Apparently they have plumbing, but water use is controlled.

I still don't move, not until Killian's pulled the curtains closed, left the room, and the door's shut. Then I'm on my feet and ripping my sticky, nasty clothes off me as fast as I can.

Shirt over my head, then two steps later my pants hit the floor, two more steps and my braies are down. I leave a trail of jam and clothes from me to the bed, more interested in pulling the lever on the wall. The water cascades from the hose cool, but not cold.

At first, the jam smudges, but when the water warms up the jam starts to wash away. Then the shower turns itself off.

I pull the lever again, but nothing happens.

Yep – very tight control on water.

No – I don't care why, I just want my shower.

Groaning, I drip out onto the floor, grab the towel the servants left on the mantle, and dry myself while navigating between my jam-covered clothes and the guys' bags. I find Seth's and begin to fish around for something to wear – when three stashed blocks of chocolate tumble out.

Naturally, I forget about getting dressed, tucking the towel tightly around myself, and sitting on the floor instead. I'm three pieces of chocolate in when the door opens.

For half a beat, I consider running for cover – but this oversized big-ass-Saber-guy towel is like a winter cloak on me and every face outside that door is one I know. One of my guys.

Three of whom just showered and are wearing towels –

like mine, only tied around their waists, not their whole bodies.

Roarke's holding the doorknob, but Pax is the first one to enter. He takes two steps into the room before his golden gaze meets mine, and he freezes in place.

"I told you to knock," Killian grumbles from the hallway.

Seth saunters past the others, stepping over the piles of clothes and searching for his bag – still not noticing me.

"Shit, Vexy. You're messier than any of us," he says, his gaze finally resting on me. "And you're naked."

"So are you," I mumble around my mouthful of delicious sugary goodness.

"I'm not currently making four guys har–" he begins, but stops himself short and instead marches from the room. "I'm waiting in the hall."

The others turn around too, and the door is almost slammed shut.

I swallow my mouthful, then call after them, "I'm finishing my chocolate first."

Darkness

My Shadow has no idea. Sitting around in a towel – on the floor – eating chocolate. Being with the four of us is never going to be safe enough to do that.

Pax has no fucking idea. Carrying that sigil in his pocket and not using it. As if things are going to change, going to get better.

Seth has no brain cells available to get an idea with. At least he got the rest of us out of the room, away from *my* naked-chocolate-eating Shadow. Shadows should not engage in any of those activities.

And Roarke has no idea. None. Can't see past his own damn nose. What does he think he's doing? Taking away her pain constantly is too dangerous.

Of course I know when she's in pain. I can feel it – ever-present. I have to actively put it to the periphery of my power, and *that's* when he uses his power. Putting her at risk again.

Worse, he knows that her mortal body can't handle it. That exposing her to his power when he doesn't have to *will* eventually kill her.

Pax puts a towel over her head as the rest of us get dressed, then ushers us all out of the cramped little room. If it weren't for her, I'd have purchased my own room – but I'm not leaving her within arm's reach of Allure without a fist ready to follow.

We return to the ground before entering Lackshir market.

The place is packed with merchants wearing swords to warn off thieves – and I love it. Something to concentrate on. Something to consider killing.

Locals move with a relaxed determination from stall to stall, collecting their needs. There's a further two categories of people here: transients with too much weaponry for a village market, and trouble.

Four boys with mischief in their threads rush between the people, upending a tray of apples and, in the distraction, taking a sweet roll from the neighboring baker. I smile at them as they run – straight into me. Looking over their shoulders and not where they're going.

The boy in the lead notices me first. He stumbles, lands on his ass, then tries to shuffle further backward. His threads of mischief become surrounded by the coppery scent of self-preservation.

"S-sorry, sir," the kid says.

His three friends come to a sudden stop. One looks nervously over his shoulder at the vendors dealing with the apples. Another searches around the markets, for exits or more trouble, I imagine. The third has his eyes firmly on me, anger bubbling up inside him. Not one of them has the ties of family or kin. My chest rumbles as I enjoy their teamwork. As a team, they have a strong chance. Survival.

"It's okay," my Shadow says, stepping up beside me and resting a hand on my chest as if to stop me from moving.

I glance down at the hand, small, delicate, gentle.

"It's okay, boys, he…" She trails off as her gray eyes meet mine, her brow furrowing. "He's amused."

She smiles up at me.

"Get home, boys," Pax snaps.

They're on their feet and off as quickly as their Silvari legs can move.

"You always amaze me," Shade says, turning to take the lead.

I grab her by the shoulder, pulling her back into place behind me, with Roarke and Seth behind her.

"Shadow," I order, and she chuckles.

Chuckles.

All of my muscles tense, but it's too late. She's already set my skin on fire, my chest, low in my torso – every-fucking-thing.

We move through the stalls. Making purchases. Giving the locals reasons to believe we're here for supplies and nothing more. Roarke takes care of the haggling. Pax makes sure Roarke actually pays the people and doesn't Allure them into just giving things to us. Which is exactly why he and Seth are banned from every gambling den in the realm – which also doesn't stop them from Alluring their way inside.

Salted meat. Solid lard. Rock cakes and crispbread. Apples and oranges. Dried fruits and nuts. A water bottle for the woman. Essentials.

When we reach an intersection where the goods turn from produce to products, everyone naturally separates. Pax to a jewelry merchant to ask about his travels and the kinds of trouble he's had. Rumors too, I assume. Anything a vendor who moves from market to market might have come across. Seth approaches a haggard-looking old man trying to sell tin whistles, and Roarke cuts across to a bookseller... Figures.

I would love to push her into one of their shadows – but I can't trust any of them, and I can only trust her when she's in *my* shadow.

On my direct right is a cloth merchant's stall, hung heavy with bolts of fabric and lengths of gossamer. The man inside is barely visible behind his wares. He makes a throaty coughing noise, spits on the ground, then looks angrily out at the crowd. The next stall down has a long table covered in

Silvari glassworks. The young man behind the counter looks confident about his product, but uncomfortable with the crowd.

Uncomfortable wins.

I approach the man, cocking my head to one side as I listen for the sound of my Shadow walking behind me.

"Oh, wow," the merchant says. "You don't look like the kind of person to buy glass."

I look over the items. A small clear dove sitting on green branches with red berries. An ink holder made to look like twisting vines. A collection of fine rings in all the colors that glass-dye could possibly come in, and a perfectly clear bracelet with five incredibly thin colored lines running through it. Around it. Never-ending circles.

I grunt. Circles are always never-ending.

And the merchant is right about me.

"News from the road. Trouble?"

"No, sir," the kid replies, his pulse quickening. He begins to lick his lips and swallow heavily – almost uncontrollably. "Saber, sir."

He might be about to piss himself. As much as I would enjoy that, we've got a job to do.

I turn to leave just as Shade steps in close and loops her arms through mine. I look down at her. Pulled in close to me, her fingers looping into mine and her other hand resting against my bicep. Half of the tape on her fingers and arms has come off. The healing nicks are thin red lines against golden skin.

Wounds I gave her.

If I didn't need this information, I'd take that hand and throw it, and her, to the edge of this damn bubble.

"What my dear friend here," she begins, oblivious to my reaction, "is trying to ask, is if you might have come across any rumors of any kind of trouble. We've been tracing a rogue Saber who has kidnapped a woman and child, and we just want to get them back safely."

A scent teases at the back of my nose, and I sniff the air just to be sure. Lilies and roses.

She's flirting with him.

The guy looks shocked at first. From the pretty girl to me and back again.

To Silvari, a mortal would feel weak. Like something *lesser*. They probably can't tell why; most Silvari have never met a mortal in their lives. Some thrive on dominating others. Some might just take pity on her. None would see her as an equal.

Not sure if there are any other emotions on that spectrum.

Don't care, either.

He steps in a little closer, his gaze so intently on her that I have to put my hand in my pocket to stop from drawing my sword. I could take the guy's head off from here. It'd be so quick, so soundless. Not even a scream. No one would know.

"There are rumors of beasts on the roads, moving toward the borders. Some say they're being called by a BeastSeed, but my grandmother swears BeastSeeds are just myths. FaunaSeeds enchant birds and deer, but these creatures are feasting on any travelers they find. I haven't seen one, and I travel from the coast to the western border then back again, so maybe they're just rumors. Even still, the merchants have begun moving in caravans – and no one dares camp on the road anymore."

I avoid meeting Shadow's gaze. She's thinking what I am. BeastSeeds are real, and the one hunting us has been hard at work sending creatures toward a force of magic that should be impenetrable to them.

"Why?" I ask.

The guy's eyes flick to meet mine. Shadow's done a good

job getting him to talk, and he starts sharing the details with me while the girl lets go of my arm and moves to explore the glass on display. She hovers her hand over the bracelet for a moment before moving further down the table.

"Rumor is they want out. That's all I know."

Seth joins us, and I thank the merchant with a few copper coins. I move toward my Shadow, rubbing the spot where her hand was resting, trying to relax the sensation of wanting her close again. I'm about to thank her for intervening when she begins to whisper.

"Is this Silvari glass?" she asks.

I nod, a 'yes' noise escaping me.

"This was in the riddle. This is what –" She waves her hand to indicate her neck. "What he keeps those souls in?"

I nod.

"But it's so delicate. This feather is so fine I can hardly see the thing."

She reaches for it. It's one of the heavier pieces on the table, the kind of thing Roarke would use as a paperweight. I take a step back, letting Seth between us. The markets are still flowing, customers coming and going. Pax is still talking to the jewel merchant and Roarke is just thanking the book merchant.

"It won't break," Seth says.

My Shadow frowns. "Of course it can break."

"Silvari glass is incredibly strong. You'd have to drop that from the top tier" – he points straight up into the trees – "onto stone just to chip it. *If* it would chip at all."

I turn my head just in time to see Shadow's fingers brush against the tip of the feather.

Brush. Soft. Shatter.

She opens her mouth to scream, but Seth covers the distance to her before the sound can escape. He wraps one arm around her waist, glass fragments still in the air.

He may have just said, "Yoink," as he snatched her away from the shattering glass, not stopping until he's down the street with her. In a blink. Pushing the deception of speed to its limits.

I growl, pull my coins out, and offer the merchant payment.

"I look like I would accidentally break Silvari glass – right?" I ask the merchant – order him, really.

He nods profusely and takes the money.

All my money.

This stuff isn't cheap.

DAY FOUR

6TH
DAY OF
SNOW MOON

ROUGHLY 76.5 MILES FROM POTION MASTER EYDIS

an you break? I ask internally, as my fingers whisper across the glass feather.

It does – instantly, shattering.

The merchant dives for cover with a squeal, and my mouth pops open to do the same. But Seth wraps his arm around my waist and lifts my feet from the ground saying, "Yoink," before the sound can escape.

He pulls me in close and uses his crazy speed to dissolve the distance between the glass merchant and the end of the street, ripping the breath from my lungs and leaving me gasping.

When we stop, he relaxes his grip enough for my boots to settle on the ground. My head spins, and my feet stumble as he turns me around and forces me to face him. He grips my chin and tilts my head back, giving me a sharp look that is so unlike him, melting my confusion into worry. Full blue-eyed intensity traces over every inch of me. He turns my head to the left, then the right, then the left again.

"What?" I ask. "Have I grown a mustache?"

My mouth is in fine form – even though my heart's racing, and my mind is terrified of his reaction. Of his fear.

A smile stretches across his lips – I love being able to do that to him.

"I'm looking for blood."

"Is there any?"

He shakes his head, just once. Over Seth's back, way down the row of stalls, Killian is paying the glass merchant. I feel the odd need to go back and claim all the untouched glass as mine. Not buy it, just take it.

"I really don't know anything about mortals," Seth says as he blows the fine glass dust from his arm.

Pax blurs across the marketplace, using his super-Saber-speed, followed quickly by Roarke and Killian. Surrounding me.

"What happened?" Pax demands, his gaze boring into me.

"Apparently when mortals touch Silvari glass, it shatters."

Killian pinches the front of his shirt in two fingers and tugs at it. Glass dust billows off of him.

"Into dust?" Roarke asks, eyes wide and full of wonder.

"Why? Is dust unusual?" I counter.

"Usually when the stuff breaks, it's thin like a razor blade and cuts deep and fast," Roarke explains. Plucking some from my hair, he rolls it through his fingers. His head tilts to one side, and his long hair falls around his face as he thinks. "This is finer than the sand that glass blowers use to begin with." He holds his fingers up and shows me the droplets of blood left there.

"Crap," I exclaim, tipping my head over and trying to shake the remnants free before I'm the one bleeding. I don't like bleeding, but I do it often enough without the help of razor sharp glass.

Roarke kneels down, looking up at me from under my hair. "You're obviously not cut, Kitten."

I freeze. *Obviously*.

"Do I look like an idiot right now?" I ask.

I'm bent over in the middle of the street. Bum in the air, hair flung over my head, dancing and shaking and jumping around.

He raises an eyebrow at me – trying not to laugh.

Seth *is* laughing.

I swallow hard. The abrasions on Roarke's fingers have already healed over. What I would give to heal like that.

"But I've touched your glass before – I washed dish after dish of it," I say from under my hair, before I straighten, pull my clothes back into some kind of order, and then act like none of that just happened.

"That was just glass. Silvari glass is made using a recipe – like a potion, it directly uses power," Roarke explains, standing up beside me. "It's super secretive. No one other than those who work it ever get to see the process. And they're sealed up, never to walk in society again."

"Let me guess – GlassSeeds are extinct too."

"There are no GlassSeeds," Seth says, but he looks to Roarke for confirmation.

"Glass magic was created and crafted by the Origins. Access is still pretty limited, very expensive trinkets except at the Black Castle."

"And OriginSeeds are extinct?"

Killian grunts in answer. A 'yep' grunt.

I wince at my lack of tact. "Are all your people dying out?"

Pax nods slowly, and my heart thumps a double beat.

The market is full of people. Three women in fine dresses are carrying baskets of lavender with five kids dancing and singing and chasing after their mothers' skirts. Colored buntings fly overhead, and a guy selling balloons sings from the corner about how a balloon is the best gift for a child. The place feels alive.

Pax does not look lively. He looks serious, solemn even.

"That doesn't make any sense," I protest, gesturing to the

crowded street. "And there were hundreds of you in the White Castle."

"Yeah," Seth says, rubbing the back of his neck awkwardly. "There are plenty of Silvari without Seeds – just not many of us left with Seeds."

"There used to be more than four thousand PowerSeed lineages," Roarke adds softly, motioning to suggest we start walking. "Eight hundred of them have become extinct. Lithael's father – Lucif – lived for eleven hundred years. The first Seed became extinct the same year he became a dignitary of the Crimson Castle."

"There is a Crimson Castle?" I ask, which completely shatters my assumption that the White Castle and the Black Castle wore good versus evil titles.

"Was. With less Seeds, the realm has needed less places for them to train and live. The castles are magical; like our borders, their existence relies on a balance of power. The Crimson Castle fell before I was born," Pax explains.

"Now it's the most feared piece of land in the kingdom. Lucif really left a stain on it," Seth adds, but Roarke quickly moves us on.

"Cobalt soon after. Followed by Jade, Amethyst, and Amber."

"They get reopened as locations for the trials. Except for the Crimson, that is. Poisoned – no one survives that one," Seth says.

All I can think is that that explains the cutthroat attitude of the servants at the White Castle. More Silvari and less Sabers means not everyone would get the opportunity to actually serve the Elite anymore. I'm not sure what the surplus of servants are off doing, but I imagine it's much less glamorous – paving roads and tending fields.

The markets sprawl on forever. Silence settles between us.

Eventually Pax stops, and the others follow suit.

"Roarke, the saddler. Seth, the canvas merchant, and Killian, do you think I can trust you with the ribbon merchant?" Pax asks.

The guys nod and move off. I follow Killian because I don't think the guy can handle a ribbon merchant at all. For one, the merchant is a woman, and for two, Killian has no charm.

I step in front of him.

"Hi, how have sales been today?" I ask, leaning in to examine a piece of pink lace.

"A beautiful day," she manages, eyeing Killian with a crease in her brow that screams her internal dialogue, 'run, run, run.'

"Oh, don't mind my…" I search for a word to settle her nerves. Bodyguard isn't going to work. "Husband. He's a big softy on the inside."

Killian grunts, crossing his arms over his chest and all but taking a step back. But the woman relaxes, taking her hands from her apron pockets and lifting a roll of red lace.

"This one is much finer quality," she says. "But I'm thinking that, with your fashion style, black would be more fitting."

I sigh down at my clothes – Pax's clothes. Again.

"Actually, a dear friend of ours was due to arrive, traveling the road from the coast, and we're afraid something has happened to her. Has there been any news of trouble?"

Her expression changes, fear turning to stress.

"The road has become terrifying. The caravan ahead of ours was decimated. We found the carts empty and several of the guards slain, all of the horses released, and the few guards that survived were bruised and scared, hiding in the trees. They wouldn't tell us what they were transporting, but it *was* in locked steel boxes and it was still stolen. They babbled that there were five who attacked them. Four men and a woman."

"Sabers?" I lean forward to whisper-ask.

She nods furiously.

"Rogues? Bandits? Surely not a triune?" I press.

"The surviving guards traveled with us until we reached Berminta. Told tales of the attackers being young, maybe even too young for the call. One was a dragon, another a ShimmerSeed. And a MagnetSeed – that's how they stole the locked boxes. A MagnetSeed – they're not even supposed to exist. And a woman who could control the world with her words. I thought they were fantasy, a new fairytale in the making. But when we reached Berminta, enforcement ushered the men in for questioning and we never saw them again – that struck me as weird. We left Berminta as soon as we could."

I feel the heat, the power, roll off Killian, but he doesn't say or do anything.

Time to end this conversation.

"Thank you." I smile at the woman.

She offers me a smile, then turns to tend a customer at the other end of her counter.

I step back to leave, but Killian doesn't move – because three men are walking straight for us.

Sabers, just by the look of them. The biggest guy is in the middle, a bow sticking out over his shoulder. The thing is huge. His brows sit heavily over his eyes, giving him an angry look even though he's smiling. The armed men on either side of him push back the waists of their cloaks, flashing the hilts of swords. The one on the left has a ruggedly handsome face, ruined by a nose that is a little too big and, at some point, had the tip sliced off. The guy on the right runs his fingers through his hair, turning in a circle as he walks to whistle at a Silvari woman in a flowing blue gown.

The woman giggles, hesitating as if she might come over to the guy. But he waves her off and she scurries down the street.

"Enforcement," Killian growls.

"Wait," I say, putting a hand on his arm before he can turn to leave, or worse – draw his weapon. "Aren't they the best people to ask for information?"

"They're long-term enforcement. They live and work here."

"So, that means they should have loads of details for us. Why didn't we go to them first?"

Killian shakes his head. "No, that means they're not doing their jobs, or worse – they are a part of the problem."

I purse my lips. He's right, but I'm right too.

"Let's just hear them out," I suggest.

The men stop in front of us.

"I'm listening," Killian growls loudly.

I roll my eyes. "What my friend is trying to say is 'hello'," I translate.

"Well, hello to you too," the whistler jeers.

I'm standing close enough to Killian that I feel him beginning to move. I wrap my arm through his before he can kill the guy. I *am* assuming he's planning on killing the guy.

"*Why don't you come along with us?*" Creepy-whistling-guy asks, drawing the words out in a kind of melodic tone that skips over my skin and makes me shiver unpleasantly.

"We can talk here," I say politely, offering him a smile.

I probably would have missed the creasing around his eyes, after all his smile doesn't falter, if Killian didn't also chuckle.

"Or we can make you," the big guy in the middle threatens.

Killian turns sharply, pulling free from my grip and practically putting his back to mine.

"What?" I whisper, not taking my attention off the three Sabers in front of me.

Something tells me that both of us turning our backs on them would be a bad idea.

"Nine," Killian lets the word out on a grunt.

Nine? Like nine armed Sabers have surrounded us? There are times when full sentences would be useful.

"Where's Pax?" I whisper.

Killian shakes his head.

I put on my best fake smile. Running my hand down Killian's arm to try and calm the man.

"Options?" I ask.

"Lots of blood."

"And these other people?" The ones shopping. The kids and the mothers and the men just trying to make a living.

Out of the corner of my eye, I see Killian nod.

"But of course," I speak up, projecting my voice in the hope that most of these Sabers can hear me. And maybe Pax too – wherever the bralls he is. "If you'd rather talk somewhere more private," I offer sweetly.

The big guy in the middle smiles, letting out a rumbling laugh that is far too dark to sound like joy. He can't be a DarknessSeed. The only one of those is standing at my back, and I'm pretty sure he's not a DeathSeed. I've been very close to a few of those, and he just doesn't feel the same. But what other options are there for Seeds that feel like evil?

He turns and leads the way.

"Follow us, sweetheart," Creepy says.

He tries to sidle in next to me, but Killian turns and steps between us. Leaving me with Broken-nose guy as my bookend. Three more Sabers follow us. There would be others among the stalls – Sabers usually travel in threes if they're triunes – but there really is nothing saying these guys are. I'm running on guess work here.

When we're thoroughly boxed in and barely able to breathe without getting glared at, I spot one more Saber emerging from behind a stall, a guy in a crimson shirt.

My heart clenches, skipping a dozen beats until the point where my vision swims.

Sromma.

I search what little of the markets that I can see between and around my escorts. No heavy beards. No sharpened teeth. No Daryan.

Yet.

And no Pax, Seth, or Roarke.

Chuck.

I really hope that whatever has gotten their attention is short-lived. My guys are pretty good at being observant, but they're not mind readers. If they don't see where we're going, how are they going to find us… save us?

Or get close enough for me to warn them.

"Killian," I hiss.

"I saw him," he grunts. And I mean *really* grunts. I feel quite proud of myself for being able to decipher that.

"Pax."

"You wanted to talk to enforcement," he says.

I sag.

Crap.

We need the information to leave town. But we need to avoid BeastSeeds more. Killian reaches for his sword as two kids with balloons run past. I grab the man's wrist, stopping him.

"No, not on the street," I whisper, and his blade clicks back into place.

I push that problem to one side of my mind as Killian wraps an arm around my shoulders, creating a man-shield.

"What's the plan?" I murmur.

"When I say duck, duck." His words are so low that it

takes me a minute of analyzing them before I'm sure I've heard them right.

I nod. Ducking is something I can do. Ducking and washing dishes.

Check.

"We still need answers," I say, but it's technically a question.

Do we? Do we really?

Should we just leave?

He makes a noise that is almost a 'herm' but could also be a 'herrr.' I don't have a translation for that one.

We're quickly led from the bustling maze of market stalls and out among the only stone buildings on the ground. The two guards in the lead, the really big guy with a bow and another with shoulder-length red hair, stream into a building with a sign over the door. Two swords crossed over a shield.

And words, but I can't read words.

The others hesitate outside the door, but it's clear Killian and I are expected to go inside. Once my eyes have adjusted to the low light, I realize there's not room for everyone in here. A metal door shuts in front of us and one behind, enclosing us in a floor-to-ceiling cage that instantly feels too small.

At least we're the only ones in here. The redhead and the big guy – who I'm guessing is their commander – are standing with smug expressions in the room beyond.

Several desks line the right, with bookshelves and filing cabinets behind them, and the center of the room is nicely decorated with three sets of manacles fixed to the solid stone floor. There's a divot down the middle of it. A drain.

For blood.

What did I get us into?

It was my idea to talk to them. Killian wanted to kill them on sight. I should have trusted him.

New rule – always trust the Darkness guy.

My Darkness guy.

I try to judge the level of fear in his expression and see none. His lips pull into his almost smile, and he nods at me – just once.

What does that mean? Is he confident we can escape without being maimed or is he looking forward to the maiming?

He does agree that there are bigger problems prowling around out there – doesn't he? Or does he know something I don't?

"Weapons," the commander orders.

"Hurry up," Red adds.

They're standing to the left and right of us, arms crossed over their chests, muscles pumped out in a very effective intimidation strategy – but they're outside the cage.

I keep my mouth shut, possibly because I'm frozen in fear. Killian begins to pull his weapons out. The big curved blade tucked into the front of his belt, broadsword at his side, knife at his back, and really big dagger strapped to the outside of his leg. He puts them all through a hole in the bars and into a metal box attached to the outside of the cage, then Red slaps the lid shut.

"Is that all of them?" the commander asks, his brows drawn in accusation.

Killian holds his arms wide and turns in a slow circle. He's not wearing his cloak; all of that kind of stuff was left with the horses at a stable on the other side of town.

Horses which we saddled, loaded our gear onto, and paid the Seduction chick to keep an eye on.

Which now makes me think Killian, or someone, knew that a mess was bound to happen.

Killian moves slowly, and at first glance it looks like he's disarmed himself. I know he hasn't. He's probably got every letter of the alphabet in weapons and at least A-J are still on him somewhere.

"Search us," he says in his low rumble.

The big guard smiles, then nods – but not at us, at the guards waiting outside. The metal door squeals sharply. The cage is filled with three Sabers, and Killian is throwing punches.

"Duck," he grunts, two seconds after he's moved to attack the nearest guard.

I duck and close my eyes against a spray of blood. The first guard goes down.

My head hits the bars and a hand reaches through to grip my hair and pin me in place. Fear explodes in my chest. My hands fly back, searching – bars, clothes, long hair, and muscles tensed ready to do damage. The information bombards me. A calloused hand with hairy knuckles, a black hilt, and the feel of cold steel against my throat.

Killian turns in the same second as the two remaining guards both throw punches. One to the temple and the other to the jaw. Killian drops like a rock. Hitting the stone floor, his body shudders from the impact.

"Killian," I gasp.

My whole body is aching to move, to get to Killian.

But I'm frozen with a blade firmly against my throat.

The hand in my hair relaxes, but I don't. I can feel Killian is still alive, *feel it*. Not sure how, but the knowledge is enough to keep me exactly where I am. The door opens, making the bars shudder and vibrate against my back, shoulders, and skull – the parts of me still pressed hard to the cage.

The two conscious guards inside this cage grab Killian by the arms and drag him into the center of the room. They fix manacles to his ankles and run their hands over every crease and pocket. More weapons are pulled out and slid across the rough floor toward the commander. He's just standing there, watching everything unfold with a critical eye, while Red picks up each weapon and inspects them.

A key clicks in the lock outside and the last guard walks into the cage – locking our exit behind him before picking up the guy Killian had knocked out and depositing him in a big cane armchair behind one of the desks. Blood dribbles from his nose and the corner of his mouth as his head lobs to the side. It's unnerving.

"You're next," Red orders.

I turn, practically crouching on the floor. There's six guards in there now. The room's heavy with power, and they're all looking at little me.

The commander, Red, Unconscious, and Creep – whose brown eyes on me are making my skin crawl – spread out across the desks. Broken-Nose has picked up one of Killian's weapons and stabbed it into the edge of the desk he's sitting on. And guy number six, who I hadn't really looked at before, his gaze jumps from me to Killian, wide with a kind of over-excitement – Crazy-eyes.

I walk like a meek lamb among lions into the center of the room and sit down next to Killian's motionless body. Then Crazy-eyes locks the final metal door. Two solid iron gates between us and freedom.

They're probably not even iron. More like some special Silvari Saber-proof metal.

Reaching over, I press my hand into Killian's. He'll be okay.

I *know* he'll be okay.

I hope.

A sensation runs through me, snapping at my fingertips, like power leaking off of him. It's almost comforting.

The room is filled with a muffled gray light, filtered through slits of glass windows on the left wall. A pattern of windows, with a row of stone, then a long, narrow section of glass – probably big enough for me to get through, but definitely not Killian – followed by a section of stone, then another window, all the way up to the roof. They offer an interrupted view of the tail end of the markets and a cleared circle of sand. I hadn't made it to the tail end of the market – and this is my first glimpse of this… place.

Tiered seating fills two sides, which also doubles as the walls. There seems to be only one way in and out – through the markets. A timber post stands tall in the center, and a rusty manacle hangs from the top of it. Shivers run over me at the sight of it. You'd think being in this room, with armed guards and Killian unconscious, would be the scariest thing that could happen right now – but that pole evokes a blackness inside me that I really don't have time for.

Four kids are playing, kicking a ball around on the dusty red sand. It's probably a quiet place to play – but the sight sends shivers down my spine.

"Why glass?" I ask, my mind grateful for my mouth's distraction.

I understand the logic behind metal and stone and bars, and a drain in the floor is just practical. But I don't understand the glass.

"Silvari glass, ten inches thick. People sitting where you are can watch their accomplices take their last breaths in front of a cheering crowd," the commander says, smiling, reminiscing, and making me want to throw up.

My bubble won't reach that far. I won't watch Killian being executed because by the time he's out there, I'll already be dead in here.

The commander sits on the corner of one of the desks and picks up a piece of paper. His companions relax a little around him. Some sitting, some standing, all of them looking satisfied.

"Rogue Saber, you are charged with the theft of goods on the trade roads and sentenced by Commander Talon – that's me – to death by blade... After you tell us where to find the goods," he reads, looking at Killian as if the unconscious guy can hear him.

"You're going to need him to wake up first," I point out.

Creepy smirks. "We plan to question you while we wait."

"Okay, well, I did hear a rumor that the Crown already sent a triune to deal with the bandit – and that they succeeded. Are we talking about a bandit here?"

"Are we?" the commander presses.

"He's the only encounter with stolen goods I've ever had. I can probably recount pretty good directions to the rest of the goods – except I ate the chocolate. Consider it payment for having to deal with him."

Creepy laughs.

The commander frowns.

"The goods in question are weapons – high grade weapons – not chocolate," Crazy-eyes growls.

"I don't know anything else. Why did you suspect him, anyway?"

"We didn't, we suspected you at first. The woman in the attack was not your normal Saber. Then we suspected him because he looks like a DragonSeed or a MagnetSeed," Red explains.

I snort and try to act like this is news to me. "Magnet-Seeds are myths."

"When armed guards from the Black Castle recount seeing a big man manipulate metal, the Seed is no longer a myth. Kieth, do your thing," the commander orders.

Great. We've got the Crown and BeastSeeds on our asses, and now some other crazy rare Seeds stealing weapons. Priorities, people – let me deal with this chuckin' bubble first.

Kieth, a.k.a. Creepy, smiles broadly. "Let's start with **why you're with him**?" he asks, and his tone goes from conversational to melodic, sending a shiver through me.

Everyone waits for my response. This feels rehearsed, like they've done this a lot. They get the suspects into their office-and-torture-space, Kieth asks them the questions, and all their secrets spill out.

And now I feel stupid.

Of course, that is exactly what's supposed to happen.

I look at the guy intently, but it's impossible for me to tell what his Seed is. Not Allure, maybe Persuasion?

"**Talk to me**," the guy insists, a flicker of impatience in his sharpening features. "**I want the details of your relationship with this Saber.**"

I can feel his strength, the compulsion brushing against me, but the effect doesn't sink beneath my skin.

Which means I can say anything I want.

I part my lips, and let my mouth do what it does best – talk shit. "I'm his fashion designer."

Kieth's jaw ticks with a sudden explosion of anger. Red bellows a laugh, and instantly gets punched in the shoulder by Crazy-eyes.

"Sorry, Sir," Red murmurs, taking two big steps toward the back of the room.

"She has to be telling the truth," Kieth insists. "She's a Silvari with so little power I'm not even sure how she's alive."

I pinch my lips, like his words have hurt me. I need him to *think* his words have hurt me.

Common sense says that letting these people find out I'm mortal would be so very bad.

"My mother gave birth to me while she was dying," I manage, not sure if that's a plausible explanation.

"She can't be a fashion designer. She looks like something

the dog left in its bowl," Crazy-eyes scoffs. "She's wearing a man's shirt."

I sigh and roll my eyes, waving dramatically over Killian's current attire.

"That is exactly the fashion I sell to my clients."

"*What's his name?*" Kieth asks, pressing his power against me.

I marvel at the sensation of it. Roarke's ability doesn't really *feel* like anything. He says something, and I obey, simple as that. Not this guy, though.

"Don't you know who he is?" I counter.

Red crouches down, looking me in the eye like a dim-witted child as he speaks. "We've spent a lot of time in some very far off places doing very specific work for the Crown. You know who *he* is, don't you?"

I nod.

"Where we've been, you wouldn't survive."

"Tanakan?" I whisper, but the word is still too loud in this small room.

He sneers. "She's not as dumb as she looks."

"What did you do?" I whisper, hoping that the question sounds like a slip of the tongue again.

"Some disbanded triunes guard the prestigious Black Castle, others patrol the halls of Tanakan. It's the luck of the draw. Now luck has brought us here, to you," Red says.

"Only the best enforcement for the Crown's most important cities. There's not a Seed who passes through Lackshir that we don't know how to deal with. Now, answer the question – who is this man?" Keith adds.

"Lilian," I answer. "His name is Lilian."

"And how did he hire you?"

"I meet all my clients at the foot salon. He was getting a pedicure, and I was getting a ten-point toe massage." *Relaxed cheeks. Relaxed cheeks,* I coach myself through

268

keeping a straight face. "I give the foot salon ten percent of my earnings, and in return they allow me to sell my services to their clients. So, I just leaned over and mentioned that his shirt doesn't really match his eyes. You can't see his eyes because you kind of knocked him out. I'm still getting paid, though, aren't I? I mean, the chocolate was only half the contract."

The men just look at me, various levels of losing-their-patience written in their expressions.

Commander Talon approaches, his steps fierce, his gaze boring down on me, and his fist clenched. I shuffle backward just a bit, drawing my feet in close to me in preparation for becoming a ball. The curl-into-a-ball defensive move has worked quite well for me in the past.

But he's off course. He's not really approaching me; he's approaching Killian.

Killian, who's laying like a dead weight on the cold stone. Talon's frown morphs into a sneer. He lifts his boot, and I move.

Not sure *how*. Not even sure *what* the plan is.

I just move.

Registering the angle of Talon's walk. The way Killian's cheek is flat to the floor. The steel plate on the sole of Talon's boot as the man lifts it into the air. And in that same second, I have my knife out of my boot and in my hand. I throw myself over Killian's body and slash upward as I sail underneath Talon's leg.

The blade buries itself into his flesh but doesn't slow my momentum. Talon falls to one side as I crash and roll to the other. Someone slams a boot down on my chest – stopping me and knocking the wind out of me.

Somewhere in that moment, Killian rolls onto his feet – great timing. The man's all wild eyes and pent-up aggression. His arms out, tense, ready to punch and wrestle. His jaw set tight. I swear a Brahman bull running at full speed would bounce off of him.

Talon is trying to grip his leg as blood pours out and flows toward the drain. I smile at that.

Even though I can't breathe.

Darkness

I've been knocked out cold plenty of times before. I get knocked out. I wake up swinging. That's the way things happen.

I'm sure I've come close to being killed a few times – but it's never actually happened.

Looking around the room, already on my feet and trying to work out what unfolded during the minutes I was unconscious – I'm trying to lay my eyes on my Shadow.

Find her. Find her. Find her.

Eight heartbeats in the room. The StormSeed is unconscious in a chair. The FaunaSeed, TrickerySeed, TrackerSeed, and TruthSeed are in defensive positions near the desks. Their commander is moaning in pain, gripping at a gaping wound, right in front of me.

I kick him in the face, removing the guy from the equation.

Shadow is on the ground.

Two arms. Two legs. None of her own blood.

And smiling at me. My lips press into an almost smile in reply.

She's gasping for breath. Holding the small blade I gave her. One of the other Sabers is standing on the tip of it so the thing's no longer any use to her as a weapon. In fact, she might be getting her fingers crushed by keeping her grip on the thing.

I smile. I don't even try to control it, just let it go, as I step toward her. The metal cuff around my ankle makes a clunking sound – the chain bumping against itself.

"No further," the TruthSeed orders.

I stop with the chain pulled tight and another few steps between us.

Shade is making short gasping noises. Gasping, but fine.

"What now?" I ask.

I probably should stop smiling and start acting serious – but this is just too fun.

Six of my smaller weapons are on the ground out of reach, but I still have two darts in the sleeves of my shirt and a knife under my left armpit. And I probably don't need any of them for these scum.

The TrickerySeed clears his throat nervously. His hands, the calluses healed over, tell me he hasn't drawn his sword in months. Not a threat. The TruthSeed and the FaunaSeed have weapons out and flickers of bloodlust fill the air around them. I pluck the darts from my sleeves and pierce both of them in the throat in the same motion.

As their bodies fall, the TruthSeed hauls Shadow to her feet, one arm around her neck to hold her in place. He wraps his other hand around hers and angles her small metal blade upwards at the base of her sternum. Toward her heart. A pretty definitive blow even for a Saber.

I hold my hands out in surrender.

Fucker has seconds to live.

CHAPTER FIFTEEN

"You okay?" Killian asks me.

I nod, the movement impeded by the giant arm around my neck.

I'm pretty sure their commander is bleeding to death on the ground, but the room is completely still.

Beyond Killian, through the window, the kids are still kicking their ball. It bounces up the tiered seating and disappears into one of the rows. Happy faces chase after it. Climbing the seating made for adults with jumps and wriggles. It looks like they're laughing as they disappear into the rows.

I smile.

Killian smiles back.

"What's so funny?" Kieth growls.

The sensation of his power barely brushes against my awareness. It has so little effect on me that I almost miss the power-getting-sucked-from-the-room sensation that follows. A clawing thing, stretching and reaching through the walls and around us. Devouring everything that should be important in this moment.

Except I can't see anything – so it can't be *anything!*

Nothing new. Nothing else. Nothing different. Just this feeling so powerful that the world slows. Almost stops.

One beat. Two.

Killian fixes his gaze on me, a look which I translate to, 'shit', or maybe 'fuck' – Killian likes to curse.

Power a million times stronger than Kieth's slams into me. Into everyone but Killian.

Kieth flies backward in a sea of papers and desks and chairs, tugging me with him for a moment, but he can't keep his grip. We're thrown apart. I slam into the wall and crumple to the ground. Kieth's on the ground beside me. Not moving, blood trickling from the corners of his eyes.

I'm alive. I'm conscious.

But crap am I hurting.

Which is more than I can say for the other Sabers. Killian has his back to me as I pull myself onto all fours. My arms are shaking, from either the power or the impact or both.

Instead of feeling guilty or horrified at the death around me, I feel relieved. One less thing to worry about.

My stomach turns – what kind of person feels relief at the sight of death?

Outside the wall of windows, the world looks just as turned on its head as it does in here. The few market stalls I can see have been torn to pieces. Distant screams and shouts filter into the room even through its thick walls.

The power that sent me flying came from out there.

And that power felt like Pax.

Killian's still just standing there, his whole body rigid except for the heavy rise and fall of his chest as he draws in breaths.

Outside, something sails through the air and slams into the sand. It rolls a few times before coming to rest.

It's a person, wearing a distinct crimson shirt.

Sromma.

What the bralls is going on out there? I manage to think, even though I can't manage to get myself back onto my feet.

Sromma presses his hands into the sand. There's a

shimmer through the air followed by the few stalls that were still standing being shattered. Fabric, leather, apples, they all go flying. People. Women. Kids.

Horror shreds at my heart.

Pax steps into view. Eyes glowing yellow. Teeth drawn and canine.

Sromma runs at him. I'm not sure what his plan was, but in a blur, Pax has him by the throat. He holds him for a second, feet in the air kicking and struggling, then he flashes from man to wolf and Sromma drops to the sand. He's barely able to shuffle backward before the wolf is gone and the man is back. Pax, now naked, stalks forward.

Pax is definitely the predator, Sromma's the prey.

But is Sromma alone? If Pax does the wolf thing again, he could be helpless against Daryan... Where the bralls is the BeastSeed?

"What's he doing?" I gasp. Becoming a wolf when it's so freaking dangerous...

Sromma buries his hand in the sand once again, followed sharply by a wave of power. The magic has the same effect as Pax's, but it feels, smells, almost tastes completely different. It grabs at me, looking for ways to hurt.

Throwing me against the wall – again.

"Is he an Alpha?" I ask – gasp – as I roll onto all fours. That's as far as I'm willing to go.

"No," Killian grunts, reaching down to crush the shackle on his ankle in one hand. "OverrideSeed."

"I don't understand," I growl, wiping at my nose and finding blood on my sleeve.

Killian grabs the commander's limp head by the hair, tossing the guy onto his back before searching through his pockets.

"Answer me!" I demand.

Killian levels his pure black gaze on me. "He's falling into his Darkness. He can't hit the bottom."

Every part of my being agrees, but I stay close to the ground as Killian pulls out a set of keys. Pax's power sent me flying, but it knocked these other Sabers out – possibly killed them. I don't know why his power went easy on me. It completely avoided Killian, so maybe it's selective.

Sromma, however, his power wants to hurt me, even though it's not as strong as Pax's. The lower I am to the ground, the less distance I'm thrown. I watch through the Silvari glass, trying to spot who's going to throw the next shockwave.

I'd like to kick my brain into gear and come up with a plan, but instinct is ruling everything right now.

Pax rolls his shoulders. His lips are moving – talking to himself, I think, because the other guy's on the ground and looks like he's screaming. Not in a rational, listening-to-what-Pax-is-saying kind of way either.

Pax flashes into wolf and launches himself at Sromma. He bites down on the Saber's ghost-white leg and tosses him into the air. Sromma's body smacks back to the ground next to the pole in the center of the sand. Man-Pax flashes into existence and approaches the cowering OverrideSeed, grabbing him by the throat again and holding him against the pole. Pax's lips are moving, and the other guy looks scared shitless – but I can't tell what they're saying.

"How do we stop him?" I ask, watching the scene outside and listening to the sounds of Killian working through the keys.

The bars are too thick to break. But he punches one with bone-shattering force anyway. He manages to bend it, then goes back to the keys, putting them in the lock one at a time and cursing constantly under his breath.

"I'm going to knock him out."

"You can't do that," I gasp.

He turns to me sharply, the black pits of his eyes swirling with smoke that seeps out over his whites.

"Something has made him lose his grip on who he is. If he falls into this Darkness, he will hunt anything and everything that is a threat to you. No reasoning, no planning. He will hunt Lithael, and he will die."

The words are barely out of his mouth before he turns back to the lock. It clicks, the gate groans open, and he starts the whole process again with the second gate.

"So if he kills this guy –"

Killian growls over the top of me. "The Override can die. But if he kills an innocent –"

He throws his whole body at the bars. His shoulder makes them bend and bow, but the snapping noise is more bone than metal.

"And the BeastSeed?" I demand. Wherever the hell he is.

"I'll knock Pax out – problem solved."

Pax lets go of Sromma's throat, but the Override's toes don't even brush the sand before Pax's pure energy smashes through him – blood and organs paint the wave of energy.

The guy's blown to pieces.

Everything slows. Right. Down.

Pax's face locks in an angry half-wolf growl.

Sand lifts from the ground. A million grains, but each one in sharp clarity.

The power tugs at the remaining tier of seating, ripping into the timber, plank by plank.

Splintering the structure seat by seat.

Each snap and crack has its own moment in time.

"Shadow!" Killian shouts. His scared gaze locks on to mine.

I should be running away, cowering in a corner, waiting for the impact. But I run toward it.

Toward the wall of glass panels – the most impossible direction. Because out there, in those seats looking for their ball, are four *very* innocent kids. I can't let him kill them. I can't let that become who he is.

Even if I have no way of stopping any of this.

I blame Killian, I think as I run in the same kind of slow motion as the rest of the world. I'm sure my body didn't have stupid ideas of its own before I met Killian.

The power ripples through the wall, shaking the mortar from between the stones. If I wasn't overcome with fear, I might find it beautiful. Cataloging each piece of mortar or chunk of stone that is blown loose. Taking notice of them in the same second as they separate from the wall.

Time is almost frozen. Moving so slowly that it's almost not moving at all.

Please shatter, I beg the wall – the glass.

Beg, then leap.

Diving forward. Hands out. Power ripples over my skin and static pricks along my arms, over my head, into my skull. For the barest second, the force of Pax's blast slides over me, then it's gone, and my hands press into the gap where the glass window was. Where the glass no longer is.

The fragments part in a pattern that reflects the light brilliantly around me. I squeeze my eyes shut against the fine glass dust, feeling it on my skin as nothing more than a soft dusting.

Air rushes past me, then I hit the sand, roll, snap my eyes open, and struggle to my feet. I chuckin' trip, then stagger again, until finally my feet settle into a run.

I don't want to look across to where the kids were. The seating is in pieces. Broken, scattered. Pax hasn't moved. He's standing with his hand hovering over the place where he held Sromma moments before annihilating him.

My Pax.

His whole body is tense, rippling, with molten gold tracing along the lines of his muscles.

"Shadow," Killian screams through the shattered windows behind me, his voice stretched as if reaching across time. "Don't touch him!"

His words fail to find meaning.

Pax. Get to Pax. Stop Pax. Save Pax.

My Pax.

I stumble, but I ignore it.

My skin pulses and burns, but I ignore it.

With my next step, the air shimmers and fire rips through my soul, but I ignore that too.

Pushing forward, distantly registering that I can now feel sand beneath my toes and air on my legs.

Pax's eyes snap to meet mine, fear and fury boring into me. I might have had time to turn tail and run – the emotions coming off of him are insanely intense – but his arms are around me before I can even consider it. His face buries in my hair as he presses me into his bare chest.

His arms completely wrap around me, like maybe he's checking if I'm real.

"You're alive," he whispers.

Over his shoulder, I spot four scared faces peeking up from behind the tiered seating. Alive. The timber is ripped and strewn about, but the framework is still there. The kids scurry from their hiding spots and off into the upturned markets. The last one is carrying their ball.

I sigh into man-Pax, the wolf nowhere to be seen, wrapping my arms around him and enjoying the sensation of his skin against mine.

His chest against my breasts.

Against my *bare* breasts...

"Crap!" I scream, pushing him away from me.

Of course he doesn't budge.

"Why am I naked?"

He growls.

"Pax!" I demand.

Finally, he relaxes his grip enough to lean back and look me in the eyes. His are still golden and glowing, mine – I hope – are screaming of confusion.

He grips my ass, lifting me up and wrapping my legs around his waist.

"**Stay**," he orders, not that I physically have the option of getting down right now.

Horses approach, making both of us turn toward the markets. There's an exit out of here now. The first tier of seating was smashed early on in the fight, but we can't outrun horses. Pax growls, the rumble rippling through his chest and into mine.

I respond for the barest of seconds before I swallow hard and stifle the ridiculous urge.

Pax is the one who can turn into a wolf. Can, but right now definitely shouldn't. I'm just the silly mortal who managed to get her clothes blown off her chuckin' body!

The sight of Seth on his bay gelding, leading Pax's dapple stallion, almost makes me cry with relief. He rides straight for us, but stops short. "Pax?"

Is he waiting for permission to approach?

Pax's body language relaxes, but his grip on me remains solid. We move toward the dapple stallion.

"What did the Override say to you? You snapped. And what the fuck did you do to Shade?" Seth demands.

Pax ignores him.

Seth curses again, pulling his shirt sharply out of the waist of his pants, then up over his head, before he drops it down onto me.

"Put the shirt on," Seth insists.

Things are bad if Seth's giving orders.

I push myself away from Pax and struggle into the shirt with his hands still on my sides. It feels so good to have the fabric slip into place – but I suspect the move was strategic on Seth's part and had little to do with my personal comfort.

Pax's attention is on the city, the road, Seth, the building I burst out of – everything.

Shouts emerge from the torn markets. People are beginning to venture from wherever they had sought shelter.

Pax throws me up onto his horse. My bare legs settle against the leather.

"Ride," he orders.

Seth obeys, and the horses lunge forward.

I struggle to grip the saddle and twist and shout backward. "They have Killian. He's locked in."

I would point too, but holding on makes that hard. Holding on chuckin' hurts. No bandage – no splints.

Seth turns the horses in a sharp circle.

Relief floods through me. Leaving Killian is not an option.

Three horses round the corner. Roarke in the lead, my horse racing to keep up, followed by Killian, who's riding slumped to the side and looking like crap.

Seth turns again.

Pax throws himself onto my horse before taking the lead through the rubble of torn-up seating, scattered sand, and the remains of what used to be market wares.

I'm concentrating on breathing and hugging the saddle. Absorbed in the rhythm of the horses, of hooves on soft soil, of my men alive.

Killian's mount moves next to me, keeping pace in a way that allows Killian to look me up and down.

"What did you do?" he demands.

One arm is slung in front of him, hanging limp, looking broken. I should know.

I swallow hard and just stare at him.

What did I do?

I have no idea how I moved through the blast. Or through a solid window without a scratch. Or how I lost my clothes. None.

So instead I ask, "Are you okay?"

He grunts, turning his head away from me. I can see he's hurting.

The landscape rushes past us until we're blocked by a river. We veer to the left and start following the trail alongside it. Pax slows to a trot, and so do the rest of the horses. The trees begin to thin, allowing more space between the river and us. The water doesn't look deep, gurgling around the odd stone.

A large red leaf floats down from the tree overhead, landing on the water's surface and flowing gently downstream – back the way we came.

Riding hard makes conversation impossible. It should have given me time to put my thoughts into order, but it hasn't. My head won't shut up.

What set Pax off? Whatever it was, it made Roarke and Seth run for the horses before they even knew where Killian and I were – or because they knew where we were?

Seth stops. My horse takes a few more steps before getting the picture, and behind me Killian does the same. Roarke pulls his horse to a stop, almost running into Seth.

To our right is the river.

To our left, Pax has thrown himself down from the saddle and is now circling around in the open space, still looking pissed. He looks like he wants to do the wolf thing, and at the same time like he's fighting himself to stay human.

I hadn't realized my heart was pounding, but as he stalks toward me I can bloody feel the thing about to burst from my chest.

It's not that I feel threatened by Pax, like I'm in some danger, but he's chuckin' scary. I'm glad Seth and Roarke, and their horses, are in front of me – otherwise, I would very stupidly run to the guy and wrap myself around him again.

My body decides to move anyway, obeying my heart.

Crap...

Darkness

She's through the broken window and running toward Pax before I can reach her.

The glass alone should have shredded her. The gap should have been too narrow for a mortal to dive through. The power from Pax should have thrown her back. The bubble should have knocked her out.

For a long second, I'm stuck.

Watching that thread of crimson-gold connect from her heart to his.

Watching as his power pulls at her – at her life.

"Shadow," I scream. "Don't touch him!"

The lock clicks. I run. All of my senses are focused on her pain – waiting for the empty sensation of her death to hit me.

Through the grate, out the door.

Roarke rushes up on his gelding. He throws my horse's reins at me, then keeps moving.

"Hurry," he shouts.

I raise my hand, the only one I can raise with my shoulder dislocated and my arm damaged, to the gelding, trying to calm his temperamental nerves as I gather the reins and draw him in to me. He settles enough to let me on, snorting and offering a buck to express how much he dislikes this commotion. I pat his neck, racing after the others.

Through the last market street and into the execution gallery.

She's alive.

She's seated on Pax's horse. But Pax still looks ready to murder someone.

His soul is tortured. His pain washes over me as I get closer. My instincts order me to keep my distance. I don't want this pain, his pain. His anguish. A Darkness eating at him. It screams of loss.

Of remembering Jessamy.

My gelding steps inside Shadow's bubble and the tension around my heart eases as I feel her again. She's on Pax's horse, and Seth is leading them. The forest offers an escape.

Pax is winning his battle because of Shadow, but he's not in control of himself yet.

People die when Pax loses his shit. Bad people – usually.

He takes the lead, and I chase them from the city, urging my mount faster to pull alongside Shade as soon as the terrain allows. Ready to grab her and run.

There's too great a risk that he'll break her if he gets his hands on her like this. No restraint. No control. Just raw energy.

Seth looks back at me from the lead horse, nodding just slightly. Roarke does the same from behind.

Pax might be in his human skin, but right now his impulses are all beast. Which makes him a sitting duck.

We can't stop. Have to keep running. Have to get away.

The Override might be dead, but the BeastSeed is not. This is not over.

"What did you do?" I demand, shouting at my Shadow. I adjust my dislocated arm, feeling the bone move too freely. Great, it's dislocated and broken.

She just stares at me for a long breath, before finally asking, "Are you okay?"

I grunt.

I can feel her pain. Her broken wrist is screaming, her flesh is searing, and she asks me if *I'm* okay.

Which twists something in my chest – something I refuse to analyze right at this moment.

We ride on, forming a pattern as space builds between us and Lackshir. A long thread of Allure trails behind Roarke, convincing the landscape that we weren't here. Tracking us will be impossible.

I'll deal with the fact that Lithael has control of the local enforcement later.

I pull my shoulder, lifting my arm, looking for the perfect spot so it'll pop back into place. The bone is definitely broken. I growl at the inconvenience of having to bloody heal.

Seth takes this as instruction to stop. The Jriinya River is beside us. Jri Forest on this side and Inya Forest on the other. Technically, we'd be safer on the other side. The night mists there are like black tar, and those mists could give us the perfect cover.

Shadow is absolutely buzzing with threads. Fear, confusion, embarrassment, and a raging thread of possession. Not what I was expecting.

Possession is what Pax has over her.

The violet hues of desire are there, entwined with the crimson-gold of her heart, but they're not her driving force.

Possession, clear and fluid, fills the space around her. Brushes against her skin and forms a glow that reaches across the cleared space.

A true mate's response.

Impossible.

Pax responds. But touching him right now would hurt worse than death.

Too much power.

The girl coils, seconds from leaping off her horse and probably over Seth and Roarke. She'll bloody fall and break something. An arm, a leg, her neck.

I grab her around the waist and pull her out of her saddle and into mine. With a click, and a flick of my horse's reins, we plunge into the river.

"Take him to kill something," I order the other two.

"Let me go," Shadow growls.

I obey, dumping her in the water.

"Pax, get on the horse," Seth orders, pointing at Pax's now riderless stallion.

"No," Pax growls, and in a flash of light he's a wolf.

Seth moans, rolling his shoulders.

"If I so much as smell a BeastSeed, I will put an arrow through you," he threatens, but the wolf would need the release just as much as the man.

Roarke looks panicked, running a hand through his hair and looking at the spot where my Shadow has sunk to the bottom.

The mortal can swim. Right?

The water is ice on my bare legs. It soaks into Seth's shirt as my ass brushes the gravelly riverbed and the current gently drags me downstream. I don't fight it, watching the small white bubbles on the surface.

Feeling my soul return to my body.

Feeling my soul return to my body?

What the chuck was I just thinking?

When I need to breathe, I push myself to my feet, and pop my head into the air not far from Killian. The water is up to my stomach, and Seth's shirt floats up around my waist. The other boys are vanishing into the trees. Roarke and Seth riding, Pax running as a wolf.

Running away.

Yep, that hurts.

"Where's the BeastSeed?" I manage as I try to swallow my feelings down, helped by the fact that I'm freezing my tits off – and everything else.

"No one followed us," Killian grunts.

It's just me, and Killian sitting on top of his gelding. Nearby, the horse I stole has its nose in the river. Horses are weird when they drink, lots of slurping.

Pax's stallion is eating grass like nothing interesting is going on. That horse acts like nothing interesting is *ever* going on. I wish.

I'm not entirely sure what just happened.

I'm not entirely sure about anything that has happened today. But I have the distinct impression that Killian may have just saved my life. Saved me from myself. Nothing new.

"Thank you," I say, swiping at my hair and trying to unstick it from my face.

"Get the horses," he growls.

He rides to the far side of the river while I wade back through the frigid water, grabbing the horses' reins and dragging them, like a child having a tantrum, after Killian. I trip up the riverbank. My fingers are shaking – from the cold.

My teeth are chattering – from the cold.

My breathing is shallow and hard work – from the cold.

"You're in shock," Killian grunts.

"I'm cold," I counter. *What's shock?*

He moves beyond the first few trees and dismounts, running a quick hand down his horse's neck before digging something out of one of the saddlebags. He's favoring one arm and has a slight limp. If he did break something, and I'm pretty sure he did, it's not slowing him down.

I seriously envy Saber healing.

He hands his reins to me with a growl, "Tie them up."

"Sure," I try to say. "Give the shaking girl three horses to care for."

He ignores me.

I latch the reins to the easiest and closest branches I can find, rubbing my arms with my hands and feeling my stomach swirl.

"Am I going to be sick?" I ask, moving slowly from behind the tight tangle that I've gotten the animals into.

Possibly should have chosen trees a little further apart.

Definitely not my priority right now.

"Probably," Killian replies.

"Because of the cold," I say.

"Shock."

My fingernails are blue, and fine lines, like bolts of lightning, have spread from under them and up along my fingers.

Shock?

Killian's made a pile of wood, leaves, and brown grasses. The sound of flint stones connecting punctuates the quiet forest.

"Why am I in shock?" I demand, holding my hand out for his inspection.

The fire catches, flames eating through the dead-looking grasses and licking along the twigs and sticks. Killian leaves it, his eyes boring into me as he approaches. His shoulder is still held at an odd angle – odd for Killian.

A hint of damage.

A hint of ignored pain.

A flash of the moment he rammed his full weight into the bars, bending them, fills my mind.

Crap, of course that's what happened. He broke his own arm trying to get to Pax.

I wasn't much better. I threw myself at a solid wall. I would have broken my neck if Pax's blast hadn't shattered the glass.

"You went through the window," he says, his gravelly tone filling the silence around us.

He grips my hand and tugs, making Seth's way-too-big shirt sleeve roll back to my elbow. I'm really, really glad I offered him my good arm to inspect.

His thumb brushes over my fingernail, tracing the lightning-like lines over my knuckles, along the back of my hand, and all the way up to my elbow.

"This is not shock," he murmurs.

He holds my gaze for a very long heartbeat. I'm not sure

what he's searching for, or if he finds it. Then he lets go of my hand and points toward the river.

"What?" I ask, because I am *not* going swimming again.

Not that it would matter much, I couldn't shiver and shake any harder than I already am.

"Find your wall," he demands.

Also not my priority right now, but if it's important to Killian… well, that makes it important to me.

"Because… Pax was too far away. I shouldn't have made it to him," I hedge, only working out what he was hinting at as the words leave my mouth.

Killian nods.

I hold out my good arm and move toward the river, tripping twice as I go. Twenty-two stumbling paces away from Killian and my hand brushes against the wall. Still solid. Still with a zing of static to it.

"It's the same," I say, using the wall to lean on.

"Get back here," Killian growls, like I'm taking too long.

"I'm chuckin' freezing," I grumble, staggering back the twenty-two paces.

Maybe it's less, maybe I should double check – or care – or maybe Killian should double check, since he's not having trouble walking.

But he's looking at me like he's waiting for more complaints, so I don't add the rest – that my arm hurts, the threads of lightning have a sting to them, riding a horse with no pants really rubs a girl in all the wrong ways, and the bruises. I really don't want to look at the bruises.

"Here," he repeats, moving to stand beside his horse.

When I get to him, he grabs my shoulder – only one shoulder, because he currently has only one usable hand – and pushes me so my back is against the horse, and he is at my front. Like maybe he's narrowing my escape options.

"Take off the shirt," he orders.

"Why?" I demand.

Not because *I* don't want the shirt off – it makes me shiver twice as hard every time the wet fabric brushes against my knees – but I want to know why *he* wants my shirt off.

"It's wet."

Right, that's simple enough. There's got to be some dry stuff in Pax's bags. I turn to search out where I left Pax's horse, but Killian's hand firms on my shoulder, stopping me before I make it anywhere.

"Now." His tone is low, the word is an order.

His hand moves up from my shoulder to rest on my neck, his thumb brushing along the length of my jaw. The light scratch of calluses from hard work feels comforting.

"Why?" I ask.

"I need to see you're okay."

Maybe it's because he's being so honest. Killian sharing feelings makes the world stand still.

Maybe it's because I've already been butt naked once today, and a second time isn't really a big deal. Whatever the reason, I grip the hem of Seth's shirt and pull it up over my head, standing completely bare and feeling his eyes brush every inch of me. Not a hint of creepy in his gaze.

He inspects my features, bare flesh, and a few old scars. The thin lines from my bad attempt at learning to wield a knife. The purple marks where Logan's men almost broke my ribs. The punctures on my shoulder left from Pax. Just thinking about those makes my insides quiver – or that could also be the cold.

Water droplets run down from my hair, over my bare breasts, and past the sting of my nipples in the cold. That, combined with the pain and the trembling, make it impossible for me to feel even remotely comfortable in front of him – but I'm not uncomfortable either.

New bruises dot my shoulders and hips. But no blood.

He motions for me to turn around. I move slowly, rubbing my arms to try and push some warmth into them. My fingers shake.

He growls, the sound sending a chill down my spine.

His horse turns its head, looking at me with accusatory eyes. Then it snorts, lowers its mouth to the ground and begins munching on the grass.

Easy for you to say, you're not freezing your ass off... And yes, I'm currently having a mental conversation with Killian's gelding.

Killian manages to smother his growl and I risk setting him off again to ask, "Can't you feel pain?"

I don't turn around, though.

He takes the wet shirt from my fingers and tosses it over the nearest bush. He pulls the cloak from its ties on the back of his horse and wraps it around my shoulders. I fasten the buttons and nuzzle into the soft lining of the collar. Then he tugs the hood up and over my wet hair.

"I didn't believe it," he says.

"You didn't believe what?" I ask, turning to face him.

His dark eyes find me. Deep and soul-warming.

I feel my cheeks flush a little. *About time!*

Standing around naked should have had an effect on me, but aside from this delayed bit of turning red, I'm still missing the common sense to be modest.

"You went through Silvari glass." As he talks, he grips the index finger on my right arm and pulls it up. Dangling my arm in front of me – which has a sharp effect on my broken bone.

I wince.

"You can't move through air without breaking, yet you went through Silvari glass without a scratch."

My arm thrums with pain, my head spins, my knees buckle. He barely lets go of me before I stagger to the side and throw up. Stumbling backward from the force. I'm just lucky Killian hooks an arm around my waist and steadies me, holding me while I heave.

And heave.

Until I stop.

"Shock," he says, steering me toward the fire.

Warmth bathes over me as I get closer, and I let him direct me to the exact spot he wants me to sit, my back to the forest and my view looking out over the river. *Let him* is an overstatement. I might be staggering and incapable of directing my own steps right now.

Killian sits down next to me and shoves a water bottle at me.

"Hydrate," he orders, trying to undo the buckles on his saddlebag with one hand.

Now that I'm looking closely, I can see his knuckles are swollen. He damaged everything from shoulder to fingertip, and the way he's favoring it only highlights his pain. If it's affecting Killian, then it would almost be killing me.

"How bad is your arm?" I ask, my voice soft against the still forest around us.

The evening sounds are comforting. The gurgle of the river, the crackle of the fire. Soft breathing from the horses, and the odd chirp from a bird.

"Dislocated shoulder, broken humerus, and three cracked knuckles – but the knuckles healed while you were having a swim. Just some swelling. And I set the arm while we were riding."

"That's not what happened. You were trying to drown me. What if I couldn't swim?"

"The water wasn't going to kill you," he replies, still struggling with the bag.

I reach over with my good hand and hold the buckle still. We balance each other's injuries and manage to make light work of the normally two-handed job. The corner of his mouth tweaks into a smile.

I like when he smiles. Like the way my muscles relax – which is even more obvious now that every muscle is trembling. Some just a little, others more violently.

"How," I have to stop and swallow against the teeth chatter before continuing, "do you know?"

He looks up, and I hold his gaze, staring at the sheen of emerald dancing across the almost black.

"I didn't. But I would have known if you stopped breathing."

"How?" I demand.

"I can *smell* Darkness approaching," he says, waving a hand in front of his face – which probably means he's not talking about a smell at all.

"Did those Sabers in the market *smell* dark?"

"Didn't matter. You wanted to flirt with that danger."

"So you let me? You just let me make a really stupid decision. Killian, you're hurt. Pax is – I don't know what. They almost killed you." I stop to gasp for air, eyes wide, watching as his smile broadens. *Stop chuckin' smiling at me. I messed up!* "And I do not flirt!"

He chuckles, pulling something from the bag. I don't even bother looking at it, resting my hand on top of his to get his attention back. This is too damn serious for him to just laugh it off. He looks down at my hand.

"You can't let me do that again. You can't let me do things that will get you hurt. Any of you," I try to order, but my voice is shaking from fear.

From the cold – and maybe from shock.

From the knowledge that I'm their weakest link.

"You didn't *do* anything. You didn't put mercenaries in the enforcement office. You didn't make Pax lose his shit," he points out, still looking at our hands like something more interesting is happening than my skin touching his. He just saw my boobs, my ass, my *everything*, and kept a completely neutral expression. But my hand on his makes him stare.

"I told you not to kill those assholes on sight – and clearly listening to me is the dumbest thing you've ever done."

Killian tilts his head to the side, seriously frowning at my hand. I pull it away.

"Sorry," I say. "You need to promise me you won't let me do that again."

"No."

"What do you mean *no?*"

He picks up two thick sticks from right beside him, obviously chosen earlier when he was prepping the fire, and holds them up. I take them from him, confusion pulling at my brow, until he holds up a bandage.

"I thought you set it?" I ask, then realize that he's changing the damn subject. "No, you need to answer me first. You need to promise."

He growls. "It needs to stay set – and no."

He drops the bandage in my lap and lifts a finger underneath my chin, holding me in place with his thumb. Power brushes along my skin, cool like an autumn breeze.

"Why not?" I ask, pushing my words through frozen lips as I struggle to put it all together.

Killian's power spreads across my cheek and down my neck.

"Because I like seeing what you do in the Darkness," he finally says, dropping my chin.

The smooth tendrils of his Shadows hover for a second before the sensation is gone.

"I don't," I mutter. "I do stupid shit."

With one tug on his collar, at the back of his neck, and a long, low growl, he pulls his shirt up over his head. His chest is smooth, with the barest scattering of hair. Tight muscles, pure tone, and that really long scar from shoulder to abs. It's still jagged and split, like the injury happened yesterday. There's the odd old scar here and there, but surprisingly few for a guy who chooses not to block half the time.

I lift my fingers and rest them at his shoulder, at the top of the old wound.

"You haven't got many scars." My voice is low, almost lost in the sudden spit and hiss of the fire.

I'm expecting him to brush my hand aside. To stop me.

He doesn't.

"Mostly we heal too fast."

"Mostly?"

"Not the scars born from Darkness."

My chest tightens. His mother being killed before his eyes certainly qualifies as Darkness.

"Why doesn't this scar heal?" I press.

I start to run my fingertips down the length of the cut.

His hand snaps up, wrapping around my fingers with just enough force and speed to make me gasp. As his hand wraps around mine, it shows a flash of the red and black design of the Release Seal on his palm.

"Some Darkness is too deep to heal."

I swallow hard and nod – even though I'm not satisfied. Maybe Roarke will tell me more if I pick the right moment to ask.

Slowly, his grip relaxes, and my hand slips free. "You," he begins gruffly. "You were good at dealing with the merchants." As he talks, he works free the beginning of the bandage – all of his attention on his hands. "Why did you call me your husband?"

I shrug, because only Killian would be confused about the obvious. "It felt right… to make them relax, I mean. What did I do to Pax?" I ask, which isn't really changing the subject because we were talking about this only moments ago.

Killian grunts at me. "Something triggered him." For half a second, I'm worried he's going to stop, but he doesn't. "Something made him fear losing you, or think that he had already lost you. Pax has triggers. Seeing the marks left from slavery on someone he cares about is one."

"What set him off this time?"

"Ask him, but if he went looking for you and couldn't find you? And Sromma, whatever he did or said. It makes sense his wolf would –"

I cut in. "Lose his shit? Because my stupid decision had us locked in some room of torture. Which is another good reason to ignore everything I say from now on."

He snorts. "Enforcement office."

I give him a 'huh?' look.

"Locked in an enforcement office; and it didn't help."

"So, you agree with me, and you'll stop me from getting us locked up again?" I press.

"No. Help me with this. If it heals wrong, I have to re-break it – we don't have time for that."

He snatches the sticks back, demonstrates what it is I'm supposed to do with the things, then jabs them in my direction again. It's a two person effort, holding the sticks to his arm and wrapping the bandage in place, especially with my fingers still trembling from the cold – or shock.

"What's shock?" I ask.

"Your body has taken too much of a beating. Physically and emotionally. It's struggling to survive."

"Oh," is all I can say.

He could be right. I could be in shock.

When I'm done with the bandage, I clench and unclench

my fists. The tingle through my palm and the shake along my fingers is getting really annoying.

"It'll go away," he assures me, gripping my broken arm at the elbow and making it clear that he wants my arm resting and motionless on his leg.

"Why am I in shock?"

"Because you killed a man."

I swallow hard. Yes, that commander is dead, but that wasn't on my mind. And technically I just cut him, I didn't actually do the killing part.

"And you lost energy to Pax."

"What does that mean?"

"Sabers suck the souls from mortals," he says, pulling on my wrist and sending a sharp stab of pain through my whole arm. "Not just from mortals. From anything not strong enough to suck an equal amount of power back out of us. We live in harmony with each other."

I growl, then gasp. My eyes clench shut.

"You need to let this heal, or you're going to be left with a weak spot that breaks every time you fight."

"I'm trying," I mutter through gritted teeth. "What did you just do?"

"Realigned the bones."

"How do bones even get misaligned?" I ask, blinking back the tears.

"Throwing yourself through a window doesn't help."

He runs his thumb firmly down my forearm, pressing just enough to see the muscle dent. I wince, and instead of releasing the pressure, he presses harder, massaging into the pain.

I clench my teeth. "That. Hurts."

But I'm not game to try and pull away.

Trying to avoid pain with Killian just equals more pain.

"You're damaging the muscles," he informs me.

"Feels like *you're* damaging them."

He cracks his almost-smile and releases the pressure. His thumb moves back in the other direction until it finds tenderness again.

"I'm going to tape your arm to your body, so you're not tempted to use it."

"Thanks," I drawl, *because that was a joke – right?*

His fingertips brush along the scabbed line of one of the seventeen cuts he left me with. I counted them.

"You break too easily," he muses.

"Yet I went through the glass without a scratch. That's weird, right?"

The low tone on his exhale almost sounds like he agrees with me.

"What does that mean?" I ask.

"You take unnecessary risks. The glass and going near Pax." He finds a new sore spot and presses into it. "Never go near Pax when he's like that."

I gasp, gritting my teeth and struggling to talk. "You said that bad things were going to happen if we didn't stop him."

"If *I* didn't stop him," he growls, pressing harder. "There was no *we*. If he'd seen you vulnerable – if the glass had cut you, if he'd felt the scars on your back... You could have made things much worse." He doesn't release the pressure, and I start to buckle at the elbow. "Promise," he orders.

"No," I snap back – which gets me more pain.

If Killian was breaking bones to get to Pax, then shit was really desperate. I want to say that there was no thinking involved – I just acted. Just ran at the stupid wall, and before my fingers touched glass, the stuff shattered.

Killian makes a noise that translates to 'promise, now.'

"I won't promise you, Killian," I gasp. "Because I can't keep it." He releases the pressure. Instinctively, I try to move, but he holds my arm against his leg. Not hard. Not rough.

Just firm. "I can't keep it because I just ran. I just moved, and I didn't have time to consider why or how," I elaborate.

Which I don't expect to help my case, I'm just a mortal soot-pentad-member and I chuckin' ran at a wall of stone and glass, but the guy huffs and lowers his eyes back to my arm. Maybe he's thinking the same thing I am, that I'm insane, or maybe he's thinking something else. Not sure, because he doesn't share.

But I didn't die.

Pax must have broken it with the same burst of power that killed Sromma – and tore my clothing to dust? Maybe?

I have no idea.

"What happened?" I ask, my words cut off as he begins to massage a muscle above my elbow.

I crumple forward, curling over myself in pain – my arm staying obediently on his leg. Letting itself get kneaded and pushed, and hurting like bralls, and at the same stupid time, enjoying his touch.

He says nothing, and I might be whimpering, but I'm not letting this conversation go.

"What was the worst case scenario today?" I insist.

He relaxes his fingers just a little. "Pax's power can rip through things. Together, we control the power. In his Darkness, he loses that control. He lost control when his daughter died. By the time he'd found himself, his wife was gone too."

"Then the risk with the glass was worth it," I decide. I would jump through a million narrow windows made of razor-sharp glass for the people I love, if I had to.

He grunts, finding a new knot, and making me gasp in pain again.

He's not watching his hands, though. He's watching my expression.

"Do you enjoy seeing me in pain?"

He grunts a 'no' sound.

"Then why – argh – are you watching – argh – me, instead of what you're doing?"

"I don't understand how you're supposed to survive this."

"A broken arm?" I say, snap really, because he's deliberately working my muscles harder than he needs to and he just exhausted the mild balance between me putting up with the pain and enjoying his touch. Suddenly, I don't think he needs to be touching me at all! "Or," I add, "because you think I'm supposed to die."

Silence.

"What's a grimm?" I press.

His thumb digs into my wrist, shooting fire through every muscle between his hand and my shoulder, even into my back.

Enough.

I smack at his hand, which hurts me more than him – but it takes him by surprise enough that I manage to reclaim my arm.

"Touch my arm again, and I'll chuckin' bite you," I growl.

He gives me a lopsided smile. "Bite?"

Yes, Shade, why did you choose bite? Not stab or punch, but bite?

"Yes! Bite," I snap, hugging my arm across my chest.

"Bite me, and I'll muzzle you," he says.

Should have threatened his balls instead.

"Muzzle me, and I'll bite your –" *Crap, no. Shade – do not finish that sentence.* Killian just looks at me expectantly, so I scramble to add something not stupid. "Face. I'll bite your face."

That wasn't much better. It's made worse by the fact that he's now laughing at me.

Damn, I love his laugh.

"Grimm," I growl, before that sound completely dissolves my anger. "Tell me about the grimm."

"The grimm," he begins, once his laughter has settled, "are creatures who guard the Veil. They stop things getting out. Lithael has the ability to open a doorway and bring them in and out whenever he pleases. Deadly speed. Incredible intuition. The leaping distance of a wieldron –"

"I need more than an inventory of their abilities," I say, cutting him off.

"People with black, tar-like skin on their hands and arms, their feet and legs. Thorns that sweat venom protrude from their flesh. They ooze Seduction and Darkness at the same time. They hold your gaze, call you to them, then do what they wish. They live solely on pain and answer to the Veil Queen. Lithael has her allegiance. He has told the council that she is helping to restore the balance, to undo the damage caused by Lucif – I don't believe it. You will die. Let me splint your arm."

"Why bother? What's a damaged arm compared to a dead body?"

I don't want a damaged arm, and I don't want to die, but if he's worried about my arm being strong enough to fight, then he thinks I can fight – right?

"I –" His gaze seeks out mine. The black washes away to reveal a pure emerald green. My breath up and leaves me, running off with every bit of common sense my heart has ever had. "I need you to live."

He holds his hand out to me, palm up. I'm too shocked to move, to even work out what his hand's there for. A shiver runs down my back, but I ignore that because the rest of me is considering whether or not death-by-kissing-Darkness would be a bad thing.

Killian, right there, shirtless in the firelight.

He is not making this easy for me.

"Give me your arm," he orders.

Ah, so that's what he's holding his hand out for.

303

"Can you do it without hurting me?" I finally ask.

But the truth is, I'm struggling to keep my arm away from him. My whole being wants to move forward and mold against his body – but this is Killian, and I really don't know what reaction I'd get if I did. Trying to kiss him could somehow end up in a battle to the death.

But I do it anyway.

I lean forward, his chest under my palm and my lips to his. Which, I get the feeling, sends fear through him because he doesn't stop me. I want him to fall backward, arms around me, hold me close, as our lips move in the softest brush of an almost kiss. But he doesn't react for three racing, stuttering heartbeats.

Four.

He grunt-groans, gripping the front of my cloak and not letting me any closer.

I can't miss the stutter in his breathing, which just makes me want to fall against him even more. But there is no falling, just that ripple that I am now *sure* is fear, maybe anger too, as he forces me to sit back on my ass.

"That was definitely your fault," I whisper.

"You're in shock. Your body wants warmth and comfort – I am not those things."

When I don't struggle or try to resist his grip, his physical order to sit and stay, he releases my cloak.

His fingers open and close, just the once, motioning for me to give him my arm. And I do, because I'm a sucker for two things: doing as I'm told and Killian.

He pulls a curled piece of stiff leather from his bag, his movements sharp. Great, now I've pissed him off.

The leather could almost be a bracelet with a crisscross of leather to tie it together, but it's too long. He slips it around my forearm, the thing just fitting in the space from my wrist to elbow.

"Good," he grunts.

The black is returning to his eyes, curling and coiling, setting in under the emerald green, as he works the ties into a neat order.

Together, we pull them tight and knot them securely. I almost want to laugh at us, one hand each, but the sense of accomplishment overrides the humor.

It's just plain nice working *with* Killian for once, instead of fumbling to keep up.

"Open the cloak," he says, as soon as the leather version of a splint is in place.

That sentence takes me off guard.

"Killian, there's a limit to the number of times I get naked in one day, and I've reached it."

A twinkle lights up his eyes.

"You need to rethink that limit. I *am* going to strap your arm to your chest, and I don't mind ripping open my cloak."

I open my mouth to argue, but he turns sharply and leaps to his feet in the same motion. I jump to my feet, much less gracefully, followed by feeling dizzy and almost falling back over.

I can't hear a horse or a person, and in the fading light I can't see anything. Just us, the forest, the river reflecting a moon slowly gaining its fullness, and the shadowy line of trees that trace the water's edge.

Killian nudges me with his elbow and grunt-chuckles.

"Made you jump," he says.

"W-what?" I stammer, my gaze still scanning the dark shadows.

Three men walk out of the trees on the other side of the river, horses ambling behind two of them.

The tall and slender silhouette on the right, with shaggy hair and a limp, is Roarke. Seth, broad-shouldered and swinging a short blade like a toy, is on the left. Moving down the middle is a still naked man-Pax. I can tell he's naked even without enough light to see their faces.

Any remnant of the cold that I was feeling is gone – pushed aside by the intense heat flooding out from somewhere chuckin' inside me.

"He, however, seems to like being naked," I whisper to Killian, or maybe to myself.

They walk toward us, straight into the river without hesitation, the horses following them. Seth and Roarke both rip their shirts off, and my jaw goes slack. It takes everything in me to keep it closed. The only light left in the sky is from the moon and the sea of stars, but there's not much of that, thank the gods. Maybe they can't see me ogling at their silhouettes.

They scrub down with their hands, wiping away something I can't really see. Roarke turns and splashes water on his horse's chest and flanks. It's only a minute or so before they amble up the bank, pants still on and clinging tight to their bodies. Water is running down their bodies. Their chests, pure hard muscle, and their abs, more hard muscle, and – *damn, I need to stop looking.*

Seth shakes his head like a dog. Then his gaze searches the tree line, and settles on our small fire. He smiles. He's all muscle, almost the biggest of the three, but with gentler definition than his brothers. And arms that are making me drool.

Roarke flicks his hair back, the silver shining in the moonlight. Tall, built for speed, and with the definition of a man whose muscles couldn't turn to fat even if he tried. He grips his horse's bridle at the jawline and uses the gelding for support. When his gaze crosses over me, he smiles, no sign of pain.

Pax cuts through the middle of them, moving half a beat faster than his brothers. His chin is lowered, gaze set on me, as he pushes forward. Sweat runs down his powerful shoulder muscles and defined chest. Every inch of him is built to attack – to kill.

My body, followed closely by my mind, aches to be close to them all in some stupid equal-proportion-ratio that makes no sense for two reasons. Reason number one is because no woman in history can keep four guys happy. The second reason revolves around the fact that these guys are amazing, deadly, skilled, royalty, and somewhere over three hundred years old. Considering the women and experiences they've had, none of them are ever going to find a soot-almost-Saber like me interesting as a partner.

A partner – not a toy, a pet, a shadow, or a mated-possession.

They've got another thousand years to live. By then, I'm going to be nothing but a speck of dust in their lives.

Doesn't stop me from wanting them, though. Or stop my jaw from falling open.

"Down, girl," Killian says in a low growl that clips into a laugh on the last syllable.

He walks out to the guys. Seth meets him, arms going wide in an animated conversation.

"Wieldron blood! I hate wieldron blood…" is all I catch.

Pax doesn't even look at his brother. All of his attention is on me. My chest is on fire, and my heart's racing – but my mind fails to function. He's in front of me, his arms gathering me against him, pulling me in close, and his lips on mine. No hesitation.

His lips taste like vanilla, and my tongue explores along them, savoring the flavor then being denied by his need, by his own tongue insisting on owning this moment. Owning me.

And all of me is begging to be owned.

My chest rumbles – I have never wanted anyone, anything, this badly – but it's soundless, and for a second I wonder what exactly my chest is doing. Until Pax's chest rumbles in return and his teeth, his fangs, pull at my bottom lip.

He straightens a little, slipping away from the kiss. Looking down at me with his eyes alive, I am sure that glowing is more than *just* Pax. I can feel it under my skin, slipping over our pressed bodies as his power begins to over-whelm my muscles.

Damn my mortality.

The glow settles, and the fangs retreat.

I am wearing only a cloak. He's not wearing anything.

"I just reset her arm," Killian grumbles.

The sounds of feet and hooves on the leaf litter move around us, but they barely register.

Just me, Pax, the need for more kissing. Right here, anywhere – I don't care.

I may have just moaned at that idea. But as I lean forward, trying to lift myself a little higher, his fingers slip through my hair, his other hand on my hip, and my whole body is pressed firmly back to the ground.

"Let me control myself," he whispers.

I open my mouth to insist, *no, please don't control yourself,* but there's a power-induced tremor in my jaw, or shock, that makes it hard to talk.

"I thought I hurt you," he says softly, breathing deeply again, and I realize he's *smelling* for something.

"What?" I manage.

He exhales. "I didn't hurt you. No blood."

"I don't care." I want to add an order for Pax to kiss me again, but even as I begin to think it, my arm jerks.

"I do. I have rules. This." He stops to wave vaguely at the space between us – which is next to nothing – and his bare abs, bare Adonis belt, bare... everything.

"Your rules are stupid," I counter.

"Your approval isn't required."

My fist clenches, then shakes open again. "I was worried about you too."

His chest rumbles in a deep chuckle. "You were worried about me?"

He's right. It sounds so ridiculous that I, from the bottom of the food chain, would ever have to rescue any of them – the all-powerful, been training for three hundred years, born with magic and badass skills, Elite Sabers in the group.

"Yeah," I whisper, because a whisper is all I can manage.

"It's coming," Killian grunts.

"What's coming?" I try to pull away from Pax, but his grip in my hair and on my hip firms, before reluctantly relaxing enough to let me turn and eyeball the other guys.

"The mist," Roarke chimes in.

Which still isn't enough information. Pax's fingers brush along the back of my neck while I wait for Roarke to realize that I'm still confused.

"You should settle by the fire. You're cold," Pax points out.

"Still in shock," Killian adds.

"I'd like to get dressed first."

"You're still naked?" Seth's gaze darts up to meet mine, crinkling from the too-big smile on his lips. He has his horse tied to a tree and is tossing dry clothes by the fire. "Why are you still naked?"

I point at Killian. "He wouldn't let me get dressed."

All eyes turn on the big man.

"She needs her arm strapped to her body, or it's going to deform," Killian says, without turning to face us.

Oh, that's right – I was trying to avoid that.

"What's coming?" I ask again, speaking a little louder than I meant to – which only makes me sound more suspicious.

Pax's hand stops stroking the back of my neck, sitting

heavily instead, and he leans down close to my ear. "Your arm is going to be strapped. You pick who's going to do it."

I break free of Pax's grip and sulk toward the horses, declaring, "Whoever gets to me first."

"Me!" Seth shouts, jumping over the fire.

Roarke doesn't get up, his injured leg stretched out in front of him, not caring that he's still wet from the river. Killian shakes his head, lowering himself down next to Roarke and offering the guy a strip of salted pork.

Seth runs for me, smiling, until Pax elbows him and sends him flying into a tree.

Killian grunt-chuckles.

"You deserved that," Roarke calls out.

Seth rolls over onto his back, groaning, "You cheated."

Pax's smile reaches up to his eyes, playful and pure – genuine.

That's when it dawns on me. I'm not keen on getting naked because I am me, and me being naked in front of people is less than comfortable. But there's an added risk to being naked with Pax – specifically. The guys have all warned me not to let him see my whip scars.

A trigger, Killian had called it – and we've had enough of those for one day.

I flick my gaze to Killian, hoping my eye-conversation skills are up to the challenge.

It takes a second.

"Seth wins. Pax cheated," he declares.

"Yes," Seth says, pumping his fist as he springs to his feet.

I would be groaning and staggering and hurting a lot, but he gets up like nothing happened. Sparking more jealousy in me over their Saber skills.

Pax's brow furrows.

"Pax, eat," Killian calls.

Seth lifts his hand and snatches a bandage that I didn't

even see Killian throw. I keep walking, moving behind the horses and trying to work the zipper on Pax's bag open. I might need to have my arm strapped to my bare torso, but I can put pants on under the cloak first.

Pax doesn't walk away, doesn't sit down, but also doesn't move any closer.

Darkness

Pax snatches Seth's dry pants off the ground and pulls them on, then he looks across the fire, placing half his attention on me. The other half is on my Shadow as Seth straps her arm beyond the horses.

The one thing to fight a grimm is something that's finally dead.

Maybe the words don't just refer to her. Maybe that's all of us.

The girl will die, followed by Pax. Chaos might survive for a while – after all, it is his area of expertise. Roarke has no hope.

"Explain," I grunt, hedging that Pax has calmed enough – that his wolf has calmed enough – to find some objectivity.

Going on a killing spree helps.

Pax turns and looks like he might actually say something when Roarke cuts over him. "The OverrideSeed was the bearer of bad news."

"What. Bad. News?" I ask, watching the wolf shimmer over Pax's muscles.

He looks sharply at Shadow, takes three measured breaths, then turns back toward me in complete control.

Or as complete as any man sharing the one biological form with another being can be.

"There is only Daryan on our tails and his BeastSeed is an issue, but Sromma had a message from Tanakan. He said that *Evil is hunting us.* Then shared the news that there is a living CataclysmSeed – and they may or may not be in the glass wing."

I still, struggling to keep the shit that wants to fucking rip through me from getting out.

Because if I lose it, then Pax is going to lose it too.

"And?" I finally ask.

"That's all the Override said," Roarke says. "All he had time to say before Thane killed him."

That gets my heart racing.

"He's reclaimed his name?"

Pax's eyes glow. Confirmation. Looks like the wolf – Thane – is here to stay. And that the animal is closer to sentience and control.

There is some hope that they will find their control before we face this BeastSeed.

Some hope.

Even after years with Jessamy, Thane still slipped into a primitive hunt and kill mentality the minute he felt grief.

Those two are a work in progress. Pax's Seed was repressed – he wouldn't have survived if it wasn't. Aeon slaves who fight on impulse would find death a welcome punishment. It wasn't until our third tetrad trial that the wolf took form. Pax called him his *monster*. Forty years later, they'd still barely found a balance when the MateBond took over – that was when Thane gained enough respect from Pax to claim a name. They'd barely worked those logistics out before a CataclysmSeed destroyed their lives. Then, when the two had burned out their rage, the wolf was gone again.

Pax's gaze drops back to the small flames devouring the kindling. Kneeling, he angles himself toward it in a display of ignoring Shadow – but he can still hear her and Seth, and every word they're saying. We all can.

"Thank you," he says.

I let out a noise that could have been the word 'anytime' if I wasn't also distracted.

Also by Shadow.

Thinking about the damage Thane will do. Even if she *is* feeling the MateBond and *is* responding to it... does Thane understand that there is no wolf hiding within the girl?

Shadow drops my cloak from her shoulders, and it falls to the ground. The horse is covering everything from her waist up, and she's already pulled a pair of pants on. Roarke clears his throat, snatching another piece of meat from the paper packaging.

"Information on the Cataclysm?" I ask.

"The Override's not talking anymore," Pax says.

"Before that?"

Pax shakes his head. Meaning all he heard was the word *Cataclysm* and lost his shit. They're all supposed to be dead. But in his rage, Pax could never confirm whether he killed the one who took his child or not. Thane was in charge – and Thane can't use words in his wolf form.

"We need to be more –" Pax stumbles over the word. "– careful with her."

"We need a system or a time limit. So we can take it in turns to keep our distance from her," Roarke suggests.

"You're fine," I tell him – he needs to hear it. Next to Pax, he's the most volatile of us.

He would be worse than Pax if Pax's damned wolf hadn't become involved.

Roarke sighs. "I'm trying."

"I hate to admit it," I tell Pax. "But you're right. She's safest with Roarke right now."

"What? How did you work that out? I *just* said I need to keep my distance. I'm trying to recommend a time limit and a safe word."

Pax's gaze is unfocused, his head tilted so he can listen to Shadow and Seth for a moment. He still looks like that when he opens his mouth to continue. "We split up. I need to inspect Tanakan Prison, but Shade needs to ride for Eydis' domain and undo this potion-bubble mess. She can't go anywhere near Tanakan."

"And you think Shade and me together for a few days is a good idea?" Roarke asks, a genuine hint of worry to his words. "Together. Alone."

Pax nods. "It's about a day to Eydis' domain, then you won't be alone. I trust you."

"Good for you," Roarke snaps. "Riding for a day is no problem. Spending minutes or hours with her is no problem. But Eydis isn't a part of her bubble. It will just be me and my power that she is feeling. I won't be able to leave her. To relax."

I mumble out the only reassurance I know. "She's stronger than that. You know she is."

Roarke frowns at the girl's feet, bare under the hem of Pax's pants.

"The problem is growing. I like being around her," he says, his words a hoarse whisper, too low for mortal ears. "I don't want to ruin that. I don't want to become that monster again. I don't want to see her eyes – her life – fade because my power has wanted something it cannot have. And it *will* want it."

The fire crackles. Roarke is speaking the truth. Pax knows it – he has to. If – when – Roarke's power latches on to her, stopping him will be like trying to force the rain to fall upwards. Or an arrow to return to its bow in mid-flight.

The wolf says nothing.

Curious.

"What did Mother leave you?" I ask Roarke.

"*Let your reflection go hazy in clear waters and see instead through a gray lens.*" He says the words immediately, well-rehearsed, but without feeling or understanding.

I point at the girl. "Or gray eyes."

Silence.

"She's changing. Enforcement's TruthSeed had no effect."

Both of them look at me. On the other side of the horse, Seth even stills for half a beat.

"What does that mean?" Pax asks. He's looking at me, but the question had to be for Roarke, because like I bloody know what it means.

"I don't know. Part of her *is* Silvari – if her memory is to be believed. She said her mother was mortal, but her father was not. To be strong enough to resist a TruthSeed, her father would need to have been Elite Saber. But her mother wouldn't have survived long enough to give birth, and even if by some potion, magic, or miracle she did, then she would be Seedless, but not mortal."

"She smells mortal," I comment.

Roarke nods. "She feels mortal too. Most children from non-compatible Seeds have no access to magic. That doesn't explain the glimpses of power she has."

"I can't tell anymore," Pax admits, still examining the grass by his feet. "She feels strong to me. So strong, and so fragile at the same time."

"The window," I say.

"What… window?" Pax asks slowly, his gaze unfocused in a clear sign that he's searching his memory. "The windows shattered in a blast of power."

I huff at him, too busy eating another strip of meat to interrupt his thought process.

"Yes, what window?" Roarke echoes.

He was fetching horses at the time. Probably didn't take note of the window when he arrived, or the wall for that matter.

"Enforcement. Execution gallery. Silvari glass. Shattered." I like keeping things simple.

Pax straightens and crosses his arms over his chest.

"My power doesn't affect Silvari glass," he finally says.

I know.

"I wasn't completely in control."

I know that, too.

"We need answers."

"Allure?" I ask, even though I think it's a shit idea.

Roarke rakes a hand over his face. "I wish she recalled more of her memory the first time. She's certainly not strong enough for me to take her back there tonight."

Or ever. That's what he's not saying. He'd do anything not to see her go through that again. Controlling someone's every heartbeat to keep them alive is not something I'd like to have to do either.

"Eydis might have answers," he offers. "In the meantime, I vote for limiting the time we spend inside her bubble. We need a way of mitigating our impulses."

"The wolf agrees –" Pax begins, but gets cut short by a sudden glow in his eyes. He smiles wickedly; clearly the thought that the wolf just put into his head was amusing. "Thane insists."

"On what?" Roarke asks, his brow drawn. "Exactly?"

I grunt, and Pax turns away.

Seems we agree on that too. The sigil goes on first – then we'll tell the others.

When it's too late for them to object.

Because even though Pax almost flattened Lackshir market, and who knows why he didn't kill her just from contact, it would have all been avoided if Pax had a second longer to think before the wolf stepped in.

Thane agrees.

SHADOW

We're surrounded by forest, night is falling, the horses are calmly grazing with what little movement they have on their reins, and the rest of the guys are chatting by the fire. Their voices are too low for me to hear much more than the odd detached word.

I keep struggling with the zip on Pax's bag. Clothing is important.

"Here," Seth says, his tone low.

Seth's voice has a kind of note to it, almost a feel, that makes me relax. Deep and playful. Hearing him speak is somehow just as good as a glass of Silvari wine.

"Thank you," I whisper.

He reaches past me to the bag still tied behind Pax's saddle and yanks out a pair of pants that are going to be way too big and a long-sleeve shirt. Roarke's pants would probably fit me better, or Pax's sleep pants. But it's dark, and I'm not fussy.

The horse shuffles and fidgets, letting me catch glimpses of the fire. Pax is kneeling beside it, his hands stretched toward the flames. He's not wearing a shirt, wet hair glistening in the firelight, and the pants look like they could be Seth's. The guy's probably cold, and waiting for me before coming over here and getting changed into his own clothes – which I keep stealing.

I'm not sure when Roarke put on dry pants, but his long hair is still out, and he hasn't bothered with a shirt.

I slip out of view, using the horse as a wall, and shimmy into the oversized pants with my cloak still on, sighing as the dry fabric begins to warm my legs. They're made from fine Silvari cotton with elastic at the sides, and they just manage to stay on my hips.

I admit I'm a little hesitant as I unfasten the buttons on the cloak.

Or a lot.

I've come a long way from thinking these guys are going to use me as sport the minute I let my guard down – but not far enough to think that nakedness is normal.

"Here," he whispers, reaching for the buttons. "You know I have seen you naked before, right?"

I drop my hands and let him finish the buttons. His eyes soften as he works down to the last one, and I don't respond to his question. This is not the same as before.

He's just strapping my arm – this shouldn't feel intimate. Right?

The cloak falls to the ground with a soft thud, which gets my heart racing. I'll admit my curves aren't much to look at. Silvari women are slender and well-defined. I've got the arm and leg definition of someone who can scrub floors and haul buckets of water all day without breaking a sweat. Mix that with eating what I can, when I can, and I'd say I'm taller and wider than most of the women in this realm. Until I met these guys, I owned two sets of clothes – both worn out and pre-loved before I got my hands on them. And both exactly the same, a simple tunic and leggings. My most prized possessions were my boots – but they're gone now.

"I've stripped enough clothes off of enough women to know what your undergarments should look like," he points out.

I have trouble getting clothes of my own, so unless the boys have a hidden habit of wearing ladies breastbands that I've yet to discover, I'm not going to have constant access to them.

But that's not the reason I'm biting my lip.

"No," I say.

He cocks an eyebrow at me as he unravels the beginning of the bandage. "You don't want undergarments?" he asks, more cheeky than confused.

"No, you aren't allowed to talk about girls. Any girls. Ever. And certainly never ones you've stripped the clothes off of."

He chuckles, lifting my arm at my elbow and resting it against the base of my ribs. I hold it in place.

"I'm serious."

"That's what amuses me."

He starts the bandage at my wrist, walking around me as he secures it into place. His fingers gently guide the fabric into position, then smooth it out. Over my arm, around my back, then over my arm again. I tune in to the gentle touch, the moments when his fingers move from the bandage onto my skin, which somehow feels intense and alive. It sends shivers down my spine – and up the insides of my legs.

I clear my throat. Then, his fingers run over the sensitive skin just under my breast, and I feel the need to repeat the throat-clearing process.

"I've had past boyfriends too, you know," I blurt out.

Throat clearing is a pretty bad distraction – mouth to the rescue.

"I'm sure you have."

"I could talk about the many ways a girl can unbutton a guy's pants with one hand or her teeth." He tilts his head to the side, his lips pulling tight to try and wipe the smile from his face, but he keeps moving – working the bandage into place. "Or the benefits of getting your kitchen bench heights just right."

He stops, fingers on the skin of my back, holding the wrapping tight, as his lips brush against my ear.

"I wouldn't mind," he says, kissing just under my earlobe.

The sensation runs down my spine. I can barely inhale through it.

Crap.

"I would even enjoy it," he adds, kissing lower.

Once.

Twice.

The soft sound of his lips fills my remaining senses. Just his touch, his warmth, his existence – and me.

"Any time you want to share details, Vexy." Kiss. "I want to hear them." Kiss. "I'll just imagine it's me in your memories." Kiss.

I squirm, but his hand presses to my stomach, and between that and his firm grip on my half-bound arm, I'm all his.

And I'm on fire.

"But Pax…" He brushes my hair aside and presses his lips to the nape of my neck. "He might ride off and kill the guy."

He lets out a long exhale that sends another hot shiver through me, then straightens.

"Just make sure you're good with the consequences before you keep talking. He can hear us," he murmurs, the vein of teasing almost completely gone.

I gulp. I'd forgotten that three other guys are just a few steps away. *How the chuck did I forget that?!*

I shift so I can dart my gaze over the back of Pax's horse, and Seth lets me, returning to his bandaging. They're all around the fire, exactly as they were the last time I looked. Pax's back is to us, still crouched with his hands stretched toward the flames.

My body has fallen back into the clutches of being in shock – not desire. Not lust. Shock.

Definitely shock.

Instead of explaining that I have never untied a guy's pants in my life – unless, of course, I was the one wearing them – I switch from trying to get a reaction out of Seth, because clearly that was too easy, to trying to get one out of Pax.

I focus to make sure there's no shaking in my voice before opening my mouth. "Did he hear the part about Peter and I dancing naked through the fields every full moon?" I'm talking to Seth, but I'm looking at Pax's back – which stiffens. That's a little more satisfying than I thought it would be. "We'd braid flowers in each other's hair. Head hair, underarm hair, toe hair, pubic–"

Pax stands sharply, turning to face me. "Not funny," he growls – not a wolf-growl, just a man-growl.

Seth chuckles. "Very funny." He tucks the last corner of the bandage in underneath itself, then hands me a shirt. His blue eyes are sparkling.

"I like your kind of funny," he says, that soft, melodic voice warming me from the inside – again. He lifts my free hand, the only one I have left now, and rubs it between his. "Your whole body feels cold. You shouldn't have gone in the river."

I offer him a lopsided shrug. "Or it's shock."

"And what did this?" He points at the sear marks that trace out from under my nails.

"I don't know – and don't poke at it."

I rip my hand free from his and begin to struggle into the shirt – which amuses him more. He's still chuckling when the shirt finally pulls into place. I emerge from behind the horses, one arm strapped underneath the shirt and the other smoothing my hair from my face. Trying to ignore Seth.

Trying to ignore the pattern on my skin that is still feeling his kisses.

I get about three steps before Seth settles a cloak around my shoulders. His cloak this time.

Pax doesn't move until both Seth and I are by the fire, then he goes to get his own clothes and get changed behind the horses.

"It's here," Roarke notes calmly.

Killian grunts in agreement.

I open my mouth to ask what, or shout it because I'm sick of not knowing what 'it' is, when thin tendrils of *something* climb up over the trees, engulfing them and leaving a solid wall of oozing, inky blackness behind.

"That?" I ask, pointing.

In seconds, we're surrounded. The horses pull and fuss on their reins, but they seem to know that there's no escape – that struggling is useless – and instead inspect the blackness with wide eyes and loud snorts. Pax moves among them, whispering hushes and stroking their necks.

Every tree, every bit of space, is covered in black ooze. I turn in a slow circle, feeling my face blanch in fear.

What the bralls is it?

The stuff reaches, curls, and spreads from treetop to treetop. Finding itself, linking, and intertwining until the sky is gone. Not even a glimmer from a single star. Nothing.

"Mist," Roarke says.

"No, it's chuckin' not," I gasp.

The fact that they're all sitting casually should make me feel better – but it doesn't.

Pax steps up next to me, his eyes on me while mine dart wildly over the solid wall of blackness. Looking for gaps, creases, any way out. Any light. I wipe a shaking hand over my face, but it does little to calm me.

"It lives here," Roarke explains. "This small pocket of forest is its home."

Pax motions to Killian. "It won't come any closer to Darkness."

"It's like a bubble I can see," I manage to voice, which surprises me given how dry my throat has gone.

I turn in a slow circle, even though it's obvious that there are no exits. The space we have left would be about as big as my bubble too, and the realization of exactly how small my world is makes my heart pound harder.

Pax grips both my shoulders, stopping me.

"Shade," he says. I let him hold me in place. The stars have gone. The moon. The trees. Everything. "Shade," he says louder, giving me a little shake.

I look up at him, resisting the urge to immediately look away again as a sound similar to 'Yeah?' slips from my tongue.

"We will find a solution to Logan's potion. We will remove your bubble, and this mist will be gone by morning," he murmurs softly.

So softly. So gently.

I manage to nod.

His hands slide from my shoulders, down my arms, and rest at my elbows. "Eat something," he presses, but he doesn't move.

And there's a wall of blackness around us, so there's no way I'm moving.

He pulls me in close. One arm reaching up my back, into my hair, the other pressing into the dip of my hips.

"I thought we had this conversation last night. Mortals need to eat."

"More. Vexy needs to eat *more*."

"What have you eaten today?" Pax practically asks my hair, because that's about where his face is nestled.

"We had sausages for breakfast, fruit for afters, rolls for lunch, honey-cream bites for lunch sweets, and then biscuits and juice when we first arrived at the markets," I recite, the list slowly helping my mind to focus.

"So you've missed tea-afters, dinner, supper, and lates," Roarke points out.

"I don't actually need to eat until midnight –" And that's as far as that sentence goes.

Pax steers me to the edge of the fire and pushes me down onto my ass. Sitting down with one arm sucks. There's no balance and this odd sensation that if I fall the wrong way I'm going to head-butt the ground. But I don't. Pax sits down right next to me, so close I could lean against him, but I don't do that either.

Seth brings over supplies. Thankfully, we had the luck of having life go to the pits of an outhouse *after* we procured supplies. Meat and cheese get stuffed into rolls and passed around the circle. The guys begin to talk, but I have a hard time believing the world still exists out there.

Which shouldn't draw me to the conclusion that, maybe, there is no world left for me outside my bubble – but it does.

"I really want to know what happened with you two," Seth says, pointing at Killian and I.

Killian grunts.

"I think we need a proper debrief. *I* need details," Pax insists.

Roarke passes me another piece of meat.

"Local enforcement…" Killian begins, and I tune out. I chew, watch the fire, finish my roll, and move on to a hard candy, until I hear my name. "My Shadow took him down."

My brows shoot up. "What did I do?" I ask, rolling the candy over my tongue.

"Dealt with the commander," Killian replies.

Pax shifts, and the tips of his fingers slip into the waist of my pants. *Just the tips, no big deal,* I tell the heat pulsing through all of the parts of me in the vicinity of his hand. Everything from knees to belly-button is on fire.

He's looking at me, but I keep my gaze on Killian and pretend not to need to deal with the emotions on Pax's face. I'm way too exhausted to try and work out if there's more fear or more admiration in him.

Seth whistles. "That's impressive."

"It was an accident," I manage.

"How do you accidentally cut clean through the main artery in a commander's leg?" Killian asks skeptically.

"Um, you throw yourself at the guy with a knife in your hand and hope for the best."

I barely get the words out before Pax picks me up and drags me into his lap. I almost choke on the damn candy.

"We have words," I cough at him.

I'm still technically sitting on the ground, with one of his legs on either side of me, his chest as my backrest. I twist to the side, pulling my legs up, pressing my elbow into his abdomen to put just enough distance between us. Trying to get his attention.

"I think she needs to spend more time with Killian," Seth suggests, ignoring me. "Training with Killian. Especially if she's going to do things like that."

He gets Pax's attention.

"Hey," I say, jabbing Pax in the stomach. That does it. "Do I have to talk to you the same as Alfie? If something doesn't belong to you, you have to ask permission first."

The yellow glow heats in his eyes. "You *do* belong to me. Who's Alfie?"

Alfie... *Where do I begin?*

I relax into Pax's chest. Resting my head underneath his chin. Letting the pain settle over my heart. It'd probably just be an ache if I wasn't so exhausted, and recovering from shaking muscles, chattering teeth, shock, and nakedness.

"My Alfie," I whisper.

Pax presses me harder into his chest. A low growl reaches from somewhere inside him to brush over my soul. It pulls a vibrating sensation from my chest – which I promptly clear my throat against and swallow down.

"Who is Alfie?" Pax asks, growls, orders.

Alfie is gone. Lost. Left behind in a life that no kid should have.

Out of the corner of my eye, I see Killian shake his head. Not sure what exactly that means, but Pax doesn't repeat the question. I don't move, even as Roarke picks up the conversation and Pax's arms slowly relax, which only makes me lean into him more. Listening to the beat of his heart. Finding comfort in the way our bodies fit together. My eyes close and my thoughts numb to about the speed of a toddler's.

Somewhere... out there... in the rest of the world... the part of the world that is not Pax... the guys keep talking. Conversation swirls around me.

"I don't understand. What did you get detained for?" Seth asks.

"I didn't get detained. He did," I mumble, stabbing my finger in the vague direction of Killian.

"I can believe that. What were his charges?"

"Having an ugly face," I blurt.

Tell me I did not just say that!

Why would I say that about the guy with a nasty scar right where everyone can see it? I peek under one eyelid. Seth's eyes are wide – not a good sign from the guy who has virtually no practical joke boundaries. But Killian – Killian starts laughing. Not a grunt-laugh. Not a chuckle.

A real laugh.

Damn, I love that sound and the way his eyes change, less black and more emerald. It sends warmth cinching through my stomach.

Everyone turns to stare at him; at least I'm not the only one. Pretty sure I *am* the only one thinking he's too damn handsome right now. And if anyone else starts making him laugh like that, I might get jealous.

"Did you guys know he could make that sound?" I ask, shutting my eyes again.

No one says anything.

The sound of his laugh dissolves before Pax speaks, "What were the commander's actual charges?"

"Something to do with stolen weapons. Expensive ones."

"The few weapons in the cave were peasant grade. Not expensive. Not worth charges."

"I didn't get anymore details," I mumble.

"Okay then, how did I meet Killian on the street, but Shade was already with Pax?" Roarke asks.

"And why were you naked?" Seth adds.

I force my sleepiness back enough to open my eyes and insist. "We are no longer talking about my nakedness."

I can't put my finger on how my clothes vanished. They were destroyed. Not even strands or threads or buttons left. But I wasn't paying attention to that. Pax's body, pulsing with anger, and with lines of gold ripping over and through him – all of that is raw in my memory, and I shiver as I try to push past those big details to find the smaller details. How the window shattered. Why I didn't get cut. And my clothes.

Killian makes a 'hmm' sound, but they're all still looking at me.

"I thought you had stripped off to get his attention." Seth points at Pax. "Because that would have worked. When he started ripping the place apart, I was at the other end of the market. I was hoping you'd stop him." Then he nods at

Killian. "And having the horses ready was the next logical move."

"I was *trying*."

Everyone looks back at me. I know there's a giant hole in this story. Things just don't make sense. Killian was way over by the door. Pax way out in the middle of the sand. Me pressed close to the furthest wall. But the bubble is still there; we checked already.

"The bubble disintegrated my clothes – when I went through it," I stumble over the suggestion.

Killian nods really slowly. How much does this man hold back? How much does he know or guess and then just sit around waiting for the rest of us to catch up?

"What do you mean? You went *through* the barrier?" Roarke's shock is clear in both his words and his wide eyes.

"I must have."

"But it's still there?" Pax asks softly.

"I think I went straight out of Killian's perimeter and into yours. I think it hurt too." I hold my hand up for Pax to get his first good look at the lightning-like lines from my fingertips almost to my elbow.

He traces his fingers along my skin, growling softly. "I'm going to have to inspect you every time we're apart, if getting hurt and hiding injuries from me is going to become a regular thing."

"I wasn't hiding it," I protest, at the same time I'm thinking, *What does 'inspect me' mean?*

"She needs to try and get through it again."

"Sure, Allure, we'll just get Pax to blow up another merchant market," Seth teases.

"Not tonight. She's too weak."

I realize I'm having a lot of trouble following their conversation and, instead of trying harder, decide not to try at all.

"Maybe the potion is running out of power?" Seth says, followed by a rushed conversation between him and Roarke.

One that is stopped by Killian. "Still. Weak."

Pax's chest rumbles with his reply. "Thane is keeping his distance."

Yep, too tired to properly hear what they're saying.

PAX'S FINGERS brush down the length of my jaw, stopping at my chin, the sensation stirring me awake. They linger, before insisting I turn to look up at him. The gold in his eyes seems to dance as it reflects the firelight. Looking at me. Just me.

"I was falling asleep," I grumble, frowning up at him.

Something flies over my head, is snatched out of the air and held down to me.

"You ate half a roll and two candies," Pax says, holding the dried piece of beef out for me.

"No food," I growl, pushing it away. "Sleep."

One corner of his mouth pulls back into a smile. "You're cute."

"No, I'm not." I'm never cute, and right now I'm just cranky.

"If there was a CuteSeed, it would be you, Vexy."

I try to twist to glare at him, but being one-armed and trapped against Pax makes that a little hard.

"No, I'm not," I grumble.

"She's pulling her cute-angry face," Roarke adds.

I stab my finger at Killian, just daring him to say something.

So of course he does, "Cute-about-to-kick-you-in-the-balls face."

I growl, a real this-is-pissing-me-off growl. "I'm not cute.

I'm a death trap. None of you should be near me. *And* I was trying to sleep."

"We've got this. Roarke will figure it out, Seth will draw it out, and Killian will kill it."

Seth shrugs. "That usually works."

"What am *I* supposed to do then?"

"Stay alive," they all answer.

All of them, in complete and annoying unison.

"Eat, Kitten," Roarke says, tossing something else across the fire.

Pax catches it, then unfurls his fingers, palm flat, and offers it to me. Another candy.

While Seth adds, "Smile."

Followed by Killian's, "Heal."

And Pax's, "Then sleep."

I groan at them. *That's so corny, guys.* But a heartbeat later, the candy is in my mouth and my eyelids are hanging low again.

"Did you see the potassium nitrate vendor?" Seth asks, shifting the conversation.

"We don't have time for that, Chaos," Pax warns, his tone vibrating against my cheek.

"We always have time for fireworks."

Roarke groans. "Don't worry, you can't get sulfur on this side of the realm."

"I've got a plan to… " Seth keeps talking.

Pax shifts, and I open my eyes to inspect my surroundings. Nothing. Just my guys and the black night.

Roarke's voice drifts across the fire, low and soft. Almost a whisper. "Pax, if she's not going to eat, let the girl sleep."

"No, I'm good," I say, wriggling my shoulder against Pax's chest, trying to find my comfy spot again.

Pax's breath skims rhythmically across my skin. The guy's

silently laughing at me. "Beautiful, you have to sleep," he murmurs.

My skin tingles.

I don't even want to repeat those words in my head, in case they realize how much they mean to me and move to live on the moon or some other distant location. Well, not *they* – just *it*. The words 'you have to sleep' are nothing in comparison.

Just that one word.

That *I* don't want to repeat, but I do want *him* to repeat.

"Say that again," I mumble out over my sleepy tongue.

"Beautiful. You. Have. To. Sleep."

Bralls, I think even my soul had a reaction to that.

Someone lifts me up, laying me down with something soft under my head. I don't even bother to look. Don't care.

Too happy.

Darkness

The girl's had six hours sleep, that's more than enough for a mortal.

I lean down as I walk past and yank Roarke's cloak out from under her head, tossing it across to the guy in a flutter of fabric. Then keep walking.

"Why?" she groans behind me.

"It's morning," I tell her.

She struggles to her feet using one arm. Her left arm. She's right hand dominant, and I'm enjoying seeing her survive on her left, more than I probably should. I managed to break my left arm – and I'm enjoying adjusting to that handicap just a little too.

Challenges excite me. It's who I am. I'm pissed that I broke it in the first place, or maybe I'm pissed that I couldn't get the keys to work and the bars wouldn't break. Either way, I'm pissed.

Roarke is using a tree downriver as a target for his bow. Pax is stretching out on the grass, warming up for a bout with Seth. The horses have been moved to let them graze, and the sun will be up soon.

I fish through my bags before returning to her. She's finally managed to get up, smothering a yawn, rubbing her eyes, and peering around with relief. The black tar-like mist has already retreated.

The weapons I purchased in Lackshir market, while Shadow watched Roarke purchase food supplies – and Pax ordered Roarke not to Allure the merchants into ridiculous bargains – land with a soft thud and metal-against-metal clink at her feet. Six kunai – small arrow-tipped darts, with red cotton wrapped around the shaft, and several ribbons trailing for balance. Six dragon darts – with twisted shafts and needle-fine points, barbed and with the potential to dip in toxins. And two blades.

"Try the darts first," I tell her, pointing at the nearest tree.

She snatches them up without hesitation – leaving the new blades in the grass.

Twirling the first dart through her fingers. Testing it. Not like a fighter, not yet, like a player. And if Seth has his way, they'll be in a gambling den making money off dart games in no time.

"Where?" she asks.

The tree is a pretty big target, and I find myself grinning as I approach it. Drawing my short dagger I carve three quick circles into the bark.

Thank you, tree.

She flicks her wrist, and before I'm even standing next to her, all twelve darts are embedded in the circles. None miss. None veer off course. None require calibration or experimenting with. All with her left hand.

I clench my jaw to keep the thing from dropping off my face.

"Fuck," I whisper.

I don't even let her retrieve them. Can't improve much on that shit.

"Arm yourself," I tell her, pointing at the knives in the grass.

The smirk on her face wipes off. Maybe I could have complimented her throws. Roarke would have. Seth would have cheered. Pax probably would have kissed her.

She doesn't need compliments or cheers or to be kissed by me.

She needs to be able to kill the person who makes it past those darts and gets in close.

Three steps backward, I draw my own short blade.

"Arm yourself," I grunt again, and wait.

Emotions tick over inside her. Confusion. Uncertainty. A hint of temptation.

Fear – but not enough to smell like ash.

And the spiced-apple scent of curiosity.

But she doesn't move.

"You swing. I block," I say.

"Then what?" she asks, still not moving to grab the knives.

"You swing again, and I'll block again."

"Why?"

I twirl my blade between my fingers. Her hesitation is annoying, grinding at my patience. She needs to learn to fight – somehow I need to do that without drawing blood.

Impossible.

I slip my knife back into its sheath and search the grass for a solid stick of about the same length.

"You swing, I block," I tell her again, holding my new weapon in the air.

Thirteen ways I could strip her skin from her bones, or slice along the length of an artery or vein, pace through my mind.

She doesn't need to know any of them because I'm not going to do any of them, and pressing upon her the fact that the weapon means nothing – it's the opponent that matters – is not going to be productive. Not right now. Not when I've only just managed to get her to relax a little.

She bends down to grab the blades. Her brow creases as she takes in their design. She would probably strike me as confused if the coppery scent of self-preservation wasn't flooding my senses. Perfect – I can work with that.

She puts one back on the ground, turning the other through her fingers.

The karambits are curved. The handle can be gripped blade-forward, or blade-facing-back along the arm. A finger loop at the end of the hilt means she can flip the blade mid-swing and cause some serious damage. They're blades made for slashing and attacking.

I need to teach her how to do that – how to attack.

"I swing, you block," she says.

And I grin in reply.

DAY FIVE

7TH

DAY OF

SNOW MOON

ROUGHLY 94 MILES FROM POTION MASTER EYDIS

I slump down next to the remnants of the fire and try to catch my breath. The sun was peeking over the horizon when Pax *finally* called an end to whatever it was Killian was making me do.

What it felt like was tripping over myself and slashing around without any success. I actually consider myself lucky that I didn't draw my own blood.

What *he* called it was training.

I think he broke some brain cells when they knocked him unconscious yesterday. His idea of effective training and mine are so far apart they're not even in the same language.

His arm didn't even slow him down. The splints and bandage are gone. If I could steal their healing for myself, I would. He is still favoring it, gripping the collar of his shirt to support the arm while we were *training*. And I couldn't even use that to my advantage.

Roarke sits down next to me – well, as far away from me as he possibly can and still be able to pass something to me.

A book. My book.

Or at least the book that I claimed. I accept it from him,

not missing the way he slips his fingers off the edges before mine are even close. No accidental skin contact here.

"Technically, there's nothing wrong with learning to read from this," he says, tapping the green cloth cover with one finger.

This book is the only non-essential thing I've ever held. Food is essential. A work tool is essential. A book is a luxury. Being told I can keep this book is a blessing, but given it holds the image of the Origin Spring, which makes my spine tingle with some long-forgotten memory, it feels more ominous than pleasant.

Which I'm not okay with. Inanimate objects, especially ones lacking sharp edges, shouldn't have any power over me. I file that away for later, a private moment, and some serious reinforcement of the natural order of things, book on the bottom and me on the top.

Okay, maybe not the top – but definitely above books.

"But," he continues, pulling something from his pocket, "here." He holds out a much smaller cloth-bound book.

My fingers brush over the faded blue fabric. The corners are worn down to nothing, and the spine has permanent creases in it. A pine cone has been printed on the cover and brown lettering spells out the title – which I can't read.

"This is the book I learned to read from," his voice whispers across to me.

I'm drawn to it, shuffling across until my shoulder is flush with Roarke's as I open the cover and peer at the faded gold lettering on the first page.

"You kept it all this time?" I ask, my voice low to match his – even though I'm not sure why.

He chuckles. "No, I found this at the book merchant yesterday. My copy would have been destroyed when Lithael burned our suite at the Black Castle. But this is the same edition." He points to a series of fine print at the bottom of the page. "Printed by the WordSeeds on the Emerald River."

"He burned down your home?" I ask.

"Well, technically it burned down in the fight. Any one of his Sabers, or the grimm, or even his son or his father, could have started the fire."

He slips the book from my fingers and thumbs through the pages, finding the one he's looking for with ease. A series of lines that look almost like a sigil, but are clearly forming the outline of a wolf, look back at me.

"AlphaSeed," he reads, trailing his finger over the bold lettering below. "Born of the Origin, you owe no allegiance, and none owe allegiance to you, for trust must be earned, and power must be protected – the beast that is leashed is one who cannot remain strong."

"Pax?" I ask, trailing my finger across the page just as Roarke had done. "How does any of this make sense to you? This word has a line straight through it, I can hardly see any of the letters!"

"That word says 'protected.' All of the possessive and coveted words have lines through them."

He flips through to a new page, and a line swirls along the edge of the spine. It reminds me of Killian turning part of the prophecy to smoke – which is probably something I should corner him to get more information about. Just not any time soon. Not while Pax is so volatile and I'm pretty sure whatever Killian's worried about in that line he turned to smoke has everything to do with Pax.

And all of that pales in the face of a BeastSeed threatening our existence.

"DarknessSeed," Roarke reads. "Turn your face to the light, let the shadows fall behind you. Turn your face to the Darkness, let those behind you see the light."

My gaze seeks out Killian, who's getting some serious

energy out of his system by throwing – and being thrown by – Seth in some unarmed fighting drills. He hits the ground with a hard thud, rolling to one side and springing to his feet. Seth circles around him, and Killian runs his hand down his injured arm.

"Should he be doing that?" I ask.

"He doesn't mind pain, but he's not stupid enough to leave himself with a permanent disability."

"What about his scars? They look pretty permanent."

Roarke shakes his head, the movement drawing my attention. His dark eyes are stormy with unspoken emotions.

"The things that take the longest to heal are the things that get broken on the inside."

His hand is still resting on the book in my lap. I wrap my fingers around his.

"I'm sorry," I say, and I know the words are hollow and inadequate, but they're all I have.

He pulls his hand from mine, fear racing over his expression before he has a chance to school his features into an almost calm.

"Wait," I tell him, catching his hand again. "You haven't read me your page."

"I was never planning to," he says, snapping the book shut but leaving it in my lap.

Then he gets up and walks away. I feel the need to throw something at him, except that would make me the ass here. The guy just cut his chest open and left his emotions bare for me, he really *does* have a right to walk away – at least that's what I'm trying to tell myself.

I flip the book open and let the pages flutter by. What would the lines for Allure look like? As the pages flutter I spot a gap, a place where a page has been roughly torn free. I glare at Roarke as he begins to saddle his horse. What's so scary about his Seed that he'd damage a book to keep a girl who can't read from finding out?

Seth ambles toward the camp, Killian patting him on the shoulder and smiling about something. Killian's eyes are a happy, clear emerald – that color they only go when he can completely let his guard down.

Even though he was just getting thrown around, Seth looks refreshed, in a remotely clean set of beige linen pants with the waist fastened by a crisscrossing string. I think I could make those tight enough to fit my hips – note to self, steal those pants.

He has a water flask in his hands but doesn't even take a sip before passing it down to me.

I drink greedily from the small leather bottle, then hold it in the air for him to take back.

"It's yours," he says, smiling as he walks over to his horse.

He begins to fish around in his bags with his back to me.

"What do you mean *it's mine*?"

I don't own anything. Except for a few sets of clothes, which technically Pax arranged for me, and so technically they still belong to him. And two books. I now own two books. The idea makes me feel a little giddy with the luxury.

Seth tosses an empty set of leather saddlebags in my direction. They hit the ground with a thump and slide to a stop next to my hand. The brown lamb-hide is so soft under my fingertips that for half a beat I just sit stroking the thing. They're finer than anything that should be wasted on bags that tie to a horse's ass. Each side is fitted with two shiny black buckles, and a design of five arrowheads in a row has been burned onto each pocket.

I'm too stunned to get answers.

And I totally don't care that I have nothing to put inside them. Just a water bottle.

My water bottle.

And two books. *My* books.

Then Roarke tosses a cloak, the black fabric swirling in mid-flight before being snatched from the air by Seth. The guy wraps it around his shoulders and smiles across at his brother.

"Does it suit me, brother?" Seth asks, fluttering his eyelashes.

His shoulders are too broad, and the hem doesn't even make it past his ass. I burst out laughing.

Seth turns toward the other two. "What do you think? Is it my style?"

While Pax and Seth debate whether the fabric matches his hair color, Killian squats down beside me and motions for me to hand over the blades and darts.

He slips them into their sheaths – short curved sheaths for the odd curved blades. The thin, twisted darts slide into a bracelet-type guard for his wrist, and the darts with red-ribbons go into the type of case that would fasten to his belt.

But then he holds them out for me.

"Yours," he says.

I point to them, leaving them in his grip and resting my finger on the rough brushed leather of the sheaths.

"No, they're not," I protest, confused.

He grunts, but he's almost smiling. A happy-grunt?

"Take them in their sheaths, or I'll embed them in your body, and you'll have no choice," he offers.

I snatch them from him, pressing them flush against my chest, so he can't get them back again.

Pax shoves my cloak down his shirt, and I groan. They all ignore me.

Yay, armpit cloak.

Seth tosses a small waxed canvas duffle on top of the saddlebags, followed by my gravy-clothes, jam-clothes, and just plain dirty clothes.

"I would have picked up some boots if I had known you would be needing new ones," he muses.

"I'm good," I say, before realizing how rude that must have sounded. "No, sorry. Thank you."

I snatch the stuff up before they can take it away from me.

Seth laughs. Killian takes his turn getting his scent all over my new cloak, and Roarke bends down to help me stow the books in the saddlebags, then unzip my new duffle and stow my clothes away – wet and dirty clothes. No wonder Seth wanted me to get a bag of my own. I have to do some washing as soon as possible, and I might need to wash some of Seth's stuff too.

When everything is in and secured I stand up, the straps of the duffle in my hand, the bag hanging limply at my side – because I only have one hand and can't possibly gather everything up at once.

"Let me get this straight. While I was trying to gather information, like we were all ordered to do, you lot were shopping?" I ask.

Pax and Roarke look amused, trying to pull their smiles down from filling their faces. Seth gives me a wicked grin.

"What made you think we don't enjoy shopping? We're in the top ten richest families in Silva – yes, we like shopping," he says.

My brow creases. That just doesn't make sense.

Seth points at himself, then his brothers. "Third-generation princes. We may have lost the title, but we haven't lost the estates. Money isn't a problem."

My eyes widen, and my jaw drops. I knew they were the old Crown's sons. I was told that early on in my life as a kidnappee, as well as the fact that Crowns are voted in in this realm, and their family was usurped. That the new Crown, Lithael, is still trying to destroy them and a good portion of the population is on Lithael's side because of some really dirty political tricks.

"Then why are we sleeping on the ground?" I ask.

"Builds character," Killian mutters as he walks toward me.

I ignore him, looking at Roarke for an answer.

"Our estates are on the lower southern side of the realm, and our safe houses are all within the major cities. We are currently trying to keep out of Lithael's sights, so we're safest if we stay out of the towns as much as possible," he answers.

Killian swoops in to take the bag from my fingers, and for a second I jerk it out of his reach... before realizing that that's a pretty silly reaction. I let him take it, and he sets about strapping it to the back of my saddle. Saddlebags first, duffle on top.

Knives, cloak, bags, water bottle, book. Way to make a girl feel like she owes you something.

"You need a belt," Killian says, waving the blades in the air and making a show of putting one in each side of the saddle-bag. "Make sure you can always reach these."

I nod dumbly.

Then he turns to me and motions toward my leg.

"Give me your foot."

"Chuck, no."

His brow creases. What did he think my reaction would be?

Kneeling down, he holds the thin, twisted darts in their bracelet-like sheath out.

"Dragon darts. I'll teach you how to poison them." As he talks, he pats his knee. "It'd be better on your wrist, but you won't be able to draw them one-handed."

I put my bare foot on his knee. He lifts the ankle of my pants, and my whole body rushes with warmth at his touch. Even though his touch is cold. Like ice. Like the guy just climbed out of the river again, and yet my body responds with warmth – it shouldn't.

His fingers stop on my calf. Pausing.

"You're not in shock," he mutters.

Damn, am I glad for that distraction.

"I feel fine," I say, lifting my fingers and showing him that even the lightning has settled to an almost unnoticeable few lines.

He grunts. Grabs my calf hard, and practically slaps the sheath against my leg.

I wobble, reaching out for something to stop me from falling over, and end up grabbing a handful of his black hair.

"What are you doing?" he demands.

"Getting revenge for the sting in my leg, I guess," I tell him.

"Pain doesn't worry me," he says, tightening the cord with sharp movements.

I nod. "I know."

"Then why are you still holding my hair?"

"Because you're still almost knocking me over."

He makes a little thinking noise, his hands gentling a little. With a final knot, he pushes my foot off his knee and stands up so quickly I'm not sure how my hand doesn't come away full of hair.

"Done."

"Fine," I snap.

"Don't take it off."

"I won't."

He grunts, turning away, and I groan as Pax's gaze narrows on his brother.

"Are we good?" Pax asks him and in true Killian style his reply is a simple nod.

I want to smack him on the back of the head. *No, we're not good.*

"Mount up," Pax calls, looking specifically at me.

Is that a '*let it go*' look?

I clench my teeth and fold my one arm over my chest. If I knew what, exactly, would get an explanation out of Killian, I would do it. But until I can kick his ass, I'm never going to have the ability to make the guy tell me what he's thinking.

Roarke leads the gelding over. The one with the creamy mane and beautiful almost black coat.

"Did I steal this horse?" I ask.

The others are checking their gear and climbing onto their horses around me, and they all chuckle – except Seth. His brow lifts in genuine excitement.

"Are we graduating to horse rustling? Why didn't anyone tell me?"

"I'm serious. This wasn't my horse. I just climbed on when everything started exploding."

"Pax purchased him," Roarke tells me, wrapping my cloak around my shoulders and fastening the buttons for me.

One-armed buttoning skills are way beyond me.

"The pony you were on couldn't keep up," Pax explains.

"Yeah, you need all the help you can get, Vexy," Seth adds.

"Sethy, that hurts," I say, copying the hand over heart motion that he used on Pax at the bandit cave.

He laughs.

I purse my lips, my mind full of the ideas for retaliation lining up and begging for attention.

"What would happen if I put sulfur in your boots – then set them alight?" I ask sweetly.

But I'm not looking at him. I'm concentrating on my next task – getting into this saddle. I run my fingers down the length of the stirrup leather, trying to straighten it.

Roarke leans in next to my ear.

"You know what sulfur does?" he asks, disbelieving.

I shrug, balancing on one foot and sticking my other in the stirrup. "Maybe."

He doesn't back off, his hair falling forward against my shoulder. His dark eyes seeking mine.

Of course I know what sulfur does. The families on the far east of Lord Martin's estate mined it in secret. They took small amounts to the markets in Drayden, in secret, to trade for food. Sometimes it was the only thing that kept them alive.

I'm not sure if I'm annoyed that Roarke thought I was too dumb to know what the stuff is, or just annoyed because he's standing so close I can't get on my horse.

He smiles, taking the edge off that feeling.

"That's," he begins, stepping back and running his thumb and forefinger over his mustache-beard combo, "interesting."

I bend my knee, ready to spring into the saddle when Killian grunts, "Wrong foot."

"Huh?" I eye the saddle and my leg, accusingly. "How do you know?" I demand, but I pull my foot out and turn around.

"Roarke, if you're not helping, leave her to fail on her own," Killian mutters.

"No, don't leave me to fail."

Now I'm facing the horse's ass and this just isn't going to work. I chew the corner of my lip for a second, then walk around to the other side of the horse. Killian grunt-chuckles while Roarke takes the horse's reins, and I struggle with the stirrup again.

Struggle to get my foot in, struggle to get my ass up, struggle to settle into the saddle.

But win. *Me and this saddle have got to get over our differences.*

Roarke guides the reins into my hands.

"Please put sulfur in his boots, and please let me watch," he says, his eyes bright.

So he wasn't surprised by my knowledge, he was surprised by the theories for its application? Whatever was going through his mind, I simply can't resist that lopsided smile.

"Do you think we could dip his boot laces in sulfur?" I ponder. "Crush it and mix it with water, then soak his laces overnight, and light them while he's wearing them? I could crawl under the table during dinner."

"You can't out-Chaos Chaos," Seth chuckles, nudging his horse in line with mine.

"Is that a challenge?" I ask.

Seth looks a little hurt. The corners of his lips turned down, almost pouting.

"Oh, don't worry, Sethy," I add. "I'll help you get revenge on Roarke. Not me, you're not allowed to play pranks on me. But we can both play pranks on Roarke."

"Traitor," Roarke calls back.

Pax makes a clicking sound, and his horse ambles to the head of the line. We follow him up the river. Pax, Roarke, Seth beside me, and Killian behind me. The silence is comfortable as the sun lights up the land, and the animals and birds come alive. A light breeze rustles over the treetops, pulling at Roarke's loose hair until the guy decides to wrestle it into a knot on the top of his head.

I play with the reins in my hand, one hand. Everyone else has two hands, and I have one. Even if I had three hands, I'd still feel unbalanced and vulnerable. I can't even ride, and now I have no way of holding on for dear life if something goes wrong.

When something goes wrong.

With me, and these guys, something always goes wrong.

We find a road, then a bridge, then an intersection with a

narrow single-file track leading off it. The thing's over-grown, like something that the cattle trample through once a year, being mustered back to the sale yards. Only I haven't seen any cattle in Silva.

We stop, and Pax nods at Roarke before guiding his horse over to me. The look in his golden eyes hints that I'm not going to like what he's about to say – or maybe *he's* not going to like it.

"Ride with Roarke to Eydis. They'll work out how to remove this bubble."

He can't possibly be suggesting this? What happened to the Elorsin brothers sticking together? We can't go a day without getting into a bloody battle. I'm going to get Roarke killed!

My mouth doesn't open, can't find the right words. His gaze narrows on me, waiting. For a split second, I see the wolf inside.

"You can't go where I'm going," he says. "Roarke's the only one that can get you to Eydis alone. It'll take most of the day, but once you're there, Eydis's domain is protected. She's powerful, Shade. Her power will help balance out Roarke's."

"I'm worried *about* him," I explain, pointing at Roarke, because any potential side effects from Roarke's Allure were not even on my mind.

"I'm not," Pax snaps.

I try again. "I'm going to get him killed. Haven't you noticed that since we left the White Castle, something bad has happened every day?"

"Twice a day, actually," Seth corrects.

Pax's expression softens. Whatever he thought he knew – it wasn't this.

"Still not worried. Go with him."

I manage to nod my head, even though I'd rather argue and convince him that this is a stupid idea.

"We'll ride hard and be at Eydis' home before dark," Roarke says, his tone trying to reassure me.

I twist in my saddle to get a good look at his expression – because that makes no sense. He looks a little resigned. I can see the way his lips are pulled even though he's trying to cover it with half a forced smile.

Some Potion Master that I've never met before is not a comforting addition to this problem.

"What's going on?" I ask.

"You and Roarke are riding to Eydis'," Pax repeats.

"Oh no, there's more to it than that. You're going to hunt that BeastSeed, aren't you?"

"No, we're not actually," Seth says, which is annoying because Seth is actually the only one in this particular conversation that I trust.

"Then why are we splitting up?"

"The BeastSeed is still hunting *us*," Killian rumbles.

"Then we should stick together. You guys are stronger together, and you said there are worse things than Daryan in Tanakan," I argue, wanting to add that Pax is the last person who should be playing cat-and-mouse with a person powerful enough to make him vulnerable, but I don't.

Because I make him vulnerable too, and keeping Roarke with them means keeping me with them.

"That's why we're not taking you there," Roarke says.

This is a horrible idea, but obviously it's worth the risk of separating if it means the benefit of not having me...

And I'm going to stop myself right there.

Whatever their reasons, and I don't doubt they include me as a lead weight, I just can't bring myself to care more about my own feelings than I do about their safety. This is a chuckin' bad idea.

Pax's horse steps sideways until my leg is crushed against the animal, and for a second I'm not sure if he's going to say something or kiss me. All he does is scan over me, from my hair to my bare toes, then clicks loudly and races off. Killian is right behind him.

"Behave," Seth says, looking directly at me before he whoops and his horse full-gallops to catch up to the others.

Um...

That's all I've got. What just happened?

I stare after them. Seth shoots me a few glances over his shoulder, almost riding his horse off the road. Pax doesn't look back – his shoulders stiff and his muscles shimmering. I swear I can almost see the wolf shifting under his skin.

Killian looks back for a heartbeat. Two heartbeats. Three.

He looks strained, and I try smiling reassuringly at him. The way his features relax in response sends a thrill rushing through me.

Darkness

My Shadow smiles at me. A soft lift of one cheek. Shadows swirl within my soul, my power looking to connect with…

What?

Not her power. She doesn't have any. Silvari blood, maybe. A resistance to glass, definitely. But nothing there for my power to find.

She shouldn't even be sparking my power – drawing it out. And she does draw it out. The kind of rush that only compares to battle. To fight. She's lucky she was in shock last night – even luckier that she tried to kiss me and not Roarke. I don't mind the pain of containing my Darkness – the way my chest contracted when I had to push her back from me.

Forced myself to.

Forced. Because as far as the Darkness is concerned – she is not a mortal.

Impossible. Even the air around her tastes mortal.

My power wants her. Seeks her with the slip of icy Shadows from under my tight grip. Holding my power in check around her is a challenge – and one that is laced with a hint of pain. That pain reminds me why I'm doing this. Because this bond she has with Pax is already breaking all the rules. But with me… unless she's magically a DarknessSeed or something bigger and badder than me…

Breaking is exactly what my power would do to her, I remind myself.

Those soft lips. The gentle way she smiles – even at me.

She barely reaches my shoulders, and when she stands in front of me and tilts her face back to look into my eyes, I can see every vein of courage in her.

So much strength. I want to wrap my hands around her and see how far she'll let me push her body.

But even if she were Saber, I would still break her. Without a desire inside of her to feel that kind of pain, I would hurt her too badly. And I couldn't bear the way she would look at me after that.

So I turn and ride away.

We ride through the day and into the dusk, moving the horses with full awareness that they might need their strength for a quick escape. We're riding into the belly of the beast.

Straight to Tanakan Prison.

The place is dark, deep within a dark forest and the black of a cloud-filled night. Nothing but ancient stone and silence.

The solid Saber-proof steel gates are locked, but there's no guard in the office next to them. No guards pacing the walls either. Last I heard, Tanakan had seventeen triunes on rotation. Seventeen of the strongest, stationed here permanently.

But I haven't been here in over a century.

My magic sprawls out over the grounds, almost lazily – over the fortress on the surface, then searching into the levels of cells stacked over cells built straight down into the bowels of the earth. The nothingness poses no challenge.

This place was a nightmare for a power like mine – when it was full. Pain and broken souls resided in every open space. Bringing my Darkness to life with thread after thread of all things best left to rot… but it's far from full now.

"I'll get us in," Seth says, and with one leap, the guy's over the wall.

"What are you doing?" I demand.

"Saber-proof bars, I'll pick the lock," he replies, and he's already on one knee using something he probably had hidden in a belt loop, or the high leather ankle of his boot, to open the gates.

Then he pops open the guards door and fishes around for a long forgotten set of keys.

Pax is bristling, the wolf shimmering over his muscles. He pulls at his shirt, considering taking the thing off, I guess.

"Are you going to behave?" he asks himself.

I'm not sure what Thane's response is, but the shirt stays on.

We leave the horses in the courtyard. My gelding skitters suddenly at a leaf being blown in the wind. There might not be anyone here, not a thing of Darkness that my power can lock onto, but there *was* Darkness here, and a lot of it. I stroke my hand along his neck, waiting for him to stop jumping around, before fastening his reins to the tethering post.

"I'm going to need to buy more clothes," Pax mutters, walking past me – his horse is already secured.

Seth puts the correct key from his chain of a hundred into the lock, first try. Chaos really pisses me off.

I rub at my shoulder, feeling the almost-healed break from my recent experience with Saber-proof bars and too many keys.

Still no sign of a single person.

Some Seeds are pretty hard to contain, those were the ones kept in pure Silvari glass.

Were pretty hard.

Were kept.

We walk toward the front doors with our weapons sheathed. My senses pick nothing up. Dead air. Empty cells.

The barest trace of the Veil having been opened – there's a burned and decaying taste to the Veil.

And maybe it's that taste that masks the presence of Sabers in the shadows until it's too late.

"Fuck," I curse, getting Pax and Seth's full attention.

We turn to face the gate and the five approaching Sabers.

Daryan is in the lead. The other four I've never seen before. Three women and one man. Warriors. Fighters. Not Sabers from the White Castle – they smell of darkness and the Veil. Sabers that belong within these walls.

And I'll happily put them in the ground.

They funnel into the courtyard, swords drawn and sneers on their faces. As if they think we're cornered.

That their victory is even an option.

Daryan runs his tongue over his sharpened teeth before speaking.

"I've found a way that I can forgive you," he says.

"Forgiveness won't make you a better man," Seth shoots back.

But it's already too late for Pax. Thane is fighting for dominance, the two of them beyond making small talk.

He lunges forward, drawing his sword as he covers the short distance. Shimmers of fur appear, then vanish.

"Control," I can hear Pax growling as I run beside him.

Seth is just as quick, Allure pooling around us even though our final brother is far away. To these Sabers, it would look like we're moving in unison. Fast and deadly.

I take down the woman on the right, a clean thrust through the chest. The movement sends pain shooting through my arm – but I ignore it. Pulling her dying threads and ramming them into the next guy. He chokes on the raw energy – the strangled look in his eyes is more than satisfying to watch.

"Sit, doggy," Daryan orders, shattering my moment. My small victories.

Pax growls. Resists. Drops to one knee. Obeys.

All of Pax's panic translates into Thane trying to surge forward and take control.

"Seth," I shout, but I'm way over here and Seth is way over there and Pax is in the middle. Seth can't get to him, he has a Saber either side of him.

Daryan leans in, whispering in Pax's ear. Slow, deliberate words.

Shadows envelop my hand. A small blade from the Aeons is forming in my grip. I toss it hard, embedding the knife in his thigh. But at the same time, I'm already running – throwing my whole body into Daryan and sending the man flying. He crashes to the cobblestones nearby. Rolls. Lies on his back and laughs.

"Now he can feel the pain of losing a brother," he says, through the laughter.

The only other sound is of Seth's sword blocking and being blocked by the cold steel of the other two Sabers. Then a scream as he cuts one down.

I turn slowly, making sure I can still see Daryan, as I seek out Pax.

He's kneeling on the stones, shoulders hunched. Thane is partly in control – the glowing eyes and molten metal through his skin is a dead giveaway. I don't need Daryan to tell me that he ordered Pax to kill us.

Told our brother to fight until one, or all, of us are dead.

I half smile at the idea – it's almost something I would do.

Seth drops his last opponent, but Daryan isn't paying attention to that. He wants Pax to attack us, and he wants to watch. Absorbed in his blood lust with his sharpened teeth sneering at us.

Thunder cracks and the sky opens up. Rain falls as if in one solid sheet, heavy and blanketing.

Pax grips his sword in his fist, fingers flexing. Then he releases it. The blade falls to the stones.

He's fighting the order. Fighting Thane and the control Daryan has over them.

Thane withdraws and in one sharp motion, the small metal token is out of Pax's pocket and pressed to his chest. Light flashes and he grunts in pain, doubling forward. The token, used and burnt out, falls to the ground. Small wisps of smoke slip from the metal.

Daryan begins to shout, something pained and disappointed, but Seth finally reaches him and buries his weapon deep enough into Daryan's stomach to pin the dying asshole to the ground, spluttering blood. Gasping. Giving up.

Seth doesn't know what Pax just did, doesn't understand it, but in a moment of clarity that only the bringer of Chaos can have, he turns his full attention to our brother. Seth's body rolls with ash-scented fear and a hint of the threads of regret.

I leave Pax to his pain, to his success, and walk the last few steps to Daryan, kneeling beside the dying Seed.

"Lithael sent you?" I demand.

He chuckles, blood bubbling in his mouth. "It's not that simple."

"Then simplify it," I growl. "Who opened the cells?"

"The grimm," he chokes out.

"Are they all hunting us?"

He barely shakes his head. "The grimm are hunting no one."

"Where are the prisoners?" I grip the hilt of Seth's sword. Seth, whose full attention is on Pax still kneeling on the stones.

"Evil is hunting you, and will never stop. The rest of

Tanakan will bring the mortals to their knees. Our border is coming down."

"And what of the Cataclysm?" I snarl.

"Lithael put her in there – see for yourself."

"And the weapons, the ones being stolen by bandits. Was the MagnetSeed in here?"

He laughs again. Like he knows his time is up and he's weaving this information into our lives to cause one last piece of destruction to our world. "If you're not stealing the Crown's weapons, then I don't know who is," he says.

Slowly I turn the blade, while asking, "What else do you know? What kind of weapons? Talk."

"I failed, but evil won't. Run, run far away, or die." He gasps. Then stops.

I turn the blade a half-inch more with no reaction. The man's dead.

Seth doesn't care, he's advancing slowly on Pax. "What did you do?"

"I," Pax gasps, "bought us some time."

Seth's on the guy before he can catch his breath. Pulling him to his feet and holding him in the air. The collar of Pax's shirt is scrunched in Seth's hand.

"What. Did. You. Do?" Seth snaps, fear and anger licking through the words.

Five dead bodies lay around us in the storm.

I wait to see who's going to hit who first, my arms folded over my chest, with just a little relief at taking the weight off my damaged shoulder. It'll be solid in a day or so, if I stop trying to fight people.

Not likely.

Pax just looks at him. He's waiting too.

The sigil is clear on Pax's exposed chest. A circle, a cross, six slashes, two dots, and the half swirl of a moon phase, though the edge is sizzling like the phase is already being burned through.

"Tell me what it means," Seth demands.

"You tell him," Pax gasps.

"It's a leash," Thane growls through Pax's vocals. Pax's body, but Thane's voice is canine, hungry, deep, with a beast's quality.

"We just killed the BeastSeed," Seth growls.

"I almost killed her. In the markets. I almost killed her. It's too much of a risk. *I'm* too much of a risk."

Seth lets him go. Turns to pace. Running his hand through his wet hair, then smoothing down the front of his shirt, then back through his hair.

"If you put her in more danger…" he finally says, furious but restraining himself.

He always got along better with the wolf than with the man. Thane has a respect for impulse – or idiocy, not sure which.

Pax, and possibly Thane, nod before saying, "I need to check the glass wing."

"*We* need to," Seth agrees.

CHAPTER NINETEEN

SHADOW

R oarke makes a light clicking sound, and I pull my attention to him.

"What's wrong?" I ask, but he just smiles.

"We need to get to Eydis as quickly as we can. We can't be out in the open like this. So we need to ride hard."

I hold my reins out to him, to be fastened to his saddle, because me going any faster than a walk on my own is likely to end with me riding straight into a solid-bubble-wall.

Roarke shakes his head. "We need to keep some distance. It could be a few days before the others get back. You and I can't spend that whole time within arm's reach of each other."

"If I ride faster than a walk, I'm going to smack into a wall," I argue.

"I won't let that happen."

He turns and pulls a length of rope from its coiled position behind him, then fastens it between both our saddles.

"I can't get any further back than this," he says, waving to about eighteen paces worth of slack rope. "Click your tongue, relax the reins, and swing your legs. Your horse isn't used to being in the lead, but he'll work it out."

I do as I'm instructed, and the horse lunges forward. A canter, I think this is.

Fast is another word for it.

Roarke stays at the end of the rope, and as my horse's rhythm becomes steady, I relax. The forest grows thick and dark around me, and once I know the horse isn't going to run me into a tree, my mind begins to wander.

Sweet Roarke, with a past full of death and the ability to make people do whatever he wants them to. Sure, the guy ordered me to strip my clothes off in his bedroom once, and he likes walking around with his shirt half unbuttoned. He flirts, a lot, and a lot of people flirt with him too. But he's gentle.

So very gentle.

And we're all stuck in this mess.

Such a giant, chuckin' mess.

The one thing to fight a grimm is something that's finally dead.

Wait until your grief has passed then – Seek the remnant beyond the border,
Speak to a man named Martin but believe the word of a bird.

Let your reflection go hazy in clear waters and see instead through a gray lens.

In Silvari glass is a blade that can pass, a soul that can kneel and a world that can heal.
This is not a battle that can be won. Before this time can pass, the mortal soul from its beginnings cannot last. There is no way a soul can rule and live.

Because I heard what the Origin Spring said to the tallest forest tree – the key will be in the last of me.

At first, I ignore the subtle change in the forest, or not really ignore it, but deem it less important than holding on and thinking about life. But the hours pass and the further we ride, the clearer it is – the trees are getting taller. I can't even see the tops of them anymore.

Then, without warning, we run out of path. It just stops.

Roarke catches up, coiling the rope as he moves closer.

"Keep riding," he says.

"Which way?"

"Straight, I'd think."

I nudge the gelding forward, around a tree, a log, and then a bush. Time passes.

We amble down a slope that looks just like any other. My skin prickles, but before I can stop or say anything, pain slams into my skull. My head pounds in time with my pulse. I squeeze my eyes shut, grip the saddle, and hold my breath. The horse takes two more steps, and as quick as the pain hit, it's gone again.

"You okay?" Roarke asks, looking me over with a concerned crease around his eyes.

I nod a little as the pain washes away.

We're no longer in the middle of a nondescript forest; we're in a really big clearing with a narrow stream flowing right through the middle of it. At the bottom of the slope is a two-and-a-bit story wooden cottage on stilts. The windows are closed, and I can't see any movement inside. Behind it, is a chicken coop made from tree branches and wire. Nearby, a yard for stock sits empty. On the other side is a large square of cleared land that might have once been a crop of wheat or corn, but it's just dirt now.

The sun is streaming straight in, bright and beautiful. There was probably grass at one stage, but the whole circle inside the trees is brown and dead. It's peaceful and sad at the same time, which unsettles my nerves. Not hard on top of the conversation that's been left unfinished since we separated from the others.

Roarke rides past me. "Let's find Eydis."

"Yes, let's find the white-haired woman who may or may not have drowned me as a baby," I mutter.

"I'm pretty sure drowning you wasn't her intention."

"In that case, putting a taco in Pax's boot was never my intention either."

A smile cracks into one corner of his mouth – mission accomplished. We turn and continue toward the little cottage, and freedom.

I hope. *Please be freedom.*

Who am I kidding – probably not freedom. I'm not that lucky.

But maybe food, possibly chocolate, and definitely answers.

Then his gaze brushes over the top of my head, and his expression drops into hard lines.

"Get down," he orders, dismounting and drawing his sword at the same time.

I swing clumsily to the ground, hobbling for a second before I get my balance and get my legs to straighten. I wrestle one of Killian's blades from my bag, which takes longer than it should, because I'm too busy searching the windows of the building for whatever danger has put Roarke into warrior mode.

He grabs his horse's reins and guides the animal to walk just ahead of him. Shielding us both.

"Keep behind me," he says.

"What is it?"

"I don't know yet."

"What do you mean you don't know?" I demand.

"I *smell* the desire to do harm. It's heavy, and it's watching us."

Darkness

W e walk wet footprints through the empty halls, each minute relaxing some of the tension from our muscles.

"We check this cell, then we ride back to Beautiful," Thane growls.

Seth crosses his arms over his chest, not caring that our brother is oozing aggression.

"Vexy," he corrects.

Thane snaps his jaws, Pax's face becoming more wolf than man for a split second.

"Beautiful Vexy," Thane relents.

I smack Seth across the back of the head.

"Hey, what?" he squeals – just like my *little* brother always does.

"Shut up," I tell him, because telling him that the bond he has with Thane makes this family feel almost whole again would have an irreversible side effect on his ego.

And maybe, even if I wanted to let those words form and turn into an unwavering truth – my voice still wouldn't be able to carry them. Strangled somewhere between the looming danger on our tails and the fact that, in about five minutes, Seth's going to do something to piss me off again.

The records in the warden's office – what's left of them, anyway – read, 'Fourth deck. North quadrant. Hall twenty-two. Room one.'

Each hall is empty. Seth and I slow, in natural agreement.

Pax falls in behind us. I hadn't realized how quickly this

sigil would feel wrong. How unguarded he is. In theory, he should be able to block, but only the first strike.

On the fourth deck, he draws his sword. His fingers are shaking as we reach room one. The door is at the very end of the hall. Seth and I are in the lead, and we can already see that it's open.

We edge closer, and I kick the thing wide.

Empty.

Pax screams. Pure animal, laced with darkness and pain. Then Thane growls. The sounds echo down the halls.

I step into the room. The stone of the building's structure is lined with glass. A solid square of it with no edges and no seams. No room for her power to leak out. A blanket and pillow are in one corner. Deck of cards. A few books. Bucket. But nothing else, no bed, no table. This woman will be glad for her freedom.

Pax is still outside the door, and I pace back toward him. Watching the glow in his eyes.

"This is what the sigil is supposed to do? Hold him back from his impulses?" Seth asks.

"Wait," I order.

"Since he has to go through me first, I'd rather not wait," Seth points out.

I chuckle at the guy.

Pax turns, focusing on the exit.

"Let's go," he growls, each syllable tainted with painful memories.

Seth steps out of his way, and I join them in the hall.

On the way out the writing on the door catches my eye. Hidden mostly in shadow, the worn-thin ink is scrawled on glass.

Hyll, it reads, and my chest tenses hard enough to make my heart skip a dozen beats.

"Stop," I grunt, and both of my brothers do, turning slowly to face me.

I pull the door closed, the full name illuminating in a flash of lighting.

Eyv Hyll.

"Eyv Hyll," Seth says out loud, then his eyes go wide. His copper Chaos tang fills my nose as he whispers, "Evil."

He would bloody find that name amusing.

Pax, however, doesn't care for the child whose parents had a sick sense of humor.

"Hyll," he roars.

He only cares that this is the woman who murdered his baby.

The Override was telling the truth. Tanakan Prison is empty, and the Cataclysm is free and hunting us.

The Cataclysm.

Pax's Cataclysm.

"We have to get back to her," Pax growls, already moving for the exit.

"We tear this Cataclysm to pieces – then we take back *our* Crown," Thane adds.

We run, all three of us, into the storm. Onto our horses. Through the forest.

Whatever it takes to get to *our* woman.

To keep her alive.

But then what?

LOGAN

Kyra ran from her family and her responsibilities months ago. Ran from me. And the grimm can't find her; she smells more like the Veil to them than the Veil itself.

That's why I'm sitting in the tavern at EastCoyt with my third daer glass empty in my hand. I even rode here like a common Saber. On a horse. All of the way from the Black Castle through the small towns. All to avoid being seen by those who matter to me. My uncle is at the top of that list, and the Veil is his prefered method of travel.

The rest of my team are in the White Castle, recovering from the beating we all took on the sands.

They're slow. Weak. Nothing to me.

I'm stronger. Better. How a Saber *should* be.

Kyra is going to slip up and come crawling back, I know it.

But I'm not a patient man.

I want blood, and I want it now.

If not Kyra's, then the servant – Shade. I'm going to pull her apart just to see what she's made of. Mortals are toys, not equals. Not Sabers, and those damned Elorsins have made a mockery of everything we are by taking that soot into their *pentad*.

Saber or soot, I'm sure they sound the same when they scream.

I could put them side by side, Kyra and Shade. Listen to them both sing with agony.

The thought makes me smile into my glass, then spurs me into action. I topple my chair backwards and slam my way out of the tavern.

Kyra or Shade.

Shade or Kyra.

Which will I see first?

Read Book 3
Kitten & Allure
HERE

Grab books 1-3
(Plus forbidden chapters)
In the box set
HERE

THANK YOU FOR READING!

Liked it? Loved it?

Got a minute to <u>REVIEW</u> it?

Reviews can be game changers for authors.

WANT MORE?

Stalk Amanda:
WWW.AMANDACASHURE.COM/STALK-ME

Join the newsletter:
WWW.AMANDACASHURE.COM/NEWSLETTER

Join Amanda in:
AMANDA'S FACEBOOK GROUP

MORE IN THE SHADOWVERSE

SHADOWS & SHADE SERIES

Prequel ~ Free with the newsletter signup *here*

Book 1 ~ *Shadows and Shade*

Book 2 (what you are reading now) ~ *Shadow & Darkness*

Book 3 ~ *Kitten & Allure*

Books 1-3 ~ *box set - plus forbidden chapters*

Book 4 ~ *The True Histories*

Book 5 ~ *Power & Pentad (pt 1)*

Book 6 ~ *Power & Pentad (pt 2)*

Books 4-6 ~ *box set - plus forbidden chapters*

Book 7 ~ *Vexy & Chaos (pt 1)*

Book 8 ~ *Vexy & Chaos (pt 2)*

(Preorder now)

HUNTERS & SECRETS SERIES

Book 1 ~ *Hunters & Secrets*

Book 2 ~ *Hiders & Seekers*

(coming in 2023)

MORE OUTSIDE THE SHADOWVERSE

The Balanced Queen (*A fast-burn stand alone*) *Your life is dictated by which side of the Queendom you're born on. House or Night, or House of Day. Unless your like me, born in the middle, which basically makes your life null and void. On the upside the scariest fucker in this place is my brother. On the downside, it's his personal mission to make sure I'm faster, stronger, and more skilled than any of my competition - the hard way. Then things go wrong, and I'm left three-quarters dead in the forest. The guys who find me aren't sure if my ass is worth saving, and without them I'm dead - but so is every other soul in this Queendom.*

Mating My Mob (*A fast-burn shifter RH*) First: I woke up
with a shapeshifting ability that I didn't know existed.
Apparently, true shapeshifting power is like a drug, and a whole
lot of fucked up people are now hunting me down. Then: my ass
gets saved by five shifters who seem to hate the fact they saved
me in the first place, but at least they're not trying to steal my
power. Followed by: some serious sexual attraction, and a deal
that has two positives - I get my own personal protection detail
and I might just have found a way out of this shapeshifting
nightmare. Make that three positives - sex. This deal contains
lots of sex. But it's not without one great big negative, I have to
become there 'mate' and in the shapeshifting world that opens
the door to all kinds of new dangers.

Dust (*Dark RH with triggers*) My magic is locked away, my
life is in danger, and I keep running into six powerful and sexy-
as-fuck shifters. I'm not complaining the sex is awesome, but I
am beginning to think fate hates me. These shifters are both my
damnation and my salvation - and they might be the only thing
keeping the true monsters from getting their hands on me.

Made in United States
Troutdale, OR
08/09/2024

21883252R00216